PRINCE: 50 ESSENTIAL BOOTLEGS

HAMISH WHITTA

Prince: 50 Essential Bootlegs
Text copyright © Hamish Whitta, 2018

Cover design and typesetting by Phil Hodgkiss, RakishDesign.co.uk

First published 2018

ISBN: 978-1543208320

"A CASE OF YOU"
Words and Music by JONI MITCHELL

© 1971 (Renewed) CRAZY CROW MUSIC
All Rights Administered by SONY/ATV MUSIC PUBLISHING,
8 Music Square West, Nashville, TN 37203
Exclusive Print Rights Administered by ALFRED MUSIC International
Copyright Secured.
All Rights Reserved. Reproduced by permission of DEVIRRA GROUP.
Unauthorized reproduction is illegal.

"For Bill Boler, who wanted to read a book about bootlegs."

ACKNOWLEDGEMENTS

Many hours were spent alone working on this project, but it took a collaborative effort to get it to print, and there are many people who I am indebted to.

First, I must thank Bill Boler, whose offhand comment in an email planted the seed that germinated into this book. I have cursed him and praised him in equal measure over the last few months; had I known what I was in for I may never have started. However, I shall forever be thankful for his support and friendship.

The stunning artwork was provided by Phil Hodgkiss, who also brought a level of professionalism to every part of the project. My original DIY aesthetic was given a professional gloss with his valuable input and invested time. I will always be grateful his collaboration and timely advice.

The adventures of James Clark and me are worthy of a book of their own. When we first meet in a Cairo hotel ten years ago, neither one of us could have imagined that one would be in the position to edit the other's book. The world keeps on turning and here we are today finishing another unexpected adventure. Who knows when our paths will next cross, but I am sure that it will be life changing and unpredictable.

I have met a great number of Prince fans over the years, online and in real life. Of those I have never had the pleasure of meeting face to face, Herman Hagan and Marco Rosenfeld are two who I look forward to having a beer with one day. Herman for his immense knowledge and good humor and Marco who kept me well-balanced with a steady diet of Beatles music and Talking Heads. He gave me a timely breather when I needed it, and I appreciate his support.

Of the fans I have met, Viv Canal and Honza Zalubil both provided encouragement and simple friendship, something that can never be underestimated.

Finally, Chris Whaley, Michael Dean, and Alex Hahn with their unswerving dedication to Prince provided great inspiration. All champion the music and are inspiring figures with their words of encouragement and personal drive. Without Michael Dean's "work it like a job" mantra, I may never have found the courage to push myself as far I did. All three contributed kind words of encouragement just as I needed it most. I thank you all.

CONTENTS

	PREFACE	10
1.	6TH MARCH 1980 - THE OMNI, ATLANTA	15
2.	22ND MARCH 1981 - THE RITZ, NEW YORK	20
3.	4TH JUNE 1981 - THÉÂTRE LE PALACE, PARIS	25
4.	11TH OCTOBER 1981 - MEMORIAL COLISEUM, LOS ANGELES	30
5.	20TH DECEMBER 1981 - THE SUMMIT, HOUSTON	34
6.	28TH FEBRUARY 1982 - SAENGER THEATER, NEW ORLEANS	39
7.	8TH MARCH 1982 - FIRST AVENUE, MINNEAPOLIS	44
8.	3RD AUGUST 1983 - FIRST AVENUE, MINNEAPOLIS	49
9.	7TH JUNE 1984 - FIRST AVENUE, MINNEAPOLIS	56
10.	26TH DECEMBER 1984 - ST PAUL CIVIC CENTER, ST PAUL	61
11.	4TH JANUARY 1985 - THE OMNI, ATLANTA	68
12.	7TH JUNE 1985 - PROM CENTER, MINNEAPOLIS	75
13.	3RD MARCH 1986 - FIRST AVENUE, MINNEAPOLIS	78
14.	23RD MAY 1986 - WARFIELD THEATER, SAN FRANCISCO	86
15.	7TH JUNE 1986 - COBO ARENA, DETROIT	93
16.	22ND AUGUST 1986 - ISSTADION, STOCKHOLM	99
17.	24TH AUGUST 1986 - LE NEW MORNING, PARIS	105
18.	9TH SEPTEMBER 1986 - YOKOHAMA STADIUM, YOKOHAMA	110
19.	21ST MARCH 1987 - FIRST AVENUE, MINNEAPOLIS	117
20.	21ST MAY 1987 - PARK CAFÉ, MUNICH	122
21.	29TH MAY 1987 - U4, VIENNA	127
22.	15TH JUNE 1987 - LE NEW MORNING, PARIS	131
23.	17TH JUNE 1987 - PALAIS OMNISPORTS DE PARIS-BERCY, PARIS	135
24.	31ST DECEMBER 1987 - PAISLEY PARK, CHANHASSEN	141
25.	19TH AUGUST 1988 - PAARD VAN TROJE, THE HAGUE	145

26.	31ST AUGUST 1988 - GROSSE FREIHEIT '36, HAMBURG	152
27.	11TH NOVEMBER 1988 - WARFIELD THEATER, SAN FRANCISCO	158
28.	1ST FEBRUARY 1989 - SENDAI STADIUM, SENDAI	162
29.	30TH APRIL 1990 - RUPERTS NIGHTCLUB, MINNESOTA	170
30.	31ST AUGUST 1990 - TOKYO DOME, TOKYO	175
31.	24TH JUNE 1992 - EARLS COURT, LONDON	181
32.	24TH MARCH 1993 - RADIO CITY MUSIC HALL, NEW YORK	187
33.	1ST SEPTEMBER 1993 - CLUB REX, PARIS	193
34.	3RD SEPTEMBER 1993 - FLUGPLATZ LÜNEBURG, LÜNEBURG	197
35.	6TH MAY 1994 - LE BATACLAN, PARIS	203
36.	26TH AND 27TH MARCH 1995 - PARADISO, AMSTERDAM	207
37.	24TH DECEMBER 1998 - TIVOLI, UTRECHT	214
38.	18TH OCTOBER 2002 - SPORTPALEIS, ANTWERP	220
39.	26TH OCTOBER 2002 - VEGA, COPENHAGEN	227
40.	29TH OCTOBER 2002 - LE BATACLAN, PARIS	232
41.	29TH MARCH 2004 - STAPLES CENTER, LOS ANGELES	238
42.	1ST AUGUST 2007 - THE O2, LONDON	244
43.	29TH AUGUST 2007 - INDIGO O2, LONDON	251
44.	22ND SEPTEMBER 2007 - INDIGO O2, LONDON	256
45.	28TH MARCH 2009 - THE CONGA ROOM, LOS ANGELES	263
46.	18TH JULY 2009 - MONTREUX JAZZ FESTIVAL, MONTREUX	267
47.	7TH NOVEMBER 2010 - VIAGE, BRUSSELS	272
48.	15TH JULY 2013 - MONTREUX JAZZ FESTIVAL, MONTREUX	279
49.	9TH APRIL 2015 - FOX THEATER, DETROIT	286
50.	21ST JANUARY 2016 - PAISLEY PARK, CHANHASSEN	293

PREFACE

The first Prince bootleg I ever purchased was *Pop*. Thirty years on and I can still recall the day I bought it: the heat of the afternoon, the silent guilt as I skipped school, the smell of the bus as we rode to the city center and the dark, cool interior of the record store. Despite owning every album Prince had released I was still drawn to the 'Prince' section of the store where I came across a CD I had never seen before, its cover an old photo slightly cheap looking. Turning it over it revealed itself to be a recording of the *Controversy* tour (New Orleans, 28th February 1982). Three times the price of any other CD in the rack, I bought it immediately and took it home. It wouldn't be until much later that I was finally able to sit down and listen to the music, and when I did it came as a revelation. I was familiar with Prince's studio work, but I had never heard anything like this before. It was live and the music was more powerful than anything else I had previously experienced. The guitars came jagged and rough, the drums louder and more dynamic while the keyboards were insistent in their melodies and underlying drive. I was immediately hooked. My mother had warned me about the evil of drugs but she hadn't warned me about bootlegs which were equally addictive and almost as expensive.

Thirty years and 1,400 bootlegs later, the world has greatly changed. The Internet has opened up the bootleg world in a way the fifteen-year-old me could have never foreseen. No longer hidden in the dark corner of the store, they are now traded online, often for free. The small groups of us that used to huddle together to discuss them have connected to online forums that stretch around the world. What once felt like a niche part of the fan community has now become a central part of most fans' collections. Some things, however, have not changed. The topic of what is best, or what has to be heard, is still a key part of many discussions. People love lists, and they love ranking what they have in an attempt to throw some logic on these vast collections.

"Which is best?" is an open question, something a dozen different people would give a dozen different answers to depending on the day. A more pertinent question is "What is essential?" It is equally subjective, but when considering essential bootlegs, we get a much better overview of Prince's career trajectory. A good starting point for what is essential would be any bootleg that you feel someone else must listen to. The parameters or qualities for "Essential" can cover a range of elements, such as: historical value, sound quality, performance quality, and rarities and oddities, along with importance to Prince's career. Some bootlegs have several of these elements; while other have only one, yet they are all equally essential when listening to Prince's live career.

Prince opening for The Rolling Stones is a great example of a historical bootleg; it captured a historic moment between two powerhouses of popular music at a key moment in their careers. It's a moment that is of great interest to fans that is released on bootlegs. This particular bootleg is one that fueled my desire to collect bootlegs. I had read about Prince's disastrous opening for The Rolling Stones, so when I found out there was a bootleg of it I had to hear it immediately. I wanted to hear for myself exactly what had happened that day. It may not be an easy or enjoyable listen, but it is a milestone in its own way and merits an inclusion in any list of bootlegs you must hear.

Other bootlegs have great sound quality and in some cases sound even better that Prince's studio albums. If anyone is going to dedicate some time to listening to bootlegs, they want to be listening to the best quality available. It is very easy to be seduced by a soundboard recording, and even an average show can become something magical with this quality. There are of course some shows that match a great performance with a great recording, and these are among the most revered bootlegs in circulation. Perhaps the most famous of these soundboard recordings is the Small Club bootleg, which is just as well-known as any of Prince's studio albums.

Equally important is the performance that the bootleg records. There are nights when Prince and his band were on fire and the concert is an experience as much as a rock show. There are many of these types of concerts in circulation with various degrees of bootlegs capturing the moment. On these bootlegs we can hear the band and Prince in full flight, and despite some poor quality recordings, the performance can still be heard and recognized as something special. Chapter 13 (*Parade* warm-up show) covers exactly this kind of bootleg; the fusion of theater, dance, funk and entertainment that provides an essential hit for a true fan.

I have always had a soft spot for the shows that capture one-off songs and odd moments. These rare appearances are equally essential, and I know many people collect bootlegs for this reason. Guest performers add a little something extra to the magic of a Prince bootleg, like at Tivoli where Lenny Kravitz joins the band onstage or chapter 44 where Prince introduces his audience to Amy Winehouse. Unreleased songs such as "Electric Intercourse" only appear in a handful of shows, and each one is worth hearing. Cover versions are also compelling, and there are a great number of these appearing on bootlegs ("Come Together" from London 2007 and "A Case of You" from First Avenue 1983 spring easily to mind): again they all demand attention in their own way.

The final element that makes a bootleg essential is the importance of the concert to Prince's overall career. The most obvious of these bootlegs would be the Minnesota Dance Benefit concert that saw Prince record the core elements of the *Purple Rain* album in a show that sets up everything that will follow. There is no denying the importance of this performance to Prince's career. Prince had many such milestones and turning points in his career, and thankfully most of these are bootlegged in one form or another. It is one thing to know that these shows were a turning point in his career, but it is quite another to be able to listen to them and experience the moment for yourself. The recording often reveals more than just knowledge of the show.

This book is unashamedly written by a fan for the fans. I make no apologies for that. There are already plenty of books on the market written with a cold journalistic eye. Bootlegs are about music and if I don't feel passionate about what I am listening to and writing about then it doesn't deserve to be one of the essential fifty. This is one of the key reasons I didn't canvas the Prince community for what should be included. If it wasn't a bootleg I was fully invested in, then I could never write about it. Yes, sometimes I am over the top and words run away with me, but music is all about feeling and the emotions it elicits.

Things change quickly in the bootleg world. New recordings surface, previous recordings are upgraded. With the passing of Prince the doors of the vault have opened a crack. No doubt this book of fifty bootlegs will quickly become obsolete as more concerts are released from the vault. Some will be better quality releases of recordings we already have; others will be new releases of shows unheard. I, like many others, look forward to coming years as these treasures are unearthed. This book is merely a snapshot of this moment in time; who knows what would appear on a list of essential bootlegs in a years' time, or even six months' time.

PREFACE

Finally, I sincerely hope that nobody reads this book from cover to cover. It is intended to be merely a quick reference, something that inspires people to add to their collection or as a companion to a wonderful hour or so with music blaring out of the speakers. It should be dog-eared and thrown to one side with the exclamation, "I have that bootleg somewhere; I should give it another listen!". To read this from cover to cover would be doing a disservice to the music, which is the main focus. At the end of the day it is all about the music and not the words. Words can never convey the feeling that live music, and music in general, can give you.

That day thirty years ago when I first heard a Prince bootleg still lives with me. Each new recording I hear is like that first one and as I push play the rush still comes as I experience a recording for the first time. I know I am not the only one, and I hope that the following pages offer something for all those who love bootlegs as much as I do. Now turn the page and rediscover some of those magical moments that only exist on bootlegs.

The following icons are used throughout this book to indicate the type of bootleg release:

- Soundboard Audio Recording
- Audience Audio Recording
- Professionally Filmed Footage
- Audience Filmed Footage

6TH MARCH 1980
THE OMNI, ATLANTA

Every story has a start, and the story of Prince bootlegs starts on the 6th March 1980 at The Omni in Atlanta. Although Prince was performing and recording long before this date, this is the earliest known live recording in circulation and as such is the ground zero of Prince's bootleg canon. To appreciate Prince at the height of his powers, one must first examine his genesis and experience some of his journey to the top.

This first bootleg sets the bar high for everything that will follow, and although it is not quite the Prince we come to know later in his career all the signs are there with some of his key traits already in place. He may be a pale imitation of Prince at this stage, but he most definitely is Prince. The band are well-drilled to the point of almost sounding cold in their playing and, although he still sounds quiet and shy when talking directly to the audience, there is a lot of confidence in his music and playing.

There is plenty on here that looks to the future, and anyone who has heard later bootlegs will recognize Prince's modus operandi. The brash rock songs brush up against smooth funk and soulful ballads, Prince playing what he chooses in which-ever style he feels for at that moment. Pop songs and ballads suddenly open up to soundscapes as the music unfurls before dropping away again and moving into previously unforeseen territories. There are well written songs at the core of a performance that threatens to be a number of things all at once: a pop show, a rock show, and a man who is playing for himself and the love of music as much as anything else.

The bootleg itself is a fine sounding soundboard recording, the audience barely audible in the background, although there is just enough in there to remind us that this is a live show. Live music is about the audience as much as the performer and adds a tension and dynamic not heard on the released record. As the audience feeds off the music, the band too feeds off the audience in a symbiotic relationship that creates the magic of a live show. Considering it is the earliest recording out there, it is a surprisingly bright example of the sound quality that could be achieved. As an early bootleg it sets expectations that will be unrealistic to maintain. If all bootlegs sounded this good, we would all be very happy indeed.

The set list is an accurate snapshot of Prince at this moment, an even balance of songs off both his albums at that time. This gives it a homogenous sound as those two albums are well paired in style and sound, and one leads easily into the other. Looking to the performance itself, it is clean and smooth, almost with a sheen to it, and is glossy and well played throughout.

There is very little spontaneity heard on the recording, and although there are jams at the end of a couple of songs, they sound more like they have been highly rehearsed rather than something that has sprung from the moment. Prince was a perfectionist, and with so much on the line early in his career, it would be hard to imagine him wanting to take a risk with an unrehearsed jam. The fact that these songs do have extended versions played with longer codas appended to them points strongly to the future when Prince becomes bolder and looser with his music. He may not be ready to let go of the reins just yet, but the intention is there. There are moments when the band threatens to disappear into the sound and music they are creating, the audience forgotten as they create their own vibe, but each time they return to the path set out by Prince, a manicured sound that lacks a ragged wildness.

> **RIGHT HERE HE IS SHAKING OFF THE DISCO FEEL OF HIS FIRST ALBUMS AND PUSHING TOWARDS A HARDER, ROCKIER SOUND**

While "Soft And Wet" serves as an introduction to Prince and the band, it is "Why You Wanna Treat Me So Bad?" that unleashes the stronger sound of Prince, with the twin attack of his and Dez Dickerson's guitars to the fore. It is the sound and look that will carry Prince through the next phase of his career; right here he is shaking off the disco feel of his first albums and pushing toward a harder, rockier sound that will win him a wider crossover audience. The look and sound of him and Dez playing shoulder to shoulder will become iconic for Prince in years to come but it is still in its infancy here and sounding

6TH MARCH 1980 - THE OMNI, ATLANTA

beautifully fresh and invigorating. The music is thrilling as Prince and Dez push it harder and harder, squeezing every drop of rock out of what is basically a pop song. Even on a thirty-five-year-old recording you can hear the vitality of the performance and the audience responding to it. Dez is the rock, literally and figuratively, behind many of these songs, and even on a song such as "I Feel For You," he gets the closing minutes to put his stamp all over it.

Dez isn't the only member of the band to get some time and a share of the spotlight - Andre Cymone too gets plenty of opportunity to strut his stuff, clearly marking this out as a band performance rather than a one-man show. In particular, "Sexy Dancer" is very much about Andre as there is a bass solo in the mix that not only demonstrates Andre's obvious abilities, but also Prince's awareness that this is a band and the music always comes first. There are always egos at play in any band but Prince has always been about the music, He is never shy to point the spotlight at another performer when the time is right. Andre rewards this confidence in him and the break for the bass rounds out the sound of the song; as well as giving the show some balance. As the bass rumbles below, there is an added depth to the sound - adult, mature, and yes, dangerous.

Through the show we have keyboards, drums, bass, and guitar all spotlighted at various stages, and best of all Prince takes time to deliver a couple of vocal performances that highlight the other instrument onstage - his voice. Especially during "Still Waiting" he sounds just as good, if not better, than anything else that is heard. His vocal performance has a luxurious quality to it as he sings his lines with a delivery that promises so much more.

Although the show is short, clocking in under an hour, Prince doesn't sound rushed at any point; he lets the music breathe and speak for itself. There are only seven songs played, and most of them get some sort of extended treatment, even if it is not a freewheeling jam like later years. Some songs flow easily into this extended treatment, although not all of them - a couple of times it does feel as if melodies have been bolted on. The show could easily have been shorter, but again Prince is setting the standard for later years and giving the audience, and the bootleg, extra value with more bang for their buck. The best two longer versions are saved for last, with "Just As Long As We're Together" and "I Wanna Be Your Lover" clocking in at twenty minutes together. "Just As Long As We're Together" brings the tightness of the band together, with plenty of interplay and tight connections to be heard deep in the song. It does sound like the era it was recorded in, coming off the seventies and the disco era, although to Prince's credit it breaks free from its disco roots late in the piece with some bass and guitar work that stretches out into new directions as the band successfully combine disco, funk, and rock into the mix. If the band intended to get people up and dancing, then it certainly achieves its mission - the beat and groove is irrepressible.

The earliest recorded bootleg of his career ends on a high, as Prince plays the crowd-pleasing favorite "I Wanna Be Your Lover." As a pure pop song and a recent hit, it is an uplifting way to finish the show, and Prince is finishing the show on a wave. It is in contrast to the long, smooth "Just As Long As We're Together" that preceded it. Prince goes from a smooth disco groove to the pop fluff of "I Wanna Be Your Lover," although this too becomes a long danceable groove that matches anything that has come before in its danceability. The show has been notable thus far for its smooth, clean sound, and it is only in these closing minutes as the song evolves into its extended coda that Prince turns up his guitar to give it some grittiness, a steely, raw sound we will be hearing plenty more of in the coming couple of years. It is the type of ending that leaves you feeling well satisfied with what you have heard; and yet wanting more. It is this hunger that will drive those collecting bootlegs, and those producing them, for the years to come.

> **THE FAME, EXTENDED GUITAR SOLOS, ALL-NIGHT JAMS, AFTERSHOWS, DANCING, AND THEATRICS ARE ALL STILL TO COME, YET THE ESSENTIAL BUILDING BLOCKS ARE ALL IN PLACE**

The fame, extended guitar solos, all-night jams, aftershows, dancing, and theatrics are all still to come, yet the essential building blocks are all in place here. A baseline has been set. The show may not jump out in either energy or ragged intensity, but it does highlight the quality of the band, the song-writing, and most importantly the professionalism and vision of Prince himself. He still has a long way to go - there will be much better performances, and subsequently bootlegs, to come - but for now he has set a standard. This is where it all started and as such it is essential listening.

6TH MARCH 1980 - THE OMNI, ATLANTA

SET LIST

1. Soft And Wet
2. Why You Wanna Treat Me So Bad?
3. Still Waiting
4. I Feel For You
5. Sexy Dancer
6. Just As Long As We're Together
7. I Wanna Be Your Lover

RELEASES

- Atlanta '80 - *4DaFunk*
- Atlanta City Lights - *Superhero*
- City Lights Remastered & Extended Volume 1 - *Sabotage*
- Prince - The Omni Atlanta - The Rick James Tour - *Premium*

22ND MARCH 1981
THE RITZ, NEW YORK

Raw is without a doubt the most overused word when talking about Prince during the Dirty Mind era, so it is unfortunate that it is also the most accurate word to describe the look and sound of Prince at that time. Rough and ready, with a hint of danger about him, he quickly moved on from the cleaner sound of the Omni bootleg recorded almost a year earlier. This bootleg video of his show at The Ritz in early 1981 is exceptional for being the first video recording we have of Prince playing live and as such it is a fascinating watch. For the first time we see his stage presentation with the unfiltered style he was sporting, both shocking and thrilling in equal measure. With only bikini briefs and a bandana he manages to look bold, and macho, and more than a little untamed. He challenges the audience with his look and his uncompromising music, as well as challenging himself as he pushes his music and band further into the unknown. He is ambitious, not just for success, but for creating his own unique musical style and look to match. This ambition sees him taking in further influences and changes in his music as he twists up funk, new wave, R&B, and pop in a heady mix. There is a lot to take in and consider with this one; it is certainly a bootleg that demands several viewings.

The video itself is well filmed: a single camera on a tripod in front of the stage. The camera operator covers the performance in an intimate way, with plenty of close-ups on Prince's face as he sings. This style of camera work gives the viewer the feeling and sensation of being there at the concert. The other aspect of the recording that marks it as essential is the clean and pure stage lighting. It complements the action unfolding onstage, ensuring that it can be clearly seen at all times. The little things make all the difference when watching bootlegs - with a great many being dark and grainy, being able to see Prince and the band for 95 percent of the time at this show means that not a moment is wasted while watching.

22ND MARCH 1981 - THE RITZ, NEW YORK

Like the Omni show Prince starts quietly, but the visuals tell a different story - he and the band look like they are ready to rock right from the start. Prince may be singing quietly, but his look marks something different about him. As he plays it is apparent that he is infused with an attitude; he may have been quietly confident before, but now he has a presence and look to match it. The rest of the band seems to have picked up on this as well as they all strut and stomp across the stage, looking for all the world like they own the place. The music and the look are inseparable and complement each other well; it is impossible to untangle the fierce look of Prince and the equaly uncompromising sound of his music at the time.

The crisp look of the video is equalled in the sound quality; the vocals sound clean and sharp as does the bass. Being easy to listen to means for the most part the main attention is focused on the visuals and the quality of the sound recording is often taken for granted. Andre in particular sounds excellent on the recording, and later when Dez gets more time to play he too can be heard note perfect.

> **THE NOTES COME DIZZYINGLY FAST, A VORTEX OF SOUND THAT IS INTOXICATING AND INSPIRING IN EQUAL MEASURE**

"Do It All Night" is a misleading start; it is the following "Why You Wanna Treat Me So Bad?" that serves as a better introduction to the band and their sound. Dez and Andre seemed restrained during the opening song, and it is during "Why You Wanna Treat Me So Bad?" that they cut loose and infuse a charge of energy into the performance. The song takes off at the chorus, and the show is elevated to another level with a rush of rising keyboards and soaring guitars. It is the sound of defiant joy in midst of a storm of music, and Prince with the band ride this joy through the song. Prince himself injects a looseness and raw sound, especially as he shreds on the guitar for the second solo, at which point there is a feeling that the band are casting off the shackles and playing as they feel. The notes come dizzyingly fast, a vortex of sound that is intoxicating and inspiring in equal measure. With the music sweeping the band up, there is a sense that the music is playing the band as much as the band is playing the music.

It is a surprise that this momentum is not maintained; things pull back and slow considerably for the next bracket of songs. "Gotta Broken Heart Again" is gentle on the ear with some delicacy to the piano playing behind Prince. Likewise, "Broken" sounds good, but it is hardly a song to incite a riot. The interesting aspect that holds the attention here is that "Broken" is an unreleased song, and as such it grabs the spotlight in its unfamiliarity compared to the other songs around it. Being an up-tempo rockabilly number, it signals the beginning of Prince's dabbling in that genre, with a couple of similar songs making it to album in the following years. It is well done without being a taxing listen, and Prince has the genre down tight, especially with Dez's brief guitar break sounding as if it could well have been lifted from any Scotty Moore recording.

Momentum is restored with the appearance of "When You Were Mine." While not the greatest version in circulation, energy is restored to the show as the song kicks into gear. Paired with "Gotta Stop (Messin' About)," both songs provide a chance for Prince to reconnect with the audience. After the fire and fury of the show earlier there is room for everyone to take a breath and reconnect with the band as they prepare themselves for what will follow. Prince's singing along with a synth squiggle soften the sound, leaving it up to the vocals of Dez and Andre to add the manlier bottom required to strengthen it.

"Sexy Dancer" is hot and sweaty, and for the first time on the recording we hear something closer to the funk Prince will later be associated with. Prince's vocals and guitar are the center of attention, although it is Andre and his bass that is the foundation to the song. Prince plays plenty of his trademark funk guitar, but yet again another band member makes the lasting impression. This time it's Dr. Fink with another bobbing and weaving solo that brings the song to a close. This serves as a reminder that they are a band of quirky individuals, each with a trademark style and sound that all contributes to the whole. As unique as Prince is, he finds people with their own unique talents and personalities to surround himself with, each member of the band able to hold attention in their own right.

The pairing of "I Wanna Be Your Lover" and "Head" is a knock-out, "I Wanna Be Your Lover" coming as a sucker punch before "Head" hits hard and leaves the audience reeling. It is easy to be lured in by the pop sound of "I Wanna Be Your Lover," only to find minutes later you are listening to something a whole lot darker and funkier as the music drops into a black hole. There is no better sound than that of Prince and the band grooving on the introduction of "Head," the opening synth stab and the delicious sound of the guitars before

Prince intones his opening lines. The early highlight is seeing a young Lisa Coleman singing her lines, the camera capturing her face as she grooves behind the keyboards. With Dr. Fink jerking and twitching and Prince prancing and strutting about like a young Mick Jagger, it is a kinetic, edgy performance that is one to watch as much as listen to. The band is definitely hitting their straps at this point, and all of them are competing for attention onstage. Andre is again the key man, his bass the glue that holds it all together. He would be the man of the moment; if not for the final minutes of the song when Prince delivers his guitar-fueled masturbation scene. The guitar playing alone is worth the price of admission. Paired with the mesmerizing show he puts on it becomes something that once seen is absolutely unforgettable. As he rolls around at the front of the stage, humping and stroking his guitar, the rest of the band, and indeed the world, disappear from view and all eyes are on Prince alone. There is something primeval about his performance: it connects to the deeper, darker parts and leaves you feeling dirty just for watching it. This one song makes this bootleg essential; Prince's unhinged and dangerous performance is not to be missed. Even as the lights darken and the band fades to silence, there is still a feeling that anything might happen.

The recording snaps out of this dark, greasy funk with a light "Still Waiting," led by Dr. Fink on the keyboards. The weight lifts with it is gentle elegance, Prince reverting back to his falsetto crooning and his vocal abilities becoming apparent as he gives it some flourishes that harks back to old-fashioned vocal performances. While channeling the vocal groups of the 1950s, we are again transported to another world. It is quite a change from "Head," but amply demonstrates Prince's ability to morph himself into whatever he is singing, in this case right before our eyes.

Unfortunately, the footage ends at this point, but there is still plenty more to come in this concert. With seven songs missing and a show stopping finale, there is much to mourn, but such is the world of bootlegs, and in this case it is better to appreciate what we have rather than what we don't, especially as what we do have is extraordinary.

Of the fifty essential bootlegs, 1980 to 1983 is perhaps over represented, but for very good reason. These are Prince's formative years, and the associated recordings lay out his early development and look that will carry him through to the next stage of his career. This early video is a fascinating first look at Dirty Mind Prince; already his early development is plain to be seen with an adaption of styles as he grows into the figure who will one day be the Prince the world knows and loves. Like anyone, he may be embarrassed to go back and look at these snap-shots of his younger years, but they are all part of who he will become in later years and worthy of the time and attention.

SET LIST

1. Do It All Night
2. Why You Wanna Treat Me So Bad?
3. Gotta Broken Heart Again
4. Broken
5. When You Were Mine
6. Gotta Stop (Messin' About)
7. Sexy Dancer
8. Sister
9. I Wanna Be Your Lover
10. Head
11. Still Waiting

RELEASES

- A Dirty Mind In New York - *Fullasoul*
- City Lights: New York Paris - *Superhero*
- City Lights Remastered & Extended Volume 1 - *Sabotage*
- A Dirty Mind In... New York - *Fan Release*
- New York 1981 - *Habibi*
- New York '81 - *Enigma/Team FDA*
- Prince Live '81 - *Global Funkschool*

4TH JUNE 1981
THÉÂTRE LE PALACE, PARIS

Like so many bootlegs from these early years of Prince's career, this one is special for a couple of firsts. Not only is it the first bootleg from a European show, but it is also the first bootleg of a one-off show. These two reasons alone make it a worthy addition, but factoring in that it is another concert captured on video makes it all the more desirable and a bootleg that must be seen. The circulating footage from New York is only three months previous, yet the jump between Prince's stage presentation on the two shows is noticeable. The Dirty Mind tour was about getting noticed and making a splash; in this one-off showcase he is toning down his wild style and preparing for the next phase of his career. The rough and ready Prince of Dirty Mind isn't totally gone, and despite his façade of respectability at the beginning of the performance, he ends the show in just his underwear and there is plenty of grubbiness along the way, which is all for the better.

Being a video as well as an audio bootleg means that the visual aspect has just as much prominence as the music. When it comes to visuals, this bootleg gives us plenty of moments and images that stick in the mind. Be it Prince, Andre, and Dez as a front line exuding effortless cool; or Prince atop the amps playing guitar god in the spotlight; or the final unforgettable image of Prince in just his bikini briefs, feet firmly astride as he passionately sings into the microphone, each one of these images stay in the mind long after the show has finished. In many ways the look of the performance is more memorable than the music heard throughout show.

Prince and the band are certainly aware of the appearance of the performance, and they do make some effort to engage in rudimentary dance moves - we see Prince, Andre and Dez moving as one from side to side in a nod to performing basic choreography. There is no doubt though; that as far as performance and dance moves are concerned, it is Prince and his prancing and hopping later in the show, especially during "Dirty Mind," that is the most memorable. Like a young horse that hasn't yet found its feet, or a teenager who hasn't grown into his skin, Prince leaps and swings about the stage in spasms of energy, both riveting and awkward to watch. Despite the awkwardness of it, there is no doubt that the man is feeling his music and he is certainly in the moment. Refinement will come later, but for now it's about the spirit of the moment and the energy of the show.

The bootleg gives us plenty of musical moments too, and we are beginning to get a broad mix of performance styles. The homogenous sound of the Omni show is now replaced with an aural roller-coaster wildly flinging the audience in one direction and then another. This is nowhere more apparent than the trio of "Why You Wanna Treat Me So Bad?," "Gotta Broken Heart Again," and "Jack U Off" that come in rapid succession. Part of Prince's appeal to the wider audience is his ability to fuse styles and mix them together. From the rock of "Why You Wanna Treat Me So Bad?," the seventies radio sheen of "Gotta Broken Heart Again" or the up-tempo rockabilly "Jack U Off," all are played and presented with a confidence that is sincere. The lyrics of "Jack U Off" may be sung with a wink, but there is a lot of passion in the music, and Prince isn't just skimming the surface with these styles - they are all legitimate. He believes in the songs themselves and the styles of music he is playing. He is not just dipping his toe; he is fully committed to whatever he is playing. It's this commitment to the song that enables him to play with styles and lyrics in his shows, styles and lyrics that another audience would not accept from a less invested performer.

> **LIKE A YOUNG HORSE THAT HASN'T YET FOUND ITS FEET, OR A TEENAGER WHO HASN'T GROWN INTO HIS SKIN, PRINCE LEAPS AND SWINGS ABOUT THE STAGE IN SPASMS OF ENERGY**

The common denominator that pulls all these threads together is invariably the lead guitar and its powerful sound, be it played by Dez or Prince. Prince and his guitar abilities are highlighted in some scorching work in "Why You Wanna Treat Me So Bad?"; the last minute he alone delivering his whole arsenal, while the following "Gotta Broken Heart Again" has him playing in a delicate, colorful style. When he loses the guitar for "Jack U Off," it is Dez who picks up the slack with plenty of fire and sharp work on the fretboard, all the while under Prince's watchful eye.

4TH JUNE 1981 - THÉÂTRE LE PALACE, PARIS

Despite a subdued crowd, Prince and the still unnamed band play a clean, sharp set that touches on the new wave sound that Prince was pushing at the time. "When You Were Mine" is Prince's best known and well-loved new wave song, and it slots perfectly into the set list. With its slightly off-color lyrics and electric new wave sound, it is at this point where the music and concert moves into a new direction. The warm-up is over; from here on in everything is turned up to eleven.

"Gotta Stop (messin' about)," "Sexy Dancer," and "Sister" maintain the energy and give the show a great push forward. The crowd maybe standing still, but the music is vibrant and has an inner energy that is undeniable. The highlight has to be when Prince, Andre, and Dez stand in a semi-circle facing one another, each playing and feeding off the other. They may not be making eye contact but there is a feeling of comradery as the music at this point is locked in tight.

A surprisingly bluesy sounding guitar rattling and shaking at the start of "Partyup" brings another genre of music into the show. It's only a brief glimpse of this style, enough to perhaps sense Prince could give more of this in future years to come. Like anything, it's easy to project these indicators from the past into the future, brazenly using hindsight to teleologically prove what would be to come, but it is intriguing to hear this guitar sound early in his career.

"Partyup" has Prince and the band back to the front of the stage - fusing two key parts of Prince's performances together, the obligatory party song along with the howl and whine of his guitar. It may not ignite the crowd, but thirty-five years on it still sounds strident and bold in its sheer noise and confidence. The shy-talking Prince of early days is gone, and here Prince angrily stomps around the front of the stage extolling the crowd to party up, at one stage even going so far to call them pecker heads. It may not be the most subtle way to encourage a crowd, but it is effective in conveying Prince's mood and attitude.

There is a feeling that the show has been building to something and that something is "Dirty Mind." Prince is suitably attired at this stage in nothing except his briefs and leg warmers. He is full of confidence and the music is strong and bold behind him, pushing him further in front with his energetic dancing as alluded to earlier. An instinctive performer, Prince leaps about with great abandon, unrehearsed with only his music as a guide for what he might do next. The song always has a lot of drive in the live setting, and the music is propelled forward as the band cut into their work. The bootleg sounds great at this stage with the visuals going hand in hand. This stands as the most memorable part of the show.

Closing out the show with a guitar heavy "Uptown" leaves the memorable image of Prince stripped down with guitar slung about him, already with the look of a rock star in waiting. The image is matched with some great guitar playing; both rhythm and lead guitar shine, and it is a credit to Prince that he lets Dez do most of the heavy lifting on the lead while he climbs atop the stacks to engage the audience. The show has plenty of memorable moments, yet it is "Dirty Mind" and "Uptown" that top them all. The final few minutes make this bootleg unforgettable as image after image and riff after riff pound out.

> **THE FINAL FEW MINUTES MAKE THIS BOOTLEG UNFORGETTABLE AS IMAGE AFTER IMAGE AND RIFF AFTER RIFF POUND OUT**

Of course nothing is perfect, and it is a shame that this recording is missing two songs that would have been key in the performance - "Head," and "I Wanna Be Your Lover." Both are staples of shows at this time, and each highlight a different strength of Prince that isn't touched on elsewhere in the show, namely the low down dirty funk sound of "Head," and the up-beat pop sensibilities of "I Wanna Be Your Lover." These are the yin and yang of Prince's oeuvre. Through the years he has constantly swung between pure pop and dirty funk, while settling on neither. Although an enjoyable show, it must be remembered that these key elements are missing and the concert is incomplete. It's not uncommon for songs to be missing on various bootlegs, and there will be further frustrating examples in future.

For his first appearance in mainland Europe, Prince must have been hoping to make an impression and he certainly delivered on that front. The performance is memorable for a variety of reasons, and it looks every bit as good as it sounds. It is hard to disconnect the visuals from the music; Prince has always excelled at combining the two into a single artistic statement throughout his career and here is no different. As always there is just as much attention given to the look of the show as to the music. With Prince creating a complete performance, the concert is a great addition to listen to and even better to watch. This is Prince again on the cusp of change giving us a lively, spirited performance with a bootleg that perfectly complements the event.

4TH JUNE 1981 - THÉÂTRE LE PALACE, PARIS

SET LIST

1. Do It All Night
2. Why You Wanna Treat Me So Bad?
3. Gotta Broken Heart Again
4. Jack U Off
5. When You Were Mine
6. Gotta Stop (Messin' About)
7. Sexy Dancer
8. Sister
9. Still Waiting
10. Partyup
11. Dirty Mind
12. Uptown

RELEASES

- City Lights: New York/Paris Dirty Mind Club Tour 1981 - *Superhero*
- City Lights Remastered & Extended Volume 1 - *Sabotage*
- Le Palais, Paris 81 - *Premium*
- Live In The City Of Light - *NPR*
- A Dirty Mind In... Paris - *Fan Release*
- Paris '81 - *GSH/Team FDA*
- Paris '81 - *Habibi*
- Prince Live '81 - *Global Funkschool*

11th OCTOBER 1981
MEMORIAL COLISEUM, LOS ANGELES

Some Prince bootleg recordings are considered more important than others. While some capture a band in peak form playing on those magical nights when you can almost feel the intensity and the sweat running down the walls, others are crystal clear quality with every element caught in near perfection for us to enjoy. And then there are other recordings, focused on neither the passion nor exquisite nature of the music, but instead a moment in history when something significant happens and becomes part of folklore. This recording is one of these moments. Although it is only a twenty-minute audience recording, it is one of the most significant bootlegs of Prince's early career.

Like Michael Jordan being cut from his high school team and then rising to complete domination in the NBA, the story of Prince being booed off opening for The Rolling Stones has now passed into part of his personal mythos, part of his struggle and his legend. Would his ascent to the throne a top of pop music in the '80s been quite as spectacular without adversary and this misstep from 1981?

Much has been written about the two gigs when Prince opened for The Rolling Stones prior to his *Controversy* tour. It has been well documented how Prince was roundly booed on both occasions and pelted with trash. Whether or not we can say he was booed off the stage on October 11 is debatable; he certainly left mid-set, but the band does finish their set, briefly and not without incident.

Listening to the full recording from that day, taking in the sets of George Thorogood and The J. Geils band, offers a more balanced experience from what can be heard during the Prince part of the recording. The person recording the show is obviously familiar with Prince and offers an even-handed assessment of his performance. The taper can be heard on the recording commenting that the band would be better in a small club and the performance wasn't terrible, despite the audible displeasure of the audience in the background. And although the recording is cut short, this isn't necessarily because the set list was cut short, but more due to the fact the taper was preserving batteries and had limited tape available to boot. With these facts in mind, the bootleg of the performance that day seems better than first appearances might suggest.

As an audience recording, it takes a few seconds to adjust to the grubby sound. At first it is just noise, before the opening riff of "Bambi" can be heard emerging from the chaos. The most striking aspect early on is how muscular and strong the song is. Prince and Dez's guitars are turned up and their playing is sharp. "Bambi" has always been a strong rock song, but here they are pushing it as far as it will go, beyond the limits of the stage, reaching out as far as they can into an audience that is here for basic rock 'n' roll - nothing more, nothing less. The other thing that stands out early is how well Brown Mark is playing. As one of his first gigs with Prince, aside from a warm-up show the previous week, and in front of 94,000 people, his playing is stridently confident despite what he might have been feeling onstage.

> **WHEN PRINCE STARTS SINGING IT IS NOT IN HIS USUAL FALSETTO AND THAT SHOULDN'T BE A SURPRISE - HE IS PANDERING TO THE ROLLING STONES AUDIENCE**

When Prince starts singing it is not in his usual falsetto and that shouldn't be a surprise - he is pandering to The Rolling Stones audience. The song is better for it. Singing in this lower register makes it solid in sound and it hits stronger. With this acoustic shift, the song hits in the chest and it hits hard. The crowd doesn't sound too hostile at this stage; they sound like any other crowd that is waiting in the hot sun for the support band to finish so they can see the main event: that is, disinterested and slightly restless.

Next up is "When You Were Mine," and while Dez addresses the audience during the introduction, acknowledging that the crowd are waiting for The Rolling Stones, there is plenty of chatter among the audience, suggesting that perhaps they don't care too much for what is happening onstage - especially as someone can be heard saying "One more song then that'll be enough for this band." As the song kicks off, for the first time the keyboards can be heard - they do not feature as prominently in the mix as they do on the album. It is again all about the guitars that are turned to eleven for the rock crowd. Wiry and jagged, the guitars bleed across everything, leaving a smear of dirty rock across the bootleg. Boisterous throughout, the crowd noise intensifies as the song goes on, before providing an ironic cheer as the song ends.

The band goes straight into "Jack U Off" without pause. It is during this song that it becomes apparent they are playing to a hostile audience. The booing is noticeable, especially as Prince sings "As a matter of fact, you can jack me off" followed midway through the song by an audience member commenting "Look at all that trash." The song may sound like it ends in a flourish, but the booing is loud and prolonged. This is the turning point of the show, and from here on in the ride gets rougher, both for the band and the listener at home.

"Uptown" follows and it is notable for the conspicuous absence of Prince himself. After whatever has gone down in the first few songs, he has cut his losses and left the stage. And here you have to give credit to the band; they stay on in front of 94,000 Rolling Stones fans and play on without Prince. It's ironic that the band should go on when the man who would be feted as a musical icon for the rest of his career did not have the confidence or audacity to continue. Best of all, they still sound good, testament to how well rehearsed and professional they were. Surprisingly the song itself doesn't suffer too much from a lack of vocals. There is more room for the instruments to play, and Dez sounds great as he crunches through the song. Normally "Uptown" is overwhelmed by the lyrics and the message, but here the music itself comes to the fore. Of the songs on the bootleg, this is one that would benefit most from a quality recording, as it is a classy performance that deserves better.

Prince is back on-board for the final song, "Why You Wanna Treat Me So Bad?" He has returned to the stage and is at his rightful place for the final song. Again he is singing lower, especially the chorus. It is in contrast to how it normally sounds, and again it makes this an interesting listen. The crowd noise isn't as prominent in this song, maybe they have settled down after his departure from stage. Unfortunately, the taper announces halfway through the song that he's had enough and stops the tape, leaving the listener to only guess at what happened next. Normally the second half of "Why You Wanna Treat Me So Bad?" takes off with the guitar solos; it would be fascinating to know how this went over with the Stones fans.

So it ends, one of Prince's most famous gigs and a compelling bootleg as well. While the recording isn't great, it is a fascinating look at one of the most significant moments in Prince's career. This may well have been the moment that gave Prince the push to continue on his own path with faith in his own music and style. The songs are obviously played with the predominantly white Rolling Stones audience in mind, and it is refreshing to hear them played this way. There are plenty of early recordings where Dez and Prince have their guitars right out front, but none more so than this. The recording has several shortcomings, but that doesn't lessen the importance of it. This is one of Prince's defining moments, and for those following his career it is crucial to what comes next.

SET LIST

1. Bambi
2. When You Were Mine
3. Jack U Off
4. Uptown
5. Why You Wanna Treat Me So Bad?

RELEASES

- City Lights Remastered & Extended Volume 1 - *Sabotage*
- The Dark Ages - *Fan Release*
- The 'Dirty' Dark Ages - *Fan Release*

20TH DECEMBER 1981
THE SUMMIT, HOUSTON

The show from 20th December 1981 (often mislabelled as 9th December) is the most exciting video of these early years and especially notable for being an excellent pro-shot video from the *Controversy* tour. With multiple cameras capturing the show from all angles, for the first time there is a real feel for these shows before Prince conquered the world just a few years later. Only months after the disaster of opening for The Rolling Stones, Prince has regained his confidence and then some; the performance he puts on is brimming with confidence, self-belief, and a heavy dose of showmanship. No longer playing a show tailored for the clubs, he storms through a set aimed squarely at the larger arenas, giving a concert that exceeds all expectations and takes several large strides forward in his development. This is Prince firing on all cylinders and ready to take on the world.

"The Second Coming" and "Uptown" signal this renewed confidence. No longer just seeking attention, Prince is now taking a step back and letting the music speak for itself. His appearance is smoother, as are his stage movements, and there is a shift to a more mainstream look with the dancing in particular already more polished.

After this appetizer, it is the next four songs that serve as the main course for the evening, a quartet of "Why You Wanna Treat Me So Bad?," "I Wanna Be Your Lover," "Head," and "Dirty Mind." Between the four of them, they make up almost half the playing time. Prince is ready to embrace this wider audience, and for the most part he looks as if he is reveling in the moment. He knows he has the audience won over from the start; the knowing smiles, cocky winks, and telling nods are apparent for all to see. He is a man who knows exactly what he is doing and why. The sly wink to the audience as he humps his guitar in "Why You Wanna Treat Me So Bad?" gives the game away, as does the cheeky "Jingle Bells" he plays to end the song.

There is the boldness of his speech over the shimmering and shining start of "I Wanna Be Your Lover," and a sassiness to his performance. The rest of the band maybe playing cool, but it is Prince who is in complete control and living in the moment, feeling the music as much as he is playing it. The segue into "Head" had previously felt like a descent into darkness; in this larger context it becomes a funk monster, an opportunity for the audience to get up and dance. The lyrics are as nasty as always, but this time Prince is fully dressed and slightly safer. Maybe not a lot safer but certainly he has moved on from the wild-looking man he was eighteen months ago. As the audience sings the key lyric, there is the feeling that they have come to his level rather than he has moved to theirs.

> **THE REST OF THE BAND MAYBE PLAYING COOL, BUT IT IS PRINCE WHO IS IN COMPLETE CONTROL AND LIVING IN THE MOMENT**

For those that focus on the music more than the look, there is plenty to enjoy, with the extended guitar jam in the darkness the obvious highlight. Under the single spotlight it is Prince who shines, his guitar whining, before sliding into a funky groove that settles on a sexy lead guitar sound that rolls up several different genres in a single sound that can only be defined by one word - "Prince." The masturbation play seems longer, more entertaining, and again is more fun than dirty.

A dynamic "Dirty Mind" ends the quartet on a spirited high. Prince and the band play a high-powered version that has the stage abound with energy, as well as providing Prince a chance to demonstrate his ample keyboard skills. Humor and entertainment are key as he speaks to the audience mid-song before indulging in some lively dance moves that are a million miles from what was seen at the Paris show. As always he is evolving right here onstage. It is important to remember that the Paris show was only nine months before this, but it may well have been a life-time ago as there is no comparison between the two. That Prince was spirited and out of control; this one is full of smoothness and speaks of a man who has found his inner cool.

The first half of the show is electrifying and it is impossible, even for Prince, to match it for intensity and ferocity as the second half commences. However, he does his best, upping the showmanship in the latter part of the concert in compensation. The songs may not have the fire of early on, but there is still plenty to entertain and enjoy.

"Do Me, Baby" is a good example of this - the song sounds great, but it is the performance that makes it what it is. Prince works the audience, and himself, into a sweat - stripping both the vocals and his clothes as he goes. His voice may carry the first minutes of the song, but it is the showmanship that carries the last few as he talks dirty to the crowd while slowly stripping clothes off. All the while the band plays a heavenly soundtrack to this seduction fantasy unfolding onstage. It works as Prince sells his performance and the song with self-belief and sincerity.

> **PRINCE WORKS THE AUDIENCE, AND HIMSELF, INTO A SWEAT - STRIPPING BOTH THE VOCALS AND HIS CLOTHES AS HE GOES**

Similarly, "Controversy" isn't as demanding as the earlier songs, despite having plenty of funk of its own. Again, Prince's performance is what keeps it interesting, including some dancing early on that is reminiscent of Ian Curtis. With arms jerking and twitching, he twists about the stage with a frenzied energy. He knows how to work the stage and relentlessly stalks back and forth, making sure everyone in the arena is engaged in his performance. If anything the performance is too good - it looks effortlessly easy, and it is as smooth as it is on the album. The visuals are just as important as the music, highlighted by the lighting that presents a lit cross and providing a back drop that hints at stained glass windows as Prince ends the song bathed in light and color.

After the intensity of the first third of the show, the smooth coolness of the second part, we change tack again for the final third of the show. It comes as a light dessert; there is nothing too demanding to listen to or watch, the main focus is sheer enjoyment. "Let's Work" sets the scene for what will follow. Over the upbeat dance groove, Prince works the audience with lively dance moves and some call and response. It is brightly lit, and now is the time when the audience can become part of the show with their dancing and singing. The song is deceptively easy, and one feels the band could play to this audience all night long.

This sense of fun and playfulness is maintained through the final encore of "Private Joy" and "Jack U Off." Prince's humor is at play,

20TH DECEMBER 1981 - THE SUMMIT, HOUSTON

ending the show with two songs about masturbation - one a delicious pop song and the other a firebrand of a rock song that jumps out of the gate. "Private Joy" has a natural warmth to it and, despite the subject matter, could easy fit on any pop radio playlist. Prince plays it as the fun song it is; he bounds around the stage as much as he dances, and the spring in his step can be heard in the music. With plenty of swagger, he entrusts Dez with a solo that includes playing with his teeth before Prince abruptly stops the song to bring us a quick "Jack U Off." The energy of the song is matched by the energy of Prince's dance moves, and the band is giving their all to close out the show. There is nothing left to hold back for, and they open the flood gates on a crescendo of noise as they sprint to the finish line. It is a storming finish that leaves the crowd breathless, even if Prince onstage isn't. The whole evening is summed up in the final seconds as Prince asks the crowd who they belong to with a gleeful look in his eye and a playful wink. Music is supposed to be fun, and he knows it.

> "THE WHOLE EVENING IS SUMMED UP IN THE FINAL SECONDS AS PRINCE ASKS THE CROWD WHO THEY BELONG TO WITH A GLEEFUL LOOK IN HIS EYE AND A PLAYFUL WINK"

A delightful video, this is high-point of any collection of Prince's early years. Some may bemoan the fact that it is only just over an hour long, although, to be fair, that is the standard length of his shows at this time. Anything longer would be adding unnecessary fat to a show that is streamlined to perfection. There is not a wasted moment and nothing feels redundant. Prince has grown into himself by this stage; he is confident and cocky and certainly looks a lot more in control of himself onstage. One can see how much he is enjoying playing to the crowd and interacting with them; in turn they are far more comfortable with his performance and accepting of his show. It is a symbiotic relationship, and Prince is perfectly at home on this larger stage and with a wider audience. Compared to the earlier shows, he is now playing with a knowing smile that suggests he is happy with where he is and knows where he is going.

SET LIST

1. Second Coming
2. Uptown
3. Why You Wanna Treat Me So Bad?
4. I Wanna Be Your Lover
5. Head
6. Dirty Mind
7. Do Me, Baby
8. Controversy
9. Let's Work
10. Private Joy
11. Jack U Off

RELEASES

- City Lights Remastered & Extended Volume 2 - *Sabotage*
- You Belong To Prince - *Observation Records*
- The Summit 81 - *Superball*
- The Summit Houston, 1981 - *Habibi*

28TH FEBRUARY 1982
SAENGER THEATER, NEW ORLEANS

The bootlegs covered so far have all been great recordings in the sense that they capture the development and on-going evolution of Prince in the first few years. With the exception of The Rolling Stones recording, they are all quality sounding recordings of decent gigs. The recording from February 1982 in New Orleans differs however. This is the first example of a dazzling show matched with a soundboard recording. That's not to say the previous bootlegs weren't good, but in this show there is an intensity and fire that hasn't previously been heard. In this case Prince plays a furious, utterly compelling set, and with the band he gives a memorable concert that connects not just musically but also emotionally. Prince is the master of injecting emotion into his music and especially so with his guitar playing. He draws emotion from his guitar that easily matches, or even surpasses, any lyric or vocal he gives in depth of feeling and pure passion. This gives Prince's guitar playing depth and sets him apart from other players of his generation. Plenty can play technically well, but very few play with heart and soul. Throughout this show the guitar is used to devastating effect, crying when it needs to cry, singing when it needs to sing, howling when it needs to howl. Sometimes it is a soft smoldering ember of a sound, while at other times it burns with an incandescent rage, all of it tapping into something that Prince cannot express with words alone. His guitar playing is not over-played though; Prince knows when to hold back and when to deliver the killer blow, the highs made bolder by the lows in between as he plays with the dynamics of the music.

The guitar isn't the only highlight on this recording. Prince has surrounded himself with a supporting cast that elevates his own abilities and gives him a solid base from which he can fly. Dez and Brown Mark get plenty of praise, as do Dr. Fink and Lisa, but at this show it is Bobby Z who is driving the music forward. Bobby Z is sometimes overlooked (with a strong front line, it is easy to forget the man at the back), but he always delivers and did more than his fair share in creating the Prince sound. Although in later years he played in and around drum machine tracks, here he is in all his glory - crisp, clean drumming propelling the songs forward at every opportunity. This is apparent from the very first moments as his sharp drum roll builds the excitement that leads directly into "Uptown." It is a fantastic opening that leaps out of the speakers and lays down the template for what will follow, songs delivered with plenty of fire and urgency. The drum sound machine guns out, giving a sense of purpose as the storm of the show swirls around this core.

Prince and the band played almost every single night on the *Controversy* tour, and while this show falls near the end of the tour, it is delivered with boundless energy and passion. The drums, guitars, and keyboards propel the music forward, and Prince himself is equally caught up in the moment with his yells, whoops, and shouts. He is rough around the edges, but that is not a negative at all and adds to the glorious live feel of the recording. It is far from what is heard on record - the smooth electronic sound replaced with a ragged passion, the vocals of "Uptown" become exclamation points and rallying cries. Prince is nailing his colors to the mast and the crowd is swept up with him. Every drum-beat of Bobby Z comes as a great crash that emphasizes Prince's stance and attitude.

The opening few minutes are frantic with the crash of Bobby Z and the grinding guitars of Prince and Dez. It is not all full throttle, and after a similar opening on "Why You Wanna Treat Me So Bad?" things pull back for the verses and allow Prince space to sing. This is where he picks up the emotional drive with his vocals, speaking some lines rather than singing them, adding more humanity along with the emotional impact. Even over the guitar solos, Prince continues with this trick; ad-libs are called out, sometimes in anger, sometimes in hurt, but always with an emotional tug. Impulsive and leaping out of the speakers, these moments capture the essence of live performance and provide an almost punk-like energy to the show. Prince is singing and playing as if this is the first (and possibly last) time he is playing to an audience.

The next two short, snappy pop songs are equally infused with these moments. "When You Were Mine" gets a chanting introduction that sucks the crowd into it before spitting them out with Prince finishing the song screaming "My babe, my babe, my babe." "I Wanna Be Your Lover" may start with an intergalactic twinkle and infectious pop hook, but it is the vocals that lend the humanity to it, the backing singers chiming in on the chorus, before the crowd pick up the baton and continue in the same manner.

There are two songs on this recording that make it the essential bootleg it is. First, the long work out on "Head." Prince plays an absolutely filthy version that more than lives up to its subject matter. Opening with bass and guitar, the song immediately takes on the heavy funk missing from the first few songs, while the synth playing is so deliciously sharp and electric it is an even better indication of what will follow for the next few minutes. The keyboard is everywhere, over and under the music, with the ever-present funk guitar filling the spaces in between. The song reeks of dirtiness, griminess, and filth, its dark tentacles reaching out to the audience and through the next few songs. Everything locks into the feel, every note, every beat; all of them build on top of one another creating a funk monster, all the while sounding every bit as dirty as the words Prince is singing. Dr. Fink's work on this song is legendary and rightly so: nobody plays the solo quite like he does - the solo at this show is just as frantic and distinctive as ever. Even Prince having the crowd chant "head" before his masturbation scene can't match the sexiness of the music itself. The guitar solos themselves achieve the desired effect, and they leave one feeling unwashed and in need of a shower by the time the song ends.

> **THE SONG REEKS OF DIRTINESS, GRIMINESS, AND FILTH, ITS DARK TENTACLES REACHING OUT TO THE AUDIENCE AND THROUGH THE NEXT FEW SONGS**

Bobby Z can again be heard all over "Annie Christian," but it is the following "Dirty Mind" that bookends "Head" and serves as the other pillar of the show. The song has an inner energy of its own, here more so than ever, as the guitar plays along the keyboard lines, giving a sharpness to the warm fullness of the keyboard. Of all the songs on this recording, this is the one that has the most life to it and is the moment when you can almost feel the sweat and the heat of the show coming out of the speakers. As great as this is, it is when Prince drops the guitars out for some dirty talk to the audience that the song becomes a more personal moment. As the music heaves back and forth, Prince speaks lines that could in any other circumstance be considered corny, but he makes them sexy and gets away with it. This lull makes the final return of the guitars and rush for the finish all the more powerful. In the closing minutes the band is flying and carrying the audience on a wave of emotional energy.

"Do Me, Baby" is in complete contrast, although it too hinges on the keyboard. The keyboard and the bass pivot back and forth, creating a tension that Prince lays his first great seduction ballad over the top of. The keyboards sound intergalactic, while the bass rises out of the ground in its earthiness. Meanwhile Prince beams his vocals in from another place altogether, managing to balance the song between futuristic and something that sounds like an ageless piece of seduction on vinyl.

> **THE KEYBOARDS SOUND INTERGALACTIC, WHILE THE BASS RISES OUT OF THE GROUND IN ITS EARTHINESS**

No Prince show would be complete without a couple of songs to get the crowd moving, and here "Controversy" and "Let's Work" fit the bill. Dez makes it clear from the start of "Controversy" with his "party in here tonight, everyone on your feet" what to expect. Although lighter than the previous songs, it nevertheless engages the audience just as much as anything else. With the continuing battle between the guitars and keyboards, there is a dynamic tension in the song that comes across well on the recording. Prince works the crowd well, with a brief break before the encore of "Let's Work" picks up from where "Controversy" left off. The difference comes with the guitar, buried in the background for "Let's Work," the bass work of Brown Mark picking up the slack and keeping things moving.

The show ends with an out of place "Jack U Off." It is lively and played with a lot of heart, but it is the redheaded step-child of the show. Despite the burst of energy and blast of guitar, it still feels like it doesn't quite fit and is a song looking for a home. It does give the show a sharp finish however, and there is a sense of finality as it ends and Prince walks off.

These are the same songs that Prince played night after night during the *Controversy* tour, and there are other nights when the performance was just as good as this one. However, this is the show that has been bootlegged, and of the circulating bootlegs of the *Controversy* tour, this is the one that stands out in regard to performance and sheer exuberance. There is much to recommend this one musically, but it is that live feel and performance that make it a must-have recording. Prince still has his youthful energy, and here it is more focused than ever, giving this show an intensity that is unmatched anywhere else in these early years.

SET LIST

1. Uptown
2. Why You Wanna Treat Me So Bad?
3. When You Were Mine
4. I Wanna Be Your Lover
5. Head
6. Annie Christian
7. Dirty Mind
8. Do Me, Baby
9. Controversy
10. Let's Work
11. Jack U Off

RELEASES

- City Lights Remastered & Extended Volume 2 - *Sabotage*
- His Royal Badness - *Men At Work*
- Jack U Off - *Swingin Pig Records*
- Live USA - *Imtrat*
- Pop - *Three Cool Cats*
- R U All Ready - *Pure Funk*
- Super Funks - *Traditional Line*
- The Second Coming Live - *Purple Gold Archives*
- Why You Wanna Treat Me So Bad - *Templer*

8TH MARCH 1982
FIRST AVENUE, MINNEAPOLIS

Recorded just a week before the end of the *Controversy* tour, this one-off show from First Avenue captures Prince at a very obvious point between phases in his professional career. The set list contains a couple of new songs that would later appear on the *1999* album, and Prince is enthusiastic and eager to present these songs and new music to his hometown fans. There are recordings from Sam's, as First Avenue was formerly known, but this is the first recording we have from the newly named First Avenue, a venue that became and is still synomonous with Prince. The concert is rough and ready - a gut-punch of a performance, and has plenty to recommend it. It is a nod to the future, and a lot closer to the loose, freewheeling, anything-could-happen performances that Prince would later exhibit at his aftershows.

From the opening "Bambi" to the final "Party Up," everything is played in a frenzied, wild manner, and there is the sense that the band are feeling relaxed and loose, exactly the sound that comes through the recording. It doesn't matter what is played; how it is played is important, and everything here comes with a grin and a wild sense of abandonment along with an exuberant love of the music.

Prince makes us well aware of what we are in for with his "This is not a concert, this is a dance" and "The only reason we're here is that there is no place else to go" quips. They sound like throwaway lines, but Prince and the band live up to these words. The next sixty minutes has the band cutting loose and playing for themselves, for their fans, and for the sheer love of being in a band and creating music.

The tone is set with a savage-sounding "Bambi." Rowdy, it has Prince's vocals struggling to be heard over the din on the audience recording of the show, while the soundboard recording delivers a far more even listening experience. There is a raucous garage band sound that leaves little room for him to be heard, the guitars and drums building a dense wall of noise from the start that is both a challenge and a statement of intent. It's no bad thing - the band has energy to burn and play with a liveliness that has the music jumping out of the speakers. The recordings may vary in quality, but the performance is still primary and rises above any audio limitations. "Bambi" has never been about the vocals; it is Prince's guitar solos that command attention and make this one of the better versions out there, each cascade of notes coming like a swarm of angry bees from the stage, stinging and buzzing in intensity.

The then yet-to-be-released "All The Critics Love U In New York" gets the same treatment. Though smooth and cool sounding on record, in this setting the band stomp all over it, providing the audience with a much harder sound. This is when the band are at their loosest, with plenty of onstage talk during the song as Dez calls for a drink while Prince calls out band members at various times. The electronic backbeat is still present, the heavy guitar the point of difference with both Dez and Prince playing exceptional solos. This is typical of what we will later hear in Prince's aftershows, the rarely heard song stretched out and played with different aspects highlighted - in this case it's the guitar, although Dr. Fink does provide a fast and intricate solo to match. From here it's not too much of a jump to the aftershows we will hear in the late '80s and beyond.

> **THERE IS A RAUCOUS GARAGE BAND SOUND THAT LEAVES LITTLE ROOM FOR HIM TO BE HEARD, THE GUITARS AND DRUMS BUILDING A DENSE WALL OF NOISE FROM THE START THAT IS BOTH A CHALLENGE AND A STATEMENT OF INTENT**

"When You Were Mine" keeps to this almost experimental, certainly reorganized theme, containing a different arrangement to previous versions with lead guitar firmly to the fore. This guitar heavy onslaught is maintained for the first three songs (which include "All The Critics Love U In New York"), and it is not until "Sexy Dancer" that the band reigns in this vibrant, almost unstoppable sound. "Sexy Dancer" is well placed, providing some variation after the metal grind of the opening numbers and giving other band members a chance to be heard - especially Dr. Fink who delivers up a solo that runs for a couple of minutes in his own inimitable style. It has a freshness to it in this setting and gives the evening some polish and shine (although some of this work is undone by Dez who dirties up the sound again with his solo that brings the song to its conclusion).

The set list ebbs and flows, the opening assault, then a come down with "Sexy Dancer" before the following "Still Waiting." "Still Waiting" has early protégé Sue Ann Carwell singing with Prince, yet another reason this bootleg is worth listening to, and her voice works wonderfully well with Prince when it comes to the chorus. This may not be the best song in this rough and tumble performance; but its delicate nature highlights the contrasting genres Prince dabbles with after the furious earlier assault. The vocal interplay between Prince and Sue Ann is a highlight, even with his bizarre ad lib of "I got cause to celebrate, because my girlfriend died."

Normally "Head" would be the showpiece of the gig with Prince drawing out the theatrics in it. On this recording it is lost in the chaos of the show and lacks the funk we normally associate with it. In terms of a long jam it is easily overshadowed by the earlier "All The Critics Love U In New York" and "Sexuality," which will end the first part of the show. Against these songs it sounds tepid, and although the guitars are strong and the enthusiastic crowd try their best to be heard, it all ends up being less than the sum of its parts.

Prince's call of "read my lips, Sexuality" ignites the band, and they burn with a fire for the rest of that song. Screams and a scratch guitar clearly mark it as a Prince performance, while the other players do their best to match him for intensity and energy. The band is playing pedal to the metal, and considering there are only six of them onstage, they are making a frightful noise. The fast and furious first half of the song is offset by a long coda, the crowd singing and clapping the chorus for the remainder of the song. The humor of Prince is highlighted with his singing "never let it be said, white people ain't got no soul," which brings the main part of the show to a close.

> **THE MOST APPEALING PART OF THIS BOOTLEG COMES NEXT, A RARE APPEARANCE OF THE TIME AND PRINCE PLAYING TOGETHER ON THE SAME STAGE**

The most appealing part of this bootleg comes next, a rare appearance of The Time and Prince playing together on the same stage. For any Prince fan, this is the part of the recording that gets the mouth watering. Prince makes the inside joke that "we share the same management, they gotta play too," which can well be appreciated now. The recording catches the bands swapping over, a relaxed atmosphere apparent throughout and there is plenty of humor and banter through this final encore. Everyone is obviously comfortable and familiar with one another, and this ease is heard on the recording. The Time plays "Dance To The Beat," upbeat and fun although not up to the standard of what we have so far heard during the show. "The Stick" is better, but still pales against the earlier Prince material. It has a much stronger groove to it than "Dance To The Beat" and works better with bass and keyboard combination. It has the vintage Time sound and is representative of what they were about, it even has Morris calling for a mirror.

The final song sees Prince joining The Time onstage for the finale of the show and the recording. Prince is heard instantly taking command, first asking Morris if he can still play the drums and then engaging confidently in some light banter. It's all light hearted and a treat to hear them interacting so casually together. With Morris on the drums they take on "Partyup," an interesting choice given the history of the song. The band and the song are enthusiastic and loose; there is a sense of fun that radiates through the performance and gives it vitality. Their familiarity, having previously played for hours together, permeates the music as they are playing, both complementing the other as the song flows on. Morris even plays a drum break that sounds as joyful to play as to listen to. For a few moments one can sense his smile as he rattles and rolls across the drum kit. It's shoehorned into the song, but it does keep with the fun, unscripted theme of the show. Brown Mark and Lisa can both be heard adding their influence on the song, but Prince steals the moment from them all with a furious incandescent guitar solo. The only downside is at this point the recording fades out and ends just as the guitar was reaching new heights.

As a one-off show this signals the way Prince will go with his aftershows in future. With its free and easy sound, relaxed attitude, and interesting set list it can be easily viewed as a prototype for those later concerts. The concert has long circulated as a poor audience recording, however the newer soundboard more than makes up for it with "All The Critics Love U In New York" and "Sexuality" being standouts and the final "Partyup" with Morris and Prince ending the show in style. Not polished and not pretty, but certainly indispensable to the bootleg collection.

SET LIST

1. Bambi
2. All The Critics Love U In New York
3. When You Were Mine
4. Sexy Dancer
5. Still Waiting
6. Head
7. Sexuality
8. Dance To The Beat
9. The Stick
10. Partyup

RELEASES

- Dance 2 The Beat - *Moonraker*
- Downtown Danceteria - *Eye Records*
- First Avenue '82 - *4DaFunk*
- International Lover - *Templer*
- Live In U.S.A. 1982 - *Golden Stars*
- Still Funky's D2tB rem. - *Fan Release*
- The Second Coming - *Eye Records*

3RD AUGUST 1983
FIRST AVENUE, MINNEAPOLIS

Of the fifty essential bootlegs, only a handful could be safely called legendary and the Minnesota Dance Theater Benefit show certainly falls into that category. Some shows are untouchable and so much a part of the Prince mythos that they become legendary from the moment they are first heard, instant classics, and this bootleg is one of those shows. This is a keystone performance of the *Purple Rain* era, and even if it hadn't been recorded it would still be talked about to this day. Recorded between the albums *1999* and *Purple Rain*, the video and audio captures the genesis of what will follow in the coming years. It is iconic on so many levels.

First of all, it is Wendy Melvoin's debut with the band, and that in itself is a key marker for the storm that will follow in the next few years. Wendy will prove to be foil for Prince to play off and someone who gave as good as she got (at least in the bootleg recordings currently circulating). She may have been young, but she was already one tough lady who could rock when she had to, funk out as required, and do both to an extremely high level that belied her age at the time.

Secondly, this recording introduces six new songs, three of them recorded for the basic tracks of the *Purple Rain* album ("I Would Die 4 U," "Baby I'm A Star," and "Purple Rain" itself). This accounts for the magnificent live sound these songs have on the album; they are fizzing with energy and have a youthful enthusiasm to them on the *Purple Rain* release. Here we see the bones of them laid bare. Again, listening to these songs as they happened is a mouthwatering proposition for any fan.

Finally, we have two unreleased songs, including the long-standing fan favorite "Electric Intercourse." The most famous song that Prince never released? Perhaps, although the classic "Moonbeam Levels" would probably tie with it for die-hard fans. I will say though, this performance lives up to its name and is truly electrifying. Likewise, the cover of Joni Mitchell's "A Case Of You" garners rave reviews and for good reason. Prince connects with the song, and he sings the lyrics with such emotion and conviction you could swear they were his alone.

Each one of these would be reason enough to rate this recording highly; taken all together the recording becomes untouchable, essential beyond measure.

From the very first notes of the show, there is the sound that something special is happening. The crowd cheers, despite the fact that none of the fans would have known the opening of "Let's Go Crazy." The frenzied anticipation that we see in the next few years isn't there (breaking out in the following year); the crowd here are expectant but not quite sure what's coming next. The most exciting aspect of the song, and the concert, is the freshness. The *Purple Rain* album and tour has been seared into memory in the thirty years since; here it still in its infancy and still has a sparkling freshness to it. Wendy makes an early impression, holding her own on the song and providing great interaction with Prince. The chemistry is apparent from the start, making it hard to believe that she is so young and has been in the band only a short time. As for her guitar playing, she steps easily into the void left by Dez. She is slight onstage, yet she holds the attention with a boldness and steely eyed look that is amplified by her forceful playing.

"When You Were Mine" has the crowd engaged again after the unknown "Let's Go Crazy," and it is just as well for the following song is one of the high points of the show. Some might even say it is among the best few minutes of Prince's live career as he takes on an outstanding cover of Joni Mitchells "A Case Of You." At the time it would have been completely unexpected for the audience, yet it makes perfect sense now looking back over Prince's career. Accompanied only by his guitar, Prince delivers a mesmerizing performance. It is hard not to be captivated by his look, his delivery, and his natural God-given talent. The song is otherworldly in its beauty, and although the lyrics aren't Prince's, he delivers them with utter conviction, more than doing justice to Joni's words. In particular

> **ACCOMPANIED ONLY BY HIS GUITAR, PRINCE DELIVERS A MESMERIZING PERFORMANCE. IT IS HARD NOT TO BE CAPTIVATED BY HIS LOOK, HIS DELIVERY, AND HIS NATURAL GOD-GIVEN TALENT**

the heartfelt delivery of the opening lines clearly come from a deeper place that connects to him.

> *Oh I am a lonely painter*
> *I live in a box of paints*
> *I'm frightened by the devil*
> *And I'm drawn to those ones that ain't afraid.*

For all his history of guitar work and rock sensibilities, Prince has never had a song quite like "Computer Blue." More than a few in the audience look on opened mouthed as it plays for the first time in public. This is a rollicking version, with more than just the guitar dark and menacing. Every instrument onstage has a sinister and heavy feel, giving it a swirling, foreboding sound. With the band pushed to the back of the stage, Prince is exposed out front, standing on the edge of the stage and pulling every guitar lick and trick that he knows as a thick, dark wall of noise is built behind him. There is no mistaking that he is the star of the show - all attention and eyes are focused on him as he steps easily into the limelight. Even with Wendy on her knees, it is still Prince wailing on the guitar that holds center stage, the expression on his face proudly displaying his obvious relish and passion while an undertone of venom escapes in the guitar's howl. It is obviously an enjoyable performance for him as he finishes with a large smile and tosses his pick to the audience.

Once again, he throws in a well-known song to keep the crowd on his side, this time with "Delirious," but again the song following leaves the biggest impression. "Electric Intercourse" is probably the most famous unreleased song in the Prince canon; a song desperately unlucky not to appear on *Purple Rain*. A lovely lost gem of a piano ballad, Prince decorates it with shrieks and screams to emphasize his emotions. There were many great songs (and a great many songs) written at this time, and this stands shoulder to shoulder with the best of them. It is testament to the quality of material Prince was recording that "Electric Intercourse" not only didn't make *Purple Rain*, it didn't even make it as a B-side.

The band is at their very best for "Automatic" and for the songs that follow. "Automatic" is missing some of its robotic coldness; the band is too good to be boxed in by the sound, and as they play with fire and passion the song ignites into a new sound. Every song on this recording is played brilliantly well and none more so than this song. The Revolution find in themselves a way to give a little more. They play with great enjoyment and a ferocity from the first moments to the last; "Automatic" is unmatched elsewhere and is riveting throughout.

The next two songs are recorded and their basic tracks used as the basis for their final incarnation on *Purple Rain*. "I Would Die 4 U" first, its distinctive drum machine an immediate highlight. The sound is surprisingly minimal, especially the chorus that has Prince releasing a single purposeful note from his guitar as he sings the hook. Asides from the drum machine, it is Prince's guitar that is the key feature; it has a wonderfully bold tone that works as the bones for the song to hang from.

Likewise, "Baby I'm A Star" was also partly used for the final album, testament to how good the rhythm section was at this time. Prince is always passionate and nowhere more so than here. "Baby I'm A Star" finds him covered in sweat and pouring his energy into the vocal performance, while a young-looking Dr. Fink bobs and weaves behind his keyboard for the solo. It is captured well by the recording, which further highlights Dr. Fink playing with a physical interpretation, much as Prince does when playing guitar.

> **IN NEAR DARKNESS PRINCE PLAYS THE OPENING VERSE BEFORE THE LIGHTS COME UP WITH THE MUSIC FOR THE CHORUS, MATCHING THE FEEL OF THE MUSIC VISUALLY AS THE SONG EMERGES FROM WARM DARKNESS**

It is a well-worn scene now, but in 1983 it was striking and new and adds a flash of excitement to the show.

The familiar strains of "Little Red Corvette" elicit squeals of delight from the crowd as Lisa is beautifully lit from behind. In near darkness Prince plays the opening verse before the lights come up with the music for the chorus, matching the feel of the music visually as the song emerges from warm darkness. Despite being a well-known song, the audience remain subdued, even with a raw performance from Prince and an even better performance from the band. The sweaty band plays hard and lets the music speak for itself. The song is strong enough to stand on its own and the band knows they don't have to do much to coax it out. As Wendy steps up to the mark to play the solo, she is strikingly young yet not the least bit intimidated; there is a cold look in her eye that is echoed in the guitar solo that follows. She plays with heavy tone; the guitar is forcefully upfront, confident, and confrontational and demands you pay attention. Wendy adds weight to the pop of the song and gives a solid backbone to the performance in what is a startling debut.

The most compelling reason to listen to this bootleg comes next with the first public performance of what will become Prince's signature song - "Purple Rain." There are many reasons that this bootleg is so highly regarded, but none more so than the next ten minutes as Prince lays down the song that will follow him for the rest of his life. The fact that this recording was used for the basic tack of the finished song tells you everything you need to know about how well it is played. Don't be fooled into thinking that this song is the same as the album however; there is a suitably drawn-out introduction to the song with Wendy playing the hanging chords as Prince indulges in some lead guitar. Foreshadowing future live performances on the tour, it is a good few minutes before Prince finally sings, walking back and forth across the stage as he prepares himself to deliver a performance that will change his life more than he could have ever imagined. The scene is set, the crowd waiting expectantly as Prince steps up to change history as he begins to sing. And sing he does, the vocals magnificent - stunning for the public debut of the song. He is sings as if the song has always existed, and he is merely the final vessel it passes through before it reaches a wider audience. It is interesting to note the expressions of the audience at the time - some of them look noticeably bored as Prince plays this new, distinctly unfunky song. Also of interest is the extra verse that doesn't make it into the final

> **THERE ARE MANY REASONS THAT THIS BOOTLEG IS SO HIGHLY REGARDED, BUT NONE MORE SO THAN THE NEXT TEN MINUTES AS PRINCE LAYS DOWN THE SONG THAT WILL FOLLOW HIM FOR THE REST OF HIS LIFE**

song. Listening here it is apparent why; it doesn't scan as well as the other verses, and the song is much more cohesive without it. There comes a joyous moment when an audience member lets out a "whoo" that can be heard on the final record, a typical live moment captured on tape forever, giving the recorded version an extra dimension and live feel. As Prince plays his impassioned final solo, there is no arm waving, no singing along, the crowd muted aside from a couple of girls near the front who seem to be feeling the spirit of it. How things will change in the next year. A stunning performance of what is still a classic. Is this one track reason enough to listen to this bootleg? The answer is a resounding yes.

After giving us a glimpse of the future, Prince ends the show in a look that is distinctly rooted in his past. "D.M.S.R." is played with Prince in his old school leg warmers, bikini briefs, long coat, and mirrored glasses. He will give these up in his conquest of a wider audience, and seeing him perform like this next to "Purple Rain" only heightens the disparity between the two eras. In many ways this is the last performance of this iteration of Prince. Everything to come in future will be tinted in purple and looked at through the kaleidoscope of fame, fortune, and all the trappings that those entail. "D.M.S.R." is a final hurrah to the era as well as a final hurrah to the show, the audience given one last chance to say good-bye to a look and sound that has carried Prince for the previous five years. The bikini briefs and leg warmers a throwback to an earlier and, perhaps, hungrier Prince. He no longer needs the attention; he has created a body of work that demands to be heard on its merits alone. With a final shot of energy and dancing, Prince and the band are leaving it all on the stage. World domination awaits and they know it, stopping abruptly before strutting off the stage with not a word to the audience.

This bootleg captures a turning point in Prince's career. The songs played here touch on his past, present, and future. Pointers are given to his influences, his future, and to what lies in the vault waiting to be discovered. The band is as cohesive as they have ever been with young Wendy Melvoin a star from the very first notes she plays. Her poise, her natural ability, and her look all compliment Prince and his vision, giving the music and band an extra sharpness and futuristic look. The blueprint for the next few years is laid out, and it is fascinating to see it unfold here before our very eyes. No words can properly do this show justice - it is truly amazing.

3RD AUGUST 1983 - FIRST AVENUE, MINNEAPOLIS

SET LIST

1. Let's Go Crazy
2. When You Were Mine
3. A Case Of You
4. Computer Blue
5. Delirious
6. Electric Intercourse
7. Automatic
8. I Would Die 4 U
9. Baby I'm A Star
10. Little Red Corvette
11. Purple Rain
12. D.M.S.R.

RELEASES

- The Avenue - *Moonraker*
- MPLS - *Dream Factory Records*
- Purple Rush Volume 5 - *Sabotage*
- First Avenue - *Ladybird*
- First Avenue '83 aka "The Avenue" - *Rupert*
- First Avenue, August 3, 1983 - *Habibi*
- Purple Rain Live Premiere - *Purple Gold Archives*
- Rain Maker - *Eye Records*
- The Makings Of Rain - *Fullasoul/Superball*

7TH JUNE 1984
FIRST AVENUE, MINNEAPOLIS

Prince used to celebrate birthdays. He did away with them later in his life, but in his twenties and thirties a birthday meant a show, and not just any show. Birthday shows always presented something special, something different. There are quite a few recordings that could lay claim to being the greatest and this recording would undoubtedly be atop of many people's lists. It oozes quality at every level: a brilliant, sparkling soundboard recording that sounds better than the recording on many of his albums; the quality of the performance by Prince and the Revolution; and, of course, those unforgettable songs played to the hilt just as Prince was about to ascend to his greatest heights. This is one bootleg that lives up to the hype and deserves all the praise it gets. "When Doves Cry" had already stormed the charts, and with *Purple Rain* just weeks away from release, this show is only one of a handful of intimate performances played before the *Purple Rain* tour, and the madness, began later in the year.

You couldn't ask for a much better opening than the spoken introduction of "Ladies and Gentlemen, Prince and the Revolution" followed by an intensely funky "17 Days" that throws down the gauntlet for all that will follow. It is better than the released version; the recording is sharp and sounds deeper and richer than it does on vinyl. The bass has an elastic feel and pulsating bouncing groove; it washes over warm and full before an aftershock of bass rumble. It is almost criminal for such a song to be relegated to a B-side, but only goes to show the quality of material Prince was producing at the time.

A slow burning "Our Destiny" follows, the keyboards being the heroes for their contributions. While the keyboards twinkle under the verses, Prince gives a casual vocal performance that has more than a hint of his true character shining through. He injects a lot of himself into the performance, and this is punctuated by the cymbals and muscular keyboard stabs during the chorus, all adding to the sense of drama the band are creating onstage.

The band is obviously well rehearsed and slip easily into "Roadhouse Garden." Yet another unreleased classic, it has a crisp guitar picking away while Prince and the girls sing with full vocals, a song that sounds like it has always existed. Although the bass line is solid, the keyboards are almost invisible, and the song well and truly revolves around the guitar and the backing vocals. It does play like one of the legendary endless jams that The Revolution generate at rehearsal, and this is reinforced as Prince tells the audience that they are just jamming. With no single member highlighted, it is an airtight jam that draws strength from its hermetically sealed sound.

In a comment that has a symmetry to his line from the *One Night Alone* tour almost twenty years later, Prince tells the crowd "Ya'll came in here expecting to drive Prince's Red Corvette, that's not going to work. We just going to play a few numbers, some of them you'll gonna know, most of them you'll won't." He ups the stakes with "Wendy wants to live forever, maybe she will" as the band plays a storming version of "All Day, All Night." The band rides on the coattails of a monster bass line courtesy of Brown Mark. This is the sound of The Revolution, and while Prince tears through the verses the music opens up spaces for the guitar and the drums to be heard cleanly.

> **" THIS IS THE SOUND OF THE REVOLUTION, AND WHILE PRINCE TEARS THROUGH THE VERSES THE MUSIC OPENS UP SPACES FOR THE GUITAR AND THE DRUMS TO BE HEARD CLEANLY "**

It has a bullet train drive and momentum to it, all gleaming and driving without let up. A pulsating song through and through, it suddenly ends with a sharp intake of breath.

The set list is balanced, and "Free" plays in complete contrast, light and airy after the dense "All Day, All Night." Equally soft, yet unforgettable, is "Noon Rendezvous," dedicated to Sheila E. Another one of Prince's famous unreleased songs (although it was recorded by Sheila E. and released on her album *The Glamorous Life*), it has an alluring, heavenly pull to it. Certainly it has a strong emotional core that belies the gentle sound. The guitar plays just enough to draw the listener in before the band lays on the smooth velvet overtones that are so intoxicating. The song laps like soft waves, two guitar solos barely raise a ripple before the final refrains of "sitting in this cafe, waiting for my baby" washes us ashore.

"Erotic City" and "Something In The Water (Does Not Compute)" are also in the set list, drawn from a deeper, darker place. Both songs are more guitar-fueled than what we hear on the recorded versions and some of the sparseness is lost. In return Prince plays with plenty of emotion and heart, which combined with the following track form the emotional heartbeat of the show. "Erotic City" runs for eight minutes, and in that time we get tight rhythm guitar as well as fiery lead guitar, both played with great aplomb, the funk of it tempered with some rock moments. "Something In The Water (Does Not Compute)" is the darker of the two - the first minutes in particular are arctic cold with the bare electronic keyboard matched with a brooding guitar riff from Prince. An atmospheric sound pervades as it is kept slow and mournful throughout. Prince captures the lonely feel of the song perfectly as he begins to sing, his "does not compute, does not compute" cold and empty. There is even a moment when he sings "what's the hang-up, bitch?" that adds a hint of desperation and feeling to the song. The song is without the drum machine heard on record, but it barely matters as Prince is sounding emotional against the icy, detached music, much like the female protagonist that the song speaks to.

> **"THE SONG IS WITHOUT THE DRUM MACHINE HEARD ON RECORD, BUT IT BARELY MATTERS AS PRINCE IS SOUNDING EMOTIONAL AGAINST THE ICY, DETACHED MUSIC, MUCH LIKE THE FEMALE PROTAGONIST THAT THE SONG SPEAKS TO"**

Of all the songs on the recording, it is "When Doves Cry" that stands above them all. Right from the first moment it is clean with the familiar drum line and the unforgettable hook from Dr. Fink marking it as unique. Prince blows his first line, mumbling "How can you...," and it is worth hearing for his fast recovery. He thinks on his feet and quickly covers with "come on, have you heard this before?" Fast and smooth; a great recovery. As Dr. Fink plays the lead line over, Prince implores the crowd to "get down" and calls the lead line several times before finally singing the first verse. This longer introduction works well, and his interaction with the crowd builds a sense of anticipation. Equally good is the outro. It too is drawn out, and after Dr. Fink finishes his solo there is a treat in store with a wonderful scratch guitar that loops over and over, adding layer after layer of funk to the recording. It is the sound often heard on rehearsals of The Revolution, finding a funky groove and playing it for what seems like forever, a sound that encapsulates beautifully the power of The Revolution. It is easily a standout of this bootleg.

After the obligatory singing of Happy Birthday, the show closes with two of Prince's tightest funk tunes. "Irresistible Bitch" and Possessed" are often paired together and here is no different as they play a crisp, tight sounding "Irresistible Bitch." It is built around the guitar, the funky riff underpins it all, and Prince takes this moment to indulge some of his band leader skills, cueing the band to stopping and start several times. "Possessed" matches it for the funk, but with a hint of pop thrown in too. There is the Vegas opening that opens to a rapid groove. Rhythm is king, the only melody coming from a simple keyboard line. With interesting keyboard jamming and Prince scatting, these songs show another side to Prince and the band. They are quite capable of stretching in different directions, the versatility of the band one of their greatest strengths, and while Prince funks and rocks with ease, the band goes with him. There will come a time when he will outgrow them altogether, but at this moment they are supporting him and pushing him every step of the way. This is the type of song that could easily be jammed on; we have plenty of other examples of The Revolution taking similar songs and pushing them to the limit, so it is surprising that the song comes to an abrupt halt on the command of Prince. It is a sharp finish to what is an exceptional show.

> **WITH INTERESTING KEYBOARD JAMMING AND PRINCE SCATTING, THESE SONGS SHOW ANOTHER SIDE TO PRINCE AND THE BAND**

This soundboard recording is one of the finest bootlegs of Prince's currently in circulation. After the release of *Purple Rain*, everything will change, and this is the last show before Prince attained mega stardom. This bootleg is a superb recording of the final step of Prince before he conquered the world. The songs are there, the performance is there, and the recording matches these high standards. There are not many bootlegs that could top this; this one is something special and as such they don't come much more essential than this.

SET LIST

1. 17 Days
2. Our Destiny
3. Roadhouse Garden
4. All Day, All Night
5. Free
6. Noon Rendezvous
7. Erotic City
8. Something In The Water (Does Not Compute)
9. When Doves Cry
10. Happy Birthday
11. Irresistible Bitch
12. Possessed

RELEASES

- 26 - *4DaFunk*
- Birthday Partying - *Horny Toad Productions*
- From The Soundboard: 1984 Birthday Show - *Anonymous, FBG & 4DaFunk*
- Happy B. Day - *Dream Factory Records*
- Purple Rush Volume 5 - *Sabotage*
- Night Before the Reign - *Eye Records*

26th December 1984
ST PAUL CIVIC CENTER, ST PAUL

The success of *Purple Rain* was a watershed moment in Prince's career and life. No longer was he an up-and-comer hungry for success; now he was a hit on a global scale and the subsequent *Purple Rain* concert tour reflected this. Playing to large arenas and stadiums, this was Prince at his most triumphant, arriving at each show as an all-conquering hero to thousands of adoring fans. The *Purple Rain* shows were delivered on a grand scale; they were large in spectacle and set pieces and as such were highly structured night after night. This is great for a concert tour, but not so great for a bootleg collector where variety and one-offs count for more than a mechanistic, less human, and repetitive set. With the same set list throughout the tour there were not many special, one-off moments - it was only during "Baby I'm A Star" that the band stretched their wings and flew, able to add their color and flair to the show. The show from the twenty-sixth (one of a series of homecoming shows over Christmas) is a concert that does contain something different and is of interest to those who enjoy bootlegs. That something is a unique performance of "Another Lonely Christmas," the much loved B-side subsequently played only this one time live. This is not the best sounding *Purple Rain* recording out there by any means, but that one-off performance of "Another Lonely Christmas" makes all the difference.

Each night the *Purple Rain* shows opened with Prince's spoken introduction to "Let's Go Crazy." It never fails to sound fresh and exciting as it announces Prince's arrival onstage. The solemnly delivered opening lines only serve to fuel the fire of pent-up excitement, so palpable in the crowd. Their reaction is the ignition of passion that will burn all night. On paper the words don't look like much, but live they sound like a sermon delivered from the mount, and the crowd is swept up in an almost religious fervor. With a whoop the band kicks in and the recording comes alive with an electric energy and passion.

As the song dissolves in a flurry of guitar and drum rolls, the door has been well and truly kicked open for the rest of the show.

Anticipation would have been building for tracks from the *Purple Rain* album, but instead three songs from *1999* follow. "Delirious" is the slightest of the three, yet retains some of the energy from "Let's Go Crazy." Likewise, "1999" has energy to it; this bootleg is great for highlighting the extra guitar being played, louder and funkier, touching on heavy when it has to. The band is on form as "Little Red Corvette" slows things down for the first time, the familiar and emotive swell of the keyboards signaling its arrival. There have been several different arrangements of "Little Red Corvette" over the years; this for many would be the definitive version. A lengthy introduction has Lisa providing some heaving swells that builds the song with a touch of piano for seasoning, and the anticipation hangs in the air in the moments before Prince sings. The band casts a magical spell that is only broken as Prince sings his first line, delivering it with a hint of vulnerability without inciting pity. Already steeped in emotion, the guitar solo unfolds with a rawness that doesn't break the dynamic of the song, an early highlight.

> **THE BAND CASTS A MAGICAL SPELL THAT IS ONLY BROKEN AS PRINCE SINGS HIS FIRST LINE, DELIVERING IT WITH A HINT OF VULNERABILITY WITHOUT INCITING PITY**

If that was a highlight, the next few minutes drop the standard as Prince indulges in the long "Yankee Doodle Dandy" instrumental break. Without the benefit of seeing what is happening onstage, the energy levels of the recording fall rapidly, and the next few minutes prove to be a flat point. It may be a case of "you had to be there" - a situation where with a bootleg, we don't have the luxury to indulge in. The piano section of Prince concerts are always well received, and this one is no different. The opening "Free" is a slow start; it is simplistic with an easy charm that makes it hard to dislike, especially as Prince sings "Be glad for what you got, I'm glad to be home," but things get even better with "Take Me With U." Although short it makes an immediate impact with the crowd and on the recording. The staple of the piano set, "How Come U Don't Call Me Anymore?" is again the centerpiece as Prince toys with the audience with his usual antics. It is enjoyable to hear, although the real highlight is the vocal gymnastics that Prince ends the song with.

26TH DECEMBER 1984 - ST PAUL CIVIC CENTER, ST PAUL

Prince swings the show back to his past with a one-two punch of "Dirty Mind" and "I Wanna Be Your Lover." "Dirty Mind" is a showstopper with an inner energy that springs out of the recording, and it captures the live spirit well. The spoken introduction is worth hearing as Prince tells the crowd:

> *Maybe she don't like men with motorcycles,*
> *Maybe she don't like men with dirty minds,*
> *If you got a tambourine shake it,*
> *If you ain't got a tambourine - clap your hands,*
> *If you ain't got hands - stomp your feet,*
> *If you ain't got feet - shake your ass.*

The band returns with a perfunctory performance of "Do Me, Baby." It is longer and fuller than the previous songs, and it gets the concert back on track, although it does sound empty. It ushers in a rather uneven part of the show as Prince stays at the piano and delivers his spoken word introduction to "Temptation." With the song yet to appear on album, the crowd is oblivious to what Prince is talking about and the momentum of the performance is lost. However, Prince explodes as he plays the first chorus of "Let's Pretend We're Married" although even with Wendy's guitar sounding great, that too ends after a minute.

Things continue on in this form - Prince playing short, tepid versions of songs that deserve better. On record "International Lover" is a metaphor-loaded extravaganza: in this concert it gets a scant few lines before Prince begins a dialogue with God. Prince has to be admired for even flirting with the idea of doing this at a show, especially an arena show with thousands of new fans. A man of conviction, it is one of his most endearing and, some might say, frustrating traits. "Father's Song" is played briefly, a lost opportunity as an achingly beautiful song is quickly put to the wayside before Prince begins "God." "God" is obviously a song that means a lot to Prince, and he plays it with plenty of reverence on this recording. The first half is particularly poignant with Prince playing alone at the piano, a surprisingly intimate moment. It would be a cold-hearted fan who could fault it, and it is a shame that the second half descends to the "who screamed" section. It is a classic piece of Prince weirdness that unfortunately isn't that enjoyable to listen to on a bootleg.

The Wendy and Lisa introduction to "Computer Blue" brings the show back into focus, and from here the straight forward concert resumes. The song is rowdy and boisterous, an unconscious throwback to Prince's younger days. The guitars show a deepened maturity, a practiced rehearsed confidence; the first guitar break suggests that the crowd may be getting something more for their money. However, hopes of an extended performance are dashed as Prince remains faithful to the original, and the song segues into the rhythmic second section. The recording sounds exciting at this point as Prince encourages the audience to "wave your hands in the air!"

There is no surprise at all with the set list and naturally enough the next two songs are "Darling Nikki" and "The Beautiful Ones." They are contrasting songs, one a chance for the audience to enthusiastically sing some dirty lyrics, while the other a more delicate ballad highlighting Prince's exquisite vocals. Dr. Fink has stated that "Darling Nikki" was his favorite song to play live, and listening here it is easy to see why - he has plenty of time to play unrestrained and loudly, the synth stabs giving a staccato and rhythmic end to the song. The fade-out is perhaps the most interesting part of the song with the background music of the album played forward so Prince can offer his message of hope for all to digest.

"The Beautiful Ones" receives a fuller introduction, with lapping keyboards sounding sublime and seductive in the first minutes. Seductive is the key word as Prince performs the song with more maturity and passion than is heard on album. He leans heavy on every lyric and inflection, pushing them to the edge before they bend

> **HE LEANS HEAVY ON EVERY LYRIC AND INFLECTION, PUSHING THEM TO THE EDGE BEFORE THEY BEND AND BREAK**

and break. This live arrangement easily rivals the album version for beauty, with the performance opening up new, deeper emotions in the song. It is the final moments when Prince racks up the intensity; as always it is the high-point of the song, and this version is just as good as any other in circulation.

These two songs herald the beginning of the *Purple Rain* segment of the recording. Following "Darling Nikki" and "The Beautiful Ones" comes "When Doves Cry," "I Would Die 4 U," and "Baby I'm A Star" in rapid succession. Of the three, "I Would Die 4 U" is the only one that

26TH DECEMBER 1984 - ST PAUL CIVIC CENTER, ST PAUL

doesn't get a different arrangement; in the live context it is the same as on the album. However, it is a completely different story for "When Doves Cry" and "Baby I'm A Star."

"When Doves Cry" is played with a crowd-pleasing joyfulness that is the trademark of Prince's biggest hits - every part of the song presented individually and broken down for the audience to appreciate, firstly with a long introduction that reinforces the keyboard hook, then with a bass heavy coda that adds a new dimension to the song. Prince sings in a subdued manner, and it is the sharp, bold guitar of Wendy that is the main attraction, giving the song some focus and a hardness that was missing in the first minutes.

Finally, on "Baby I'm A Star" the band has a chance to breathe and play to their considerable talents. *Purple Rain* shows are highly structured and uptight, and it is only with this track that the band gets a chance to demonstrate what they are capable of. There is a second wind at this stage of the show and another surge of energy can be heard in the recording

> **THERE IS A SECOND WIND AT THIS STAGE OF THE SHOW AND ANOTHER SURGE OF ENERGY CAN BE HEARD IN THE RECORDING AS THE BAND TAKES FLIGHT**

as the band takes flight. An infectious enthusiasm fills the air; Prince sings with great gusto as Eddie M adds his welcome tone to the song. The band is sharp and the horns come to the fore; Eddie M plays hot and fast, giving some spice and sizzle to the performance. At this point the concert and bootleg has a swing to it that is irrepressible.

The next part of the recording is the reason this bootleg makes it into the top fifty essential Prince bootlegs - the only live performance of "Another Lonely Christmas." It is special, and Prince provides a worthy performance. It is an appropriate song choice given the date, and there is an extra element of emotion present in the room as they play. Considering this was the first and only time it has been performed live, it is an amazing performance as the band nails it with perfect rendition. With a gentle guitar break, presumably by Prince, it has a sharp and clean finish that paves the way for what comes next.

"Purple Rain" gets the full treatment, and the introduction is a full five minutes before Prince sings. "Purple Rain" is always the emotional high-point of these shows, and the lead guitar in the introduction emphasizes this as it touches on sentimental and gentle beauty as it plays. The song is played full length, and the guitar solo stretches on seemingly forever - but always balanced and always enjoyable. Prince never overdoes it as he plays, and as the last notes shimmer and fade, there is the sense that this is the perfect finish to the show.

Purple Rain concerts are structured and tight, but Prince and The Revolution still find ways to inject energy and a celebratory tone to proceedings. They shake off the constrictive set list, and the last forty minutes is when they show the world how great they are. Listening to too many *Purple Rain* shows can get repetitive, but this is Prince at his very best and as such deserves a closer listen. There are plenty of good bootlegs from the *Purple Rain* tour, but this is a cut above the rest.

SET LIST

1. Let's Go Crazy
2. Delirious
3. 1999
4. Little Red Corvette
5. Yankee Doodle Dandy
6. Free
7. Take Me With U
8. How Come U Don't Call Me Anymore?
9. Dirty Mind - I Wanna Be Your Lover
10. Do Me, Baby
11. Temptation - Let's Pretend We're Married
12. International Lover
13. Father's Song
14. God
15. Computer Blue
16. Darling Nikki
17. The Beautiful Ones
18. When Doves Cry

26TH DECEMBER 1984 - ST PAUL CIVIC CENTER, ST PAUL

19. I Would Die 4 U
20. Baby I'm A Star
21. Another Lonely Christmas
22. Purple Rain

RELEASES

- Another Lonely Ex-Mas - *FBG*
- City Lights Remastered & Extended Volume 4 - *Sabotage*
- Purple Majesty - *Empress Valley Supreme Disk*

4TH JANUARY 1985
THE OMNI, ATLANTA

Only two pro-shot shows are circulating from the *Purple Rain* tour, the released Syracuse concert and this Atlanta show recorded a couple of months prior. The Atlanta show is filmed from a single stationary camera, yet that doesn't make it any less enjoyable. Prince plays a high energy, albeit rather typical, *Purple Rain* concert. Like the rest of the *Purple Rain* performances, it follows a formula, and there are very few surprises in the show. However it does look glorious in terms of costumes, dancing, and the feeling of exhilaration and excitement as Prince plays. As a record of the *Purple Rain* tour, this is fantastic viewing as Prince plays his most successful album to an adoring audience.

The *Purple Rain* concerts may suffer from being overly familiar, but even after thirty years there is a thrill of excitement and electricity in the air as Prince speaks his opening lines of "Let's Go Crazy," silhouetted in white light and shrouded in smoke. As the organ swells, there are audible screams from the audience at every pause or softer moment, and there is no doubt on the recording that the audience is just as ready as the band is. The bootleg is of a high standard and despite being a single camera, it looks just as good as the officially circulating concert, highlighting every nuance onstage and the attention to the smallest detail. Things take off as the spotlight hits Wendy for the main riff before the show explodes in a shower of flowers, light, and noise. The band has the youth and energy of rock revolutionaries as they blaze through the song; they are storming the barricades from the start, winning over the audience with their life-affirming show. For all their energy, it does lack the killer blow, and with no piano break or drawn out solos it is true to the record. This hardly matters a jot as the song ends with Prince and his guitar, leaning back, face contorted with the music while his pink stole billows behind him, one of the most iconic images ever seen in rock ending one of the greatest show openers of all time.

The band generates noise next, allowing Prince to hand off his guitar and shed some of his clothes. With a shout from Prince things take a pop turn as The Revolution strike up "Delirious," a song that is an almost throwaway next to the bombastic "Let's Go Crazy," although the visuals carry it with Prince prancing about the stage. It is fast paced and builds the momentum, keeping the show moving forward until "1999."

Although played in an identical fashion to the video clip, "1999" still elicits a loud response from the crowd. Prince is cleverly playing to the MTV generation and giving them exactly what they expect with both "1999" and "Let's Go Crazy." They are both presented in a way that the audience has already seen and are familiar with, cocooning the audience in the familiar pop hits they've eaten their breakfast over. "1999" gets the full treatment rather than the truncated, watered down arrangement heard in later years, and it is all the stronger for it. Prince finds an extra spark, and his guitar break ratchets things up before the song ends in a crescendo of sound, light, and smoke.

> **PRINCE FINDS AN EXTRA SPARK, AND HIS GUITAR BREAK RATCHETS THINGS UP BEFORE THE SONG ENDS IN A CRESCENDO OF SOUND, LIGHT, AND SMOKE**

These opening songs see Prince running through some of his pop hits and he stays on this tack with "Little Red Corvette" and "Take Me With U." The opening swells of "Little Red Corvette" are imbued with a warmth that lures the listener in before Prince seductively sings his opening lines. As the song opens up, it becomes lighter as the stage changes from being bathed in red light to a brightly light forum for Prince to engage in some dancing. "Take Me With U" ups the stakes even further with what must be every light in the building turned on as Prince and the band romp through the song. Although Wendy and Lisa sing, they are lost in the chaos as Prince dominates the stage with his look and fierce guitar solo; it's the first moment of the show where he cuts loose and plays with an unrehearsed passion and fire. With guitar ablaze he stomps impatiently across the stage directing all his energy out into the audience.

The "Yankee Doodle Dandy" section of the show is an unnecessary distraction, and the energy and bravado of the opening numbers is lost as the mist swirls and disappears in the darkness of the stage.

Redemption comes in the following piano section as Prince plays a soft and delicate introduction before properly tackling "Free."

Prince is back on his feet for "Do Me, Baby," with plenty of stylings and moves to boot. There are better versions out there as Prince's vocals are overwhelmed by some of the other instruments, but visually there is some excellent showmanship on display. Again, it looks glorious on the recording, and for a couple of minutes the music is secondary to the visuals.

"How Come U Don't Call Me Anymore?" pulls Prince back to the piano, this time interacting with the crowd as they clap as accompaniment. Prince displays some of his theatrics with a vocal delivery that is matched with coy looks to the crowd that tease and seduce in equal measure. The ante is upped with his "I'm going to stand over here until you make up your mind" shtick. A crowd-pleasing moment, it hasn't aged well and gives credence to the phrase "familiarity breeds contempt."

The piano set becomes a grab bag for the next few minutes. "Let's Pretend We're Married" starts with a spoken introduction that would later become the song "Temptation." Prince teases with vocals and piano before finally playing a quick fire yet expressive, "Let's Pretend We're Married" while on his feet and shaking his hips. The downswing comes as he jumps to "Father's Song," a tender moment on the piano that comes as a shock after the previous set. In almost complete darkness Prince plays the main refrain filled with a melancholia that haunts the show for several minutes after it is finished.

The show comes back into the light with a reverential "God." With the smoke swirling at his feet, the stage takes on a heavenly appearance that matches the song. It is hit and miss, the first few minutes divine before Prince unleashes some screams that introduce the spoken conversation with the audience. Anyone who has seen *Purple Rain* or knows something about Prince would expect some sort of weirdness and here Prince is true to form - melding spirituality, music, and a concert show together in a form that doesn't always work but is always brave. This burst of spirituality finishes with Prince baptizing himself in the bath as the religious part of the show ends and the purple part of the show begins.

The next seven songs come off the *Purple Rain* album. Prince knows what the crowd has come for, and he is going to give it to them. As Lisa asks Wendy if the water is warm enough, Prince rises from the stage for a powerful "Computer Blue." A song normally associated with guitars, it is surprising how prominent the keyboards are. They form a thick, dense wall of noise for the guitars to play against. There are no surprises from the rest of the song; Prince gives a strong, serviceable solo as per the album and even Wendy simulating fellatio offers nothing that hasn't been seen before.

A wash of red light across the stage introduces "Darling Nikki" and a chance for the audience to sing its X-rated lyrics. Prince knows this and gives them plenty of opportunities to sing lines at the appropriate moments. Musically, the best moments come late in the song as Dr. Fink plays his solo. This is one of the lighter moments of a show that is often over the top.

"The Beautiful Ones" is, well, beautiful. Prince plays from a pedestal lit in soft reds and blues, and there is no mistaking that this is the emotional high point of the show. While it is Prince's piano that is to the fore, it is the other keyboards that are carrying the load with Dr. Fink and Lisa using plenty of swells and swirls to fill out the sound. This is Prince's best vocal delivery of the night - he leaves the piano to sing and the payoff comes near the end of the song as he caresses the melody before the final climax that reverberates around the arena. With no distraction of talking to the audience or guitar playing, it is all about his vocals and the emotion he can inject into them. With some showmanship he falls to his knees for some passionate screams and whoops before rolling on his back for a final howl at the moon.

> **WITH SOME SHOWMANSHIP HE FALLS TO HIS KNEES FOR SOME PASSIONATE SCREAMS AND WHOOPS BEFORE ROLLING ON HIS BACK FOR A FINAL HOWL AT THE MOON**

The show has some momentum now after the lull in the middle, and things continue to ascend with "When Doves Cry." The band works the crowd with the music, the bare beat and piano hook stringing them along for a minute and building anticipation. The lyrics and vocal delivery fail to live up to these opening moments, however the lure of the song is undeniably crowd-pleasing. The plus for the audience is Brown Mark's bass line that runs through the song and takes it to another level as the bottom end ties the song down and grounds it in a solid groove. Brown Mark may be the man of the moment, yet Wendy manages to upstage both him and Prince with a guitar solo that is glassy and electric while playing with a look that is cooler than cool.

Wendy is again prominent in the following "I Would Die 4 U," as her vocals stand strong next to the vocals of Prince. It has a lightness and pop sound that gives to some spirited dancing by Prince. It is reminiscent of the twelve inch version, with some funky guitar from Wendy, but it is much shorter and gives way to "Baby I'm A Star" after a couple of minutes.

"Baby I'm A Star" highlights the quality of this video; musically it is brilliant, but watching it is an absolute joy. Eddie M is on-board to contribute with his saxophone, and this gives the music an added edge. With the extended line up, Prince is able to channel James Brown, and he is infused with his spirit as he indulges in dancing and band leadership for the next few minutes. The Revolution could jam all right, but they could stop on a dime, and watching them move to Prince's command speaks to the hours of rehearsal and practice they had put in. After the highly choreographed show thus far, now is the time when the band begin to soar, and there is the feeling that musically anything might happen. "Baby I'm A Star" disappears into a long funk workout with the band finally playing to their full potential. Eddie M almost steals the show; he is a demon on the saxophone throughout, but in the end this is all about The Revolution, and they take this moment to shine. Not to be forgotten, Prince gives a little bit of everything to the performance - singing, dancing, piano playing, all the while never stopping the groove and the relentless beat.

> **"WITH THE EXTENDED LINE UP, PRINCE IS ABLE TO CHANNEL JAMES BROWN, AND HE IS INFUSED WITH HIS SPIRIT AS HE INDULGES IN DANCING AND BAND LEADERSHIP FOR THE NEXT FEW MINUTES"**

Eventually the moment arrives that everyone at the show had been waiting for, "Purple Rain" itself. The movie, the album, the concert, and now finally the song itself played before 14,800 screaming fans. There have been many different versions of Prince's signature song over the years, and for many the definitive version will always be the one played during the *Purple Rain* tour. With Wendy alone playing on the empty stage, the opening chords hang, shiver, and sparkle in the darkness. The soft chords may have been heard thousands of times, but they remain undiminished in their power to conjure up deeper feelings and emotions. The performance by Wendy has a powerful allure to it, and the song is mesmerizing from the start. Prince's opening guitar break matches her for emotion and delicacy, the shock and awe of his early guitar playing replaced by a guitar that plays as if it is softly weeping. An opening verse sees Prince leave the stage, returning soon after with the cloud guitar and a hard rock sound steeped in anthemic guitar shrieks and howls. It is not all about the guitar; Prince does give equal consideration to his vocal delivery, giving a performance that is every bit as good as the guitar, if not better. The vocals are solemn and deliberately just as emotionally packed as any of the guitar playing. With the vocals and guitar in balance, it is a well-rounded and fitting end to the show as it ends with yet another iconic image, Prince atop the high point of the stage delivering a final salvo on the guitar as the keyboard twinkle signals the end of the show.

Purple Rain shows may be well-known and intimately familiar, yet that doesn't in any way lessen the power of the live performance. The *Purple Rain* tour is heavily bootlegged with almost fifty shows in circulation, although very few are recorded as well as this. The real attraction of this show is the video recording; the audio bootlegs are good, but the show is just as much about spectacle and theater as it is about music. This bootleg is stunning in its quality and essential for anyone wanting to see more of the *Purple Rain* tour aside from the Syracuse concert. It is not perfect, but it is unmissable.

SET LIST

1. Let's Go Crazy
2. Delirious
3. 1999
4. Little Red Corvette
5. Take Me With U
6. Yankee Doodle
7. Free
8. Do Me, Baby
9. How Come U Don't Call Me Anymore?

10. Temptation - Let's Pretend We're Married
11. Father's Song
12. God
13. Computer Blue
14. Darling Nikki
15. The Beautiful Ones
16. When Doves Cry
17. I Would Die 4 U
18. Baby I'm A Star
19. Purple Rain

RELEASES

- Atlanta 85 - *Superhero Records*
- It is Raining In Atlanta - *NPR Records*
- Purple Majesty - *Empress Valley Supreme Disk*
- Purple Rain at the Omni - *FBG*
- Purple Rush Volume 4 - *Sabotage*
- The Beautiful Ones: Radio Broadcast 1985 - *Laser Media*
- The Omni, Atlanta '85 - *Premium*
- Atlanta '85 - *Habibi*
- Atlanta '85 - *Ladybird Records*

7th JUNE 1985
PROM CENTER, MINNEAPOLIS

June 7 - Prince's birthday and yet another classy show with a fitting bootleg to suit. March 1985 saw the *Purple Rain* tour come to an end, which had the expected knock on effect with no new bootlegs as Prince concentrated his efforts on filming and recording *Under The Cherry Moon* and *Parade* rather than playing live shows. However, this bootleg features a recording of the birthday show that sees Prince presenting a raft of new material, still seven months before most of it will be heard by the majority of his fans. It also features Sheila E. and Eddie M adding their respective abilities to the show. They add some color and demonstrate some of the palette Prince was drawing from at that time. This is a recording with more funk than heard during the *Purple Rain* shows and this signals the direction Prince will be going in the next year as he expands The Revolution and strikes out in new directions.

The bootleg is drawn from an audience recording that opens with "A Love Bizarre," a long bass introduction appended to the front end, and although missing the great jump-start that "A, B, A, B, C, D!" provides, it still manages to be attention grabbing. It goes without saying that it is funky and already Sheila E. and Eddie M. make an impact on the overall sound. Sheila with her vocals and Eddie M with his saxophone push the music further into the light, setting the standard that all future performances will strive to live up to. Here on tape we can hear Prince adding new players to the mix and experimenting with new band combinations. It is just as well that the saxophone and Sheila are on the recording because either due to the mix or the recording, the bass is heavy and smothering and very low-end sounding.

"Mutiny" begins with Prince asking for a D minor and the band slips easily into it. Eddie M is still present, front and center as he throws solos under Prince's instruction, making up for the missing deep organ groove. Prince had previously toyed with a saxophone player in the band, usually for a couple of songs during the Purple Rain shows, but this is markedly different as Eddie M is key to the music being shaped onstage. As he hits the riff, it is apparent how quickly Prince has assimilated this into his music and made the horns part of his ever-expanding arsenal. Fittingly Eddie M gets the final say in the song with a snotty solo that commands attention.

The bootleg has a wonderful live feel, especially the moment Prince misleadingly says, "Sometimes It Snows In April" as Sheila delivers a drum solo out of nowhere. Things get back on track as he does in fact play "Sometimes It Snows In April" next, but only after forewarning the audience that this is a new song and if they wanted to get a drink that's cool. The song itself is delicate, the pacing is just right with the guitar playing slightly longer, leaving room for everything to breathe and settle into its natural place. The backing vocalists sing as one; they back Prince wonderfully and as always less is more.

The funky guitar of "Irresistible Bitch" is unmistakable as it begins. All guitar and heavy bass, it sounds as if it is lifted straight from a *Purple Rain* show. As it vortexes into an all-encompassing jam, with Bobby Z and Wendy playing in the eye of the storm, and every band member is highlighted as the song moves swiftly through its paces. The next few minutes are interesting as Prince throws a few lyrics from other songs into the broth, a couple of verses from "The Bird" are heard with some call and response before Prince further pushes the crowd with "Drawers Burnin." The crowd clearly responds well to these new elements, singing enthusiastically along to most things, and there is no doubt they are greatly enjoying it. Prince is pushing his boundaries, and his audience is prepared to follow him as he moves into uncharted territories. With the luminous horns of Eric Leeds and Eddie M, there is a radiance to the performance that elevates it above the quality of the recording.

> **"PRINCE IS PUSHING HIS BOUNDARIES, AND HIS AUDIENCE IS PREPARED TO FOLLOW HIM AS HE MOVES INTO UNCHARTED TERRITORIES"**

One of the shortest bootlegs of the fifty essential, this is worthy of its place as it points to the future Prince is pushing into. The show gives us an early insight to the new instruments Prince is bringing to his music and the overall show is more colorful than anything we have

7TH JUNE 1985 - PROM CENTER, MINNEAPOLIS

heard previously. There are plenty of bootlegs from 1986 that fill out this sound and direction more fully, but this is the first marker to what is coming next. There are two different quality bootlegs of this show circulating; try and hunt down the more recent release if you can.

SET LIST

1. A Love Bizarre
2. Mutiny
3. Drum Solo
4. Sometimes It Snows In April
5. Irresistible Bitch
6. Possessed
7. The Bird
8. Drawers Burnin'
9. Holly Rock

RELEASES

- 27 - *4DaFunk*
- 27 V2 - *4DaFunk*
- Birthday 85 - *Universal*
- Purple Rush Volume 6 - *Sabotage*

3RD MARCH 1986
FIRST AVENUE, MINNEAPOLIS

There are great recordings of good shows, and then there are good recordings of great shows. The *Parade* warm-up concert at First Avenue definitely falls into the second category. It is quite possibly one of his best and although not a perfect recording it is good enough. What elevates this performance to mythical status is the fact it is also circulating on video. As a sneak peek of the *Parade* tour it is astounding. Prince is playing on his home ground, and the material is still fresh with a sense that Prince is itching to get it out there and share his new vision with the fans. A lengthy show, it captures all that is great about Prince - the song writing, the musicianship, and the showmanship. Here he demonstrates all three as he delivers a performance at the cusp of his creative peak.

"We have only been rehearsing a week so we a little rusty" Prince informs the crowd as the show starts, "but here we go." The opening "Around The World In A Day" belies that comment as the band are well drilled from the opening note. "Around The World In A Day" doesn't fit with anything Prince has done before or since and as such is an interesting oddity whenever it appears on bootlegs. It opens the *Parade* shows, yet since then has vanished from set lists. This performance is of two halves - the first light and delicate, the second brightly lit as Prince and the band run through some rudimentary dance moves. It's a clear sign of what's to come in terms of showmanship and a bright start.

With a shout, "Christopher Tracy's Parade" springs forth. Fun is key to the performance, the audience relaxing in the light mood. Prince is obviously feeling relaxed too, with the ad-libbed line, "Jimmy Jam, I don't want to hear this on your record!" It may be a throwaway line, but it does offer some insight to Prince's state of mind as he moves away from the people he was previously surrounded with and embraces new players and instruments. There is another signpost to

3RD MARCH 1986 - FIRST AVENUE, MINNEAPOLIS

the future *Parade* shows as Prince jams on the keyboard. It's only half a minute, but again it's a sign of what's to come during the next hour, and the tour that follows.

The recording and performance sounds like a rehearsal, exactly as Prince described it, with the band running through the standard *Parade* set list - next up being "New Position." These opening three songs work very well together and they offer a colorful view of Prince's musical style at the time. All three are infused with energy as well as sharing a clean sound that carries to the bootleg well. The extra members are slotting in seamlessly from the outset. This is the first live appearance of the extended Revolution and an early look at how they play together; already they are a close-knit unit, and there is further interest in the bootleg as we see how they interact with one another.

"I Wonder U" brings another musical genre into the concert and is a reminder of all the different styles Prince was dabbling with at the time. The band has started well, but even so Prince again reminds the audience that they are still rehearsing before another completely different style is played, a rarely heard live version of "Paisley Park." With Prince on the guitar for the first time at the show, the song takes on a raw feel, and this is matched with his throaty vocals and naked guitar taking prominence. It may not be a perfect recording, but it does remarkably well at capturing the feel of the show. The sound of all the instruments working together strengthens the community theme of the song, although the best moments belong to Prince as he plays finger cymbals during the final seconds.

> **"THE SOUND OF ALL THE INSTRUMENTS WORKING TOGETHER STRENGTHENS THE COMMUNITY THEME OF THE SONG, ALTHOUGH THE BEST MOMENTS BELONG TO PRINCE AS HE PLAYS FINGER CYMBALS DURING THE FINAL SECONDS"**

Bootlegs not only capture great performances but also intimate stage moments that offer insights to the band and Prince. What happens next is an example of this as Wendy launches into "Alexa De Paris," only to stop when she realizes she's the only one playing. Prince covers with "oh man, you let someone new in the band and they wanna solo," which seems like a strange comment considering Wendy had been in the band for almost 3 years. Undoubtedly a seasoned live performer by this stage in his career, Prince is nonetheless human. His generic rebuke come joke was almost certainly off the cuff and not meant to insult Wendy, a key member of the group. With so much on his mind, he probably said the first thing that came into his head, demonstrating his easy affinity and relationship with the audience.

After the collage of styles, there is finally some good old-fashioned pop as they play "Raspberry Beret." Refreshingly Prince sings all the lyrics himself rather than leaving it to the crowd. He engages in some choreography in addition to some straight out joyful jumping around. There is also some fantastic face pulling by Prince and some banter between himself and Jerome, mostly about wiener size (seriously, guys?!)

Post male genital conversation, Wendy gets her moment in the sun with "Alexa De Paris" and it is worth the wait. She speaks through her music, and although her body language doesn't show it, she plays an impassioned guitar break. She prowls back and forth across the stage holding the audience, and the camera filming, enraptured.

The recording has very little funk until this point, but that all changes with the pounding stomp of "Controversy." The funk of the original is still there, with the horns adding to the song without being too brassy and overwhelming. It is well-balanced with the new members adding a further dynamic tension and giving an urgency that propels it forward. Prince is full of energy - he elects not to play guitar, instead content to dance and sing, energy naturally pouring out of him during the song.

The shout of "Get Up!" sees a storming arrival of "Mutiny." Many things vie for attention: Prince's dancing, Eric Leeds's sass, the funky guitar lines, the driving beat, the biting lyrics. It does sound good, but it is not quite perfect; somebody misses a cue midsong, and Prince points out to the audience they are still rusty. However, Eric Leeds saxophone solo is a joy to behold, especially while Prince and the backup singers have fun chanting "Paul, punk of the month." Prince teases those in the know and those listening in the future, singing "This is what it's like in the dream factory." It is a stellar performance, with many strands to pick up on, and all of it is played with passion and fire.

The recording takes a nostalgic turn as "Soft and Wet" and "I Wanna Be Your Lover" are the next two songs in the set list. Although not as complex as the other music he is working on at this time, these songs have their place in the roots of Prince's music. Prince easily plays through these songs; he isn't pushing them too hard in terms of performance. He moves as he feels the music, no chorography or stage show to match, simply letting the music pick up his body and take it as it will. The show takes on a party atmosphere, especially the latter part of "I Wanna Be Your Lover" as the crowd becomes swept up in singing and clapping, the moment too much to be contained onstage.

Prince dips into the back catalogue again for "Head." It rolls out effortlessly, and Brown Mark is a rock through the song with his ever reliable bass the foundation the song is built on. The horns add strength, but nothing can match the keyboard solo of Dr. Fink, a fact that Prince acknowledges with "Don't play no keyboard unless you can do that." It is amazing that a man bobbing and jerking behind a keyboard in surgical scrubs can be so cool, but that is part of the legend that is Dr. Fink. Simply untouchable.

With a keyboard placed center stage, Prince reclaims the spotlight with a rendition of "Under The Cherry Moon." Only a minute ago he was moaning his way through "Head," now he is delivering a delicate piano-led performance. Such is the contrast, scope and versatility of Prince.

"Pop Life" oozes pop with just a touch of funk underneath. Not many songs have a flute solo, but this one does, and somehow Eric Leeds manages to look cool as he plays it. In this case it is the video bootleg that captures the moment better than the audio as the song breaks down to a long dance routine that looks better than it sounds. Eric Leeds garners further praise as the next song is another chance for him to shine - "Girls And Boys." This version is a cohesive band performance, even with the guitar low in the mix. Again Prince stalks back and forth across the stage with plenty

> **"PRINCE STALKS BACK AND FORTH ACROSS THE STAGE WITH PLENTY OF AUDIENCE INTERACTION AND AD-LIBS; EVERYONE HAS THEIR HANDS IN THE AIR BY THIS POINT, AND YOU KNOW PRINCE IS IN COMPLETE CONTROL"**

of audience interaction and ad-libs; everyone has their hands in the air by this point, and you know Prince is in complete control. Prince even has time to play more organ as the song runs for nine minutes, never repeating an idea while showcasing all his styles and talents in a performance that is stunning in its demonstration of his raw talent. In a show full of unmissable moments, this one trumps them all in a song that is a tour de force of Prince and his pure genius.

The recording doesn't let up in the slightest as "Life Can Be So Nice" comes right on top of "Girls And Boys." Prince has endless energy, and he plays and dances without pause; whether it's the song fueling his spirit or his spirit fueling the song, I just don't know.

The show to this point has been outstanding, and the next moments maintain this high standard. "Purple Rain" is undoubtedly the most over-played song of Prince's career - it has been played at almost every concert since 1984 and has appeared on countless bootlegs. However, the arrangement played at this show is exceptional and is unlike other versions out there. "Purple Rain" begins with the simple familiar guitar signature, but it lifts off with Eric Leeds playing saxophone over the introduction. "Purple Rain" isn't a sacred cow that shouldn't be messed with, and here there is new life breathed into it, the new elements lifting the song in unexpected ways. Eric's playing gains passion and feeling as he goes, and adds yet another emotional layer to the song with its well-intentioned sensitivity. It is not Prince providing all the highlights, but rather his music and the people he has brought into the fold. He does however provide some beautifully intricate guitar runs.

> **TOUCHINGLY MOVING, THERE IS A LOT OF FEELING HANGING ON THOSE FEW NOTES, AND EVEN AS THEY SPARKLE AND FADE THE EMOTION SHIMMERS IN THE AIR**

Touchingly moving, there is a lot of feeling hanging on those few notes, and even as they sparkle and fade the emotion shimmers in the air. The rest of the song is a blur of singing and guitar heroics, but of all the "Purple Rain" performances this is perhaps the most sensitive recorded, coming dangerously close to outshining even the original.

After all that "Whole Lotta Shakin' Goin' On" is a comedown, but anything would be after what has just been heard. To its credit it is short and has energy to burn. Both the horns and piano shine, giving the audience a lift after "Purple Rain." A tough act to follow, this isn't a bad choice to bring the buoyancy back to the room.

The deep and expressive tone of Eric Leeds introduces the following "Anotherloverholenyohead." The crowd understands what is coming and is primed from the start. This is a new song for the band, yet they make it another showcase of their talents. With Wendy and Susannah sharing a mic for backing vocals and Eric and Atlanta delivering some nice runs, it is very much a total band performance.

The big songs just keep on coming as "Mountains" is heard. Again it is lively and a chance for Prince to engage in more dancing. Early in his career he wasn't much of a dancer (see the Paris 1981 show in particular), but by this stage he has ironed out all the kinks. He is excellent in this song and every song seen on this recording. Wendy and Miko provide the highlights; while Wendy is upfront and prominent for most of the gig, Miko is anonymous in the shadows - a shame as his slippery, slimy funk playing is excellent throughout. During the long fade, his playing is heard more clearly, a bonus before Prince ends the song with his finger cymbals, something to bring a smile to most people's faces.

The shout of "A, B, A, B, C, D!" heralds the arrival of "A Love Bizarre," an astonishing song that was written for somebody else. Songs were coming to Prince effortlessly during the course of 1985/1986, and it is testament to his talent that he was able to give away such songs as this one. "A Love Bizarre" is classic, and the performance here is brilliant - not just the audio but also the visual aspect that has Prince all over the stage with his dancing and singing. The band doesn't miss a beat, and they turn the club into a party as the audience and the band become one in the desire to live in the moment. The whole band is bouncing as Eric plays a solo, but it is Prince who has the final word with some great guitar work that flows into the riff of "America."

"America" deserves more live performances than it ever got. The live video recorded in Paris is one of the best documents of Prince and The Revolution playing the song, and this recording stacks up well against that. They play as if there's no tomorrow, and nothing is spared as Prince demonstrates that he hasn't forgotten how to play guitar. It is The Revolution that elevates this song to such heights; no other band could play it like this - every member gets a moment and they play furiously. Finally, Prince puts down his guitar to dance as the band marches on. At this point it becomes an all-in jam with everyone contributing something to an ever-evolving song. Just as things look like they can't get any better, Prince shows us his mastery of another instrument as he takes the drums for a brief roll around the kit.

Prince knows how to play the home-crowd and his promises to come back and build a club-house so they can do this every day hits the right note. The crowd appreciates it, and it is not just an empty promise if Paisley Park could be considered a club-house of sorts. Prince loves building communities around himself, and this simple comment says a lot about him and the world he created. Then with a call of "who's house, Prince's house," the band play the final song of the night - "Kiss." After some of the songs heard previously, it is light, nevertheless it is utterly enjoyable. The final moments with just the guitar and beat sees Prince dancing with his wooden leg, and it is with this sense of causal fun that the recording ends.

Despite not being one of the great recordings, this bootleg is still one for the ages. Prince is revitalized and plays with a spring in his step through the whole show. The introduction of new music and new band members adds a freshness to the recording and serves as an excellent introduction to the next phase of Prince. The recording may not be 10/10, but the performance certainly is. 1986 is jam packed with essential bootlegs, and this has to rank as king of them all.

SET LIST

1. Around The World In A Day
2. Christopher Tracy's Parade
3. New Position
4. I Wonder U
5. Paisley Park
6. Raspberry Beret
7. Alexa De Paris
8. Controversy
9. Mutiny
10. Soft And Wet
11. I Wanna Be Your Lover
12. Head
13. Under The Cherry Moon

3RD MARCH 1986 - FIRST AVENUE, MINNEAPOLIS

14. Pop Life
15. Girls And Boys
16. Life Can Be So Nice
17. Purple Rain
18. Whole Lotta Shakin' Goin' On
19. Anotherloverholenyohead
20. Mountains
21. A Love Bizarre
22. Kiss

RELEASES

- City Lights Remastered & Extended Volume 5 - *Sabotage*
- First Avenue '86 - *4DaFunk*
- Parade America - *Eye Records*
- Veni Vidi Vici - *Uptown Productions*
- Warm Up - *Universal*
- First Avenue Warm Up - *Camille*

23RD MAY 1986
WARFIELD THEATER, SAN FRANCISCO

The show from May 23 is the longest circulating show of the *Hit and Run* tour, and in a year already full of essential shows (1986 is represented more than any other year in these fifty essential bootlegs) it is another worthy addition. Although all the shows are similar, Prince's style continues to evolve over the twelve months providing fascinating moments and new songs through the year. Prince sprinkles his new creativity evenly over the year, and many shows contain one-off moments that call for a closer listen. This show is the longest, and while it contains many of the same songs that are heard at every concert, it does feature "♥ Or $," in addition to a long version of "America." The cherry on top is an appearance by Andre Cymone to play "Dance Electric," an unmissable moment if ever there was one.

San Francisco has a lot of love for Prince; nearly every bootleg from San Francisco highlights a great show. This recording has plenty of evidence of that love with the opening "Around the World In A Day" getting a passionate response from the crowd as the band play to their impeccable high standards. "Christopher Tracy's Parade" has the same response; Prince's vocals aren't recorded well due to limitations of the taper, but the crowd carries the moment on the bootleg by giving it some liveliness and spirit. The recording is uneven for these first few songs, but it does even out later, giving the recording some balance.
The uneven sound is still a problem for the following "New Position" and "I Wonder U." The real problems lie in the vocals, which have a murky thick sound. In reality the band are storming through the set, tearing up the stage in their highly focused intensity, so the less than perfect recording can be forgiven.

With Prince counting them off, the band steamrolls into "Raspberry Beret." The sound problems dissipate, and as the crowd claps and sings their way through the song, there is a more promising tone to the recording. "Raspberry Beret" is light and easy as The Revolution draws the best out of it without overworking the moment. The classic pop is present and a radio friendly vibe fills the recording.

With no vocals, "Alexa De Paris" is the best-sounding song of this opening bracket. Prince has a clever balance to most of his songs, and here is no exception with the horns offsetting the guitars. The dynamics of it are held in equilibrium, presenting another quality to be admired.

The concert, and subsequently the recording, becomes funky for the next portion of the show with a series of Prince's best funk tunes. Kicking off this block is the irrepressible "Controversy" as the glassy guitar line comes in, shining in its brilliance. With the bass and drum operating as one, it has incredible momentum, and the best follows with a break-down featuring some terrific riffing by Miko that slips and slides across the recording. Wendy joins and matches him stroke for stroke in the funkiest moment of the whole show.

The band rolls along with an unstoppable groove, barely breaking a sweat through "Mutiny." Eric rides this wave, and he is the star of the show for the next few minutes, playing his own style all over "Mutiny," as the band stops and leaves him playing alone, encouraged by the background singers. The Revolution plays as if this was their last show on earth, never wanting the song to end as they give it an endless drive, and the outro is played almost reluctantly as they wind down over the horn riff.

> **THE REVOLUTION PLAYS AS IF THIS WAS THEIR LAST SHOW ON EARTH, NEVER WANTING THE SONG TO END AS THEY GIVE IT AN ENDLESS DRIVE**

There is no way the band can top this, and they don't try to as they play the short medley that normally appears at this time in the *Parade* shows. "How Much Is That Doggie In The Window?" "Lady Cab Driver," and "Automatic" get little more than lip service in the performance, but it hardly matters as the concert maintains momentum.

The highlight of the show, without doubt, is the appearance of Andre Cymone for a rendition of "The Dance Electric." It is hard to know what is more special: Andre appearing onstage with Prince, or the song itself. There is a novelty value to the song appearing in the show, but the arrangement surpasses this feeling with a flaming hot guitar, the bass matching the intensity as the song cements its place in the set list. The song is packed with this ferocity, the band holding the groove, letting the guitar range out as it fills the spaces with its power. It is a show-stopping moment and the one that catapults this recording into the essential collection

The concert swoops and soars; after the fire of "The Dance Electric" the mood changes as the contrasting "Under The Cherry Moon" begins. It demonstrates how far Prince has come with his music in the previous few years, confident to play this after all that has transpired in the last ten minutes. The song works well as a break from the ferocity of the show, a quick breather before the whine of the guitar opens the door on "Anotherloverholenyohead," which again ups the intensity. The climax comes with a false ending as Lisa plays her usual keyboard run, picking the music up for another minute as the crowd chants "You need another lover, like you need a hole in yo head"

The set list gets some balance as Prince digs into the back catalogue for a pop song. "Soft And Wet" fulfils a necessary role with the show being light on out-and-out pop songs. Along with the earlier "Raspberry Beret" and the following "I Wanna Be Your Lover," it brings some sunshine to the show. The recording remains an average audience recording, but the quality of the music is beyond any taping issues, and it is easy enough to listen past any problems.

Having horns in the band give some songs a completely different arrangement, and at first they seem to detract from "Head" rather than add to it. The nastiness and dirtiness usually associated with this crowd-pleaser is initially missing as the horns add their vibrancy, and it is only once Dr. Fink plays and Lisa sings that this classic returns to its truest form. Prince does indeed 'burn it up' as he works the microphone with plenty of croons and squeals. He can be heard introducing the wooden leg, but what the recording captures best is the slimy guitar running underneath. Prince begins his "chopping down the oak tree" spiel as the music stays focused, but he continues. "I wish Morris was here to see this; would he be mad or what?" he questions.

> **THE NASTINESS AND DIRTINESS USUALLY ASSOCIATED WITH THIS CROWD-PLEASER IS INITIALLY MISSING AS THE HORNS ADD THEIR VIBRANCY, AND IT IS ONLY ONCE DR. FINK PLAYS AND LISA SINGS THAT THIS CLASSIC RETURNS TO ITS TRUEST FORM**

Fans at the time would be all too aware of the history between Prince and Morris, along with Morris's "Oak Tree" single from the year previous, and were probably thinking the same thing themselves.

The pop theme continues with "Pop Life" and "Girls And Boys." The quirky keyboard and deep saxophone rub up against each other, but Eric Leeds is the star of the performance, his signature sound driving the song onwards. Prince leaves him to it, allowing Eric the space he needs to have his vital impact before cutting back in with his own vocals at the end.

"Life Can Be So Nice" comes as a rush after "Girls And Boys" winds down, uplifting, revitalizing, and rocking the audience. What a pity though the recording fails those who couldn't be there at the time or those hoping to recapture the experience. Instruments, band members, and vocals all take a hit to the extent that some die-hard Prince bootleg fans might disagree with the inclusion of this particular bootleg. But with a performance more reminiscent of the theater and less a music concert, it makes it in as a testament to Prince and The Revolution's physicality and expression.

"Purple Rain" is the odd man out in a concert like this. There is no other song like it in the Prince canon, and it is completely different from anything else heard at the show. The most well-known song of Prince's, indeed his signature song, it is completely unrepresentative of his sound. For all that, it is always great live, and the version played here lives up to the history of the song. A long introduction with soft lead guitar by Prince opens up for the crowd to begin their singing early before Prince finally begins to sing. Any issues with the recording are forgiven as Prince delivers a sublime vocal performance with a weight and emotion in his voice that sells the song. The guitar break picks up where the vocals left off, the flurry capturing our imaginations and delivering an emotional depth that matches Prince's voice. The cascading keyboards bring the music back to earth after yet another high point in the performance.

There is no time to dwell on "Purple Rain" as some furious guitar work by Prince opens "America." The opening explosive burst kicks the song off in style, with Prince playing the main riff before the band come and drive the beat home. *Intensity* is an overused word when it comes to Prince shows, but it is entirely appropriate as the band plays everything with a driven ferociousness. Previously unmentioned Atlanta Bliss is well in the mix with his trumpet matching some fiery guitar work by Prince, again giving the performance another dimension and color. But the surprise comes at the end as the song abruptly runs out of gas and comes to a rather limp finish.

The show has a playful aspect to it, and this becomes more apparent as the band play "Whole Lotta Shakin' Goin' On." It is short and light, the fun coming as Prince calls for a beat as the crowd begin to bark. The casual way he calls Bobby Z "Bob" is unexpected, a rare moment of authentic friendship caught on tape.

This show has a looseness to it, each song getting progressively casual in its delivery. "A Love Bizarre" is almost a jam, with the unstoppable Eric Leeds to the fore. Wendy is not to be outdone; she can be heard playing some great lines, before Prince has the crowd chant "who's house, Wendy's house." There is another moment of friendship onstage as Wendy calls out "wasn't that great?," before Prince comes to the microphone to speak highly of her playing. It is candid and real, adding some more humanity to the show. These aren't just highly skilled robots playing, nor are they individuals manufactured into a pop group; they are real people with real relationships.

> **THESE AREN'T JUST HIGHLY SKILLED ROBOTS PLAYING, NOR ARE THEY INDIVIDUALS MANUFACTURED INTO A POP GROUP; THEY ARE REAL PEOPLE WITH REAL RELATIONSHIPS**

"Kiss" sounds tepid, suffering from the problems already mentioned with the recording. Wendy comes across well; she lives up to the praise Prince has just given her and along with Brown Mark, she holds down the sound.

"♥ Or $" closes the show and is another great example of how good The Revolution were. Each member of the band can be heard clearly, playing their part, without being individually showcased but all making a valuable contribution. The horns deserve special praise as they scramble over the top of one another to be heard, this pall-mall rush adding some energy to the recording. The show ends as it should with the band suddenly stopping, leaving the audience cheering and barking for more (literally).

1986 was quite a year in Prince's world. Not only did he play some amazing shows, he also recorded a fantastic catalogue of songs in the same calendar year. It is an unmatched achievement, and listening to these live shows in the broader context is mind-blowing. This show, although not the greatest recording, is just as good as anything else from the era. Featuring a set list chock full of goodies, Andre making a guest appearance, sweet personal moments, and music that is both challenging and danceable, it is a bootleg that can be enjoyed for many years to come. Musically brilliant, historically interesting, and contextually essential, this one earns its place.

SET LIST

1. Around The World In A Day
2. Christopher Tracy's Parade
3. New Position
4. I Wonder U
5. Raspberry Beret
6. Alexa De Paris
7. Holly Rock - Controversy
8. Mutiny - Dream Factory
9. How Much Is That Doggy In The Window? - Lady Cab Driver
10. Automatic
11. D.M.S.R.
12. The Dance Electric
13. Under The Cherry Moon
14. Anotherloverholenyohead
15. Soft And Wet
16. I Wanna Be Your Lover
17. Head
18. Pop Life
19. Girls And Boys
20. Life Can Be So Nice
21. Purple Rain
22. America

23. Whole Lotta Shakin' Goin' On
24. Holly Rock
25. A Love Bizarre
26. Kiss
27. ♥ Or $

RELEASES

- Baddest Band In The Universe - *FBG*
- San Francisco 1986 - *Sabotage*
- The Dance Electric - *Fan Release*
- The Dance Electric I & II - *Fan Release*
- The Warfield - *Persic*

7TH JUNE 1986
COBO ARENA, DETROIT

Of all the shows in circulation from 1986, none is more well-known or bootlegged than the birthday show from Cobo Arena, Detroit. Professionally filmed for broadcast, it captures better than any other bootleg the thrill and color of the *Parade* era shows. It has an extra glow of special due to the fact that the show deliberately coincides with Prince's twenty-eighth birthday, and he delivers a performance worthy of the occasion. The circulating bootlegs don't cover the whole show, but what we do have is essential viewing. This is Prince and The Revolution at their finest and a bootleg that matches the moment in terms of quality and pure unadulterated joy.

"Around The World In A Day" may start in darkness, but it soon explodes into a brightly colored world that matches the music. In a cascade of orange and yellow lights, Prince springs forth to delight the audience. Filmed for TV, this show is noticeably brighter and better lit than the other shows in circulation and all the better for it. Although it is Prince's name splashed garishly across the marquee (in honor of his birthday), The Revolution are integral to the party bringing with them the gifts of timing, personality, responsibility, talent, and more besides. They hand them over immediately at the opening number, but as with the best kind of gifts, they keep on giving.

The inner joy and energy of the *Parade* shows is highlighted with "Christopher Tracy's Parade," where Prince sings and dances with boundless energy while Wendy and Brown Mark add plenty of bounce and pop of their own. The *Parade* shows are well-known for showcasing Prince's dancing and while this is true to an extent, he does take some time to make an effort to jam on the organ set up at the front of the stage. This performance demonstrates many of the things we have come to expect from Prince at this stage of his career: the singing, the dancing, and the all-round musicianship.

The pop of "Raspberry Beret" engages the audience early on, and with Prince in an upbeat mood, he lifts the crowd. It may only be a couple of minutes, but the pop and exhilaration rains down. Prince personalizes the moment as he tells Jerome that all these folks came to his birthday party, and it adds to the human feel of the show.

The twin guitars of Wendy and Miko slip and slide through the introduction of "Controversy," before a serious 'funk-faced' Prince takes to the microphone. The greasy sound is brightened with the horn section, and this lifts "Controversy" to another level before The Revolution roll on with the funkiest moment of the show - a driving balls-to-the-wall rendition of "Mutiny." With this performance Prince nails his colors to the mast - he is a legitimate funkateer.

> **IT IS NOT JUST PRINCE WHO IS SWEATING FUNK, THE REVOLUTION ARE WITH HIM EVERY STEP OF THE WAY**

It is not just Prince who is sweating funk, The Revolution are with him every step of the way. Wendy was sharp on the *Purple Rain* tour, but now she is playing against Miko, and together they seem to drive the funk even harder. Likewise, Eric Leeds brings all he has to the table; much like Wendy he seems to connect with Prince on another level. Again Prince revels in his versatility, and the several minutes he spends grooving on the organ serves to demonstrate his innate ability to take something funky and make it even more so. The band may be well rehearsed when it comes to the dance steps and moves, yet musically they can do anything on the fly as Prince challenges them through several stabs and changes.

Prince and The Revolution have been jamming together for many years by this point and Prince's birthdays have become synonymous with another cracking show. It's touching that their commitment to the fans and the music doesn't get in the way of their commitment to one another. Wendy leading Prince to the front of the stage so everyone can sing him a Happy Birthday is a gentle, touching moment in the otherwise tempestuous cacophony of noise, sweat, pop, and funk.

The show throws up a diversion in the form of "How Much Is That Doggie In The Window," which then becomes "Lady Cab Driver" before morphing into "Automatic." Compared to everything else the band plays, this is stripped back, which works well for the medley. The combination of Wendy and Brown Mark carry the music before the band joins for a chorus that spins off into uncharted territory. In the live performance it was Prince's dancing that drew the most gasps of admiration and excitement; the bootleg though tells another story with Miko and Wendy's guitars being the grease that everything slides across.

The next part of the bootleg is widely known, the footage of it used for the official video of "Anotherloverholenyohead." There is the added bonus of Wendy's sister, Susannah, joining her to sing, along with the appearance of Atlanta Bliss adding his horn to what becomes an extended version. As with previous songs, all eyes are on Prince, but it is the band that is doing the heavy lifting, not only the funk of Wendy and Miko but also the brassiness of the horns and the color of Lisa's piano. Prince is trusting of the band, and he leans on them for most of this show.

"Soft And Wet" is a welcome addition, although it is not on every bootleg of the show, allowing Dr. Fink to get his groove on with the synth. It is a song that ties the concert back to an earlier era and goes to show how far Prince has come in a relatively few years, contrasting with the newness of the previous song.

Similarly, "I Wanna Be Your Lover" has Prince asking who remembers "seventy-nine!" His cheeky comment "check the lyric change, I ain't got no money - that's a lie" could be seen by some to be indicative of his obsession with money, yet in this context it is said in jest (and accuracy). The rest of the song sounds as if it could have been lifted straight from the album, if not for a few moments where Prince extolls the audience to sing along.

Things slip back into a darker, dirtier time with the appearance of "Head" in the set list. Prince may have reached a global audience, yet here he reverts to his earlier ways with a performance that is just as sleazy as he has ever performed. The song may start out as a dark and funky jam, but it is the second half where it builds from a slow burning start to an incendiary performance. As the band eases to a barely breathing funk groove, Prince slowly undresses, all the time commanding the band through several stabs. Some of this sexiness is undone by his tooth brushing mime and dance, but this is blown away by the sexy performance that follows. Writhing on the floor,

> **THE SONG MAY START OUT AS A DARK AND FUNKY JAM, BUT IT IS THE SECOND HALF WHERE IT BUILDS FROM A SLOW BURNING START TO AN INCENDIARY PERFORMANCE**

stroking the microphone and himself in equal measure, he exudes sexiness through the rest of the song in a spellbinding few minutes. This 'burn-it-up' sequence gathers intensity as Prince sings Muddy Water's "Electric Man." While the music sinks deeper into grimy funk, the audience disappears from view as Prince loses himself in the moment and the music. Prince humping the floor as the stage darkens is a fitting end to a breathtaking performance that takes the nastiness of Prince's early performances and updates it for the larger audience.

There comes a glimmer of light in the darkness as the shimmering opening of "Pop Life" rises into view. A door is suddenly opened, and the show takes on a purity and uplifted spirit. This is no doubt helped by the fat pop of Brown Mark's playing and the flute solo of Eric Leeds. It comes as a complete contrast to "Head." Prince was the master at making stylistic changes so radically in a show and yet making them a natural fit next to one another. The girls give the song a soft landing with their vocals and the stage is again full of light.

"Life Can Be So Nice" has The Revolution injecting themselves early on before the music strips back on the chorus. Wendy and Bobby Z are the obvious heroes; Wendy's vocals are all over the song, and Bobby Z gets a shout for his break. It is fast and intricate, and the band seems to play it with great relish; they never once stop with the energy as they play with a smile.

One has to agree with Prince as he hails the band with his comment "I got the baddest band in the universe" before the quick fire "Whole Lotta Shakin' Goin' On." An unusually workmanlike choice for a band as funky as The Revolution to take on, it is only notable for the element of showmanship Prince adds.

There comes a breath of fresh air with the appearance of "Mountains" in the set list. It is a spirited performance from The Revolution, which plays a vibrant rendition while Prince stands out front playing to the crowd. The strength of the band is emphasized as Miko and Wendy play a rhythmic break that showcases all they are good at before Bobby Z takes a moment to shine. It is an entertaining performance, helped in a large part by Prince and his dancers who deliver some of their most choreographed moves of the night.

"Kiss" highlights the fun the band have onstage and the comradery between them. With plenty of eye contact and smiles, the band provides an irresistible groove while Prince sings his lines. This is where the bootleg is at its best, with the camera offering plenty of close-up shots of Prince in a segment that is filmed in an organic and natural way. The camera starts from an audience perspective before becoming more involved onstage and giving Prince's view of the show. It may not be the strongest song of the show, but it is amply compensated by the filming. A fitting final song for the bootleg.

The Cobo Show is talked about in the same terms that are usually reserved for the '84 Birthday Gig or the Small Club concert. It is generally hailed as one of the finest videoed performances in circulation and is regarded as a must-have for any true Prince fan. It is almost criminal that this exists as a bootleg; if there was any justice in the world it would have been officially released years ago. The phrase "lightning in a bottle" is a perfect description for bootlegs such as this - Prince playing a celebratory show that is strong on soul, funk, and downright fun. It is beyond essential; a bootleg that all Prince fans should have in their collection.

SET LIST

1. Around The World In A Day
2. Christopher Tracy's Parade
3. New Position
4. Raspberry Beret
5. Controversy
6. Mutiny
7. Happy Birthday
8. How Much Is That Doggie In The Window?
9. Lady Cab Driver
10. Automatic
11. D.M.S.R.
12. Anotherloverholenyohead
13. Soft And Wet
14. I Wanna Be Your Lover
15. Head

16. Pop Life
17. Life Can Be So Nice
18. Whole Lotta Shakin' Goin' On
19. Mountains
20. Kiss

RELEASES

- A Very Special Day - *Madhouse Records*
- Birthday '86 - *Fan Release*
- Birthday Parade - *Sabotage*
- City Lights Remasterd & Extended Volume 5 - *Sabotage*
- Happy Birthday - *Moonraker*
- Happy Birthday - *Rarities Special*
- Live Documents - *Benadette's Disques*
- Prince's Birthday Parade - *Purple Gold Archives*
- Birthday Parade - *Habibi*
- Birthday Show Detroit '86 - *Brave*
- Cobo Arena 86 - *GSH/Pimpsandwich*
- Parade Live - *Ladybird Records*
- Prince's Birthday Parade - *Purple Gold Archives*

22ND AUGUST 1986
ISSTADION, STOCKHOLM

There is not a single bad show from 1986, and that perhaps explains why that year is over represented when considering essential bootlegs. Bookended between the warm-up at First Avenue and the final Revolution performance in Yokohama are two pro-shot shows, one from the *Hit and Run* tour of the US, and one from the European *Parade* tour. The concert from Isstadion, Stockholm, is similar to the Cobo birthday bootleg from the US leg, yet every bit as essential as it captures Prince and the extended Revolution at their very best touring the *Parade* album. Anything pro-shot is worth its weight in gold, and seeing The Revolution in full flight in 1986 is always a sight to behold.

The classic "Please welcome Prince and The Revolution" opens the concert while the band plays "Around The World In A Day" in darkness. There is plenty to enjoy in the music at the beginning with lots of instruments to pick out and appreciate and all senses are heightened by the fact the band is playing behind a curtain. It is Prince's voice that is the strongest instrument onstage, it is well-rounded with a warm sound in contrast to some of the instrumentation in the background.

Next, some great bass work, as well as some fanfares from the band, opens the door on "Christopher Tracy's Parade," a song full of sounds and textures. Lisa is at her best with both her keyboard and vocals backing Prince, while Prince himself takes a solo at the organ later in the song with a warmth and fullness.

"New Position" and "I Wonder U" keep the show moving through stylistic changes. Both are stronger than on record; "New Position" is the more colorful of the two and has plenty of horn work to appreciate, while "I Wonder U" upstages it with some singing from Wendy before Atlanta Bliss and his trumpet play a solo that is easily the best thing on the first ten minutes of the bootleg.

"Raspberry Beret" is Prince's opportunity to engage with the audience, first asking them if they are ready to rock 'n' roll before encouraging them to clap and sing. Usually he lets the audience take on most of the vocals, but this show differs in that he sings most of it himself. The downside is he cuts some of the verses, leaving the song lacking the charm of the storytelling original. Prince ends it on a high as he again teases the audience with some of his playing on the organ, something always worth hearing.

Prince and the band tear through "Delirious"; it becomes a fun dance number before quickly moving on to something substantially funkier in the form of "Controversy." At this moment the concert becomes a celebration of Prince and the band at their finest. With the guitar, keyboards, and horns all coming in heavy, it has a full funk sound that avalanches over the crowd.

Prince owns "A Love Bizarre" during these live performances and here is no different. The song is still funk, yet there is a heavy dose of pop thrown into it as well. Prince and the band deliver it with a genuine intensity, not just in the music but also the performance. While Wendy and Lisa provide solid backing vocals, the keyboards and guitar maintain a relentless groove with the horns adding a splash of color. It is yet another performance that ends with Prince on the drum riser, leaving one wondering how he could possibly top that.

> **IT IS YET ANOTHER PERFORMANCE THAT ENDS WITH PRINCE ON THE DRUM RISER, LEAVING ONE WONDERING HOW HE COULD POSSIBLY TOP THAT**

The tempo drops as Prince delivers a slow burning classic rendition of "Do Me, Baby." As always the vocal delivery is top shelf, but on the recording it is the backing vocals that shine through. They are right behind him on the chorus and complement him perfectly - Prince, Wendy, and Lisa have a wonderful mix of vocals that work incredibly well together. The bootleg is a fine example of quality recording, and Prince's vocals are clean enough that every note and inflection can be heard. With the horns giving an extra push and adding to the seductive nature of the song, it has a breathtaking finish as Prince sings while the crowd gently supports him through the final moments.

The 1999 medley of "Lady Cab Driver," "Automatic," and "D.M.S.R." get the show moving again. From the soft finish of "Do Me, Baby" it accelerates the show back to a party, all in anticipation of the next song.

22ND AUGUST 1986 - ISSTADION, STOCKHOLM

Following the medley the simple keyboard riff of "When Doves Cry" is enough to get the crowd screaming. It is played true to the album and has a stripped down sound; the beat Prince sings over is very sparse. The beauty of this song arises from Prince's voice out alone in front of the music. Normally this would be the defining feature of the song; however, the best is yet to come in the guitar solo from Wendy. The tone of the guitar wails as a lone voice and over the barren beat the solo plays as a great rock moment. The arrival of the full band and horns for a final coda is distracting, out of place against the soundscape created by "When Doves Cry" and could well be another song, although it does have an equally funky sound with Prince playing organ to close it.

The show gets better as next Prince takes to the piano alone for several minutes of improvising. Even if he is only warming up, it is elegant, and when he does settle to play "Under The Cherry Moon," it is heavenly. It is his vocals and piano playing that provide a lush sound that is just perfect.

Eric Leeds and Atlanta Bliss add their usual brassy weight to "Anotherloverholenyohead," although initially it is the backing vocals that get the attention. Lisa and Prince work hand in glove together, their vocal stylings intertwining and their friendship translating into some beautiful musical moments. Eric Leeds and Atlanta Bliss live up to their billing with a shattering blast, but Lisa holds her own, a long break highlighting her piano playing with some full chords matched by fast, delicate finger work, elevating the bootleg above most others from the year.

> **LISA HOLDS HER OWN, A LONG BREAK HIGHLIGHTING HER PIANO PLAYING WITH SOME FULL CHORDS MATCHED BY FAST, DELICATE FINGER WORK**

The Revolution is a band and every member earns their place. The next two songs are where Brown Mark gets plenty of well-deserved praise. His bass line on "17 Days" is strong and rumbling; it sinks into the shadows getting lower and increasing in power as the song progresses. The following "Head" is even deeper and darker, his bass becoming impossibly thicker. "Head" by name, head by nature as the bare rhythm guitar and dirty horn stabs sound suitably nasty. The only time Brown Mark is outshined is when Dr. Fink plays his solo, different from what is usually heard yet compelling and worth hearing. The rhythm section is the backbone of the song, and they allow Prince plenty of room to perform. Prince takes advantage, rolling on the floor and then picking up his guitar for some dirty sounds before walking off stage leaving the band to play out in darkness.

The tone is lightened again as the band strike up "Pop Life." Live, it sounds just as joyous as it does on record. It starts off with Prince singing "life it ain't too funky, life it ain't too funky" as the music lives up to the promise of the chorus. The rest of the song is almost as heard on record, except for Prince's stronger vocals and a keyboard riff that is more to the fore. There is pop in the air with Eric Leeds's flute and Prince's ragged yet uplifting vocals. There aren't any surprises musically or performance wise for the rest of the song; it does exactly what you would expect from the title - it is pure pop.

Prince maintains his ragged vocal delivery for the next two songs, "Girls And Boys" and "Life Can Be So Nice." With Prince singing throatier, both songs gain a fuller live sound; he is never rough, but he is passionate. There is an energy and pace to both songs, even coming late in the set list, and The Revolution has to be admired for maintaining their energy levels and professionalism. "Life Can Be So Nice" is an ambitious live song, and during the second half the band comes into its own, grooving on it effortlessly in a way that suggests they could keep going for hours.

The band romp easily through "1999" - they could sleepwalk through it at this stage and still sound great. There is only a touch of horns to it rather than the full horn treatment that it will receive in later tours, and the balance is right as it retains the synthesized "1999" sound.

The encore comes with "Mountains," the deep organ sounding before Prince sings in a manner that brings a further solidness to the song. The song doesn't deviate too far from the original, although Wendy's guitar has a raw feel that isn't heard on the album recording. The arrangement of "Kiss" is in contrast to "Mountains." "Kiss" does differ from the album track from the start; the main riff is played on the keyboard while the guitar has only a low-key presence. The horns sharply begin the solo, reminding the audience that they are very much part of the band, before Wendy plays her bold solo, a solo that becomes a stronger guitar riff that will continue for the rest of the song. The final minute is guitar heaven as Wendy and Miko play together; they both have a different style yet work well together as they play in and around each other.

A single spotlight on Wendy playing guitar takes us to "Purple Rain" and the finale. The introduction is short; Wendy plays the opening chords only once before Prince starts singing. The bootleg reveals some surprises; there is a sharpness to the recording with the keyboards louder than expected, as too are the backing vocals. There are no surprises with the guitar solo however. Prince plays a long, blazing, solo with little crowd singing and he carries the final minutes on his guitar alone - a fitting way to finish a show that has a touch of everything.

The *Parade* tour is well covered by bootlegs, and looking at the set list for this show it would seem that there isn't much there that hasn't been heard elsewhere. What lifts this bootleg above others is the fact that it is pro-shot and, along with the new arrangements of familiar songs, it has something new to give with every viewing or listen. One of the best recordings of the *Parade* tour, and being pro-shot, it is an unmissable part of the 1986 experience.

SET LIST

1. Around The World In A Day
2. Christopher Tracy's Parade
3. New Position
4. I Wonder U
5. Raspberry Beret
6. Delirious
7. Controversy
8. A Love Bizarre
9. Do Me, Baby
10. How Much Is That Doggy In The Window?
11. Lady Cab Driver
12. Automatic
13. D.M.S.R.
14. When Doves Cry
15. Under The Cherry Moon

16. Anotherloverholenyohead
17. 17 Days
18. Head
19. Pop Life
20. Girls And Boys
21. Life Can Be So Nice
22. 1999
23. Mountains
24. Kiss
25. Purple Rain

RELEASES

- City Lights Remasterd & Extended Volume 5 - *Sabotage*
- Stockholm - *Superhero*
- Stockholm/Are You Hip To The Funk? - *FBG*
- Stockholm August 22nd 1986 - *Fan Release*
- Stockholm Isstadion - *Premium*
- Stockholm - *Habibi*

24TH AUGUST 1986
LE NEW MORNING, PARIS

One of the great trade-offs in listening to bootlegs is quality of the show verses quality of the recording. The most frustrating aspect of collecting bootlegs is there are some fantastic performances circulating on terrible recordings. A lot of people shy away from these bad recordings, but there are cases where the concert features one-off moments that demand listening, no matter the quality. The show from 24th August 1986, is just such a show. Recorded at Le New Morning Paris, it is a recording of a one-off performance that although not an aftershow carries all the hall marks of such a gig. Played in a smaller venue, it begins a tradition that will continue for the rest of Prince's career. We have previous bootlegs of Prince playing one-off shows at small venues, but this is the first that has a set list and performance that matches expectations for such concerts. The set list is attention grabbing, including gems such as "Purple House," "An Honest Man," "Strange Relationship" (still a year away from being released), "Last Heart," and "Susannah's Blues." Then there is the small matter of Prince's father appearing to play piano on a jazz jam, something that is only heard twice on bootlegs. Taken together, these facts easily outweigh the rough recording, and this is definitely an essential, although difficult, recording.

From the first moment, the bass has a distorting buzz that will be constant throughout. Prince and the band can be heard clearly, although the buzz is a distraction that needs to be overlooked. The cover of "I Can't Get Next To You" has a hypnotic beat and bass line and it takes careful listening to unlock its nuances. From the very beginning, the crowd can be heard on the recording, without ever being too intrusive. Miko makes an early impression with a clean guitar break that has a strong tone that makes a mockery of the poor sound.

Any reservations about the recording are put to one side as "♥ Or $," prompts the band to hit their straps, starting a groove that sweeps aside the distortion with a sharper sound. There is a contrast between the tightness of the band and the looseness of Prince and the horns, creating a tension and an air of anticipation that is only heightened as Prince threatens, "We about to get funky in here." He is as good as his word as he unleashes Eric Leeds, his horn fat against the subtle guitar line.

The first live performance of Jimi Hendrix's "Red House" (appropriately retitled as "Purple House") follows as the band swings back to the blues. "Purple House" has been played at various shows over the years, and this recording is notable for being the first time it appeared in the set list. Prince claims the song as his in the first line as he sings "there's a purple house over yonder," and it is unfortunate that the ever-present distortion steals some of his vocals. The song isn't as guitar heavy as expected; there is plenty of vocal work

> **THERE IS AN INEVITABLE GUITAR BREAK THAT IS KEPT SHORT, SOMETHING YOU WOULDN'T EXPECT ON A HENDRIX COVER**

from Prince. However, there is an inevitable guitar break that is kept short, something you wouldn't expect on a Hendrix cover. The song is rounded out by Eric's horn, which gives the performance balance and warmth.

"An Honest Man" is another eye-catching addition in the set list. With Prince playing alone at the piano, he captures just the right side of vulnerable. The distortion eases due to the lack of bass and the sound improves. While Prince adds some flourishes on the piano, it is the addition of Eric that creates the magic moment. As Eric and Prince play together they complement each other beautifully - a wonderful moment captured on tape.

With Prince finishing the song with a croon and piano twinkling, there comes another magic moment with the first public airing of the now familiar "Strange Relationship." Although slower and missing some of the energy of the finished product, it is nevertheless close to the fully formed song. A long, elastic introduction heralds in a series of "do, do do do" that are instantly recognizable. The only detraction is the reappearance of the distortion in the recording. There are very few bootlegs from the year 1986 where Eric Leeds doesn't feature heavily, and this one is no different as he is a key component of this track, adding a fullness to the song as it stretches out. There are further surprises as

Prince begins to sing "Last Heart"; with the piano prominent Prince creates yet another memorable moment.

The show becomes grounded with the appearance of "Head" and "Anotherloverholenyohead." As mainstays of the main shows, they don't offer anything new and certainly don't match anything else on the recording. From a bootleg point of view, these songs have become filler.

With a simple "and for my next trick," Prince and the band strike up "Soul Power." The band are well suited to this James Brown groove, with the guitar and organ leading the charge while Prince channels James Brown for the next few minutes. Eric Leeds playing is frenetic, although criminally kept relatively short. The show becomes a jam again, with Prince leading the band through a series of changes before essentially playing the audience in the same way, leading them through several chants and toying with them.

"Controversy" comes and goes with its pounding beat, and it is the "A, B, A, B, C, D!" introduction of "A Love Bizarre" that follows, together with a fantastic horn riff that draws an intake of breath and shout from the crowd. Excitement and energy is obviously high in the room as the band play with a roar. Sadly, the verses are lost to the distortion; the choruses survive and along with airy horns make the song. There is respite from the distortion with a dropout for the ladies to sing "Love Bizarre" before a glorious sounding Eric Leeds plays with the organ behind him. The band has a great rumble to them, but unfortunately it is a rumble that only heightens the distortion and leaves one wishing "if only".

"Jazzy Jam" is perfectly titled and is exactly that. The first half of the song is missing from the recording, although what we are left with is interesting with a strong saxophone and trumpet. The horn section plays with an obvious jazz sound, but it is another lost moment as we only have half the song. This is a clear pointer to the other music Prince was dabbling with at the time, and for the first time his jazz leanings appear in a live show. Jazz will be heard much more in the coming years as he seeks new directions and dimensions. It is

> **THIS IS A CLEAR POINTER TO THE OTHER MUSIC PRINCE WAS DABBLING WITH AT THE TIME, AND FOR THE FIRST TIME HIS JAZZ LEANINGS APPEAR IN A LIVE SHOW**

on this track that John L. Nelson makes an appearance, although he doesn't leave a strong impression and can barely be heard.

"Do Me, Baby" is far more recognizable, Prince elects not to sing, instead playing with the vocal melody on his guitar. The melody is only the starting point as Prince stretches it out and begins to branch into new directions, new depth, and emotions found as he gets further from shore. It is only in the final moments when we hear something familiar as Prince sings a series of "do me baby, all night longs." The song becomes a thing of beauty, the delicate guitar trickling down as the song ends in soft darkness.

> **THE SONG BECOMES A THING OF BEAUTY, THE DELICATE GUITAR TRICKLING DOWN AS THE SONG ENDS IN SOFT DARKNESS**

The tempo and mood is again uplifted with "17 Days." Prince plays with the song, allowing the rhythm to carry it. With a stripped back arrangement, the guitar is sharper and funkier, while Brown Mark is prominent with his bass holding down the sound. In the spirit of the show, Prince keeps his singing to a minimum, and it is once again the horns that make their mark, playing a delicious break that leaves the audience wanting more.

There is one final surprise as Prince calls a change and the band segue into "Susannah's Blues." It is loose, with Prince chatting to the crowd and Miko during the song, and this part of the show feels informal and close. With a gentle riff, a scat, and a jazzy piano break the final fade of the recording comes. It all comes and goes very quickly, but for rarity value and interest has the bootleg ending on a high.

There is no denying that this show is a tough listen for a casual fan. Even for a hardcore collector it can be challenging with the heavy distortion. The payoff comes with the set list peppered with gems and rarities. These are songs that demand to be listened to, new songs in new contexts, there is plenty here that can't be heard elsewhere.

24TH AUGUST 1986 - LE NEW MORNING, PARIS

SET LIST

1. I Can't Get Next To You
2. ♥ Or $
3. Purple House *(retitled cover of Jimi Hendrix's Red House)*
4. An Honest Man
5. Strange Relationship
6. Last Heart
7. Head
8. Anotherloverholenyohead
9. Soul Power
10. Controversy
11. A Love Bizarre
12. Jazz Jam
13. Do Me, Baby
14. 17 Days
15. Susannah's Blues

RELEASES

☰ Burn It Up - *Premium*

9TH SEPTEMBER 1986
YOKOHAMA STADIUM, YOKOHAMA

This is one of the most important Prince bootlegs in circulation. It's the final show of the *Parade* Tour which also serves as the final performance of Prince and The Revolution together; truly the end of an era. For historical significance alone it is a standout served with a worthy performance and recording to match. People often deride audience recordings, but when they are done well they are a joy to listen to. This recording is surprisingly good for an audience recording and has a small and warm sound. The concert too has plenty to recommend it, and when we factor in the historical context, it becomes absolutely essential.

A nice touch to the bootleg is the few minutes of audience noise beforehand that adds to the sense of expectation and anticipation. There is some chat, a couple of cheers, and with little effort by the listener the scene is set. With the benefit of hindsight it is difficult not to read too much into what is happening, and when the announcer introduces the band, there is a hint of melancholy and resignation in his voice. As always "Around The World In A Day" is a great first track for the band, with the horns making themselves heard early on, along with the fantastic Brown Mark bumping and buzzing along the bottom.

The girls' voices aren't heard well as "Christopher Tracy's Parade" begins; it is Prince and the band that come through strongest, but the balance is restored as the song goes on. Later the power of the backing singers and Prince's voice come together in a synergy that is something to behold. This is an early indication of how the rest of the show will go, the power of the performance coming from the combined efforts of Prince and the singers. In fact, it is the interplay with Prince and the band that glues the mixture of styles and textures together, highlighted by "New Position." It is unbelievably smooth and easy, testament to how tight the band was musically. There are plenty of new genres and instruments in the mix, and they manage to weld it all together and make it work without sounding disjointed or forced.

There is a particularly psychedelic and alluring tone to "I Wonder U," and another new instrument appears in the music, this time a flute giving it a floating quality that is offset by Wendy's guitar. The band knit it all together wonderfully; even when Prince isn't there, the band and the music are strong enough to stand on their own without his powerful stage presence.

The next few songs come in a flurry of sound and excitement. "Raspberry Beret" is first out of the gate, working as a crowd-pleasing singalong, although the crowd is fairly muted. On a positive note Brown Mark's bass is strong and energy levels are kept high as the band runs through an equally brief "Delirious," complete with a "one, two, three" count off in Japanese. It comes and goes in the blink of an eye before a snippet of "oww wee oww" that segues into "Controversy." The medley is a run through of high-octane crowd-pleasers but it is the next song that brings the magic.

With a count of "A, B, A, B, C," Prince is joined onstage by Sheila E. for "A Love Bizarre" in one of those magical concert moments. Their vocals playfully dance around each other; Sheila sounds cool, and Wendy and Brown Mark even better. The breakdown of the vocals is sublime, the recording good enough that every voice is easily identifiable. Eric Leeds sprinkles some of his fairy dust over the performance with a solo that lives up to the high standards he sets at each and every show. The intensity increases, and the song finishes with wave after wave of horn blasts and a final shout of "Ice Cream."

A sultry "Do Me, Baby" lowers the intensity and the energy, yet is perfectly placed in the set list. With the pop of bass and some sass of horns in the introduction, it comes like a warm breeze. For all the glory of the introduction, everything is irrelevant as once Prince sings - the experience lies in his lyrics and delivery. The music rocks back and forth, and he croons and emotes as he has never crooned and emoted before. Despite appearing hundreds of times at other shows, this is one of his standout performances of the song. There is the feeling that he is putting plenty of emotion in every song, lyric, and breath for this show.

> **WITH THE POP OF BASS AND SOME SASS OF HORNS IN THE INTRODUCTION, IT COMES LIKE A WARM BREEZE**

Next up is the trifecta of "How Much Is that Doggie In The Window?" "Automatic," and "D.M.S.R." It is something of a let-down to have two killer tracks off *1999* relegated to a medley like this, especially as they are paired with "How Much Is That Doggie In The Window?"

The ship rights itself as "When Doves Cry" plays, the opening keyboard riff as beautifully chilling as always. It has a clinical delivery, and over the cool electronic music Prince sings dispassionately, which heightens the sense of loneliness the song exudes. It is a cold world indeed, and it is only in Prince's singing of the chorus do we feel the humanity and hurt at the center of the song.

The concert has an easy ebb and flow to it, from energetic high-intensity numbers to soft heart-warming moments. "Little Red Corvette" has Prince alone at the piano tugging at the heartstrings. Any other show and this may well be an emotional highlight, but on this occasion it will be overshadowed by what comes later. Likewise, "Do U Lie?" seems to simply rise out of the ground, the band joining for a song that swings and sways its way through the next few minutes. It has a lilt to it and seemingly has appeared from out of nowhere or from another concert entirely.

Prince doesn't disappoint the fans as he stays at the piano for an emotionally charged "The Ladder." "The Ladder" has the obligatory piano and a whole lot more, with the backing singers making an impression and horns that lift it to the heavens. In a stadium show Prince finds a way to make it feel like he's playing in the living room. There is a lively intimacy in the recording, and Prince finishes on a classy note - thanking the audience in Japanese.

> **THERE IS A LIVELY INTIMACY IN THE RECORDING, AND PRINCE FINISHES ON A CLASSY NOTE - THANKING THE AUDIENCE IN JAPANESE**

Prince is alone again for the next couple of songs, "Condition Of The Heart" and then "Under The Cherry Moon." Prince delivers a performance that does both songs credit, although of the two it is "Under The Cherry Moon" that is breathtaking. With some flourishes on the piano, Prince gives it some pizazz, and the music has a magical quality that is rarely heard, mesmerizing throughout as it dips and turns.

The band and the funk return for "Anotherloverholenyohead." The bootleg is phenomenal thus far and the performance of this

9TH SEPTEMBER 1986 - YOKOHAMA STADIUM, YOKOHAMA

song proves to be no exception to the high standard. It returns to the heavier sound of the band and is dark and brooding as Prince begins his "another lover" talk midsong. The horns and piano match him for attention, but it is the piano that finally nails it - Lisa is a treasure. She is magnificent as she plays her piece, and it is distinctly, and uniquely, her. Even better, she plays for several minutes and provides a chance to swim in the music flowing from her fingers.

"♥ Or $" is unexpected. Rarely heard, it is Eric Leeds who puts his mark on the song, although to be fair, it is a total band performance. The show becomes more focused and intense at this point; all medleys are dispensed with and there is some proper, heavy funk. Keeping with this direction the band funk up "♥ Or $" before turning their sights on "Head."

"Head" sounds at its very best with the slippery guitar sound, plenty of which is heard on this bootleg; with Miko and his guitar giving it grease. It could easy be a dark funk jam, but Prince toys with the crowd bringing some lightness as contrast. Don't be fooled, the guitar is key to the song and it is the center of attention until Dr. Fink sets things on fire with his synth solo. "Electric Man" also gets an outing, with Prince surprisingly throwing in some lyrics from "Hot Thing," recorded barely a month previous. It is always interesting to see how willing Prince is to get his new ideas out to the audience, and this is typical of him - dropping lines and hooks of future songs into his concerts before they appear on album. The song ends with the music rising and some ominous guitar that is the equal of anything else that is heard in the song.

> **IT IS ALWAYS INTERESTING TO SEE HOW WILLING PRINCE IS TO GET HIS NEW IDEAS OUT TO THE AUDIENCE, AND THIS IS TYPICAL OF HIM - DROPPING LINES AND HOOKS OF FUTURE SONGS INTO HIS CONCERTS BEFORE THEY APPEAR ON ALBUM**

"Pop Life" banishes the darkness of "Head" in the first moments; after a twinkling opening it bursts into life with its uplifting pop. For all the melody of it, Brown Mark is the important player here, his bass adding an infectious bounce to proceedings. Something to get the crowd to their feet, and no doubt they are up for it, as is the following "Girls And Boys." Eric Leeds features on both, first with his flute and then his saxophone. The energy levels are again up, and Prince can be heard performing hard, seemingly catching his second wind.

The concert is on its upswing at this stage, these songs and the next few propelling it to the end. On the back of "Girls And Boys," "Life Can Be So Nice" comes quickly, almost too quickly, and it is not until the first chorus that the music slows. The verses are crowded while the chorus is sparser, Prince almost playing the loud/soft game long before it was popular in the '90s.

Against this colorful parade of music, "1999" is already sounding jaded and dated. The crowd enjoys it, the recording full of cheers and singing, and it certainly has its place in the set list because of this. The ending goes with a bang, the horns and the band tear through the last minute, making sure the main show ends on a high.

The encore begins with an underwater sounding "America." The recording gets better, and it is worth hearing for the dual guitar assault of Wendy and Miko. When Prince joins the fray with his vocals, there is a fire to his performance that the recording doesn't quite capture. Bootlegs catch a lot of great moments, but they don't always catch them well. Elsewhere, Eric is great and Atlanta even better as his trumpet scorches through the song. A lead guitar appears in the mix, and the music becomes smoking hot. It is almost unfair that Prince has Wendy, Miko, and Eric on his team funking up the stage as the solid bass of Brown Mark keeps things firmly on the dancefloor.

"Kiss" is more evenly balanced with the stripped back sound of Prince and Wendy's guitars taking lead roles, nothing else bolted on or tampered with. The vocal delivery is a shade downbeat, and it is up to the crowd to provide a boisterous "Kiss!" The ending brings the best moment as Prince thanks the crowd, leaving a bare guitar playing for the last few moments that wraps it all up in a bow before the next encore.

What comes next is the emotional and musical highlight of the show, a gut-wrenching rendition of "Sometimes It Snows In April." The opening with Lisa and Wendy is simply stunning, the delicate guitar and piano playing together. The emotion comes as Prince begins to sing, his voice has a melancholy tone that is real rather than performed. The three voices come together for the final lines, and it is hard not to think about the times these three had together. Prince ends the song thanking Wendy and Lisa, and even thirty years on it sounds like a definite full stop.

9TH SEPTEMBER 1986 - YOKOHAMA STADIUM, YOKOHAMA

"Purple Rain" is a beautiful song that sounds so big it threatens to overwhelm all that has come before it. The guitars are warm, the piano clean, and Prince's vocals heavy with emotion. The guitar solo starts with a quiver and a shake before settling on its familiar howl. The recording is laden with feeling; Prince is pouring everything into the guitar solo with a sustained whine that only ends as he throws it to the floor. Picking up another guitar, he continues with this howl of anguish, before it too is thrown to the ground. The emotion of the moment and the show are clearly written large in these few minutes of the performance. Prince regains some composure and thanks the crowd before he exits the stage, leaving the keyboards to play out the final minutes to a stunned audience.

It is impossible to divorce this recording from the context surrounding it. Many people admit to having a tear in their eyes as they listen to this, and that is understandable based on what the recording represents. There are plenty of fantastic recordings of The Revolution in circulation, and even thirty years on it is sometimes hard to grasp why Prince broke up the band at this moment. There are many words that spring to mind in regard to this recording - essential, historical and emotional surely top that list. There are no two ways about it, this recording demands listening to. A fitting send off to The Revolution, this bootleg delivers on all counts and is an essential keystone for any collection. There is no more fitting way to remember The Revolution than this final performance.

SET LIST

1. Around The World In A Day
2. Christopher Tracy's Parade
3. New Position
4. I Wonder U
5. Raspberry Beret
6. Delirious
7. Controversy
8. A Love Bizarre
9. Do Me, Baby

10. How Much Is That Doggy In The Window?
11. Lady Cab Driver
12. Automatic
13. D.M.S.R.
14. When Doves Cry
15. Little Red Corvette
16. Do U Lie?
17. The Ladder
18. Condition Of The Heart
19. Under The Cherry Moon
20. Anotherloverholenyohead
21. ♥ Or $
22. Head
23. Pop Life
24. Girls And Boys
25. Life Can Be So Nice
26. 1999
27. America
28. Kiss
29. Sometimes It Snows In April
30. Purple Rain

RELEASES

- Septembre - *Paper Corn*
- The Final Parade - *Zion*
- Yokohama 86 - *Fan Release*

21st MARCH 1987
FIRST AVENUE, MINNEAPOLIS

Most fans would feature *For Those Of U On Valium* high on an essential list and with good reason. Prince has played several warm-up shows at First Avenue over the years, and every one of them is a special occasion, each performance seeing the introduction of a new band, a new look, and a new sound. The music is fresh, the crowd eager to hear it, and Prince is always happy and at ease. This bootleg has Prince introducing a new band after the demise of The Revolution and a raft of new material from the *Sign O' The Times* album. *For Those Of U On Valium* is one of the classic Prince bootlegs, and although it is the subject of much speculation, analysis, and column inches over the years, it is surprisingly short. This is a bootleg bringing the audience quality over quantity, and the quality of the material is outstanding - some might say untouchable.

The show opens with one of Prince's most quoted and beloved introductions (for those of you on Valium); he is unhurried and there is a sense of drama as he speaks to the crowd. Completely at ease and unrushed, Prince takes his time to introduce the new band and explains that this is just a rehearsal. The real fun starts as Prince introduces the new band with a "these are my new friends" as he goes through them one by one, before coming to "that's an old friend, Dr. Fink - this is a new friend, polka dot suit." Prince's look is one of his more well-known styles, hair slightly longer, polka dot suit and glasses. He finishes his introduction with one of his most famous quips "and for those of you on Valium, my name is Prince"

"Shut up already, damn!" is the line that starts the music, and what an opening line it is. "Housequake" is brilliant at most shows; in this smaller setting even more so. The band may be new, but they are already cohesive and indicative of the style Prince will next pursue. The Revolution had the advantage of working with Prince day in day out for ten years, and you could be forgiven for fearing his newest acolytes might be slow on the uptake. But they have obviously been rehearsing hard because initially there is no sign of the shift. Within thirty seconds of starting, the glasses and suit jacket are gone as Prince works the stage, demonstrating considerable stage craft with his dancing. The band is well drilled in the choreography already, and although Prince excels when it comes to playing an instrument, here he demonstrates his physical proficiency.

> **WITHIN THIRTY SECONDS OF STARTING, THE GLASSES AND SUIT JACKET ARE GONE AS PRINCE WORKS THE STAGE, DEMONSTRATING CONSIDERABLE STAGE CRAFT WITH HIS DANCING**

The song is stronger live, with a captivating beat and horn lines courtesy of Eric Leeds and Atlanta Bliss - both of them crucial to his overall vision. In true Prince style he doesn't hide his emotions, treating the audience to wide, easy smiles and laughter.

Sheila E. drums things into "Girls And Boys" as Prince encourages the crowd to clap their hands. The hypnotic guitar and Eric Leeds's horn are the obvious highlights. Despite Prince's gesturing, facial expressions, and ass wiggling, the coolest guy in the band is Eric Leeds. Not just in the band, maybe the coolest guy in the world, as he steps forward to solo he is the epitome of cool, immaculate suit and sunglasses underlining his style. With Cat on his shoulder, it stands as one of the most memorable images from the show.

It is a Prince cliché that stands true; three songs in and we have a ballad. "Slow Love" on another album would be a focal point. On *Sign O' The Times* it is surrounded by some of Prince's finest work and gets a little lost in the crowd. The performance at this concert restores its status as Prince moves into full seduction ballad mood. It doesn't deviate from the recorded version, but it does sound full and strong with Prince's voice forward and the horns adding some extra sheen.

Prince began the concert reminding the audience that it was a rehearsal, and it is during "Hot Thing" that this rings true. "Hot Thing" is excellent in sound, the downside being that Prince and the band are trying too hard to get their dance moves right and working on the stage routines. As a result it feels over-rehearsed and in complete contrast to "Girls And Boys," which was loose and joyful. Eric Leeds provides a solo that does kick things up a gear as Prince bangs away at a keyboard, but rather than heralding something new, it signals the end of the song. The song that hasn't come of age yet, but by the start of the *Sign O' The Times* tour Prince and the band get the contrast right and it settles down.

"Now's The Time" brings a costume change from Prince. As enjoyable as it is, the concert does sag when he disappears from stage. The band to its credit is fantastic and the song gives them a chance to show off their individual credentials. Atlanta Bliss and Miko are the pick of them; two players we don't normally hear enough from yet here they prove they are deserving of more time than they normally get. Sheila E. on the other hand gets her big moment at every show and her drum solo here, although technically very good, isn't anything we haven't heard before. However, it is an exciting way to finish the song, and it puts an exclamation point on it all.

The next song, "Strange Relationship," is undoubtedly the highlight of the gig. It cannot be overstated how great this version is, it is rated highly among all fans. With a beat and some Stevie Wonder inspired keyboard, "Strange Relationship" gets an extended introduction. There is even time for the audience to chant "oooh way ooh" under Prince's command. As good as the band is in every aspect, Prince playing the keyboard is the stand out. The song and the band are wild, and it is Prince jamming on the keyboard that holds the attention and keeps the groove on track. As he adds more keyboards, the song reaches its climax, Prince driving the groove into the ground with his calls over and over of "is he good to ya?" This would be enough for most, yet Prince keeps pushing it further before he comes with "we have some new shit for you, squirrel meat." Yes, it is completely mad and doesn't make any sense but at the same time is total genius. The song dances to the edge of reason, touching on madness, yet the groove holds it just on the right side of sanity. You can let go of the steering wheel; Prince has things under control.

Another classic, "Forever In My Life," comes next in this show of ever increasing highs. For a song that is slight on record, it certainly packs a punch live. Prince jumps straight in without an extended introduction, but it doesn't become interesting until he picks up his guitar. Even thirty years later it is still one of the funkiest acoustic guitars ever heard; Prince squeezes plenty of soul and funk out of those strings in a sound that is completely moving in every sense of the word. A Prince show is as much a visual experience as an aural one, and in this case it is a blessing that the video is circulating. Nothing comes close to the live experience of a Prince concert (even the video pales in comparison to the real thing), but is still essential viewing as Prince confounds expectations with another stellar performance.

"Kiss" is a great song looking for a great live arrangement. This one comes close to capturing the magic with the strong first section drawing on the spirit of the original. The dancing between Prince and Cat is fun and works well as it anchors the entire song. The shortest song of the show, it closes with the solo sound of Miko on guitar, a solo that is as close to pure funk as you can get.

Prince thanks the crowd at the end of "Kiss," but there is one more song to come: "It's Gonna Be A Beautiful Night." The energy levels go through the roof, and the band gives a spectacular performance to match. The version played here is identical to what is seen in the *Sign O' The Times* movie, with every dance step, every move, as seen night after night during the concert tour, including Prince taking his turn on the drums. It feels very rehearsed and yet is completely believable and fun. A final chance for the band to shine, they make "It's Gonna Be A Beautiful Night" something that will keep fans listening for years with the horns giving it plenty of life and soul. It is only fitting that the horns end the song with a final flourish as Prince finishes one of his most famous shows with "Thank you, good night."

With a new band, new songs from the critically acclaimed *Sign O' The Times* album, and the iconic First Avenue venue, this bootleg is unmissable. Yet it is much more than those elements - this show has the magic x-factor so often sought in bootlegs. It has a soulful and passionate performance to match, not only from Prince but also his band as they strive to make their mark on his music. They are all playing with something to prove, playing to vanquish the lingering ghosts of The Revolution. The resulting performance is Prince at his very best and the fact it is pro-shot makes it all the more miraculous. This show should be essential for not just Prince fans but all fans of great music and performances.

SET LIST

1. Housequake
2. Girls And Boys
3. Slow Love

21st MARCH 1987 - FIRST AVENUE, MINNEAPOLIS

4. Hot Thing
5. Now's The Time
6. Strange Relationship
7. Forever In My Life
8. Kiss
9. It's Gonna Be A Beautiful Night

RELEASES

- 4 Those Of U On Valium - *Moonraker*
- Blue - *Play With Me*
- For Those Of You On Valium - *Chapter One Records*
- Housequake - *Swingin' Pig Records*
- Kiss - *Pipeline*
- Live In Minneapolis - *Headliner*
- Live In Minneapolis - *Music Tape*
- Live In Minneapolis - *Starbox*
- Live In Minneapolis - *Vaivens*
- Live In Minneapolis, March 21, 1987 - *International Pop*
- Live USA - *Imtrat*
- Minneapolis 21/3/1987 - *Polyphone*
- Sign O' The Times Live - *Sabotage*
- Testing One, Two - *DFB*
- This Is A Rehearsal - *FBG*
- Victory - *CDM*
- 4 Those Of U On Valium - *Digital Cruciality*
- First Avenue March 21, 1987 - *Habibi*

21st MAY 1987
PARK CAFÉ, MUNICH

The soundboard bootleg of this show is astounding on many levels. The fact that it suddenly appeared after twenty-eight years is itself a minor miracle - to have a lost recording like this unearthed is akin to suddenly stumbling across a pirate treasure washed up on the beach, plentiful in its riches yet completely surprising to appear. Then there is the sound quality of the recording that captures the complexities of the heavily jazz-influenced show. The icing on the cake though is an emotional element as Prince's father makes a surprise appearance playing the piano for a jazz jam. It may not be a great moment musically, but as a personal moment for Prince it rates highly. The show itself is an oddity, being a Madhouse performance with a short Prince set tacked on the end. The Madhouse sound and jazz influence permeates through the show as Prince toys with his more experimental music, making this one of his most unique shows in circulation. This bootleg would be essential with any sort of recording, but being a soundboard is what pushes it to greatness.

To set the scene there are some Madhouse songs at the start of the recording. They aren't on every bootleg release of the show, but they do provide context to the overall performance when they are present. The Madhouse songs lead the recording smoothly into the Prince songs that follow, a natural flow between the two that clearly points the direction the show will go. Opening with "Two," the drums, piano and saxophone all play in the initial circular motif of the song with the recording picking up every nuance coming from stage. The buzz and vibration of the cymbals are a fine example, sounding exactly as they should without even a hint of distortion. This is Eric Leeds territory all the way; he plays with a lightness not present before in his work on Prince songs. Another familiar face in the form of Dr. Fink also makes an impact early on with a synth solo that overshadows anything played on the piano earlier.

The following three Madhouse songs all continue in the same vein, with Eric Leeds and his smoky saxophone leading the way. "Three" has a summery vibe to it, while "In A Sentimental Mood" is complex and maudlin. Eric is impressive in his ability to express the sentimentality in his playing, and his saxophone is moody throughout.

"Sixteen" ends the Madhouse set and for many is the highlight of their performance. With a saxophone refrain that conjures up images of adventures past, it is a final opportunity for Eric and the band to display their abilities. Dr. Fink matches Eric Leeds for cool during the song with Eric's saxophone solo eclipsed by Dr. Fink's synth solo. The organic sound of the horn plays off great against the futuristic electric sound of the keyboard, and both are stronger for having each other in the mix. The final minutes are where it all comes together as Eric and Dr. Fink both indulge in wild passages that are dizzying in effect. Madhouse is even better live than on record and this is a superb performance that demonstrates that fact.

"A Conversation" follows, and it is at this point that Prince joins the concert. The song begins with a light cymbal run before Prince's guitar unmistakably sprinkles notes here and there as required to add ripples to the pond. The first minutes have a cool atmosphere, with the music building slowly as it comes into focus. The stronger electric guitar of Prince is finally released at the seven-minute mark, with a tone and sharpness to it that is tempered and held in check. He is not extravagant with his playing, which heightens the constrained feel of the song; the music is fighting to contain itself. With an insistent guitar coming to the fore, the song continues to expand, allowing time and space for everyone to take a solo, including Atlanta Bliss. The twenty minutes of song feels more like five, with plenty of changes and textures keeping it forever evolving and undulating, never quite revealing what might come next. A little experimental, a little jazz, a little funk - Prince covers all the bases in an opening song that is everything a Prince fan could ask for.

> **A LITTLE EXPERIMENTAL, A LITTLE JAZZ, A LITTLE FUNK - PRINCE COVERS ALL THE BASES IN AN OPENING SONG THAT IS EVERYTHING A PRINCE FAN COULD ASK FOR**

A horn riff, a dog bark sample, and some Stevie-Wonder-sounding keyboards introduce "Strange Relationship." Although different in style from the previous song, it is still every bit its equal. With the innate funky bounce of the keyboard there is added color and this is heightened by the horns and keyboard. "Strange Relationship" is a highlight on the *Sign O' The Times* album; in the live setting it is a monster. Prince invests a lot into the song, even going so far as to curse, which gives the song more bite and a hint of venom. As it descends into a jam, Prince injects the word "Leviticus" - something that only Prince could do and make it sound cool. With Prince and the song accelerating, it disappears in the rearview mirror as the next jam appears on the horizon.

This show is all about jams, and another long jam is next in "Groove In F (An Argument)." In Prince's typical style he replaces the horns with some longer notes from the keyboard. This sound can be heard in many rehearsal jams, a quick beat and a horn refrain with the keyboards filling the other spaces. With a rhythm guitar running underneath, it is the horns and keyboard that take center stage with a particular choppy sound. Entirely typical of a rehearsal, it is a treat to hear this in a live setting.

The crowd claps a steady rhythm calling the band back for more, and they are rewarded with the downbeat keyboard of "The Ballad Of Dorothy Parker." It is all about contrasts, and Prince's singing is bright and up-sounding, all the more striking against the darker music. This works well, as does the sharp horns and the quick piano solo that come later, all adding textures to the song. The arrangement has several extra pieces thrown in, and yet it still finishes after four minutes, delivering a surprising amount in that time.

"Just My Imagination" is laden with synth and piano, giving a lush warm sound. One of Prince's favorite songs to cover at this time and a favorite of his fan base, he lays it out from the start with the synth playing strong strokes while the piano improvises over the top. It exceeds expectations, and as Prince sings, it is still the piano that holds the attention. His singing is fine and delicate, almost too delicate for the heavier keyboard and piano as they continue to play around him, filling the air with a dense sound. As Prince finishes his verses, the music swells while Eric Leeds delivers the best saxophone solo of the recording, and in a show full of saxophone solos that tells you everything you need to know about it. The music rolls beneath him, Eric riding the wave and providing a sharp counter point to the fullness of the song, neatly bringing the music to an acute point. This bootleg is one of his finest performances captured on tape, and even as Prince's heavier guitar comes to the front, it is still Eric Leeds that provides the lasting impression.

Prince calls for "Blues In G," and that is exactly what he delivers. Things take an interesting turn when Prince calls "ehhh, substitution" switching to a very different piano performance. This is the most fascinating part of the recording as we clearly hear for the first time Prince and his father playing together. His style is markedly different from anything else heard, and as the bass walks along, he keeps the piano banging. Prince sings several verses, but any fan will be listening to John L. Nelson in search of clues for Prince's inspiration. Prince requests Little Steven join them on guitar, and although that promises to throw further fuel on the fire, it fails to ignite into anything more with only a short guitar solo and some interplay between the piano and guitar. There is no denying that the song rates high on novelty and personal value, yet it fails to fire musically, and despite featuring both John L. Nelson and Little Steven, it is the weakest part of the show.

> **THIS IS THE MOST FASCINATING PART OF THE RECORDING AS WE CLEARLY HEAR FOR THE FIRST TIME PRINCE AND HIS FATHER PLAYING TOGETHER**

"What are we gonna do now, Prince?" Levi asks, "Whatever it is, it got to be funky" comes the reply as the familiar introduction of "Housequake" begins. For a show where horns have featured strongly in every song, it is surprising to hear them subdued for this final moment. The concert may have opened with several jams, but "Housequake" is by the numbers; Prince doesn't play with the arrangement at all, making for a flat finish. It all comes to an abrupt end with a simple "Thank you, good-bye" that signals the end to one of Prince's more interesting and curious shows.

Although the final couple of songs of the bootleg don't live up to the opening salvo, it is nevertheless essential. The *Sign O' The Times* shows only made it to Europe yet are universally held in high regard. With the *Sign O' The Times* band, Prince was able to stretch his wings further and with his secret weapon in Eric Leeds, he was able to further push toward his jazz leanings. This bootleg contains all you could wish for when it comes to Prince's dabbling's in jazz and the Madhouse project. The opening "A Conversation" alone would have made this essential, and the fact it is a soundboard and we have a guest appearance from John L. Nelson only adds luster to an already stellar set list. The partnership between Prince and Eric Leeds here is the real attraction and is key to understanding the direction he was moving toward at the time. All these reasons, along with the music itself, is what makes this essential listening to anyone wanting to hear more of Prince's jazz oeuvre.

SET LIST

1. Two
2. Three
3. In A Sentimental Mood
4. Sixteen
5. A Conversation
6. Strange Relationship
7. An Argument
8. The Ballad Of Dorothy Parker
9. Just My Imagination
10. Blues In G
11. Housequake

RELEASES

- München - *Irukandji*
- Park Café - *Silverline*
- Park Café One-Off - *Fan Release*

29TH MAY 1987
U4, VIENNA

The aftershow from Vienna in 1987 is another concert that doesn't follow conventions or expectations. At first appearance it looks like a regular aftershow from the tour, when actually it is a charity show played by Madhouse, Prince only appearing after for a short set himself. With a rough recording and short performance, it wouldn't normally merit a mention in any list of essential recordings. However, this bootleg scrapes into the top fifty because of the stand out performance of two songs: "The Ball" and a touching rendition of "Adore."

With a boisterous crowd, scratchy recording, and some fantastic music, the landscape for the recording is set. Everything that you need to know about the bootleg is in those first few moments. The recording is rough and ready, yet it provides a feel for the size of the venue, and the audience talk is loud and frustratingly clear, almost distracting, from the first minute. Although the Sabotage release attempts to clean this up, it is still a problem on all releases.

"Housequake" starts things off simply, building expectations for what will come next. Prince relishes small shows like this and is clearly in a playful mood as he teases the start several times without ever jumping right into the song. It is kept as a slow-burning groove; it never bursts out of its skin as it so often does, but even in this form and as an opening jam it works surprisingly well, especially with the horns adding their substance to it. It serves as a good enough opening that the quality of the recording is temporarily forgiven.

The most interesting part of the bootleg appears early as the band tackles the unreleased "The Ball." Rarities such as this are the reason Prince bootlegs carry the currency they do; it is a delight to find a song such as this on the bootleg, and it is the main draw card of this release. It is made even better by the fact that the band jams on it for a good long time with several minutes of steady groove before Prince sings and begins to engage with audience - primarily by having them chant "Ball." Aside from the beautiful groove, the heroes of the song are again the horns. The recording unfortunately fades in and out partly diminishing Prince's otherwise clear voice. The tape continues with this uneven sound as Sheila E. raps her way through "Holly Rock," and the crowd feeds off this performance as the chat quiets down noticeably with singing and clapping taking its place.

The segue to "Girls And Boys" is barely perceivable, only the bass line gives the game away. In fact, the bass line is all that remains of the original song: the band use this sole element as a jumping off point to move into the song across a variety of genres. Horns come and go, the bass drops in and out, guitars rise up from nowhere as the song continues to evolve in weird and wonderful ways. Never once does it let up in the funk stakes, remaining captivating until the final moments flicker and fade. It has a trance like effect and any reservations about the quality of the recording drop away as it plays.

> **HORNS COME AND GO, THE BASS DROPS IN AND OUT, GUITARS RISE UP FROM NOWHERE AS THE SONG CONTINUES TO EVOLVE IN WEIRD AND WONDERFUL WAYS**

"Adore" is led by a heaving organ before the horns arrive to lighten the tone and usher in the song as it is more widely known, even as the tape hiss becomes more noticeable and does its best to ruin the moment. It is not as smooth as it appears on album, and with Prince calling some chord changes, it has a raw, live feel. It is a song of feeling and vibe, and it is well served by the performance that shrugs off the quality of the recording to provide a soulful moment. There is some wonderfully delicate guitar work that is the equal of the soulful vocals provided by Boni Boyer, and with all these pieces coming together the song ends on an all-time high.

"I Got My Mind Made Up (You Can Get It Girl)" retains the original and infectious bass line, but in this case it is subverted by the keyboard solo of Dr. Fink that makes the original song just a memory. Instant Funk would barely recognize their song, so buried under all the sounds that this band brings to the table. With a steady platform to play against, Dr. Fink is at his best for the next few minutes he indulges in funky flights of fancy, the audio equivalent of a Picasso painting. The bass does leave its mark however, giving some bottom to a show that is otherwise dominated by horns and keyboard.

The following song is listed as "Guitar Rock Jam," a somewhat misleading title early on as the band grooves the first minute sans guitar. When the guitar does arrive on the scene it begins with a snake charmer solo before working steadily into a frenzy. The band moves with the guitar, the pace of the song quickening as the guitar becomes a blur at the center of a flurry of notes. The recording heats up with Prince's fingers ablaze by midsong, each note flaring from the guitar, burning incandescent for a split second before disappearing into the darkness. To say it is stellar is underselling it; interstellar would be closer to the mark.

Anything after this would be a comedown, and the gentle opening of "Purple Rain" feels out of place for the first few moments. It does have its charms, and although it can't be compared to the jams surrounding it, Prince still delivers a sincere performance with a powerful vocal delivery. The songs that precede it can't be shaken though and "Purple Rain" is labored and heavily structured in comparison, all heavy architecture in comparison to the nimbleness of the song before. Things pick up with the guitar solo, although it is unfortunate that the recording ends during the solo, a frustrating moment all round.

Although this would be one of the poorer recordings covered in this book, it is still worth a second listen. It is highly flawed, yet the quality of the material and the band carry the day. "The Ball" and "Adore" are the two pillars the show are built around, two entirely different songs that are indispensable. This bootleg captures the band again playing a loose show and stretching out across some interesting song selections, playing an interpretive and free set. Of more interest than a main show, this is Prince and the *Sign O' The Times* band playing a show that sees them pulling in several musical directions at once, covering a lot of ground in the short time they are onstage. It is easy enough to overlook the audience recording when Prince is playing at this level, but I'm sure there are more than a few people who would love to see this appear as a soundboard. This may not be one of the first bootlegs people would reach for, but it nevertheless earns its place among the top fifty.

SET LIST

1. Housequake
2. The Ball
3. Girls And Boys
4. Adore
5. I Got My Mind Made Up (You Can Get It Girl)
6. Guitar Jam
7. Purple Rain

RELEASES

- City Lights Remastered & Extended Volume 6 - *Sabotage*
- Funky Crystal Ball - *SIT Records*
- Masquerade - *Giotto/4DaFunk*
- Pink - *Play With Me*
- Vienna Ball - *Eye Records*

15TH JUNE 1987
LE NEW MORNING, PARIS

The attraction of the Le New Morning show from 1987 is immediately apparent, a short set list that touches on all the aftershow crowd pleasing favorites. Playing in a small venue, the songs have an extra intensity that cuts through the audience recording, making them the prime focus. The recording may be poor, but the show and the music contained within are anything but. It is held in high esteem by the Prince community, and although the more casual fan may be discouraged by the audience recording, it is rewarding for anyone who listens more carefully. The set list tells you all you need to know about the show - rock tunes, funk songs, jazz-flavored songs and a band that could take on any genre and make it seem easy. The *Sign O' The Times* band was highly adaptable and could cover plenty of genres; this bootleg demonstrates that and is a great document of another one of Prince's great bands.

From the first moments of the show, Prince's guitar acts as a clarion call for all, delivering the highlight of the opening number - "Purple House." This retitled cover of Jimi Hendrix's "Red House" was first played the previous year at the same venue, "Purple House" is a tour de force of Prince's guitar playing and his ability to morph the blues. It is considerably quicker than the version played in 1986, and after a spluttering start Prince scorches all before him as he plays a white-hot solo. As the song swings beneath him, he has the guitar crying out in the first of several inevitable solos. Prince defies expectations and displays great confidence in the band as he steps back from his guitar to let Eric Leeds take over. The second half of the song sees the guitar give way to horn solos, the band pulling it in a completely different direction for the rest of the song, giving it a new focus and freshness.

Some heavy bass and a robotic funk guitar loop introduce the following "I Got My Mind Made Up (You Can Get It Girl)." It is both electrifying and mesmerizing, its funk punching out of the speakers.

The horns and Prince are both low in the mix, leaving the guitar and bass carrying the load - something they do with great finesse. Like the previous "Purple House," this is a showcase for the entire band, with a piano solo in the mix and a saxophone run from Eric that raises the energy heard on the recording. There is also the organ swell that is a trademark of the era rising and falling underneath, laying the ground work for a guitar solo that stays in a deeper tone rather than the expected shrill and whine.

"Just My Imagination" is recognizable from the outset, the soft introduction featuring some flowery playing from Prince before his whispered "two, three" introduces the song proper with the wall of keyboards rising as a backdrop to further cascading guitar runs. A responsive crowd draws a mock humble "thank you" from Prince as the song continues on in its own majestic way. There is a lot to recommend Prince's vocals, although clarity of lyrics isn't one of them. As great as the vocals are, it is hard to understand exactly what he is singing, although that in no way detracts from the performance itself. The vocals are of course secondary to the guitar, and here Prince has it singing like a harp. He elects not to go for the scorching setting on his guitar, instead keeping it sweet and sharp without the need to unleash a flurry of notes. With the guitar several notches lower on the intensity level, there is more room for Prince to engage with the audience, and the sing-a-long finish is a perfect match for the mood of the rest of the song.

The bootleg gains further credibility as the following song is a once-only performance of the unreleased "What Did I Do?" It has been listed under several different names on various bootlegs, including "Wasn't My Faith" and "Wasn't My Face," although current consensus is the title "What Did I Do?" This one-off appearance makes the bootleg special, but to be fair the song itself is powerful enough to have been special without that fact attached to it.

> **" WITH A HYPNOTIC BASS LINE, COURTESY OF LEVI SEACER, IT IS MESMERIZING AND THE FEEL OF THE SONG IS AMPLIFIED BY THE MOODY LYRICS OF PRINCE "**

With a hypnotic bass line, courtesy of Levi Seacer, it is mesmerizing and the feel of the song is amplified by the moody lyrics of Prince. The song is dense and heavy with a darkness pervading, the lyrics hinting a love lost. With a repetitive circular motion, the song seeps emotionally through everything, leaving a heaviness in the room and on the bootleg. This is tempered by a guitar solo by Prince, this time playing a smoldering solo that builds to an incandescent finish, a clean tone prevalent and played with laser-point accuracy that contrasts to the rest of the song.

"Mutiny" sweeps away all the swampy darkness of the previous song as it bursts out of the speakers, and the pace of the show lifts considerably with a shot of energy. There is nothing new or different about the song itself, full of horns and swagger. While being the shortest song of the set, it is just as important as anything else heard, and its appearance lifts the show to yet another peak.

As it fades to a beat Prince strikes a "get on up" chant that will signal the start of the final song and the rush to the finish. "Sex Machine" is the jam that he chooses to close the show with, the crowd voicing their approval and appreciation with a full-voiced chant. The performance is notable for the trumpet sound that Atlanta Bliss brings to the mix. Usually overshadowed by Eric Leeds, here he gets an opportunity to make himself heard, an opportunity he grasps with both hands. They easily morph into "Housequake," but not before Prince lavishes it with a fierce guitar break that underlines everything that has come before. Contrast is again key as the guitar of Prince and the horns add their individual parts to the mix in a final romp. A final hit out for the band, they inject a fierceness into the performance that encapsulates everything that has been heard before and is a fine way to wrap up the show.

> **CONTRAST IS AGAIN KEY AS THE GUITAR OF PRINCE AND THE HORNS ADD THEIR INDIVIDUAL PARTS TO THE MIX IN A FINAL ROMP**

Fans have spoken of this bootleg for years in its various guises and for good reason. It is entirely representative of the era and the aftershow experience of that time. It may have ended on an extended funk jam, but before that there was a little bit of everything and something for everyone, rock and blues sitting easily besides heavy funk and jazz horns. Prince and the band excelled at performances such as this one, and this bootleg catches them at full flight and is worthy of all the years of praise it has had. The audience recording is misleading; it is definitely essential.

SET LIST

1. Purple House
2. I Got My Mind Made Up (You Can Get It Girl)
3. Instrumental Groove
4. Just My Imagination
5. What Did I Do?
6. Mutiny
7. Sex Machine

RELEASES

- After Midnight - *Royal Sound*
- City Lights Remastered & Extended Volume 6 - *Sabotage*
- He's Got The Look - *Rock Solid*
- Le New Morning '87 - *4DaFunk*
- Private Show '87 - *Hot Stuff*
- Peach & Black - *Thunderball*
- Red - *Play With Me*
- The Paris Aftershow - *Back Door Productions*
- The Spooky Electric - *NEC Records*

17TH JUNE 1987
PALAIS OMNISPORTS DE PARIS-BERCY, PARIS

This show represents one of the most well-known and beloved bootlegs in circulation, a magnificent soundboard recording of a *Sign O' The Times* show in Paris. It is a lively and infectious show with a recording to match; it is easy to see why it is held in such high regard from the first moments it crackles and fizzes with energy. The *Sign O' The Times* shows are among the best Prince played, and the tour itself was hailed as a European triumph. The music, the performance, the costumes, and the songs themselves are all fantastic and come together in a singular artistic vision. There is not a single weak point in the whole show from top to bottom. With the *Sign O' The Times* tour never playing in the States, bootlegs are particularly popular with Prince's American fans; this bootleg is the best bootleg of the tour and as such can be consider one of the best of his career.

There is no better sound in the world than the throaty, guttural sound of Prince's guitar opening to "Sign O' The Times." It has a charge that completely changes the song from the cool, passionless record to something that has a fire in its belly. The cold, electronic beat is present, along with Prince's headlining lyrics, but the guitar adds a new dynamic, giving a passionate response to those cold soundbites. It howls in anger, weeps with sadness, and gives a human reply to the chilling news that Prince recites. Whatever weight the lyrics carry, Prince manages to capture the same with his guitar giving the music some emotional muscle.

The recording is crisp and has depth, and during "Play In The Sunshine," the band sounds as if they are in the same room as the listener. The song spins out thick and fast with Prince playing his guitar break over the frantic music, while Eric Leeds's saxophone plays crystal clear on the other side. The recording itself is the star, the music fresh and clean thirty years after the event.

Things slow with "Little Red Corvette." While the band and the vocals are good, it is the piano that is unique and worth clinging onto. It is an early carrot for those that have come to hear the hits, but Prince pulls the curtain down on it with a sharp "shut up already, damn!"

"Housequake" has been heard in many forms over the years, and while each version is good in its own way, nothing comes close to the original arrangement that appears on this bootleg. The song is great, the band is on fire, and the bootleg does it all justice. The recording captures the beat in complete clarity, and Eric Leeds has never sounded so good as he adds his aggressive horn parts to the mix. Compared to the thin sound of the *Sign O' The Times* CD, this version is full and leaps out of the speakers.

Eric Leeds is all over the following "Girls And Boys"; after the foreplay of a couple of verses and chorus, he gets his big moment and plays a delightful solo over the top of a funky guitar. It is revitalized as for the next minute Eric blows new life into a familiar song.

After Eric, it is Atlanta's turn as his trumpet croons the beginning of "Slow Love." Prince may be the center of attention but it is the little things that make this song, be it Atlanta Bliss and his shining trumpet, the drums of Sheila E. that accent every point, or the divine vocals of the women in the band that provide a fullness to Prince's vocal performance. It comes together in a way that is completely natural, a calmness falls; everything has its place. Prince's soft, pillow-like vocals alone are worth the price of admission with their warm and inviting feel.

> **PRINCE'S SOFT, PILLOW-LIKE VOCALS ALONE ARE WORTH THE PRICE OF ADMISSION WITH THEIR WARM AND INVITING FEEL**

"I Could Never Take The Place Of Your Man" harks back to a familiar rock sound, yet it is injected with a thrilling excitement with a longer introduction that racks up anticipation. With the talking in the background, the twinkling piano and the swell of the horns all build to that moment when Sheila drives it forward into the song and the band is unleashed. It is a story-telling song at its very best and the drama of the song unfolds with the music as well as the lyrics, culminating in the moment when words can no longer express the feeling and Prince resorts to some of his most inspired and uplifting guitar playing. He swoops, he soars, he turns the solo into a celebration of life. Then, demonstrating his complete mastery of the guitar and moods, he plays a mournful few minutes as the music pulls back to a melancholy place before one final surge to the finish.

The organ at the beginning of "Hot Thing" signals a change in styles. With Levi and Prince doing their spoken interplay, it is a fun opening without ever becoming distracting. The mix on the song is good, the guitar more forward with a robotic funk sound. The song becomes fuller later when the horn lines lift it beyond this cold, electronic sound and take it to a higher level. A song of two halves, it keeps the listener engaged until the end.

The band comes into their own with "Now's The Time," a showcase for all their skills. The band is its own animal; they demonstrate what they are truly capable of as Prince lets them off the leash. The concert turns on this point; without Prince on the recording every band member contributes something unique. Initially holding down their own corners they each come to the fore taking turns to push each other further. Levi is immense in his bass performance, and the finale with Sheila playing a solo that gathers momentum before ending in a hearty cheer is a fitting finish.

"Let's Go Crazy" is a revelation; the keyboard swell that announces the opening gives it a new dimension, and the rest of the performance that follows is equally uplifting, shaking off any staleness the song might have. The guitar is neutered, but with this band it doesn't matter at all; they are a different band with their own sound, and they make "Let's Go Crazy" fit their unique personality. The latter part of the song with the "go, go, go" chants by the crowd doesn't work well on the recording, but that's just a minor point that fades into memory with Prince's final searing notes.

"When Dove's Cry" is swiftly dealt with, an abridged version satisfying those who want to hear more from the Purple Rain era. It is a tidy arrangement, although only a couple of minutes long. The lead line is still a heart starter and the highlight of the song, while the vocals are disappointing with Prince barely intoning the lyrics before it ends.

This bootleg is not a complete recording of the show. "Purple Rain" appears surprisingly early in the set list, where we would normally expect to see it later in the show. However, with the recording running barely an hour, it is perfectly placed. Prince doesn't play around with it; he heads straight for the guitar solo to give the people what they want after a single verse and chorus. The solo is lively and energetic without ever offering up anything new; there is the sense it is only there to satisfy those fans from the *Purple Rain* days.

"1999" comes as a surprise after "Purple Rain," the music coming down and then rising up. Like everything at this show, it is horn infused and more colorful sounding, its purple hue given a makeover by a band that has a much larger palette. There is plenty crammed into the few minutes it plays, and most of the band has some input at various stages. True to form it ends this part of the show on a high and ushers in the first break before the encore.

The returning encore of "The Cross" takes the concert and the recording to yet another high. The comparisons between "The Cross" and Lou Reed's "Heroin" are valid, but by the time "The Cross" reaches it is zenith all comparisons are moot. Prince's vocals are stronger, while his feverish guitar playing leaves "Heroin" pale in comparison. He may be singing about God, but he plays guitar like a man possessed, the music flowing through and out of him, the final few minutes being an electrifying mix as Prince steps onto the pedestal reserved for rock gods. The guitar quivers and shakes in a frenzy against the more measured horns and the band, threatening to shake the group apart at any moment, before ending it all in a show-stopping performance.

With a simple call of "encore" the band fly into "It's Gonna Be A Beautiful Night." The recording is sublime to listen to, with plenty of instruments that can be individually picked out, each one sounding crystal clear and easily placed in the wider context. The wondrous thing about Prince in his live shows and recordings is they stand up to repeated listenings over the years and there is always something new to find. This song is full of such moments: Prince even name checks Jill Jones with "the Jill Jones crawl," a nice nod to a former band member. The song is in full bloom with a funky, thick sound that closes the show on an all-time high, and it has to be said that this is one of the best versions of "It's Gonna Be A Beautiful Night" in circulation.

This bootleg is much revered among the bootleg community and for good reason. Although it is incomplete, it is a devastating performance matched with a sublime recording and as such must be hailed as one of the greats in the bootleg canon. *Sign O' The Times* only toured Europe, and with this bootleg we have a beautiful document of that tour; it is certainly worthy of all the praise it gets. There is no need to listen to all the bootlegs of the *Sign O' The Times* tour - this is the only one you'll ever need.

17TH JUNE 1987 - PALAIS OMNISPORTS DE PARIS-BERCY, PARIS

SET LIST

1. Sign O' The Times
2. Play In The Sunshine
3. Little Red Corvette
4. Housequake
5. Girls And Boys
6. Slow Love
7. I Could Never Take The Place Of Your Man
8. Hot Thing
9. Now's The Time
10. Sheila E. Drum Solo
11. Let's Go Crazy
12. When Doves Cry
13. Purple Rain
14. 1999
15. The Cross
16. It's Gonna Be A Beautiful Night

RELEASES

- 87 Laments - *Minotauro Records*
- 87 Laments - *Speedball*
- Live And Alive In Holland - *Imtrat*
- Live Documents - *Bernadette's Disques*
- Live In Paris 1987 - *International Pop*
- Live USA Volume 3 - *LSD Records*
- Nothing Compares 2 U Volume 2 - *Banana Productions*
- Paris 17.06.87 - *4DaFunk*
- Paris 1987 - *Arriba*

- Paris Affair - *Kiss The Stone*
- Sign 'O' The Times Live! - *Sabotage*
- Unauthorised Live Vol. 2 - *Joker Productions*
- Wonderboy - *A Library Product*
- Wonderboy - *Moonraker*
- Wonderboy In Paris - *Premium*
- World Tour In Concert - *Joker Productions*

31ST DECEMBER 1987
PAISLEY PARK, CHANHASSEN

As far as Prince bootlegs go, 1987 is a stellar year. Starting with the *Sign O' The Times* warm-up show at First Ave, through the main tour itself, the excellent aftershows of Le New Morning and Park Café, there is a bounty of high quality and variety. The year is capped off with one more legendary bootleg, the New Year's Paisley Park show that sees the iconic Mile Davis joining Prince and the band onstage. Prince had experimented with jazz over the previous two years and one feels that having Miles Davis onstage with him was a validation of his work. Miles doesn't feature through the whole concert, and the performance itself isn't as jazz infused as some of the other shows earlier in the year, but it is still a monumental moment. The set list is an interesting mix, while there are some standard renditions as heard throughout the tour, things become more interesting near the end as the band indulges in one of their longest jams, incorporating a fascinating mixture of songs, colors and textures. The recording is missing the first few songs, which is unfortunate, but what there is more than makes up for it as the show ignites in the final thirty minutes.

The first songs of the concert are missing and the bootleg jumps starts as the final moments of "Jack U Off" are heard before Sheila E. builds into a drum solo, slowly working her way around the kit and picking up pace as she goes. With a sharp snare the solo builds to its peak, Sheila passionately crashing away on the cymbals, forgoing drum sticks to instead smash away with her hands.

After a perfunctory performance of "Hot Thing," successfully recreating what is seen on the *Sign O' The Times* movie, the bumping bass of "If I Was Your Girlfriend" takes the show to the next level. With the fantastic bass line setting the mood, Prince draws out a masterful performance. The extended introduction consists of the bare beat, a hypnotic bass and washes of organ, and there is plenty of time to savor the moment and wallow in the textures of the song. Prince gives the appearance of a casual delivery, hand in pocket, while in reality he serves up a focused vocal performance. Prince is full of character as he speaks his lines, lending to the lonely subject matter, before returning to his excellent singing voice without skipping a beat. As per *Sign O' The Times* movie, he picks out Cat midsong and lures her away, leaving Eric Leeds and Dr. Fink carrying the load now that the main focus is removed until even they pull back to the bare beat ending.

The organ refrain that begins "Let's Go Crazy" is unique to this tour, unmistakably from the 1987 era; one keyboard holding a long-sustained note with the other playing a sound that rocks back and forth. With Prince picking up his guitar, a traditional sounding "Let's Go Crazy" follows, pulling the bootleg back to 1984. It fails to connect for the first few minutes, but Prince ditches the usual song arrangement and indulges in a long guitar break that raises the music immeasurably. The second part of the solo in particular has some wild licks that add a lot of freedom and soul to the performance, erasing the sterile opening minutes from memory. Prince ends in the best way possible, guitar howling and head thrown back in the most Princely of poses.

"When Doves Cry" is more satisfying; much of the original remains, and there is the added sheen of horns that gives it a polished finish. A great vocal performance by Prince compensates for the sedated keyboards, bringing a spark to the song that isn't heard in the music behind him. Although crowd-pleasing, Prince keeps the song short, electing to play an abridged version.

The full royal treatment is rolled out for "Purple Rain," played with plenty of reverence as Prince and the band dwell on the opening. As Dr. Fink provides a keyboard backdrop, Prince stalks the stage making this a New Year's Eve to remember as he rings out the "Auld Lang Syne" refrain on his cloud guitar. The show begins to snowball as Prince begins to improvise a little, adding more color and fullness to the song as he

> **THE SHOW BEGINS TO SNOWBALL AS PRINCE BEGINS TO IMPROVISE A LITTLE, ADDING MORE COLOR AND FULLNESS TO THE SONG AS HE BUILDS TO HIS WORK**

builds to his work. The revelation of the song is Miko who plays a solo far removed from the slippery, dirty funk sound that he has long been associated with. Without playing fast, he delivers a crisp, sharp break that contrasts with the crunching "Purple Rain" solo that Prince ends the song with a few minutes later. The song's own weight of emotion carries it, and the band plays around the song rather than carry the emotion themselves.

In a show so full of color and tones, "1999" is strangely out of place and is firmly rooted in the early '80s where it came from. It is clean and smooth with its synth sound, but it lacks the fire to elevate it to the level of the songs surrounding it.

With the keyboards rocking back and forth, the tension builds in the dark as the band work up to the next song. The beat of "U Got The Look" and the rhythm guitar is heard, Prince initially singing without the guitar. This negates some of the rockiness that sometimes overshadows the song. The crunch of the guitar finally arrives late as Prince clambers aboard the piano and, with full rock god showmanship, plays as the dancers scurry beneath him.

What comes next is extraordinary and is not only the highlight of this show, but perhaps one of the highlights of his career. The band briefly leave the stage, only to return with a thirty-minute rendition of "It's Gonna Be A Beautiful Night" incorporating Miles Davis and almost every music genre Prince has ever touched upon. After the usual opening, Prince takes the drums for an extended period, setting the stage for what will unfold next as he moves onward. With Eric Leeds playing a snippet of "Six," the scene is set for the appearance of Miles Davis. The moment that follows is indescribable as Miles quietly paces back and forth, his look and music both cool, as he solos. He may not be playing the greatest Miles Davis solo, but the sound of his horn playing with this band is every Prince fan's dream come true, and no doubt Prince's dream too.

It is disappointing when Miles steps back into the shadows, although the funk of the band is undeniable, a fact that Prince acknowledges with "someone tell me we ain't got the funkiest band in show business; we will take on all comers." The band is certainly worthy of the praise as the song twists and turns through several different grooves and styles. It has everything; Eric Leeds's horn solos, Prince on drums, organ and piano, Boni singing, Prince commanding the band, as well as his humor on display with lines such as "ya'll expect a lot for $200" as he stops and starts the band through another change. The final call of "Confusion" is fitting, as this song leaves one's head spinning in its brilliance and coverage of styles and musicianship. Of the moments this show provides, none are as great as this last thirty minutes, and everything that you need to know about Prince and his music is there - an entire career condensed and distilled into one track.

The period encompassing 1984 through 1987 was the pinnacle of Prince's career. There will be plenty more great moments ahead but nothing comes close to these years in terms of success, creativity, and unbridled happiness and joy. This show is the exclamation point, a fantastic band coming off a magnificent year, and with Miles appearing alongside Prince, his place among the greats is legitimized. "It's Gonna Be A Beautiful Night" alone makes the bootleg worth having, and when we factor in the quality of the recording, the set list, Miles Davis, and a wonderful pro-shot video, it all adds up to a show that is essential in every way.

SET LIST

1. Drum Solo
2. Hot Thing
3. If I Was Your Girlfriend
4. Let's Go Crazy
5. When Doves Cry
6. Purple Rain
7. 1999
8. U Got The Look
9. It's Gonna Be A Beautiful Night

RELEASES

- City Lights Remastered & Extended Volume 6 - *Sabotage*
- Miles 2 Nowhere - *Thunderball*
- Miles From The Park - *Sabotage*
- Miles 2 Nowhere - *Thunderball*
- Miles From The Park - *Brave*
- Miles From The Park - *Global Funkschool*
- Live at Paisley Park New Years Eve 1987 - *Habibi*

19TH AUGUST 1988
PAARD VAN TROJE, THE HAGUE

The most famous Prince live bootleg of all is *Small Club*. In a year of fantastic aftershows this performance is the best - not only the best aftershow, but also the best recorded concert, making it one of the most desirable bootlegs in circulation. It captures Prince at the height of his powers, all in a pristine soundboard that is better than a lot of his studio releases. Every inflection, breath, and note is captured in a clean yet full sound. The Prince fan community is usually fractured when it comes to opinions on almost everything, but this bootleg unites all in agreement that this is one of the best. Having been in circulation for many years and in many different releases, it is found in most people's collections. This book covers the top fifty essential bootlegs, but this show would easily feature in any top ten bootleg list, or even a top five. Universally loved and revered, Small Club is the pinnacle of the Prince bootleg experience and is what all other bootlegs are measured against.

The bootleg opens innocuously enough with a simple drum roll and soft percussion. Prince and the band are showing some of their influences early with a jazz percussion feel provided by Sheila E. The piano adds to this jazz club vibe; Prince may have dabbled with the genre in previous years, but here is it is in a different form with the music incorporated into his own style rather than him overtly playing something jazz inspired. The difference is subtle yet crucial. The piano leads the way; however, it is washed away as some bold and loud guitar playing from Prince changes the agenda and makes it clear that this is going to be a show of extremes. It is the final third of the song where Prince lets go of any inhibitions and plays in a wild, improvised manner, to be commended - not just his guitar playing, but also the guitar tone that is clean and strong, with a muscular fullness. Prince may technically be a great player, but he is also very good at setting up the sound to achieve something unique and complimentary to his playing.

The show isn't just about the music and the band; there is also plenty of personality and character present in the performance. Before "D.M.S.R." he asks the audience if they're drunk and teases "you aren't gonna make the notes up in your mind," while later in the show he has the audacity to tell a knock-knock joke that any dad would be proud of. It is not the greatest comedic moment in the world, but it does show that Prince is enjoying the performance as much as anyone listening. This joyfulness carries the joke and the moment with the audience.

The funk arrives in the form of a loose, rolling "D.M.S.R." At first it closely follows the original album version, although soon enough there are differences to be heard and plenty to keep the listener interested. The most interesting portion comes late in the song as Prince first has the band "rumble, Minneapolis style" - they do indeed rumble, before he takes it to Hawaii with a shiny sliding Hawaiian guitar. The following guitar solo is closer to what one expects from a Prince show and additionally neatly takes in the main riff of "America." The band is worthy of all the praise they get; they keep "D.M.S.R." chugging along underneath as well as working their way through a couple of Prince false endings before it all wraps up with a bare guitar strum.

Prince has received praise from all quarters over the years for his ability with the guitar, and no song or solo has garnered more praise than the following few minutes on "Just My Imagination." The hours of performing, rehearsing, and playing all come down to the next minutes when he distils it all to a solo that stands above all others. The simple guitar riff that begins "Just My Imagination" is deceiving, for what will follow will be a tour de force of guitar heroics. The lush keyboards pick up the cause as Prince sings, a great choice for a cover version as his voice works the mood. Listening to him sing for the first minutes it is hard to imagine what is coming; he is slowly but surely luring the listener in before the storm blows up in the following moments. The listener is standing in the mouth of Aladdin's cave as the first notes stretch out like a flashlight in the darkness, gems and treasures revealed as Prince warms to his work and the guitar rises in volume, pace, and intensity. This is more than a virtuoso performance,

> **THE HOURS OF PERFORMING, REHEARSING, AND PLAYING ALL COME DOWN TO THE NEXT MINUTES WHEN HE DISTILS IT ALL TO A SOLO THAT STANDS ABOVE ALL OTHERS**

it is a soulful one. Prince's playing is technically brilliant, but that's not what makes this song connect with people. He is not playing with his hands or his head but from his very heart and the guitar is not playing music, it is the sound of raw emotion itself. Prince plugs the guitar into his soul, and from the first stabs of the solo to the moment when the last embers fade, it is loaded with more heart and passion than most can muster over a lifetime. Of all his guitar solos, this is the most essential and key to his playing - the ability to elicit emotion from his instrument.

After setting the bar so high, Prince does what he has all his career - play something completely different. That something is the unreleased "People Without." Played in the dark, it takes on an ominous tone as Prince speaks and sings over a mournful synth that only heightens the seriousness of his lyrics and their tone. The music becomes heavier with the arrival of the bass and more keyboards, making the song punchy and forceful while retaining the dark mood set earlier. Appropriately enough the song ends with the music quietening as Prince sings, "I thought you wanted to do it in the dark, turn out the lights."

"Housequake" rarely disappoints, although in such esteemed company it isn't the expected highlight. With Eric Leeds back at the hotel (having elected to skip this show due to tiredness), the weight of the load is carried by Atlanta Bliss. He gives the song the sparkle it needs, adding extra color and brightness to a show that so far has been a swirl of dark and foreboding music. Interestingly enough, "Housequake" is the shortest song of the concert, clocking in a barely five minutes, which gives some indication of how it is played - straight down the line and close to the album. Compared to the other long jams of the evening, it passes by in a blink if the eye, short but eminently enjoyable.

Atlanta Bliss stays in the limelight as it is the fine sound of his trumpet that introduces Boni Boyer and "Down Home Blues." It plays exactly like its title, and Boni is in her element as she sings it, backed with the crisp blues of Prince's guitar, mirroring the blues he mined in the main shows from this era. In this setting it is pure and lends authenticity to Boni's vocals. The solo from Atlanta Bliss is also in this style as the band stays with the genre for Boni to sing "Kansas City." Initially it has a timeless and uniform tone, until Prince's solo moves things up a notch as the groove becomes deeper and insistent.

Prince is on the drums for "Cold Sweat" and, as good as he is, it doesn't add anything to the recording. Atlanta Bliss shines but is let down by the unnecessary Transmississippi Rap from Sheila E. that derails the groove. At ten minutes there should be more to say about it, but there isn't. The song does its job in the set list, without adding anything extra to the show.

After the briefest of guitar introductions, the heavy organ and drumbeat of "I Wish U Heaven (Part 3)" begins the next part of the recording. Over this heavy groove, Prince provides one of the highlights of the show as he sings an unforgettable and epic "Forever In My Life." The song is dominated by an organ groove and the rattle of the guitar that never lets up as both instruments push each other further into a duel that propels the song along. The call and response guitar between Prince and Miko is fantastic, with a mesmerizing interplay between the two of them the climax of the performance. The finale comes with a call to "put a snare on it" as Boni comes to the microphone and rocks the house, taking over with a powerful vocal performance that comes from deep inside. The more she gives, the more Prince and Miko respond on their guitars, and the song gains a life of its own. Every scream is met by a pause and then a heavy response from the guitars and organ building a crushing momentum that squeezes the air out of the room. As the song ends in a frenzied crunch and howl, Prince can only respond to with "Boni Boyer, ain't nobody can mess with that girl."

> **EVERY SCREAM IS MET BY A PAUSE AND THEN A HEAVY RESPONSE FROM THE GUITARS AND ORGAN BUILDING A CRUSHING MOMENTUM THAT SQUEEZES THE AIR OUT OF THE ROOM**

Prince returns to the well of emotional ballads for his song "Still Would Stand All Time." Similar in structure, a ballad with a haunting guitar solo, it would be easy to compare it with "Just My Imagination," yet Prince takes it in a different direction with its fresh sound. Still two years away from official release, the song still has yet to be overworked, and the version played here is fresher, cleaner, and less syrupy than what later appears on *Graffiti Bridge*. There is a perfect time to record a song, after all the kinks have been worked out and it has been crafted, yet before it is overworked and overpolished. It is unfortunate that "Still Would Stand All Time" falls into the second camp, and the album version is sterile and tepid compared to this. The rawness of Prince's voice gives it the humanity it needs to become soulful in the live performance. This passion shines through as Prince sings his lines and nowhere more so than the breakdown as he sings in a throaty rasp. There are only a few lines, yet they are enough to signal the intent and emotion of the song. Of course there is the famous moment when he corrects one of the band with the lone "who's the fool singing *will*, it's *would*." The guitar solo that follows and closes the song is shorter than the previous pyrotechnics on guitar, which is no bad thing as it adds a balance to the song that could have easily been overwhelmed with a histrionic guitar break.

One feels that Prince is giving himself a chance to catch his breath as "I'll Take You There" features Boni, keyboard, and an organ to begin with. Soon enough he returns to the fray leading the band from the keyboard driven "I'll Take You There" into the guitar led "Rave Un2 The Joy Fantastic." "Rave Un2 The Joy Fantastic" itself is a guitar fueled groove that features the band chanting (obviously enough) "Rave". It is upbeat and typical of the type of jam that Prince likes to finish his shows with, all rush and downhill energy. The rapid-fire solos come in quick succession, and Miko and Atlanta both contribute furious moments before Prince tops them all with his own solo. Just as it seems to be coming to a halt, Prince calls "kick some ass" and the band takes off again, sounding more frantic than before. There comes one final burst of unrestrained energy before Prince brings it to a close with a simple "Thank you; God is Love."

> **THE RAPID-FIRE SOLOS COME IN QUICK SUCCESSION, AND MIKO AND ATLANTA BOTH CONTRIBUTE FURIOUS MOMENTS BEFORE PRINCE TOPS THEM ALL WITH HIS OWN SOLO**

When it comes to essential bootlegs, none is more essential than this show. It is quite simply the first and last word when it comes to aftershows and soundboard recordings. Anyone who is starting out on their bootleg journey is best to start here, and although it sets impossibly high standards that all bootlegs aspire to reach, it is the starting point for all collectors.

SET LIST

1. Instrumental Jam
2. D.M.S.R.
3. Just My Imagination
4. People Without
5. Housequake
6. Down Home Blues
7. Cold Sweat
8. Forever In My Life
9. Still Would Stand All Time
10. I'll Take You There
11. It's Gonna Be A Beautiful Night
12. Rave Un2 The Joy Fantastic

RELEASES

- After Concert Show - *Fan Release*
- Dance, Music, Sex & Romance - *Turtle Records*
- Forever In My Life - *Bundy Records*
- Golden Hits - *Clarence Music Group*
- Green - *Play With Me*
- Just My Imagination - *On Stage*
- Just My Imagination - *Red Phantom*
- Nightclubbing - *Swingin Pig Records*
- Nothing Compares 2 U - *Banana Records*
- Orange - *Play With Me*
- Secret Gig - *Living Legend Records*
- Small Club - *Beech Martin*
- Small Club - *Insect Records*

- Small Club - *Moonraker*
- Small Club - *STE*
- Small Club - *Thunderball*
- Small Club, 2nd Show That Night - *X Records*
- The Trojan Horse Aftershow - *Sabotage*
- Trojan Horse Remastered - *Sabotage*

31st AUGUST 1988
GROSSE FREIHEIT '36, HAMBURG

Recorded during the height of the *Lovesexy* tour, the bootleg of this aftershow ticks all the boxes. A late-night aftershow, inspired cover versions, a surprising guest appearance, and some fan favorites make it a standout from start to finish. Although over shadowed by the *Small Club* gig recorded around the same time (see chapter 25), it deserves more coverage and praise than it has previously received. There is plenty to recommend it; Prince and the band are in fine form, and the show is fantastic. It certainly earns its place among the essentials and can look any one of them squarely in the eye.

"Just My Imagination" is well documented across a variety of bootlegs, although this is the only time when it actually opens a recording. There is very little in the way of buildup; Prince is into the song from the start, leaving listeners no time to catch their breath. The rawness of the recording is immediately apparent - the audience is right there with the band in the microphone and audible through the song. As with contemporary bootlegs, this extra audience participation can corrupt the musical impression; however the quality of the song outshines the recording quality, and Prince's vocals are strong and steady early on before he lets his guitar do the talking for him. It is not as soaring or as sheering as other examples, but it is still captivating in its intensity and intent.

It is tempting to compare this rendition to the *Small Club* bootleg; this one doesn't come close in terms of recording quality, but the music can't be faulted and is just as good as anything heard on *Small Club*. The guitar solo has its own personality and is quite different from *Small Club* (worth listening to closely and comparing) before a second solo appears dreamlike, far more relaxed and clean, pointing perhaps to Miko's playing. Miko brings a lot to the band and is an unsung hero; his playing stands up after all these years and still provides something interesting to latch on to.

31st AUGUST 1988 - GROSSE FREIHEIT '36, HAMBURG

The comparisons to the *Small Club* show continue as the band play an arrangement of "Rave Un2 The Joy Fantastic." After a brief introduction of the band, and his "new friend, the Blue Angel," two funky rhythms strike up, intertwining and gaining strength together. They run in and out of each other, working well together as they lace up a web of sound. As Prince starts to sing "Rave" the song lifts off, with Eric Leeds back in the front line and very much leading it. After his previous absence, he obviously tries to make up for it here in Hamburg by being everywhere with his unmistakable style permeating every track. He twists the song in new ways and shines a different light on a track that is already so well-known by the other performance. This arrangement contains a shifting landscape of improvisations and jams shaping into song as the crowd rides on the back of it, less frenetic and more inclusive.

> **THIS ARRANGEMENT CONTAINS A SHIFTING LANDSCAPE OF IMPROVISATIONS AND JAMS SHAPING INTO SONG AS THE CROWD RIDES ON THE BACK OF IT, LESS FRENETIC AND MORE INCLUSIVE**

Without pause Prince sings the first lines of "Girls And Boys" a cappella. The rest of the band joins as the funk levels go up considerably for the next few minutes. Off the back of "Rave Un2 The Joy Fantastic," Eric stays at the center of things, his saxophone solo longer and funkier than anything that has come before. He arrives early and gets several chances to play before the song boils over with a head-spinning solo from Prince that has him turning the world upside down with his guitar. One wouldn't normally associate "Girls And Boys" with a fiery guitar solo, yet it works and adds to a song that most people are overly familiar with.

After such a dynamic song, things take a gentle twist with the piano and "Venus De Milo." It is as brief as it is beautiful and serves as the perfect way to introduce the piano set. "Starfish And Coffee" is equally as good, and the crowd is readily feeling it, clapping along as Prince plays, creating an intimate moment where one can almost feel the heat coming off the stage. This too is short, Prince opting for a single verse and chorus before the segue into "Raspberry Beret."

"Raspberry Beret" benefits greatly as a solo piano piece, the melody shining brightly on the piano and the lyrics holding the center of attention. With just a verse and chorus, Prince acknowledges the crowd with a "oh, you guys are too nice; I'm going to stay here a while."

The biggest surprise of this bootleg is the appearance of "People Without" in the piano set. It lacks the weight of the *Small Club* recording, yet is every bit as enjoyable. It is not yet a fully formed song, and what we have here is it in embryonic stage, nothing more than a couple of lines and the main refrain repeating. Still, even in this state, it is special and another reason to rate this bootleg highly.

Prince hits the emotional heart of the show with the next one-two punch. "Condition Of The Heart" sees Prince singing the first verse before the crowd join him for the chorus. They are too loud, leaving Prince to dryly comment "oh my goodness, how many singers we got?" before he continues with "now I'll play one you don't know."

The following "Still Would Stand All Time" is a showstopper. The album arrangement doesn't come close to the live versions circulating, and this version is one of the best. On record the soul of the song is absent; it has been so polished and overworked that the emotion we hear in the live performances is missing entirely. The arrangement at this particular show is full of soul and could well be another song entirely. Prince sings gently, but his voice aches with emotion through the first chorus. It is a breathtaking performance as he works the audience into it, coaching them through the chorus before delivering the lines himself, dripping with an emotional quiver. The introduction of surprise guest Taylor Dayne is a boon for the crowd and for the bootleg as she delivers a phenomenal solo. This is Taylor Dayne at the height of her popularity, and she channels great singers of the past as she sings her part. Her vocals are full yet crystal in purity, and even though her time is short on the microphone, she certainly makes her presence felt. This is the high point of the song; from here it meanders before an upbeat, swinging coda.

"One, two, three" brings another fan favorite in "Strange Relationship." It is irrepressible with Prince's sharp vocals and a drum sound to match. Rather unusually, it features a bass solo that adds to the

> **"IT IS A BREATHTAKING PERFORMANCE AS HE WORKS THE AUDIENCE INTO IT, COACHING THEM THROUGH THE CHORUS BEFORE DELIVERING THE LINES HIMSELF, DRIPPING WITH AN EMOTIONAL QUIVER."**

flavor of the show (there is always something unexpected happening). The segue from the bass solo to Dr. Fink's solo is absolutely seamless, a solo that is distinctly twitching and hyperactive. It harks back to Prince's early years, and it says something of Dr. Fink's style and ability that he played with Prince for so long. The final minutes are perhaps the best as they are filled with grooves and chunky piano that carry the funk.

The elastic bass kicks off the next song and a trademark Miko guitar riff plays before the song emerges as "A Love Bizarre." In true aftershow fashion the song is drawn out as the band gives it their own flavor. Eric plays with more freedom than previously heard, and the strong bass line underpins the whole thing. It is much less of a pop song in this context; it has a life and vibrancy of its own as it sprawls out across the recording. The song unfortunately and predictably becomes like all other jams, it loses focus with first an Eric Leeds solo before Prince adds his guitar to the cauldron, producing a soup of odd flavors.

With Boni Boyer singing "I'll Take You There," the intensity of the show wanes. There is no denying she is a fine singer, but the song never takes off and stays in a low gear throughout. Despite some great vocals, it remains the poor cousin compared to the earlier tracks. However, the song ends with some big-hearted screams from her, and this sets the scene nicely for "Down Home Blues."

Starting relatively slowly, Boni reveals the meaning of the song to the crowd. The song is obviously a great fit for her voice and style. With the keyboards and horns playing swells underneath, we are transported to another time and place. For the next few minutes this could come from anytime in the last fifty years, it is ageless in its sound and delivery. However, Prince later snaps the song out of this nostalgic glow with a guitar break in his own Prince style.

"Cold Sweat" takes its time to settle and properly begin, as a variety of different drum patterns play before it climbs into the groove. The first section of the song contains little of Prince as Eric Leeds provides a relaxing solo. The song twists through several stops and starts, never quite building momentum, before coming to an extremely funny moment as Prince briefly sings the bass line of Michael Jackson's "Bad" - it is short but highly amusing and makes for an interesting listen.

The concert moves quickly on as the guitar chugs and grooves along with the keyboards to bring in "God Is Alive." As a finale this can't be beaten; it is the high-point of a show that has already had an outstanding track with the performance from Taylor Dayne. The groove is heavy and strong, grounding the song with its crawl, while Prince sings with a passion that is infectious and spiritual. His vocals have a growl to them, singing straight from the heart, which makes the performance all the more powerful. Even the guitar break can't match the vocals for emotion. The intensity is ramped up further as Prince sings "God is alive," the song offering several insights into Prince and his spiritual beliefs. Later he gives a candid and interesting speech about *Camille*, then a longer talk about *Lovesexy*. To hear Prince speak about his beliefs is an insight to his inner world and is a must-listen. Never once does it cross the line into preaching though; it is a fascinating moment that says a lot about his character and how his beliefs shape his music.

"Purple Rain" is a mainstay of Prince's main shows; yet rarely heard at aftershows such as this. To have it played at this concert marks it as something special, and even though the performance of the song is average by normal standards, it still adds to the appeal of this bootleg. The audience senses there may not be much in it, and they sing their part almost as soon as the guitar break begins without waiting for prompting by Prince. The guitar break comes to an end as Prince sings with them, and at this point the recording and bootleg suddenly stop.

This bootleg has obvious flaws but easily surpasses them. A set list full of highlights, it is the final "God Is Alive" that stands above all else as the high point. "Still Would Stand All Time" is the other track that deserves special mention. Taylor Dayne gives good account of herself with a performance that belies her pop status at the time. The 1988 aftershows are similar to one another in some ways, yet each is different and offers something more for the careful listener. There is some tough competition for what could be considered essential in these aftershows, but this one is worth the time to listen to.

31st AUGUST 1988 - GROSSE FREIHEIT '36, HAMBURG

SET LIST

1. Just My Imagination
2. Rave Un2 The Joy Fantastic
3. Girls And Boys
4. Venus De Milo
5. Starfish And Coffee
6. Raspberry Beret
7. People Without
8. Condition Of The Heart
9. Still Would Stand All Time
10. Strange Relationship
11. A Love Bizarre
12. I'll Take You There
13. Down Home Blues
14. Cold Sweat
15. God Is Alive
16. Purple Rain

RELEASES

- Driving to Midnight Mess - *Sabotage*
- The Story Of Camille - *Fan Release*

11TH NOVEMBER 1988

WARFIELD THEATER, SAN FRANCISCO

There are many great 1988 shows in circulation, however it is the aftershows from that era that are of most interest as far as essential bootlegs go. Superficially the aftershows are alike, but closer inspection reveals them to more different than first listen suggests. There is a wide variety of tracks played at these shows, both covers and originals, and the songs that do appear several times are often different arrangements featuring other sounds and styles. The Warfield show of 1988 is short, yet in the hour it runs several songs appear that haven't been widely heard and that is a plus in its favor. With this concert coming later in the year the band is well versed in the way of aftershows, offering a bootleg of high quality and interest.

Like so many other Prince shows, this one begins with a single steady beat before a touch of bass reveals the final song from *Lovesexy* - "Positivity." A slow burner, the song builds as it goes, drawing in the crowd and the energy in the room like a musical black hole. A quiet first verse; followed by a second sung full throated, it has a full thick sound, giving it more humanity than the mechanical beat heard on the released record. True to form, Prince has Eric Leeds provide not one but two of his distinct solos. It is typical of Prince and these aftershows; he takes the song in a direction not heard before with simple additions. Eric isn't as cool and laid back as one might expect, electing to play in a punchy style that adds some force to the piece. This opening hand closes with a "hold on to your soul" statement of intent from Prince.

The muted chord progression of "The Ballad of Dorothy Parker" plays and it immediately conjures up images of a dark, smoky room. With the horn and piano carrying the song, it has an inner light that uplifts it beyond its muted roots. There is a jazz vibe that permeates through the song, and an ad-lib by Prince name checking Madhouse before a cool jazz-infused piano solo further highlights this point. The piano and horns remain the bones of the song, settling on a riff that takes it to the finish, both of them adding an inner structure to a downbeat song.

Prince is heard taking time to thank the crowd for coming out, saying "this beats hanging out at the hotel watching Letterman" before launching into "Housequake." Like everything on this bootleg, it is a strong version and has a steeliness to it that is underlined by Prince's singing. With an impassioned vocal, he is in the moment as he gives it a full voice.

Some soft lead guitar follows, introduced by Prince with "I think I want to play guitar," but proves merely a warm-up for what will follow as he tests the waters with further lead lines. With a hushed "one, two" the familiar opening of "Just My Imagination" begins. The opening minutes of guitar set the bar high, and it is almost disappointing as the song begins proper. However, Prince's singing is warm and inviting and casts a spell as he begins to weave his magic. The guitar break is equally alluring, drawing the audience in before Prince cranks up the pressure with some bolder strokes; it is perfectly paced and soaked in passion, never too fast or furious and always full of emotion. There is a moment for fans of rarities on bootlegs with a surprising and impassioned singing of "Noon Rendezvous." This is a gem of a moment and makes this aftershow stand above others from this era.

> **THE OPENING MINUTES OF GUITAR SET THE BAR HIGH, AND IT IS ALMOST DISAPPOINTING AS THE SONG BEGINS PROPER**

With the lead guitar still playing the band introduces a relaxed "I'll Take You There." It is an enjoyable rendition with the crowd obviously lapping it up with plenty of hand clapping and some whoops. The guitar is slight yet worth listening to, but the strongest player is easily Boni and her voice. These shows sometimes suffer when Prince isn't on the microphone, but in this case Boni commands attention with a strong, soulful performance that keeps the show on track. Nicely backed by Miko's funk, Boni and the band gather momentum and push harder as the song continues, finishing suddenly but on a high.

"Take this beat, I don't mind" signals the beginning of "I Wish U Heaven (Part 3)." The band play to their strengths with a funk fueled upbeat groove that is irresistible. The song accelerates as the band fleshes out the basic groove, before they morph into "Cold Sweat."

The opening drum break by Prince is less than spectacular, but it does add another dimension to the recording. With the bass joining him, it becomes a brief jam before Sheila relieves him of drum duties with a percussive sound that she should trademark. Her solo is every bit as good as Prince's, if not better, and it is distinctly hers all the way. She plays with plenty of flourishes, adding a richer percussive tone to the band rather than a conventional straight rock solo.

To close out the show and this bootleg, there is a well received, full rendition of "Lovesexy." The opening twinkling of piano gives nothing away, and it is as Prince begins to sing that the song reveals itself. With the guitars and bass more prominent than the recorded version, it gains an inner strength and is all the more powerful for it. Despite the kaleidoscope of sounds throughout the song, the groove remains fundamental, and it never lets up through the performance. Prince can be heard throwing in snatches of other lyrics. "Hollyrock," "The Glamorous Life" and "A Love Bizarre" are expected, but a line from Bruce Springsteen's "Born In The U.S.A." comes bizarrely into the mix, as does a line from Michael Jackson's "The Way You Make Me Feel." Both are pleasant surprises, although only a line from each is heard. This is the climax of the show and the band take on "Chain Of Fools," before a fast and furious saxophone carries through to "It's Gonna Be A Beautiful Night." It is an awe-inspiring performance and the band is awesome in the truest sense of the word. If not for Prince's final call of "Vegas," they would still be jamming on this song until late into the early morning.

There are several bootlegs circulating of this show based on different recordings. It may not be on everyone's radar, but this show is another aftershow from the 1988 golden period, and as such is colored by the same magic as Small Club. With a higher quality recording, it would be better known and even with the recording limitations it is still a wonderful show. The recording is average, but the show itself is anything but, with a couple of *Lovesexy* songs as standouts. This is an underrated bootleg that is worth the time to listen to.

11TH NOVEMBER 1988 - WARFIELD THEATER, SAN FRANCISCO

SET LIST

1. Positivity
2. The Ballad Of Dorothy Parker
3. Housequake
4. Just My Imagination
5. I'll Take You There
6. Take This Beat
7. Cold Sweat
8. Prince Drum Solo
9. Lovesexy
10. '80s Medley
11. It's Gonna Be A Beautiful Night

RELEASES

- Just Another Aftershow - *Fan Release*
- Lovesexy USA - *Sabotage*
- Take The "W" Train - *4DaFunk*
- Take The Other "W" Train - *4DaFunk*

1st FEBRUARY 1989
SENDAI STADIUM, SENDAI

The Dortmund show of the *Lovesexy* tour is the go-to show as far as capturing the energy and spirituality of the tour. However, as it was released as *Lovesexy Live* on VHS and laserdisc, I am going to overlook it as a bootleg. There are several other fantastic bootlegs of the tour circulating, and the most essential of these is the soundboard recording of the Sendai show. It is almost as well-known as Dortmund and an excellent soundboard. The set list differs ever so slightly from the Dortmund show, making for an interesting listen after the heavy rotation of the Dortmund VHS over the years. As for the *Lovesexy* shows, they are an experience in themselves as Prince presents his latest material in a manner that lets the listener know how important it is to him. The concert is a spiritual journey as Prince bends his old material in a medley that fits with the story he wants to tell. As a medley, it presents just enough of each song that the audience never feels cheated. It works as a clever way to get the weight of history off his back, leaving him to concentrate his (and the audience's) attention on the new material.

"Snare drum pound on the two and four, all the party people get on the floor - bass!" is a simple yet effective introduction to "Housequake." "Housequake" sounds thin on record but on this recording it is round and full of drums from the start. "Housequake" could only have been written and conceived by Prince; there is nobody else who could put all these pieces together in a way that would work. The recording is such that every piece can be heard, and the song can be broken down and heard individually or as a whole. It is all built around the horns and drums with the bass being much stronger in the live setting. As the longest song in the first half of the set, the band has a chance to play as a unit before the medley that will follow.

Prince slips easily into "Slow Love" as the song ends, and the next forty minutes are a roller-coaster ride as he blitzkriegs his way through his catalogue. "Slow Love" sets the standard - it is barely a couple of minutes and Prince cuts it down just as the mood is being set. However, "Adore" is the following song and a natural progression as he cleverly pairs two seductive jams together. Prince's vocals are getting an early workout, and his vocal gymnastics are more than matched when Boni intercedes for some interplay between the two of them.

A sudden shout and things speed up for the next three songs. Prince has the set list cleverly constructed; the songs are all suited to what has come before them and what comes next. In this case "Delirious," "Jack U Off," and "Sister" all come tumbling after one another, each seemingly trying to outdo the other in break-neck speed. "Delirious" is a flash in the pan at thirty seconds, while "Jack U Off" gets a longer outing. It is sprightly with the horns adding a nice element in contrast to the guitar heavy version of previous tours. There is even time for brief organ and guitar solos before it rolls into "Sister." Unbelievably, it is even faster with just a verse and a chorus, although the band is all aboard with some guitar work that raises it to a higher level. A quick dash to the finish line and then a lovely and surprising segue into "Do Me, Baby."

"Do Me, Baby" is a chance to catch our collective breaths as it is slower and longer than many of the songs in this first half of the show. There is beauty in the recording as Prince and his magnificent vocals are captured with every nuance and inflection. A couple of squeals introduce his deeper voice for some laid-back cool seduction talk. He has done it all a thousand times before, but it always sounds good; he knows how to draw the ladies of the audience in and no doubt more than a few men. Then, in a move that ties it back to the start of the show, he finishes with a couple of lines from "Adore."

> **A COUPLE OF SQUEALS INTRODUCE HIS DEEPER VOICE FOR SOME LAID-BACK COOL SEDUCTION TALK**

The energy levels are restored with the opening notes of "I Wanna Be Your Lover." The pop doesn't last too long as things immediately take a nasty turn with the appearance of "Head." Although nasty, it isn't anywhere near as dark and dirty as it is on earlier tours; in this settling it is clean and sharp, which negates some of the lyrics coming from Prince. However, the ever reliable Dr. Fink is onboard for his trademark solo that harks back to the earlier era and gives it some credibility for older fans.

"On the one" brings "Girls And Boys" into the show. It is unfortunately a pale imitation of itself, and thankfully there is only a minute of sterile sound to be heard. From the same era, "A Love Bizarre" is a different story. The bass and drums are thicker and the horns stronger than ever as it surges into view. Having Sheila E. present is a bonus, and her vocals on "A Love Bizarre" add to its authenticity. The funk is turned up to eleven as Miko plays a funk infused break that tears the roof off, encouraged by Prince and the band chanting "who's house, Miko's house!"

"When You Were Mine" is as fresh as the day it was recorded. With the guitar identical to the album version, it is the singing of the band that is the difference. The song gains a lot from the soundboard recording, and as the crowd sings "hey, hey" to Prince's command, the horns are heard, adding an excellent update to the back catalogue.

The following cluster of songs begins with the pound of "Controversy" stomping into view. It is only a minute in this form before it quietly slows to the mournful keyboard of "Little Red Corvette." The change of pace is well-placed, bringing some respite to the breakneck medley heard thus far. "Little Red Corvette" is itself unremarkable and as Prince did for many years he shuts it down after the guitar solo, jumping directly into "U Got The Look." The funky rhythm guitar underneath and the louder rock guitar over the top battle it out for supremacy, but the outcome is undecided as it ends soon enough with the introduction of "Superfunkycalifragisexy." It is surprising to see *Black Album* songs in the set list, yet it makes perfect sense in the wider context of the show and Prince's life at that time. The first half of the show features a selection of Prince's dirtier, darker songs before the rebirth midshow and the redemption of the *Lovesexy* album that makes up the second half of the show. "Superfunkycalifragisexy" is a natural fit to this story that Prince is portraying. It is as fresh as it is on record, and it deserves to be heard by a wider audience such as this. In a neat symmetry the medley ends with the song that started it all, "Controversy," and we end right where we started.

> **IT IS SURPRISING TO SEE BLACK ALBUM SONGS IN THE SET LIST, YET IT MAKES PERFECT SENSE IN THE WIDER CONTEXT OF THE SHOW AND PRINCE'S LIFE AT THAT TIME**

The first half of the show, some might say the dirty half, is rounded out with the most interesting song of the set - "Bob George." Again, it makes perfect sense in this setting; it is dark and funky as its protagonist reaches an all-time low. In the context of the set list it sets the scene for the rebirth and redemption that follows, providing a dark contrast for the second half to shine brightly against. Creative and dark, it ends with the Lord's Prayer and literally a bang!

There are a few seconds of silence and dark noise before the show resumes with Prince solo at the piano playing the opening chords of "Anna Stesia." The most intriguing *Lovesexy* song, it signals the end of the first half of the show and heralds the beginning of the second half as it washes the stage with its clean, pure sound after all that has come before. From here on in, there will be no more medleys and shortened versions - it is now all about *Lovesexy*, positivity, and full songs played to the hilt. It is the perfect way to close out the opening hour of the show, and as the song ends with Prince singing "God is love, love is God," there is no doubt about where the rest of the show is going.

Prince bursts out of the speakers with his "aw-oa" as "Eye No" begins strongly. The song isn't as busy as it is on record, which is in its favor on this bootleg as all the parts are distinguishable and clean; one can see how the individual pieces fit together, and when they are all taken together the only conclusion is that this must have been written by a mad genius.

The opening beat to "Lovesexy" is loud, and like so many of these *Lovesexy* songs it is a pleasant surprise to hear how strong it is live. "Lovesexy" is full of different layers and textures, but the rhythm section is the most impressive, outstanding in this song and the songs that follow.

The concert and bootleg dips with "Glam Slam." While the second half promises more than the first half, it is only "Glam Slam" that gets the short treatment. It is barely two minutes, essentially a throwaway moment, especially considering the songs around it. However, that is a minor quibble in a concert that delivers so much else.

"The Cross" is a perfect fit to this spiritual aspect of the show, and it is sounding better here than it did on the *Sign O' The Times* tour. It is less reverential and more uplifting in tone. Before it was a spiritual song lyrically; in this context the very sound of the song itself is spiritual and the music just as uplifting as the message. It is all about context, and surrounded by these other spiritual songs it takes on a new life, testament again to Prince's set list. It is only to be expected Prince's guitar playing is a highlight, and he delivers an absolute joy to listen to, playing as if infused by a higher power. The tone of the song is uplifting as it shines some light into the dark of the first portion of the show.

The beat of "I Wish U Heaven" is soothing, and it is a cool balm after the heat and furious finish of "The Cross." Sheila E. is in fine form - a star in her own right, she contributes on many levels through this show. This song is yet another highlight for her, and along with Miko, she brings a different aspect to the show and this song.

Prince begins the next song with "Sendai, come here and give me a kiss." No surprises at all then as the familiar "Kiss" rings out. However, it is a disappointing version as the guitar is buried low and the polished and sharp mix is frustratingly lacking the creativity of the original.

"Dance On" gets an introduction before it quickly disappears under Sheila's Transmississippi Rap. This is where the show lacks in that magical quality that makes the rest of the performance so special. It is good, but it lacks the sparkle that is heard in the other songs.

The keyboard swell, so familiar from the 1987/1988 era, serves as the opening for "Let's Go Crazy." Prince delivers an abridged introduction before the crunching guitar cuts in. While not providing anything new or innovating, it does give Prince a chance to show off his guitar skills and as always he delivers. Showy and angular, the guitar adds to the intensity as Prince pulls out all stops. Foregoing further guitar heroics later in the song to instead encourage the crowd to sing "go, go, go," the song loses momentum as the intensity drops, leaving only the first portion memorable.

This is obviously the purple portion of the show as the classic riff of "When Doves Cry" plays. With more horns in the song, there is an extra element of funk that hadn't been in the show earlier. The short arrangement played doesn't do the song justice, but it does have some great additions of bass, horns, and samples.

The guitar introduction to "Purple Rain" is also kept short and is fleeting compared to some of the long, drawn out versions that have been heard over the years. Predictably it is a verse and a chorus before the onslaught of the guitar solo that obliterates all else. There are other songs on the set list that carry the emotional weight of the show and that leave "Purple Rain" oddly cold and empty. It would be easy to say it had been overplayed, but there are plenty more powerful versions in later years.

"1999" is horn infused, yet it still retains its signature keyboard. Prince skips over the bulk of the song and heads straight to the fade out where he can engage the audience for the trademark "party!" singalong, something all too common in later years. Even with this party ending it is all over by the three-minute mark with a rumble and Prince thanking the crowd, assuring them God will take care of them.

The show has one more twist as after a minute Prince is back for a final encore of "Alphabet St." He leaves the concert on a high as the song is just as good, if not better, than all that has come before. With Prince singing playfully, the band weaves in and out around him keeping the music cohesive. This is a great example of the versatility of the band - they are playing a highly rehearsed and choreographed show, yet they always sound as if they could cut loose at any moment, something they do indeed do at the aftershows of the era as they let go and stretch out. On this recording they are well reined in, all the while the potential is there for something more to happen.

> **WITH PRINCE SINGING PLAYFULLY, THE BAND WEAVES IN AND OUT AROUND HIM KEEPING THE MUSIC COHESIVE**

The show ends on a religious and spiritual note with the sound of running water, the sound of baptism and purity. Prince's journey through the show is complete, from someone who is in need of saving to someone who has indeed been saved by his spiritual beliefs.

This is a highly enjoyable concert from one of the most interesting periods of Prince's career. The shows may not offer much difference from night to night, but the beliefs and spirituality behind them are fascinating and an insight to Prince's inner workings and motivations. On paper it is highly choreographed, rehearsed, and restrained, with little room for the band to display their character. In reality it is a joyful, uplifting show with Prince believing in every note he is playing. As he said himself "People won't think you're naïve if you play what you believe," and during this tour he was doing exactly that, playing directly from the heart. That shines through the songs, giving them a strength and brightness that isn't always heard elsewhere. As a record of the *Lovesexy* main shows, there is no doubt that this is 100 percent essential.

SET LIST

1. Housequake
2. Slow Love
3. Adore
4. Delirious
5. Jack U Off
6. Sister
7. Do Me, Baby
8. Adore
9. I Wanna Be Your Lover (intro)
10. Head
11. Girls And Boys
12. A Love Bizarre
13. When You Were Mine
14. Little Red Corvette
15. Controversy
16. U Got The Look
17. Superfunkycalifragisexy
18. Bob George
19. Anna Stesia
20. Cross The Line
21. Eye No
22. Lovesexy
23. Glam Slam
24. The Cross
25. I Wish U Heaven
26. Kiss
27. Dance On

1ST FEBRUARY 1989 - SENDAI STADIUM, SENDAI

28. Let's Go Crazy
29. When Doves Cry
30. Purple Rain
31. 1999
32. Alphabet St.

RELEASES

- 89 - *African Shark*
- Black Funk Invitation - *Watch Tower Records*
- Sendai - *Premium*
- Sendai 89 - *Sabotage*
- Sendai 1989 - *Zion*

30TH APRIL 1990
RUPERTS NIGHTCLUB, MINNESOTA

Prince is sometimes (unfairly) perceived as being cold towards his former friends and employees. It isn't strictly true: there are countless examples of his generosity toward former employees once they leave the fold. He can be both sympathetic and empathetic; the benefit concert for Big Chick a few weeks after his passing a perfect example. It is not a remembrance show (although Prince does talk about his passing); it is a benefit show with all proceeds going to the Huntsberry family. The concert is reported to have made more than $50,000 for the family, a much-needed sum as Big Chick died without life insurance in place. Admittedly the recording is not of the greatest quality, but the main attraction of the show is the significance of the Big Chick connection as well as the live debut of three songs from the *Batman* album. The first live performance by Prince of "Nothing Compares 2 U" is a bonus and yet another reason that this bootleg makes the list.

The standard of the recording is laid out early as Prince begins by speaking of Big Chick. It is muffled, and Prince is difficult to make out. It doesn't matter too much as it gives way to the DAT intro, something familiar now but at the time was new and full of different snippets that heighten the sense of anticipation.

What follows is a recording dropout and then a surprisingly sharp rendition of "The Future." As a live debut it is well rehearsed and as polished as later performances; already the band has a good handle on the song. The recording continues to drop a couple more times during the song, but it does improve as the bootleg progresses. There are still crackles and pops though, and these persist through the entirety of the recording. On the performance front, Prince's vocals have a smoothness to them, and there is plenty of warmth in the keyboard swells, making amends for the muffled sound.

"1999" is a crowd-pleaser, played in this incarnation over the top of "The Future" drumbeat. There is plenty of time for the band to make themselves heard, in particular Rosie Gaines's voice cuts through the noise and brings a large dose of humanity to the song. It is a pleasant change to hear "1999" early in the set; a song too often relegated to the party section near the end of the show in this case it has its moment early in the concert.

"Housequake" is disappointingly tepid. It is plastic sounding and has been neutered to fit the beat of these opening songs. The soul has been stripped out of it from the *Sign O' The Times* tour, and here it is barely a shadow of its former glory. Some of the small, nuanced sounds have been taken out, leaving the subtlety of the song missing; sadly it is not much more than just a pounding beat and the vocals. On a generous day we could say that this is due to the recording rather than the performance itself, which may be close to the truth.

> **SOME OF THE SMALL, NUANCED SOUNDS HAVE BEEN TAKEN OUT, LEAVING THE SUBTLETY OF THE SONG MISSING; SADLY IT IS NOT MUCH MORE THAN JUST A POUNDING BEAT AND THE VOCALS**

The following "Sexy Dancer" is little better in terms of recording. It is truncated and serves as a mere coda to the trio of songs that open the show. There is no doubt that it is a fine song that deserves better treatment than it gets at this show, and there are other circulating bootlegs that see it get the recognition it deserves.

"Kiss" is treated much better and gets a solid pass as it retains the key elements of the album recording along with a healthy dose of fun from Prince. It isn't overworked and manages to retain the simple charm of the original, its basic form surviving intact. Again the recording lets the performance down. It drops a few seconds mid-song and this, coupled with the muffled sound, neutralizes the positive aspects of the live performance. A magnificent-sounding Rosie Gaines is in fine voice though as she delivers "Let's Jam." Disappointingly though the recording can't match her for power and solid strength.

"Purple Rain" has a slow, sentimental sound that is purpose-built for a show like this. Prince takes time to talk about Big Chick, frustratingly it is again difficult to make out what he is saying as there are several people chatting near the taper. Prince gives the "Purple Rain" 'highlights' package, that is the opening verse and a chorus before letting loose with his much anticipated guitar work. Some might rail against this sort of thing and demand the full, uncut masterpiece, however, there is nothing to fault it for, and as his guitar wails it is just as good as the full arrangement.

Prince stays on the *Purple Rain* trip as he breaks out "Take Me With U." It is all a lot of fun, and the energetic crowd participation is noticeable. The song is lightweight but is something people can't help but respond to with its own inner energy.

A fast and furious "Alphabet St." has the audience enthused even further and the energy levels remain high. The band sticks with the live arrangement that served them well through the *Nude* tour with the "It Takes Two" middle section dominated by Rosie and her distinctive vocals. This arrangement is still harmonious to a modern audience with Prince as energetic as ever as he spits his lyrics, and with Rosie the song is well-endowed with fine voices.

The live debut of "The Question Of U" features a longer guitar-infused opening, a slow burn of a beginning that runs for some time. The smoldering guitar flickers and flames; one wonders if Prince is going to sing at all as the guitar continues to grip the listener's attention.

> **THE SMOLDERING GUITAR FLICKERS AND FLAMES; ONE WONDERS IF PRINCE IS GOING TO SING AT ALL AS THE GUITAR CONTINUES TO GRIP THE LISTENER'S ATTENTION**

Finally he comes to the microphone and begins to sing the "Electric Man" lyrics. This works well; "The Question Of U" musically is adaptable for what is sung over top, and the slightly silly "Electric Man" lyrics have an intensity to them. The only down side is that it leaves us shortchanged when it comes to both songs.

Rosie takes control of the show with a cover of "Ain't No Way." On a soundboard recording this would be breathtaking and even with the static and audience noise it is outstanding. Rosie's voice commands respect - it is full with a pureness that is undeniable to every listener.

Prince follows this with a live performance that reclaims "Nothing Compares 2 U" from Sinead O'Connor. It is a special moment as for the first time he plays his rendition for a live audience. There is no doubting whose song it is as he puts his stamp on it, the performance briefly outshining the recording as Prince strokes the lyrics, making every line ring true. The piano break lifts the song higher and lightens the slightly deadened recording - make no mistake this is a masterful performance.

"Batdance" is glorious live, and the guitar is especially loud. Another song making its live debut at this show, it is an enthusiastic performance with the Gameboyz making themselves heard. Prince whips the crowd up, but it is mostly the Gameboyz that are heard later in the song.

Things change dramatically with the appearance of "Scandalous." For a seductive ballad such as this there is a surprising amount of audience chatter, although this could be put down to the fact that it is a new song. There is a hint of guitar as the keyboards swell, and this gives it a sharper sound that plays well with the lushness and Prince's dripping vocals. Several drop outs in the recording threaten to overshadow the performance, but when he is heard, Prince sounds marvelous.

"Baby I'm A Star" signals that the end of the show is near. Prince is well in his stride, and the energy coming off the stage is captured on the bootleg - his enthusiastic scream is case and point. The song spins into the jam often heard on the *Nude* tour with the Gameboyz providing both rhythm and fun. The song does sag at the midpoint: it eases into a slow jam with Tony M. on hand to encourage the crowd to "make some noise." Once he steps back, the song casts off the shackles with Rosie belting out "Respect" and the band ratcheting things up for the final few minutes.

There is a celebratory mood to end the show, with clapping and cheering before an action-packed "Partyman" arrives, complete with a long introduction that is lifted straight from the video clip. Despite the muffled recording it is hard not to enjoy the song. It starts off fun, and then gets better with plenty of piano that stays through the song giving it a jazz sound. As a jam it works much better than the previous "Baby I'm A Star" and ends the show in a celebratory fashion.

This may have been a benefit show for Big Chick, but it was no morbid memorial. Prince played an enthusiastic and upbeat show that cuts through the poor recording. This is one concert where the performance, and the feeling behind it, outweighs any negativity about the quality of the recording. The songs debuted are played with great gusto, sounding well rehearsed and betraying no hint of being new to the band. This is an interesting performance and ticks just enough boxes to make it as essential part of the collection.

SET LIST

1. DAT Intro
2. The Future
3. 1999
4. Housequake
5. Sexy Dancer
6. Kiss
7. Purple Rain
8. Take Me With U
9. Alphabet St.
10. The Question Of U
11. Ain't No Way
12. Nothing Compares 2 U
13. Batdance
14. Scandalous
15. Baby I'm A Star
16. Segue
17. Respect
18. Baby I'm A Star
19. Partyman

RELEASES

☰ In Memory Of Big Chick - *Fan Release*

31st AUGUST 1990
TOKYO DOME, TOKYO

The *Batman* soundtrack never received a proper tour to promote it, although several songs from the album did get played regularly during the *Nude* tour. The *Nude* tour itself is a strange beast; falling between the release of *Batman* and the subsequent *Graffiti Bridge*, it captures the spirit of neither. With no album to promote, the tour is a greatest hits package, and the set list draws from across the board rather than leaning heavily on one particular album. At the time this was a departure for Prince. Until this point he had always strongly promoted his latest material in concert, and although the show opens with a song from the *Batman* album and features a couple more, the bulk of the concert is a hodgepodge of songs from his career. The clue is in the title - this is the *Nude* tour, not the *Batman* tour. It is well served by several soundboard recordings and a couple of pro-shot videos in circulation and of these the Tokyo concert is the most essential. Prince has paid plenty of attention to detail for this leg of the tour. Of particular note are the tour costumes he and the band wear, complete with Kanji characters (Rosie's says "Soul" while Prince's outfit reads "Love" down the side, with cuffs that say "Nude"). They only play five concerts in Japan, yet they make an effort to make a new stage presentation and give the local audience something special.

The concert itself is a slick, modern production far removed from the impassioned rock shows of early years. This is an arena show featuring all the modern trappings: a big stage, plenty of dancers, and a light show to match. The recording is just as sharp as the performance, and the opening "The Future" sets the standard. With a heavy low end, the music is just as muscular as Prince's vocals. There is a sense of darkness and foreboding in the music that suits the lyrical content. The recording has just enough of the live audience to enhance the live feel, and despite the cavernous arena Prince doesn't get lost, instead projecting himself outward from the center.

Prince dips into the back catalogue for "1999" and "Housequake," both of which roll over the same pounding beat. Prince may be sporting a completely different look and playing with a different band, yet "1999" sounds as it always has. The mood is set early for a party with the funk and roll cruising straight into "Housequake." The horn section is absent, so it is the bold keyboards that add the stabs and fills that drive the song, each stab coming as a flash out of the darkness. The band is almost invisible onstage, but their musical presence and talent overcomes this, especially the powerhouse voice of Rosie. With the band playing in darkness it is Prince and the Gameboyz that provide the dancing and visual aspect of the show, further highlighted as "Sexy Dancer" comes in the mix. It becomes all about the dance routines, and the next few minutes are given over to Prince and the dancers.

> **THE HORN SECTION IS ABSENT, SO IT IS THE BOLD KEYBOARDS THAT ADD THE STABS AND FILLS THAT DRIVE THE SONG, EACH STAB COMING AS A FLASH OUT OF THE DARKNESS**

"Kiss" is in a similar vein, with the band in the background as Prince sings out in the front with his dancers. It is far removed from The Revolution shows five years before, Prince is a solo performer here, the band kept at arm's length. He is in step with what his contemporaries were presenting at the time, and although it sounds and looks good, it lacks the magic of his earlier years. The redeeming feature comes in the form of Rosie Gaines - she injects an element of soul into an otherwise sterile performance with a rendition of "Let's Jam It" that demands you sit up and take notice.

The largest cheer is reserved for the following "Purple Rain." Prince doesn't spend too much time with it: the introduction is brief, especially compared to what's heard on the *Purple Rain* tour, and the main body of the song is barely a verse and chorus before Prince blows his load with an early guitar solo. With the first part of the song dispensed with in such a fashion, it loses a lot of its emotional weight, and rather than the guitar solo being the emotional release and triumphant climax, it is instead merely the musical equivalent of masturbation.

Things perk up with "Take Me With U" and the bootleg gains a boost of energy at this point. It is joyful, and hums along with Prince playing with plenty of bounce and the blue cloud guitar.

31st AUGUST 1990 - TOKYO DOME, TOKYO

The highlight of the performance follows with one of the great renditions of "Bambi." A song often heard over the years, in this concert it is harder and louder than ever before. Prince plays a smoking rendition with the guitar on fire for the next few minutes as he makes it not only cry but also sing while he indulges in every boy's rock god fantasy. It is not just about the poses and the looks; Prince delivers a screaming solo to match that raises the roof of Tokyo Dome.

Equally good but completely different is "Alphabet St." With a swift start Prince and the band race through the song with a fair measure of showmanship and playfulness. Every pause brings a rousing cheer from the crowd before a Rosie Gaines interlude sees the song jump out the starting blocks on the back of plenty of audience encouragement. Everything Rosie touches turns to gold, and nowhere more so than here as she spins a straightforward song into something soulful and earnest with the power and breadth of her vocals alone. The best is saved for the final minutes as the organ grooves while Prince breaks it down for his own vocal gymnastics that bring a level of sexiness to the song.

> **EVERYTHING ROSIE TOUCHES TURNS TO GOLD, AND NOWHERE MORE SO THAN HERE AS SHE SPINS A STRAIGHTFORWARD SONG INTO SOMETHING SOULFUL AND EARNEST WITH THE POWER AND BREADTH OF HER VOCALS ALONE**

The next portion of the show begins with Prince on the piano, teasing with "The Question Of U" before "Under The Cherry Moon" gets a longer rendition, complete with the audience offering a high-pitched sing along. "The Question Of U" returns for a heavier band performance, the drumbeat in particular sounding almost too strong as it keeps time. With the *Graffiti Bridge* album released just the previous week, this is already familiar to the crowd and they respond well, especially to the guitar solo, which is insistent and forceful in delivery. The performance becomes intoxicating as Prince sings the "Electric Man" lyrics. He is enthralling in the next few minutes as he prowls the front of the stage, molesting the microphone stand and humping the floor in a direct throw back to his performances of the 1980s.

"When Doves Cry" is timeless, and this performance, if not for the look of it, could be straight from 1984. The obvious difference is the Gameboyz bouncing on their heels beyond Prince, but elsewhere everything is in its place musically. With a bass line that rumbles through the arena, Prince turns it into a celebration as the final minutes see him emphasizing the dance aspect of his performance. He covers the entire stage as he marches back and forth before climbing atop the piano, eventually ending the song with piano runs that sweep across the keyboard.

The show may be slick to the point of being soulless, but "Do Me, Baby" restores the balance and is the emotional heart of the concert. The opening guitar of Miko is opulent and sweeping, bringing forth emotions previously buried deep. He has time to indulge the audience, and it is some time before Prince begins his lines. Prince matches Miko, delivering a sultry performance laying on top his piano, softly lit in reds.

Red is a recurring theme as "Little Red Corvette" enters the building. Although not as emotional as it sometimes is (and certainly not as emotional as the preceding "Do Me, Baby"), it still draws a nostalgic feeling as it plays. Even as an abridged version, it retains enough of its original charm to win over the audience.

Things turn darker, onstage and in the music, with the appearance of "Batdance." Miko is the key, his guitar riff being the backbone of the song. With not much happening vocally, Prince has plenty of time to dance and interact with the Gameboyz. It may not be for the purists, but it is undeniably entertaining. An interesting song live, although it doesn't quite fit with everything else, it is pleasing to have a *Batman* song on the set list.

You wait all day to hear a *Batman* song, then two come along at once. "Partyman," which follows, breathes new life into the show and lifts the level of fun immediately. This is Prince's most striking look of the evening as he struts to the stage clad in an orange striped suit and sunglasses, tipping his hat to the look of The Joker in the *Batman* movies. Prince sweats music, and nowhere is it more apparent than here as he moves effortlessly across the stage before jumping to the piano and instantly providing an engaging piano solo.

The rush to the finish comes with "Baby I'm A Star." The band manages to put their own spin on it, and it is quite different to arrangements heard on other tours. The sound is distinctly early '90s, which could be attributed to the Gameboyz, who spend some time imploring the audience to "rock the house." Even as the original riff plays, it is tempered by a modern sound, and one can easily date it by the gloss and sheen of the music. As a finale, the song sees the band finally come out of the dark and step into the limelight. They are a tight unit of classy players delivering an understated performance, and it is only during the final song does the show feel like Prince and the NPG rather than Prince and the band.

The *Nude* tour is neither here nor there for many people. It falls between the cracks of his '80s high and his early '90s renaissance. This, however, is an excellent production and recording of a show from a transitional period. Prince will bounce back in a couple of years with *Diamonds And Pearls* and the accompanying tour before the craziness of the '90s arrives, and this concert sees him treading water between the two periods. This may not be the most interesting concert in terms of music, but it is one of the best filmed and circulating. The footage is of the highest standard and, although dated, is still entertaining to watch after all these years. When it comes to pro-shot concerts, this is one of the best.

SET LIST

1. The Future
2. 1999
3. Housequake
4. Kiss
5. Purple Rain
6. Take Me With U
7. Bambi
8. Alphabet Street
9. The Question Of U
10. When Doves Cry
11. Do Me, Baby
12. Little Red Corvette
13. Batdance
14. Partyman
15. Baby I'm A Star

RELEASES

- 🎵 ooSex Licence To F... - *Four Seasons*
- 🎵 Do U Love Me? - *Fan Release*
- 🎵 Funkin' Around - *New Keruac Line*
- 🎵 In Japan - *Fan Release*
- 🎵 Live In Japan - *On-stage Records*
- 🎵 Live In Tokyo '90 - *ITM Records*
- 🎵 Nothing Compares 2 U Volume 3 - *Banana Productions*
- 🎵 Nude Tour '90 - *Beech Martin*
- 🎵 Nude Tour 1990 Live In Tokyo - *Deep Records*
- 🎵 Stripped Down - *Sabotage*
- 🎵 The Ride Dyvine - *Fan Release*
- 🎵 Tokyo '90 - *Confusion/♥ Or $*
- 🎵 Tokyo '90 - *Moonraker*
- 🎵 Tokyo '90 - *Premium*
- 🎵 Tokyo 1990 - *Fan Release*
- 🎵 Tokyo 1990 - *Gossip*
- 🎵 Tokyo 1990 - *Live Storm*
- 🎵 Tokyo 1990 - *Red Line*
- 🎵 Unauthorized Live Volume 2 - *Joker Productions*
- 🎵 World Tour In Concert - *Joker Productions*
- 🎞 Prince In Tokyo '90 - *Fullasoul*
- 🎞 The Question Of U - *Ladybird Records*
- 🎞 Tokyo '90 - *♥ Or $*
- 🎞 Tokyo 1990 - *Brave*
- 🎞 Tokyo 1990 - *Fan Release*

24TH JUNE 1992
EARLS COURT, LONDON

The late '80s and early '90s saw a downturn in the availability of quality Prince bootlegs. The amazing shows of the '80s turned into the not-quite-so-amazing shows of the early '90s as the *Batman* soundtrack and *Graffiti Bridge* album didn't get the concert tours they deserved. The *Nude* tour was enjoyable enough, but it didn't have an agenda to push and served as a placeholder more than anything else. However, with the release of *Diamonds And Pearls*, Prince was back on the top of the world. Although not as artistically challenging as his earlier material, it still proved to be a commercial success, and Prince toured the world promoting it, giving the album a tremendous push. The show from 24th June 1992 comes during his run of concerts at Earls Court London and is the closing performance of that series. What makes this bootleg so desirable is the fact that it is a pro-shot show, one that Prince himself recorded with the intention of releasing. We therefore see Prince as he wants to be seen, at his best with every move and note pitch perfect in anticipation of reaching a wider audience. This may be Prince at his most commercial and aiming his music squarely at a global audience, but it still retains some artistic integrity and makes for a great video.

Rosie's vocals on the opening "Take My Hand, Precious Lord" are divine and make an immediate impression. The show is spellbinding from the onset, as in the darkness she brings depth and passion to a concert that will later feature a shallow glitz and glamour performance. "Thunder" plays powerfully in the live setting, gaining more gravitas with the weight of the band fleshing it out. Most noticeable on the recording is the power of the guitar. Prince may look thin and almost sickly, but the sound he generates on the guitar is anything but. The dancers are a distraction; the star of the show is the sharp solo Prince plays with a glassy, clean tone; nothing else matters apart from those moments when he is working the guitar.

With the guitar gone, the dancers use "Daddy Pop" as an opportunity to strut their stuff. The song is far from the greatest Prince has ever written; however, the music and the band become secondary as the performance aspect of the show takes over. With the dancers and Prince leaping across the stage in all directions, the music briefly takes a backseat, until Rosie Gaines steps forward and gives a vocal performance that knocks the song sideways and restores the balance of the show.

The music is back to the forefront as "Diamonds And Pearls" receives an enticing guitar hook introduction that draws the audience's attention. With Prince and a ballerina dancing onstage, it does threaten to be another dance number; however, he takes time to sit at the piano and play, giving the song a focal point. The following song, although loud, is worth waiting for. With Rosie Gaines singing beside Prince, there is the gentle reminder of just what they could produce together, along with the thought of what could have been had she stayed in the band longer.

> **"WITH PRINCE AND A BALLERINA DANCING ONSTAGE, IT DOES THREATEN TO BE ANOTHER DANCE NUMBER; HOWEVER, HE TAKES TIME TO SIT AT THE PIANO AND PLAY, GIVING THE SONG A FOCAL POINT"**

The next two songs are throwbacks to Prince's vast back catalogue. Prince punches through "Let's Go Crazy" and "Kiss" in quick succession; "Let's Go Crazy" blazes like a comet before giving way to a performance of "Kiss" that is more about stagecraft than the song itself. Prince still manages to instill a bucketload of funk into the song and this arrangement thrills in its reinvigorated sound.

"Jughead" could be a whole lot better. Musically it is almost there, and with a funk groove it could on a good day be another "Sexy M.F." The main stumbling block is Tony M. There is no problem with Tony himself (I'm sure he's a great guy), it is just that in this live performance, and indeed in many more, he comes across as a bit shouty. While the song is potentially cool, especially as Prince sings from the dressing room, most of the good work is undone by Tony M. yelling and hyping the crowd.

The bootleg throws up a real surprise next in "Purple Rain," which comes as a complete contrast to the previous "Jughead." It is a performance that grounds the concert after some of its flashier moments, and the Prince guitar solo that opens the song also introduces sincerity into the performance. He speaks from the heart to the audience, although the words are swept away by the fantastic guitar break that he plays right after - the guitar a blow-torch that tortures the notes until the emotion bleeds out of them in a performance that draws a line right back to his '80s heyday.

Signposting the next track in this eclectic performance Prince whips the audience into a frenzy with a backward and forward chant "Live 4 Love, Live 4 Love." It opens with blistering guitar work that lays out a scorching path for what will follow in the coming minutes. The song maintains the fury of the opening assault as it soars with a Sonny T. solo. The following dual guitar attack stamps its authority all over the song and is one of the most powerful moments of the show.

The guitars and rock are put to one side as the funk arrives with horns, hand clapping, and some of Rosie's full-hearted singing. The next few minutes become a blur of sound and vision as Prince takes the piano for a burst of "Delirious" with the horns matching him every step of the way for energy and excitement. They continue to blast their way through "Willing And Able," with Tony M.'s rap being completely overshadowed by the horn section. which is simply on fire.

> **THE GUITARS AND ROCK ARE PUT TO ONE SIDE AS THE FUNK ARRIVES WITH HORNS, HAND CLAPPING, AND SOME OF ROSIE'S FULL-HEARTED SINGING**

"Damn U" would have been a song that was completely new to the audience, yet on the recording they can be heard responding well to it. Six months out from its release, it gets a rousing reception from the crowd, something that must have been extremely gratifying to Prince. While Prince's vocals are exquisite, he is equally matched by the horn section that maintains their own high standard throughout.

The audience seems to know the words to "Sexy M.F." far too well and they take great delight in singing the chorus back to Prince. Prince is again bettered by the horns and the audience in a song that is full of surprises - such as the solos played by Levi and Tommy Barbarella, both full of heart and adventurous beyond the confines of the show.

The next ten minutes are the high point of the bootleg as Prince plays a rendition of "Thieves In The Temple" that is breathtaking in its pure funkiness. There is the mystical introduction before Prince brings forth an extended funk-fueled "Thieves In The Temple." This is a barn-burning performance that is only heightened further by the series of screams he unleashes at the end. However, he is not done yet and takes the music to yet another level with an acoustic guitar funk jam. The playing is so hot that it is a surprising the guitar doesn't spontaneously combust; these few minutes are among the funkiest heard on any bootleg and unmatched by any artist.

> **THIS IS A BARN-BURNING PERFORMANCE THAT IS ONLY HEIGHTENED FURTHER BY THE SERIES OF SCREAMS HE UNLEASHES AT THE END**

Prince had to follow with something, and he chooses a performance of "Strollin." It has an easy way about it that sways naturally into "Insatiable." It is fresh; with a smooth alluring sound, and it works well as a comedown from the previous few songs. With an appealing warmth, the summery solo that Levi adds to it is a natural fit, and in its own way this pair of songs are the second-best part of the show.

"Gett Off" gets off to a jump-start with seemingly all the main parts playing at once - the scream, guitar riff, and Tony M. rapping right away. Compared to other parts of the show, this is a letdown; for all its lewd lyrics it comes across as tame and can't match the intensity or pure showmanship from earlier in the concert.

There is a brief break in the recording before the encore begins with the crowd-pleasing "Cream." The look and sound of it is suitably creamy, Prince looks the part, and his vocal delivery is buttery throughout. However, the song doesn't offer much more. The bootleg recording ends at this point, but not before Rosie has a minute to sing "Chain Of Fools." It is a fitting bookend to show, and not only does Rosie open and close the bootleg, she brings it to an end on a high. It is regrettable that the next encores aren't present, but one can't complain when the quality of the rest of the show is this good.

Diamonds and Pearls brought a new audience to Prince while the older audience fell in love with him all over again. This concert features the bulk of the *Diamonds and Pearls* album and just enough of his hits to keep the older fans interested. The circulating footage is typical of the shows at this time, and this is one of the most well-known bootlegs currently circulating. Therefore, it should not be a

24TH JUNE 1992 - EARLS COURT, LONDON

surprise that it makes the most essential list: not only is it a pro-shot from one of his most commercially successful periods, but it is also a quality show delivered with professionalism, passion, and an eye to the wider market. With that in mind, this is one bootleg that should appeal to everyone.

SET LIST

1. Take My Hand, Precious Lord
2. Thunder
3. Daddy Pop
4. Diamonds And Pearls
5. Let's Go Crazy
6. Kiss
7. Dead On It
8. Jughead
9. Purple Rain
10. Live 4 Love
11. Delirious
12. Willing And Able
13. Damn U
14. Sexy MF
15. Arabic Interlude
16. Thieves In The Temple
17. Strollin'
18. Insatiable
19. Gett Off
20. Cream
21. Chain Of Fools

RELEASES

- Earls Court '92 - *Premium*
- Prince & The NPG - Earls Court - *Onion Records*
- The Complete Live Recording - *Fan Release*
- The Ryde Dyvine - *Fan Release*
- Thieves In The Temple - *Sabotage*
- Thunder - *Moonraker*
- Diamonds & Pearls In London - *Fan Release*
- Earls Court Live - *Brave*
- Thunder - *Ladybird Records*

24TH MARCH 1993
RADIO CITY MUSIC HALL, NEW YORK

After the success of *Diamonds And Pearls*, Prince continued to evolve, and the following years threw up an array of twists and turns as he rediscovered his muse. The ⚥ album is a sprawling collection of eclectic music that is largely unfiltered. At this stage in his career Prince could produce whatever kind of album he wanted without regard for commercial viability. Not only does it contain some of his most interesting material, but it also has plenty of spectacle and theatrics mixed into the music; from the storyline that plays out between the songs, or the songs themselves in the case of the "3 Chains O' Gold." The accompanying *Act I* and *Act II* tours are likewise full of this drama and over the top theater. It is refreshing, as with the *Diamonds And Pearls* shows, to see Prince drawing the bulk of his set list from the current album he is promoting, engaging with his freshest music and not resting on the laurels of his global hits. Although some of the music hasn't aged well, Prince does play it with plenty of feeling, and the accompanying performance is an extravaganza of color, dance, and dramatics.

The show is a visual feast as Prince and the band play out various subplots, providing a visually exciting ride that matches the thrilling music he is presenting. It doesn't always make sense, but it doesn't have to when it looks this good. "My Name Is Prince" sets the tone for the show with plenty of Prince braggadocio as he struts across the stage with his chain hat and cane in hand. The opening song is an onslaught of sound and visuals, Prince putting all his cards on the table from the start. With a choppy guitar underneath, Tony M. spits his lines while an Arab princess appears with a couple of other Arabs. It is completely unconnected and over the top yet sets the tone and scene, raising expectations for the series.

Music threatens to become the focus of the concert as "Sexy M.F." plays; however, this too falls into the background as the stage comes alive with dancers while Prince and Mayte engage in several dance sequences. This early part of the recording features plenty of entertainment and flash, and these opening two songs are typical of how the rest of the show will progress.

"Damn U" does bring a sense of decorum to the performance, and for the first time the show settles as Prince connects with the music. Although there are still dancers and other distractions, finally we see Prince singing alone. The best parts come when he is singing alone onstage, much to the delight of the crowd.

The songs from the ♀ album are presented well in the concert, and the following performance of "The Max" is a real treat. With thick and powerful music behind him, Prince produces his best dance moves so far. Over the following few minutes, there is plenty to look at as Prince sits at the piano, snapping Polaroids of the band, before finishing it all by playing out a seduction scene with Mayte.

The reporter sequence is as unnecessary here as it is on the ♀ album, but there is a payoff in a welcome rendition of "The Morning Papers." Prince starts at the piano before he climbs atop it for a guitar solo full of bluster and bravado. By Prince standards the solo is tame, mostly hot air, although the second solo ups things considerably and is closer to the fans expectations.

Prince keeps the guitar strapped on for a lively "Peach." The introduction provides a good insight for what will follow; the guitar is full and loud as it grunts and chugs through the introduction. "Peach" is young and fresh at this time, and as Prince releases the guitar frenzy, the quality of the show and the recording goes up several notches.

From left field, the reggae-infused "Blue Light" appears as Prince switches moods in an instant. It may seem a strange choice in this show, yet it manages to find its place with its light groove. If it was Prince's intention to capture a summer feel, then he succeeded.

"The Continental" is great to watch, but not so good to listen to. The guitar plays with a swagger, and the song begins strongly. It has an obvious intensity that the bootleg doesn't quite capture; we can see it onstage but it doesn't translate to what we are hearing. The stage presentation is the key element, and the final minutes as Prince performs some lewd dance moves while Mayte sings are particularly captivating.

The concert becomes dreary for the next few numbers as Prince and the dancers just go through the motions. "Everyone Get On Up"

24TH MARCH 1993 - RADIO CITY MUSIC HALL, NEW YORK

is lackluster, while the following reporter segment is annoying. "The Flow" starts well; but derails as Tony M. takes the microphone. The saving grace is the trumpet solo that makes up for some of silliness and theatrics performed onstage.

"Johnny" is much better; slowed down Tony M. has a heavy delivery, and the lyrics are amusingly tongue in cheek. The show breathes at this point as the slow groove brings things to a gentle pace.

Sitting alone at the piano Prince intimately plays the opening piano segment while staring into Mayte's eyes. One feels almost voyeuristic watching, but Prince's lyrics cover a range of songs that center on "And God Created Woman/3 Chains O' Gold." By the end of it, one is left wondering how we went from this tender moment to something so wildly unhinged. It is off-the-wall crazy and something that only Prince could do. And do it he does, playing at the piano while the band and the dancers carry the weight of the visuals. The scope and vision of the ♛ album is all here, and Prince gives a compelling performance that is equal parts genius and madness. He condenses the breadth of the album into this short part of the show, and over the course of the next ten minutes welds it all together in a manner that works. The theatrics match the music, and it all comes to a head as Prince plays his guitar while a row of performers point pistols at him. Like I say, bonkers and brilliant.

> **"THE THEATRICS MATCH THE MUSIC, AND IT ALL COMES TO A HEAD AS PRINCE PLAYS HIS GUITAR WHILE A ROW OF PERFORMERS POINT PISTOLS AT HIM"**

Any other rock concert with a woman dancing with a sword on her head would be classed as mad; in this context it seems perfectly normal and something of a letdown. The dance and the Arabic introduction lead perfectly into "7." The current hit of the moment, it gets a great reception from the crowd as Prince gives a lively performance. It is close to the recorded version, with Prince opting to play it safe and giving the crowd what they want in a satisfying performance.

The encores begin with a busy arrangement of "Let's Go Crazy." With so much going on, Prince and the singing are lost in the noise; there is simply too much happening to focus on the music. The thrills eventually come as he stands in the spotlight, guitar strapped on, but the music doesn't sound as iconic as the look.

"Kiss" is similar in that the sound lacks clarity, but the performance looks fantastic. It is undemanding, an enjoyable part of the show, especially as the groove slips into "Irresistible Bitch." This song is a good match for 1993 Prince, and it stands up well when compared to songs like "Sexy M.F." The song ends with a full, round funk sound that makes it timeless and lifts it above other parts of the show that have dated badly.

The funk doesn't last as Prince returns to his guitar for a driven version of "She's Always In My Hair." With so much happening onstage, it is a relief to see Prince returning to a heartfelt song, and he can be seen pouring his all into the guitar. It grounds the show after some previous flights of fancy, and the concert is reconnected to its musical heart, the chaos of the stage show finally finding a focus in a blazing version of an old favorite.

An interesting guitar interlude conjures up all sorts of thoughts of what might follow next, although I doubt many people would have guessed at "Insatiable" and Mayte on a pair of roller skates. Prince takes on the role of balladeer as he sings bathed in blue light. All the other distractions count for nothing when the music is this good, and things become even better as it turns into a doubleheader with "Scandalous" added on the back of it.

The concert and bootleg improves, and "Gett Off" offers another strong performance. With Prince and his guitar in fine form, the audience response becomes more vocal as he segues into "Gett Off (Housestyle)." There is a twist in the tail as the music slows to "Goldnigga," a nod to his other projects at the time, and the song ends with this slower groove.

"Purple Rain" swells and floats into view, and the audience are ready, welcoming it with plenty of singing before the song starts proper. It is given time to breathe and takes on a solemn air compared to the over-the-top show that has preceded it. Kneeling onstage to sing, or arched back playing guitar, Prince physically plays the song, and seeing the performance is key. The highlight of the song comes in the final coda as Prince plays with a lone guitar before finishing the song with one last refrain; a dazzling performance, it gains further power as a respected elder on the set list.

The final encore has a sense of inevitability as it opens with a frantic sounding "Partyman." A lot of the subtleties are lost as it is pounded out, and the following medley will carry on in a similar fashion. "1999" follows, its uplifting synth riff an air-raid siren warning all that the party is about to start. The rest of the song amounts to very little, the main attraction being the "party" chant. "Baby I'm A Star" suffers the same fate; the horn section is bright and sharp, but the song is subservient to the show. Prince is showboating at this stage of the recording, his dance moves carrying him back and forth across the stage as a sense of fun pervades. There are some musical moments that surface, for example the purpleaxxe jam he plays, but for the most part it is an all-singing-and-dancing routine. There is one further interesting development as Prince plays the part of a puppet master to the dancers during the final moments. Some people may read a subtext into this, Prince being the controlling person he is, but at the end of the day it is all part of what has been a colorful and adventurous evening.

This bootleg captures a moment in time when the show itself takes precedence over the music. There are several moments through the performance where Prince is channeling his creative energies into the stage show, whereas previously the music was always first and foremost. Not everything works, but given the variety of different ideas presented, it is to be expected that not everything will stick. Most admirable is the way Prince is fearless in his creativity and willingness to try anything. The results are interesting to say the least, and this makes for a fascinating show and a scintillating bootleg.

> **THIS BOOTLEG CAPTURES A MOMENT IN TIME WHEN THE SHOW ITSELF TAKES PRECEDENCE OVER THE MUSIC**

SET LIST

1. My Name Is Prince
2. Sexy M.F.
3. Love 2 The 9's
4. Damn U
5. The Max
6. The Morning Papers
7. Peach
8. Blue Light

9. The Continental
10. Everybody Get On Up
11. The Flow
12. Johnny
13. And God Created Woman
14. 3 Chains O' Gold
15. 7
16. Let's Go Crazy
17. Kiss
18. Irresistible Bitch
19. She's Always In My Hair
20. Insatiable
21. Scandalous
22. Gett Off
23. Gett Off (Housestyle)
24. Goldnigga
25. Purple Rain
26. Partyman
27. 1999
28. Baby I'm A Star

RELEASES

- Licence To funk - *Red Phantom*
- Live And Alive Volume 1 - *Imtat*
- Live USA... Volume 1 - *LSD Records*
- Live USA... Volume 2 - *LSD Records*
- Peaches - *Front Row*
- Acting Up In New York: 1st Night - *Fan Release*

1st SEPTEMBER 1993

CLUB REX, PARIS

The band of 1993 added more horns to Prince's music and further strengthened the sound of the ☥ album and the territory Prince was moving toward. With a fully-fledged horn section consisting of two saxophones, two trumpets, and a trombone, a classic funk sound that harked back to the 1960s and 1970s was added to his arsenal. Prince drew from this as he created new music that straddled the past and future. This bootleg from Club Rex in Paris features many songs and genres that will feature over the next couple of years as Prince forged into the ☥ era*. Serving as a strong indicator of the future, the performance is an important marker in Prince's evolution.

The horns are the most obvious sign of this new vein Prince is mining, and he leaves his earlier music behind from the start. "House In Order" is the epitome of this new music, the band swinging and funking with ease. These shows often open with a number that signals what will follow, and here is no different as Prince and the band give a brassy tone to the music. It also demonstrates the mood of Prince at the time; he is far more aggressive, and the shy Prince heard back in 1980 is long gone. However, there are some funny lines opening the show, along with a stage dive into the crowd during the first minute of the song. It can be heard on the bootleg with a loud cheer generated from the action.

The horns are present through every song, and the following "The Undertaker," although normally a guitar-driven slow burner, is brightened with the horns adding their shine. Their sound is infectious: even Levi's solo is cleaner and almost hornlike as he is caught up in the moment. Prince has a lot of faith and trust in this band; he sinks to the background as the relentless groove is carried by various other members, especially the keyboards.

---

*Although Prince changed his name to ☥ on 7th June 1993, for the purposes of this book he'll continue to be referred to as Prince.

Prince's humor has always been one of his greatest assets and nowhere more so than "Black M.F. In The House." With its hilarious lyrics, Prince sends up racists everywhere. He exaggerates the lyrics further, singing them unaccompanied before the crowd joins for the chorus just as the band jumps onboard. It still sounds good after twenty years, the music undeniably smooth and funky while the lyrics bring a smile to the face. There are only 400 people in the room, and they sing and dance through the song, ending in another rousing cheer.

Prince is at his socially conscious best, another political statement coming in the form of "Race." Prince didn't just pay lip service to these causes; he made sure they were in his songs and their meaning enhanced by the music. The song is bolder than the album version, with Prince making sure the lyrical message is heard and understood.

The show continues to evolve in surprising ways with "Blue Light" appearing out of the darkness. Suddenly the funk of earlier has dissipated and been replaced with a head-bobbing groove and Michael B's heavy drumming. "Blue Light" and the following "Delirious" both spotlight his input. "Delirious" has plenty of his swing and ends with a lengthy drum solo as the mood lightens. This performance displays the strength of Michael B. and the horns - they are key to understanding the direction Prince is moving toward.

> **THIS PERFORMANCE DISPLAYS THE STRENGTH OF MICHAEL B. AND THE HORNS - THEY ARE KEY TO UNDERSTANDING THE DIRECTION PRINCE IS MOVING TOWARD**

Compared to the opening thirty minutes of the show, "The Ride" is almost pedestrian. Normally the cornerstone of a show, here it is only six minutes long and never reaches the guitar-saturated climax that it regularly delivers. However, the segue into "Bambi" injects some fury into the performance. Prince pulls inspiration from another band and another era as he rips through one of his finest guitar-laden songs, making the crowd and the guitar squeal with delight. The recording may not be at its best at this point, but the onstage performance is.

The display of guitar prowess continues with a headlong rush through "Jailhouse Rock" before switching to a sweaty, crowd-pleasing, "Poorgoo." It flows effortlessly through the opening lines before rising steadily as Prince ups the intensity with some punchy guitar playing that is the very heart of the song itself. Without being fast and furious,

Prince demonstrates the power that can be extracted from his guitar as he solos for several minutes, a quiet storm that rewards repeated listens.

The following "Come" brings some levity to the recording after the heaviness of the guitar, but even that finishes in a flurry before the opening roar of "Endorphinmachine" sees the show reach new heights in excitement and thrilling guitar work. All this energy and excitement is encapsulated in the moment when Prince asks the audience to scream, and they respond with a hearty cheer. This energy is maintained well into "Peach"; both the crowd and Prince sound like they are having the time of their lives.

"Pope" takes on a completely new skin at this particular concert as Prince strips all the hip-hop out of it, leaving it as a laid-back funk jam. With the rhythm guitar and horns adding vibrancy to the song, it is far removed from the recorded version. The horn solo makes the greatest impression and again only highlights how important the horn section was at this time.

The band romps through "America," again impacted by the furious horn section. It is the jump-off point for a frenetic jam as they play with an intense pace for the next ten minutes. With "Gett Off" and "It's Gonna Be A Beautiful Night" making cameo appearances, the horns stay at the center of attention until the very end.

The last song of the bootleg is "Johnny," and this time it is the audience that steals the moment. "Johnny" runs for ten minutes with the last four minutes given over to the audience entirely. They chant out the NPG chant long after the music has finished. Bootlegs are normally all about the music; to hear the audience chant and sing is something unusual and made all the better by the fact that it adds to the performance. As they chant and clap the bootleg comes alive, and it is easy to imagine what is happening in the room.

Club Rex is essential not just for the show itself, but also for what it represents. It captures Prince at a time of change as he turns his back on all he has created in the 1980s and reinvents himself as a new artist. This bootleg is a fine record of that moment, with Prince finding strength in the band and the audience as they support him through this change. The two key elements heard on the recording are the dominant horns (tempered by the guitar of Prince) and the powerhouse drumming of Michael B. Both propel Prince forward, and with the audience clearly loving his new output, he is ready to take up the next challenge of his career - the ⚥ era.

SET LIST

1. House In Order
2. The Undertaker
3. Black M.F. In The House
4. Race
5. Blue Light
6. Delirious
7. The Ride
8. Bambi
9. Jailhouse Rock
10. Poorgoo
11. Come
12. Endorphinmachine
13. Peach
14. Pope
15. America
16. Johnny

RELEASES

- A Time 2 Dream - *After Dark*
- America - *Fan Release*
- Black MF - *Pluto*
- Intermission - *Clinton*
- Live At The Rex - *Live Storm*
- Live At The Rex - *Red Phantom*
- Paris Aftershow 1993 - *Fan Release*
- The Rex Club - *Universal*

3RD SEPTEMBER, 1993
FLUGPLATZ LÜNEBURG, LÜNEBURG

With the ☥ era looming on the horizon, this bootleg covers one of the last shows of the *Act II* tour and one of the last shows before Prince disappeared from the live circuit for a year. The battle with Warners had already started and was about to become far more bitter and time-consuming, leaving this concert as one of the last big shows to be played before his reemergence with the *Gold Experience* album in 1995. This bootleg is well-known, a classic soundboard recording released by several well-known labels, and is taken from the Rock Over Germany festival date in early September. It is the only soundboard recording of the tour and as such is a fantastic document of that time.

The rock 'n' roll introduction by the announcer is clichéd, but there is no denying it energizes and excites the audience. From the first moments the band is wonderfully in sync; coming near the end of the tour we would expect nothing less, and they create a powerful rhythm for "My Name Is Prince." The music may be solid, but Prince himself is relaxed and his rapping flows naturally. It serves him well as he raps in a deeper, more authoritative voice and resists the temptation to yell.

Michael B. is an early hero of the recording; he hammers his way through the opening number before switching to a lighter style for "Sexy M.F." With a silky guitar line, "Sexy M.F." has a timeless quality - something that is further enhanced by the horns. The band all make an early impression, Tommy Barbarella with an organic perforamnce that brushes against the shiny, smooth funk and Levi with a solo. The horns play the final notes of the song, and they make a lasting impression with their contribution to the show.

There is an early surprise with the inclusion of "The Beautiful Ones." It is updated with the addition of the horns while the keyboard swells pull the song back to its roots. The song does not paint a perfect picture as the lyrics imply, the "paint a perfect picture" lines are too contrived and overworked, but Prince makes amends by closing the song with some full-blooded screams as the band contribute a final flourish.

The organ intro of "Let's Go Crazy" follows, full and rich from the start. The recording is excellent but does suffer with the overall sound being a little off - Prince and the pounding beat can be heard but the other instruments are buried in the mix. Balance is restored with Prince's guitar solo, which is front and center as it turns from a howl to the funky rhythm of "Kiss."

The trademark funk guitar may start "Kiss," but it is backed with heavy bass and a gang of horns. The delicacy of the original is replaced by the insistent push of the brass section, and Prince sings in a stronger voice to match them. This is the strongest-sounding song in the show early on and is consistently powerful until the very end.

"Irresistible Bitch" is shortchanged; it is an electric performance that is all too short. The following "She's Always In My Hair" is every bit as good for the full performance it receives. With a crisp and clean guitar, it is a standout, and for all the dancing and costume changes, it is this classic rock moment that glues the show together. The initial guitar becomes swept up in the moment and washed into the longer jam that plays out the rest of the song. Prince gives a light, playful, sometimes heavy but always fun-sounding solo. As it gathers pace, Prince plays faster and faster in a masterful display of musicianship.

> **PRINCE GIVES A LIGHT, PLAYFUL, SOMETIMES HEAVY BUT ALWAYS FUN-SOUNDING SOLO**

There is very little pop in the concert up to this point, but that changes as the band strikes up "Raspberry Beret." A feel-good song if ever there was one, this lives up to its reputation. It sounds as if it is straight out of 1985 in its freshness and is only disappointing in that Prince plays barely a single verse and chorus.

Prince stays in his '80s catalogue with a raw-sounding performance of "The Cross." In the live setting it has an almost garage-band element to it; that is until Prince begins to solo and unleashes a maelstrom of guitar noise upon the audience. It floods across the recording, and even as he sings in a half scream later, he can't match this moment for pure rock.

Surprisingly, he does manage to top this in the next couple of tracks. First, "Sign O' The Times" gains some guitar work that fleshes out the bare bones of the song. The music is beefed up with this sound, and Michael B. also makes himself heard as he provides some drumrolls as a backdrop to Prince's guitar work.

He then follows this with "Purple Rain" and a heavenly guitar line as an introduction. The guitar is the weapon of choice as Prince switches from this delicate moment to heavier crunch that will carry the rest of the song. He opens the door on his main solo with a "live for love" call before laying it all bare with an impassioned guitar break. As the final notes fade, there is the feeling of satisfaction and that Prince has delivered a worthy rendition.

With the sound of thunder, Prince intones the opening lines of "Thunder," before playing a cool rendition of "Nothing Compares 2 U." As an instrumental it has new life and serves as a change of pace in a show that has so far been nonstop.

The following "And God Created Woman" is good, not just the band performance but also on the recording. Again, it is a shortened instrumental that gives a taste of Prince's wider platter of songs and styles. After the guitar work of the previous few songs, the horn section make a welcome return and gives it some extra shine before a snippet of "Diamonds And Pearls" ends this diversion.

The recording resumes with Prince at the piano for a medley, beginning with longtime favorite "Venus De Milo." As part of a longer medley, it is little more than an introduction of what's to come. "I Love U In Me" has Prince singing questionable lyrics, but the music is undeniably good, his piano playing smooth as it leads into "Strollin" with barely a breath. The full band returns for "Strollin," and it is enhanced by the sunshine feel of the horn section. The drums are a little too much, but the song glides by easily.

"Scandalous" ends the run of shorter songs as it sees the return of full arrangements and performances. It is not as smooth as expected; the horns are the dominant factor as both they and Prince compete to be the center of attention. It should belong to Prince, but the horns steal the moment from him and truly dominate the proceedings.

Prince opens the next song with a couple of lines from "Girls And Boys" before he introduces the old cliché "I'm gonna stay over here until you make up your mind." It is old and corny, but it still raises a cheer from the crowd. When the song returns, it is with a slower, heavier, yet still funky sound. There is a surge of energy as the crowd gets to sing along, and Prince himself can be heard with plenty of passion in his voice during the performance.

There is a confusing start to the next part of the show as the introduction music of "Around The World In A Day" is heard, but it soon gives way to Michael B. and his drumming. This too is a red herring as a fresh "7" is played. The opening minutes retain the Arabic feel and seem to be from another song until Prince's vocals confirm that it is indeed "7." There is a twist in the show as yet again Prince swings this way and that in his repertoire.

The encore begins with Prince yelling "what's up y'all" before presenting Mayte who does a much better job, addressing the crowd in German. What follows is a helter-skelter rendition of "1999" with some monster drumming coming fast and beastlike through the speakers. The band flies through it; Prince sings the first verse and chorus before the party continues with the crowd singing "party." It is a disservice to a classic song, but at the same time it is a party moment.

That party feeling is enhanced as the band rips through "Baby I'm A Star." With vibrant horns this keeps the momentum and party atmosphere going as the music careens into a surprising "America." The band is loose and plays a wild "America" with plenty of swing to it. This party-time medley continues with "D.M.S.R." Like the previous songs it doesn't stay long, but it does keep things moving. "Gett Off" swiftly follows, although it is far removed from the original. With a groovy keyboard playing and horns stuffed everywhere, it keeps things jumping along. It retains the lyrics, but without the screams, classic beat, and guitar riff, it is just a pale imitation of itself. The

> **THE SONGS FLASH BY FOR THIS SECTION OF THE SHOW, TOO FAST TO BE PROPERLY ENJOYED, ALTHOUGH PRINCE'S HUMOR DOES BRING A SMILE TO THE FACE**

songs flash by for this section of the show, too fast to be properly enjoyed, although Prince's humor does bring a smile to the face. He tells the crowd he can't sing anymore and maybe he should lip-sync. He quickly banishes that idea with a "fuck that shit!"

"Pope" is slowed down, highlighting Prince's rapping, which is disappointingly uneven. That doesn't diminish the enjoyment of the song however; there is plenty to appreciate in the performance.

After a quickfire couple of verses, the band takes control with some instrumental work; the guitar and piano are present with the horns adding their tone before a smooth transition to "It's Gonna Be A Beautiful Night." This is the final rush as Prince finishes with a simple "what's my name? - confusion!"

The heavy crunch of guitar brings the audience back to life after a minute's pause. Prince speaks the opening lines of "Peach" before the inevitable guitar onslaught begins. Prince tries to match the guitar with some ragged vocals, but the best moments are when he's not singing at all and the guitar is doing all the talking for him. There is some call and response, but that's not what this song is about, and the final guitar solos are where all the real excitement and danger are.

It is surprising that there aren't more bootlegs of this recording in circulation. Only four labels have released it, and considering it is one of the best recordings of the '90s, that is unusual. The bootleg is of the highest standing, and the performance itself is nothing short of spectacular. Some might grumble that it is a greatest-hits show, and while I can understand where they are coming from, there is nothing wrong with a greatest-hits show - after all it is what the majority of people pay their money to see. There is much to enjoy about this bootleg, and it is an essential part of Prince and his early '90s output.

SET LIST

1. My Name Is Prince
2. Sexy M.F.
3. The Beautiful Ones
4. Let's Go Crazy
5. Kiss
6. Irresistible Bitch
7. She's Always In My Hair
8. Raspberry Beret
9. The Cross
10. Sign O' The Times
11. Purple Rain

12. Thunder
13. When Doves Cry
14. Nothing Compares 2 U
15. And God Created Woman
16. Diamonds And Pearls
17. Venus De Milo
18. I Love U In Me
19. Strollin'
20. Scandalous
21. Girls And Boys
22. 7
23. 1999
24. Baby I'm A Star
25. America
26. D.M.S.R.
27. Gett Off
28. Pope
29. It's Gonna Be A Beautiful Night
30. Peach

RELEASES

- Lueneburg '93 - *Premium*
- Lueneburg '93 - *Quickline*
- Rock Over Germany - *Purple Gold Archives*
- Rock Over Germany - *Sabotage*

6TH MAY 1994
LE BATACLAN, PARIS

Prince played at Le Bataclan in Paris three times and each time saw a special show and worthy bootleg to suit. The bootleg of the May 1994 show is the first of this trilogy, and although an audience recording, it has a warmth to it that gives it an appealing, natural quality. The audience is audible, in this case adding to the recording rather than detracting from it. The year 1994 saw Prince put his back catalogue to one side, instead choosing to plough on in his new direction as ⚥. As such, the shows from these years feature all new material as Prince reinvented himself as an entirely new artist. The set list from Le Bataclan features many of the usual suspects of the time ("Days Of Wild," "The Ride," "Peach") as well as a debut of another new song - "Gold." With "Gold" in the set list Prince is laying the groundwork for his next two projects, *The Gold Experience* and *Come*, and the bulk of the show highlights the songs he will playing for the next couple of years.

Some fine lead guitar is the first thing on the bootleg as Prince can be heard preparing his guitar setup for the first song. The opening keyboard of "Gold" transports the bootleg back to this era instantly; the song is indeed golden in this setting with a celebratory feel coming through the recording. The crowd rejoices in singing the chorus and the rest of the song, and it is apparent that this song belongs just as much to the audience as it does to Prince.

"The Jam" has featured in Prince's set list's since the mid-'90s, making its first appearance in early 1994. It is an obvious favorite of Prince's, and he often uses it early in the set to warm up the band. The recording here captures what is typically par for the course. Morris Hayes and Tommy Barbarella both add their pieces, though it is Morris Hayes who does the heavy lifting, while Prince provides the sharp rhythm guitar that drives through the heart of the song.

"I Believe In You" moves the performance quickly onward and has Prince singing in a tone that is natural. Without vocal gymnastics he sings with plenty of character, and that is the lasting impression left. Despite some guitar moments, the song rests on the vocal performance of Prince.

There comes a great bootleg moment next with a rendition of "Interactive." Although it lacks the firepower of later performances, it still has a brightness and is well received by the appreciative crowd. It gives the recording an extra sense of sparkle with its appearance.

"Days Of Wild" is muted, mostly due to the quality of the recording. The bass comes through well, as does Prince's vocals, but it is the rest of the band that is washed out and the song is weaker for it. Although the bootleg doesn't live up to the moment, the performance captures what Prince was all about at that time. This is a new, wilder Prince bringing a heavier, darker funk to the audience. The pop star of the 1980s is a distant memory as Prince and the NPG crunch and roll "Days Of Wild" over the audience.

> **THIS IS A NEW, WILDER PRINCE BRINGING A HEAVIER, DARKER FUNK TO THE AUDIENCE**

After the heaviness of "Days Of Wild," "Now" adds a lot of fun to the show. Prince's vocals are light as he spits his lines, and although they may not sound great on record, in the live setting it has a party vibe. Like many of these shows, it is a chance for the band to move into a jam and, as the organ slows it down, they weave "Babies Makin' Babies" in and out of the groove. It is a captivating few minutes, and the band is spellbinding.

There is plenty of guitar noodling to keep the guitar aficionados happy before Prince finally settles on the steady beat of "The Ride." Normally a solid blues number, this performance sees it played with lightness of touch. With Prince singing playfully and the audience adding an upbeat clap, the song is unshackled and is uplifting in the recording. Prince is a long time in coming to his guitar before succumbing with solos that more than make up for the wait.

There is more guitar from Prince as things take a break at the beginning of "Acknowledge Me." His spoken introduction has a delicious sound that is both inviting and scary at the same time. This is heightened as the band sudden leap into the song, giving it a powerful, muscular drive. There is plenty happening in the last few minutes as the bass, drums, and audience clap, pulling it through to the conclusion of the song. As with some of the other songs, there is plenty of audience interaction that captures the beauty of a live recording.

There is silence as Prince solemnly delivers up a spoken introduction before the song opens up to "Dark." The title maybe "Dark," but, the song is anything but and it is a ray of pop sunshine to an already joyful show. Prince is in fine voice and he gets better, injecting more passion and fire as he goes before pulling back into a deep, laid-back voice. The song is pitched just right and is perfect in restoring balance to the concert.

The instrumental that follows is an up-tempo jam that flies along at a clip. Morris Hayes and his organ excel at this type of thing, and his playing holds it together as the crowd claps along enthusiastically. Within this quick jam, Sonny T. gets his moment to shine with a solo that makes you wonder why he hasn't had more chances like this on the recording.

The following performance of "Solo" silences the audience as Prince plays the live debut of the song. It maybe the debut, but Prince gives the song a sense of importance that carries across to the audience.

"Race" has the crowd singing loudly as Prince leads the band in a tight performance. Morris Hayes is the standout. He is the lynchpin of this band; his keyboard playing giving the shows a richness of sound while his ability to jam captures the spirit of the band. Morris has the ability to add a seriousness and sincerity to whatever is being played while being versatile enough to fly when required.

> **MORRIS HAS THE ABILITY TO ADD A SERIOUSNESS AND SINCERITY TO WHATEVER IS BEING PLAYED WHILE BEING VERSATILE ENOUGH TO FLY WHEN REQUIRED**

Praise has routinely been given to many of Prince's band members over the years, but Morris Hayes remains a somewhat unsung hero despite having been vital in conveying Prince's vision through the '90s.

A couple of minutes of the "oh way oh" chant bring the band back for a noisy and wild "Peach." As always it is dedicated to Mayte, but the real star is Prince's guitar as he makes it exhilarating and exciting every step of the way. The song ignites the audience, who can be heard cheering on Michael B. who dutifully finishes the show with a cameo of a drum solo.

This show is for me what live music is all about. The recording isn't great, but that's irrelevant when the show is as good as this. Joyful and celebratory are often words associated with Prince concerts, and they have never been more appropriate than in this case. Nothing can beat that joyful feeling as the band soars and everything drops away leaving the audience swimming in the music. That sense of celebration and togetherness seeps out of the recording at every turn; there are not many live recordings that recreate the feeling of a show like this one. Listen to this bootleg and revel in that feeling that only the magic of a live show can give you.

SET LIST

1. Gold
2. The Jam
3. I Believe In You
4. Interactive
5. Days Of Wild
6. Now
7. The Ride
8. Acknowledge Me
9. Dark
10. Instrumental
11. Solo
12. Race
13. Peach

RELEASES

- Dark - *Way Out Records*
- Le Bataclan '94 - *4DaFunk*

26TH AND 27TH MARCH 1995
PARADISO, AMSTERDAM

The Gold era is one of the more interesting periods of Prince's career as he shed his '80s skin and reinvented himself as a funkateer worthy of George Clinton's mantle. With an outpouring of material across a variety of projects, he buried his old "Prince" under a pile of new releases and music. The youthful pop he once produced was subverted by darker, more mature music that demanded the audience listen close. *The Gold Experience* tour and aftershows are well represented in the bootleg market, and there are an array of different quality recordings and shows available, ranging from soundboard recordings to scratchy audience recordings. The release of the Paradiso aftershows sees the two shows from Paradiso paired together in a single package, and although at first appearance it isn't as polished as some other bootlegs circulating, the audience recording touches on brilliant as it captures two of his best shows of the period. As a bootleg it is one of the best and is essential listening for any fan.

The first concert from the very early morning of the 26th sets the high standards that will follow, and as far as show openings go, it doesn't get much better than the "go Michael, go Michael" chant. The quality of the recording is apparent from the start as it captures the party atmosphere that hangs in the air. The song "Funky" kicks things off as the crowd cheers Michael through the song. The band are hot and the bootleg is equally sharp from the start.

"18 And Over" sees Prince dwelling on the chorus. The somewhat questionable lyrics strike the right chord with the audience, and they take delight in singing them loudly. The song maintains a late-night vibe and ends on a crowd-pleasing high as they happily sing the chorus again under Prince's guidance.

There is a world of difference between the "Now" heard at this show and the "Now" heard on record. With a deeper tone and chaotic feel, it is more of a jam, the main feature being the hand clapping and a passionate howl from Prince. It carries the sound of a band having a lot of fun onstage and Michael B. personifies this feel with his drumming bringing an energetic roll to the show.

"I Believe In You" was a staple of the set list at the time, and this performance of it is notable for the squelchy bass that underpins the song. The guitar break by Prince is rather pedestrian by his standards, and even as it shudders and shakes it never gains the spark of energy it needs. This is the second-shortest song of the recording, but it is surrounded by worthy jams.

Before these jams though, there comes a hi-tempo "Proud Mary," drenched in guitar runs from Prince. It is kept short, and the rush comes as the song finishes with a final burst from Prince. It is all very sharp and not a note is wasted in an efficient performance that is tidy in delivery.

The longer jams begin with a "The Ride" and a smoky start from Prince. He ratchets it up as he plays expressively and passionately, although steadily in control. A great late-night burner, this is an extended performance that delivers.

Glam Slam Boogie comes next, conjuring up the word *groove* as the guitar takes a backseat while the crowd and the keyboard carry the song. It is not quite the long jam it promises to be, although the song is freewheeling. It has an uplifting way, and Mayte's tambourine solo is definitely an interesting moment that adds life to the bootleg.

"Days Of Wild" has a different feel, not so aggressive, and with its laid-back overtones it fits in nicely. The recording captures the live spirit of the show and the togetherness of performer and crowd, especially as the audience can be heard singing with plenty of vim and vigor. This is the essence of the recording - Prince and the audience together in a sense of comradery, the music binding them together.

Things move from one wild-titled song to another as Prince kicks off "Get Wild." This is a great performance with the vocals catchy and infectious and carrying plenty of bounce. Mayte's input is equally fun on the recording (although the moment she jumps into the audience can't be heard), and one can hear how happy she and Prince are onstage together. The crowd is again involved as Prince introduces them to the "play the motherfunkin bass" chant that captures the spirit of the night. It becomes a jam that threatens to go forever - guitars come and go, as does singing and chanting, the occasional chorus, and some interesting keyboards. The show finishes the only way possible with a final roll from Michael B. providing symmetry with the opening.

During the show Prince speaks to the audience: he can be heard on the recording at one point saying, "If I come back tomorrow will you be there?" True to his word he did return for the second night, which completes the bootleg. As a companion set it is great to have the two shows back to back, hearing them as they were intended to be heard.

The second night (morning) picks up right where the first show left off. The crowd participation is again vital; right from the start they can be heard singing the "ow we ow" chant. It ends soon enough as the gentle chords of "People Get Ready" begin the show in a more traditional manner. It is a smooth, seductive performance as the soft "owww owwww" of Prince draws the music in around him. With a touch of organ underneath and an audience-led handclap for accompaniment it becomes a delicate moment. Using only the simple chords of the guitar, Prince begins to sing the opening lines before it all comes to a sudden noisy stop as the entire band jumps in and everything is turned to maximum.

> **USING ONLY THE SIMPLE CHORDS OF THE GUITAR, PRINCE BEGINS TO SING THE OPENING LINES BEFORE IT ALL COMES TO A SUDDEN NOISY STOP AS THE ENTIRE BAND JUMPS IN AND EVERYTHING IS TURNED TO MAXIMUM**

The band is right in from the start as they monster "The Jam." "The Jam" is infused with something extra on this recording, the magical x-factor that everyone attends concerts for. With a squelching bass and crisp guitar keeping the music focused, Prince has the audience chanting "Prince is dead," setting the agenda for the rest of the show. He is a man comfortable with himself and his newfound lease on life. A large part of this could be put down to Mayte, who receives cheers and applause as she is introduced; she brings a stability and focus to his life. There is both a party and family feeling to this recording as Michael B. and Sonny T. play solos, before the band meld together tightly, demonstrating again their worthiness to the claim of one of the all-time greatest bands.

"Get Wild" follows close behind with a chunky piano prominent at the start. The recording lets things down here - Prince's voice is distant. The song follows the template set down on the previous night, with Prince leading the audience in "play that motherfuckin bass," before each member takes a turn to play a break. Prince encourages the audience with "we just come from London; are you as wild as them?" before a humorous moment when a chant of "go Mayte, go Mayte" has Prince replying with "oh, ya'll just gonna run the show huh? I ain't got nothing to do?" This is the strength of both these shows; Prince is at total ease with the audience and they are equally enthusiastic for him to do whatever he pleases.

Prince's choice to cover "Jailhouse Rock" is an interesting one. After Elvis was dismissed by Public Enemy a few years earlier with "Elvis was a hero to most, but he didn't mean shit to me," Prince's cover seems oddly out of step with the mood of the times. Maybe he was staking a claim for the music and song himself. His cover is decent, giving it a rasp as the rockabilly edge harks back to some of his own early '80s material.

A flurry of guitar sees the introduction of "Zannalee." It is played with a swing, even as the guitars continue with their buzz-saw attack. The vocals are secondary to the music, the guitar featuring heavily as Prince bends it to his will. It is merely a taster as the band warms to their work for the following "The Undertaker."

This band is all about "The Undertaker." The performance on this bootleg points to the sound Prince and the NPG were trying to achieve at the time, with the band playing with a closeness that gives them the power of one, a strength deriving from their cohesiveness. Prince begins with a speech about gun control during the opening groove that might lumber a lesser song but "The Undertaker" has its own powerful force and rises above any morality speech. It is heavy, but Prince's guitar work lightens it with bright notes lighting up the sky in flashes of brilliance. The music opens out to the guitar break, and this is when the song becomes the heavy hitter that it is, the guitar laying down a river of fire that is the essence of the performance.

> **THE PERFORMANCE ON THIS BOOTLEG POINTS TO THE SOUND PRINCE AND THE NPG WERE TRYING TO ACHIEVE AT THE TIME, WITH THE BAND PLAYING WITH A CLOSENESS THAT GIVES THEM THE POWER OF ONE, A STRENGTH DERIVING FROM THEIR COHESIVENESS**

The funk goes up several notches next as the bootleg continues with "Funky Design." This is one of Prince's heavy funk periods, and the song oozes funk from every pore. To temper this there is a sizzling guitar break that never quite boils over but constantly threatens to. There is plenty of noise and fury going on, but the recording doesn't quite capture all of it.

The next song starts off innocuously enough with the drumbeat and the crowd clapping along while chanting "Go Mayte," before Prince gets on the microphone with a "ooooowww pussy control." It is more laid-back than on record, and the introduction is drawn out with some nice organ and a rubbery bass. The fun levels increase through the song as the crowd comes aboard with more clapping and singing, making it something that everyone can enjoy.

The kick drum comes to the front again as Prince dives into a brief instrumental, led by the chant of "can't get enough; of that funky stuff." The action is once again up-tempo, and like every other song there is a lot of audience participation, this time chanting "can't get enough of that funky stuff" as the band stops.

"Johnny" sees the band play slow with a swing to their sound. Once again there is no keeping the audience out of this one, and there is a chant at the beginning of "N...P...G in the mother-fucking house." Prince's mood is obvious - with a cheeky swagger he relishes his lines, adding to the pervading sense of a fun. There is a lot of personality throughout this show, and it gives a good sense of what it would have been like to be there. Prince's guitar playing is soulful and has just as much character as his singing, adding emotion and warmth.

There is a pause in the music next as Prince takes his time to address the audience. He reminds them the new album Exodus is coming out next week, along with his line that Prince is dead and the only ones who think he is alive is the record company. This leads to a very funny moment as the crowd breaks into a loud chant of "fuck Warner Bros." It is made even funnier by the fact that they chant "Warner Bros," rather than "Warner Brothers." Prince seems to take great delight in it and asks the crowd if he could bring the President of Warner Brothers next time so they can do it again for him.

"Endorphinmachine" begins with a rush, and there is no denying the energy of the guitar playing as Prince launches into it. The band plays behind with plenty of power, and for the first time in the recording the quality of sound is forgotten as the music takes over. An excellent performance of a keystone song of that period, this is one of the most important moments at the show.

There is plenty of guitar and noodling before the Prince says, "I'm hungry, is there any peaches in the house?" The recording has plenty of anticipation hanging in the air before the roar of "Peach" finally begins and delivers all as promised. The song only has one purpose and that is to maximize the guitar storm that Prince conjures up. The opening verse is quickly dealt with, no more than a diversion, before the guitar takes over with its furious sound. It is not the funkiest of songs, but it does close the show in a spectacular way, Prince and the band storming the barricades in a final all-out attack.

Considering these are audience recordings, the subsequent bootlegs have a fantastic sound to them. Credit must be given to the source material, and these two shows rank among the best of 1995. This bootleg carries a sense of warmth and community uncommon with contemporary gigs. As a double set there is plenty to take in, but this is a recording that stands up to repeated listens. Prince may have been at war with Warner Brothers, but the show is lighthearted and fun, making it this one of the most enjoyable bootlegs out there.

> **THIS BOOTLEG CARRIES A SENSE OF WARMTH AND COMMUNITY UNCOMMON WITH CONTEMPORARY GIGS**

SET LIST

1st Show - 26th March

1. Funky
2. 18 & Over
3. Now
4. I Believe In You
5. Proud Mary
6. The Ride
7. Glam Slam Boogie
8. Days Of Wild
9. Get Wild
10. Funky Stuff

26TH AND 27TH MARCH 1995 - PARADISO, AMSTERDAM

2nd Show - 27th March
1. People Get Ready
2. The Jam
3. Get Wild
4. Jailhouse Rock
5. Zannalee
6. The Undertaker
7. Funky Design
8. P. Control
9. Funky Stuff
10. Johnny
11. Endorphinmachine
12. Peach

RELEASES

- Paradiso - *Superhero Records*
- This Is What We Do 2 Have Fun - *Midnight Beat*

24TH DECEMBER 1998
TIVOLI, UTRECHT

Although there are a lot of good aftershows from the mid-'90s in circulation (some of which in pristine condition), they all follow a template, especially as the decade progresses. They are exercises in great music and musicianship, but the set lists recur, and despite the sheer funkiness of the performances, they are predictable. What brightens up these shows and the accompanying bootlegs are the guest appearances that add a touch of unpredictability and a different version of already well-known songs. Not all guest appearances have that spark of magic - more than a couple don't provide the guests with the chance to show off their talents, and the listener could be forgiven for missing them or mistaking their contribution for those of the regular band. The bootleg covering this show from late 1998 is different. Lenny Kravitz makes a guest appearance and leaves a strong mark. He drums for the first few songs before later joining Prince for an unmissable performance of "Are You Gonna Go My Way?" The show also features Larry Graham and a host of familiar covers (and some less familiar ones too), which all adds up to another classic bootleg that should take its place in any collection.

The opening "Cissy Strut" does in fact strut, and it is classic start to the show as they build the groove from the ground up. It is a steady build, made all the better with Candy Dulfer on saxophone. The song follows the usual Prince structure for an opening number, with the swirling organ of Morris Hayes and some of Prince's guitar playing in a high whine. The concert has yet to ignite, and this is the sound of the band warming up... the real fireworks are yet to come.

The mood takes a turn toward the funk as the band begin to play "Superstition." However, Prince calls "wait a minute, we didn't write that," and the song collapses upon itself.

"Chameleon" is a cover of a Herbie Hancock song and is led by the horns and an attention-grabbing bass line. With a saxophone and punchy keys leading the way, the music is rounded out by Morris Hayes and his organ. The recording promises more than it gives, an enthusiastic audience chant appears "go Lenny, go Lenny" but not a lot more is heard on the recording at this early stage.

Lenny is replaced on the drums by Kirk Johnson for the following "Asswoop." "Asswoop" is a staple of this era, and these aftershows often feature it as a jam. Like so many of these songs, everyone takes a turn to solo and the recording has comes alive. Without ever becoming spectacular, it does provide plenty of entertainment and offers a well-rounded experience. The keyboards are outstanding, but it is Candy Dulfer and Hans Dulfer who steal the show with an expressive break that brings a kaleidoscope of color to the song.

Larry Graham is well and truly in the fold by the time this show was recorded, so it is not unexpected to hear Prince say, "Y'all want some Larry Graham?" What is unexpected though is the pulsating groove of "The Undertaker." With Larry on the bass, it carries a forceful yet groovy rhythm that sustains the momentum. The song is plenty of fun, and Prince uses it as a platform to step into other songs. As he sings "Joy And Pain," the audience join him effortlessly before they follow him into "I Know You Got Soul." These arrangements draw from soulful roots, and with Larry Graham, Cynthia Robinson, and Jerry Martini onstage, they have plenty of firepower to play with. Larry Graham delivers some of the bass he is renowned for as he sings the aptly named "Groove On," and the grooves keep on coming.

Prince stops the band on a dime and they pick up straight into "Hair." Larry plays fast and funky, and with a shout of "turn his mic up!" from Prince, he begins to sing "Hair." It is played with conviction and enthusiasm from Prince, and this gives it a vitality that jumps out on an average recording. It sometimes sounds stale, but at this show it goes from good to great.

The concert doesn't let up as Al Green's "Love And Happiness" follows, keeping with the nature of the last two songs. Larry is still the main draw; with plenty of bounce in the room, he sings and provides the underlying rhythm. It is timeless and could have appeared at any aftershow in Prince's career and slotted in easily. With the horns and keyboards playing off each other, it highlights the strengths of the band and the scene is set for what comes next.

The following song is both expected and yet completely unexpected. There was never any doubt that with Lenny Kravitz appearing they would play one his songs, and it would be reasonable to assume that it would be "Are You Gonna Go My Way?" or another one of his rock guitar numbers. The unexpected comes as Prince plays the main riff of "Are You Gonna Go My Way?" not on the guitar, but on his piano. This is the attraction of aftershows and bootlegs in general; hearing familiar songs spun in different directions. With the main riff banged out on the piano, the song becomes magical as it unfolds. The band bring a swing to the song as the guitar solo is replaced with a saxophone solo by Candy Dulfer that makes any thought of the guitar irrelevant. As a rock moment it has an otherworldly quality and makes the bootleg essential.

> "THE BAND BRING A SWING TO THE SONG AS THE GUITAR SOLO IS REPLACED WITH A SAXOPHONE SOLO BY CANDY DULFER THAT MAKES ANY THOUGHT OF THE GUITAR IRRELEVANT"

Larry picks up where he left off as the anticipation builds for "The Jam," played as a series of solos orchestrated by Prince. Mike Scott and Larry Graham are the stars before the song ends with Morris Hayes playing an organ solo that would be better described as a solo organ. Morris Hayes excels at this sort of thing, and there is no better example of what he does than this.

"Mad" receives a rousing cheer from the crowd. The star of this is the guitar - it is a constant in the background riffing. The song is busy but the balance is brought out as Prince sings in a relaxed manner bringing a lighter tone to the song than the original version.

A segue into an instrumental of "I Want To Take You Higher" is played in a laid-back summery manner and is also incredibly short. With a quick tempo change, the bass builds into a murderous rendition of "Days Of Wild." With its ominous bass line rumbling, it builds momentum and menace as the crowd chant along. The band adds lighter touches - a guitar here, a saxophone there - but for the most part it steams ahead in its own way. It does threaten to build into something momentous, making for disappointment when Prince quickly ends it.

With this band, it is no surprise that "Days Of Wild" becomes "Thank You (Falettinme Be Mice Elf Agin)." Over the bass and swirling organ of "Days of Wild," Prince enthusiastically sings Sly's song in a way only he can. He throws in a few random lyrics, but that is irrelevant as the music is the most important element.

"Forever In My Life" is a rarity for an aftershow. There are notable exceptions (*Small Club* for one), but mostly it is played for the main shows rather than an aftershow. With the full band involved, it has a hip-shaking swing that is charming. This is not the greatest rendition ever played, but it is hard to complain when it is only a minute and a half.

The crowd evidently loves "Everyday People," singing along heartily throughout. The song is functional without ever growing into something essential. It threatens to become another anthem but remains thin. Larry Graham is always good, the song is great, the band is fine, but it never becomes more than the sum of its parts.

With a call of "bring it down, just the drums," Prince begins to play some rhythm guitar that drives the groove home. It begins to loop over and over and this compounds the feeling of the relentless groove. The set list has this down as "Guitar Jam" and that is exactly what it is - a rhythm guitar overload that borders on fabulous. While other elements come and go, the guitar remains a constant, providing joy and funk to all.

There comes another break, and then after much noise from the crowd Prince returns with a proper "rock god" guitar break. Playing alone he pulls more than a few tricks out of his guitar-playing bag as he solos for the next couple of minutes. Without a song or emotional center, it doesn't feel satisfying, even if the guitar playing is out of this world. It is almost a disappointment.

The guitar playing in the "Santana Medley" that comes next is much more rewarding to listen to. The "Santana Medley" suits Prince, and his style is attuned to the type of music that follows. In the smaller venue it sounds even better as Prince bends and shapes the guitar solo around him. Candy is a counterpoint to the guitar, and with her contribution the song becomes balanced and more enjoyable.

The guitar line of "The Question Of U" is rousing from the first moment, strong and proud in the darkness. Prince doesn't sing; instead his guitar does all his talking for him, and the following few minutes are a reminder of just how great Prince is at drawing a strong emotional response from his guitar. "The Question Of U" is often played, yet here it is fresh and inviting even after all these years.

The next twist comes as the squeal of "Gett Off" begins before the guitar plays the main refrain. With the main riff played by all the band, the arrangement is bright and refreshing. Prince has time to inject guitar lines where he pleases and doesn't bother with the lyrics, singing a single verse before letting the crowd take the chorus. It is a crowd-pleasing moment that comes off well, especially as Prince solos again.

The sound strips back again as Prince takes up the opening riff of "When You Were Mine." It is pure pop joy, something that isn't heard very often at this show. After the long jams of earlier, it is almost a throwaway, yet its well-crafted pop is more than welcome. The point of difference comes at the end where instead of the final guitar break, Candy plays her saxophone. This brings some fun to the song and the show, and as always Candy is full of enthusiasm.

The final song of the show begins with Prince telling the crowd he has to go home "to America, get ready for the bomb," before he begins to sing "Osama bin Laden getting ready to bomb." He sings this several times, nobody at the time realizing how the future will unfold. It is interesting to hear that he is aware of what is happening around the world and he already knows of bin Laden, hinting that he is a man who reads more than just the newspaper headlines. He sings this several times for the first few minutes of the song, telling the crowd "that's the new groove." The song serves as a call and response with the audience, and this is where the recording ends, a wail of a siren signaling the end of the show.

This bootleg has a serviceable audience recording, but what makes it stand out above others is not only the appearance of Lenny Kravitz, but also the piano cover of "Are You Gonna Go My Way?," the funk of Larry Graham, Cynthia Robinson, and Jerry Martini and then the final song where he 'foretells' the events of 9/11. There are interesting moments throughout. Prince may have been relatively quiet in the late '90s but he still had the ability to produce fascinating performances. An oddity on many levels, this is one bootleg that needs to be heard more than once.

SET LIST

1. Cissy Strut
2. Superstition
3. Chameleon
4. Asswoop

5. The Undertaker [Instrumental]
6. Joy And Pain
7. I Know You Got Soul
8. Baby Let's Go
9. Hair
10. Love And Happiness
11. Are You Gonna Go My Way?
12. The Jam
13. Organ Solo
14. Mad
15. I Want To Take You Higher [Instrumental]
16. Days Of Wild [Instrumental]
17. Thank You (Falettinme Be Mice Elf Agin)
18. You Can Make It If You Try
19. Forever In My Life
20. Everyday People
21. Guitar Jam
22. Guitar Solo
23. Santana Medley
24. The Question Of U [Instrumental]
25. Gett Off
26. When You Were Mine
27. Also Sprach Zarathustra

RELEASES

- R U Gonna Go My Way? - *Sabotage*
- Tivoli 2nd Show That Night - *Quickline*

18TH OCTOBER 2002
SPORTPALEIS, ANTWERP

The *One Night Alone* tour is one of the more interesting tours as Prince brought a variety of shows and experiences to his audience, along with an artistic rebirth that saw him produce some of the most challenging music of his career. Although not everyone enjoys *The Rainbow Children* album, there is no denying that it is a bold artistic statement and a lot stronger than the albums that preceded it. The tour that supports it demonstrates Prince had a lot of faith in this new music; he plays the bulk of the album throughout the shows and puts this new music front and center. They maintain an intimate feel, and they give the audience value for money with most being in excess of two hours. The European tour is well covered by the bootleg market - there is a variety of sound checks, concerts, and aftershows available. The Antwerp concert is perhaps the best sounding of these, and at two and a half hours long there is plenty to listen to. Prince and the band were undoubtedly getting better as the tour progressed, and the *One Night Alone* tour is represented by three shows in this book, coming from a ten-day period at the end of October. The *One Night Alone* period saw the renaissance of Prince and his continued resurgence that carried him through the decade.

The opening song lets the audience know what to expect as "Rainbow Children" introduces the concert. With twists and turns at every corner, it doesn't settle and leaves the listener wondering where it might go next. This feeling is further heightened by the distorted vocals Prince uses in the song, unsettling and unnerving for those that have come for "Purple Rain." The band is well suited to this type of music, and with Renato Neto, Candy Dulfer, and Eric Leeds in the band they give it a freefalling sound. Prince's guitar adds some direction and sharpness, but the music of the band is far more representative of what to expect. At thirteen minutes long it eases the audience and the listener into the concert without feeling rushed.

"Pop Life" is night and day compared to "Rainbow Children." It is straightforward and poppy, a complete contrast to the first ten minutes. Prince makes it fit with his current vision, and it is Renato Neto with a solo that acts as a bridge between Prince's past and present. The pop aspect of the song is there, but the jazz side of it is highlighted with Renato's solo, and Prince makes it more explicit when he says "life - it ain't too funky, unless its got that jazz" as Candy Duffer takes a moment to play.

Prince declares pop music is dead as "Xenophobia" begins. The crowd is subdued when Prince asks them (somewhat confrontationally) "Who came to get their "Purple Rain" on? You at the wrong party."

> **THE FOLLOWING MINUTES ARE WEIRDLY BRILLIANT AS THE MUSIC SNAKES AND TURNS BEFORE PRINCE TOYS WITH AN AUDIENCE MEMBER WITH HIS "LEADER OR FOLLOWER" SPEECH**

"Xenophobia" keeps with this ominous tone, sounding fascinating and a touch scary. The song fuses several different styles together, the band playing to Prince's command as he calls various members to solo. The following minutes are weirdly brilliant as the music snakes and turns before Prince toys with an audience member with his "leader or follower" speech. It all comes to a happy ending as the guitar takes up an aggressive stance that eventually comes back to the lead line. Any other performer and it would be bafflingly weird, but here it is just Prince being Prince.

The *Diamonds and Pearls* album seems a million miles away, especially as Prince says, "Music is art - for it to remain that way it must ask hard questions, and that's what we're trying to do tonight," but "Money Doesn't Matter 2 Night" is the next song in the set, and it sits well with its jazz overtones and plays to the band's smooth poise. The song also manages to strike a good balance between music and political lyrics, something Prince doesn't always get quite right.

Another long funk jam next with "The Work (Pt 1)." It anticipates the music that will be heard on the Musicology album, with horns and turnarounds wherever you look. Prince is in his element as he encourages Candy to play and he commands the stage. There is more interaction with the audience, this time dancing, and although it can't be seen on the recording, it does sound like a lot of fun.

"Purple Rain" begins with the simple piano riff as with a quiet cheer from the crowd the band comes in. This is in contrast with Prince earlier saying people who wanted to hear "Purple Rain" were at the wrong party, and he is clearly hedging his bets. Although not a great version, it is still enjoyable at a basic level. As the crowd sings the chorus Prince begins to work the guitar before he begins his trademark solo. This one proves true to form but still with a twist or turn to latch on to, just enough to keep it interesting. It is typical of the *One Night Alone* shows, with Prince rallying the crowd with a final speech before they sing as one voice.

"Turn this guitar way up, Scotty" signals what to expect from "1+1+1 Is 3." It is strong on rhythm, and it is Prince's guitar that keeps the song and the crowd moving. The recording is great; not quite as clean as a soundboard but good enough. It picks up all the elements coming together, especially as Prince calls Eric in for the "Housequake" refrain. "Housequake" is warped to fit the band, and although far from the original, it works in this context. This funky medley continues with the addition of "Love Rollercoaster" and "Get Up (I Feel Like A Sex Machine)," although neither can match the intensity of earlier in the song.

The show slows again with "Strollin." It is easy, with the highlight being a guitar break by Prince that is to the point. All the band shows their chops, with a piano break and saxophone solo that adds plenty of depth to what started as a light song. The band plays with finesse, something that this bootleg highlights.

"Gotta Broken Heart Again" gets off to a slow start but then draws in once Prince begins to sing. He's on form here; his vocals are smooth and velvety giving a richness to the performance. It has a level of sophistication not heard on the original *Dirty Mind* album. The song opens up with a lush midsection that gives way to an Eric Leeds saxophone solo far removed from the original song.

With the arrival of "Strange Relationship," the energy is restored to the show as it gets things moving with its upbeat, funky groove. The piano and bass are the foundation, and it is played with a blast of enthusiasm by Prince and the band. Prince seems to derive extra energy from the song; he is lively on the recording, especially as Rhonda comes to the fore with her bass.

Things take a guitar turn as Prince calls "turn me up Scotty; crank this up" and his guitar introduction to "When You Were Mine" begins. This song has never dated, and it still has a freshness to it that is hard to ignore. Prince gives it a standard run through, his guitar crisp and sharp all the way through, and for the next few minutes he rolls the years back with a youthful rendition.

"Sign O' The Times" is a quiet storm as the first minutes features Prince building the intensity with some fiery guitar work. It snorts and howls under his command, giving added emphasis to the lyrics as he begins to sing. It is not just about the guitar though; the crowd adds their voices to the song, giving it some depth before Prince returns with some more guitar that underlines everything that has come before.

"Take Me With U" is far more easygoing and lifts the clouds of the preceding song. The audience sings along, although they are never overly loud and the recording stays focused on Prince's voice. It skips by light as a breeze, and the show is purified by it. There is the obligatory segue into "Raspberry Beret," overplayed through the years and verging on stale. However, the enjoyment factor for fans and the audience can't be overlooked, and it adds to this lighter part of the recording.

"The Everlasting Now" is an upbeat song that follows on nicely from the previous pop moments. It is a double blow - the horns shine brilliantly in the first half of the song before Prince reclaims the spotlight with his Santana medley midsong. It is only a couple of minutes, but what a great couple of minutes they are - not only Prince and his guitar but the horns providing their weight to the medley, turning it into a New Power Generation jam.

> **"IT IS A DOUBLE BLOW - THE HORNS SHINE BRILLIANTLY IN THE FIRST HALF OF THE SONG BEFORE PRINCE RECLAIMS THE SPOTLIGHT WITH HIS SANTANA MEDLEY MIDSONG"**

The following piano set starts off well with a quick fire "Delirious" before Prince seduces with "Adore." The piano version is slight and gentle as Prince doesn't push his vocals too hard. Even so, he still takes his time and makes sure that every high note is hit. The lyrics are clever, and the transition into "I Wanna Be Your Lover" is as smooth as glass as Prince drops the opening line into the song. It is a sweet moment as the piano set rolls on.

"Do Me, Baby" gets a reverential performance, Prince melting the lyrics in his mouth as he sings them. The performance sounds sexy, and one can almost smell the incense and candles.

"Condition Of The Heart" goes further down the sentimental route, and the audience sounds in awe on the recording as Prince feels his way through the song. "Diamonds and Pearls" is paired with "Condition Of The Heart," and the sentiment is lovely although the song is more lively and not quite as heart-tugging as "Condition Of The Heart."

Things become more conventional as the band backs Prince for a full rendition of "The Beautiful Ones." The song's power remains undiminished over the years, and Prince gives it some soul with an impassioned plea that connects it back to the *Purple Rain* era.

The crowd gives an appreciative cheer to "Nothing Compares 2 U," and it gets a full performance with the band and the horns adding to it. As the audience trades lines with Prince, it becomes a campfire singalong moment. Candy Dulfer comes to the party with an exquisite sax solo that contains just as much emotion as any of the lyrics. Not to be outdone, Eric Leeds gets to draw the curtain on the moment with a busy solo that matches Candy.

"The Ladder" takes on a seriousness with the theme of the show, and Prince uses it to hammer home his sermon. Midsong Prince delivers a monologue that comes back to some of the themes he has already commented on earlier in the evening, and it makes for interesting listening. The song is versatile, and Prince uses it to carry his spiritual message in a manner that doesn't derail the show. It is uplifting, and with Eric Leeds again playing, it is a classic concert moment.

"Starfish And Coffee" makes a cameo appearance before Prince returns to sentimentality in the form of "Sometimes It Snows In April." It is poignant, and he doesn't overplay it; just him at the piano with the merest hint of the band behind him. His voice is smooth, and he finishes with the audience singing softly and respectfully behind him in a touching moment.

The best, however, is saved for last - an incredible seventeen minute jam around "Days Of Wild." It is a knee-trembling, earth-shaking performance that is everything anyone could possible wish for and more. To say it is wild is an understatement - this is the type of song that the phrase "off the chain" was invented for. It takes on a life of it is own, and Prince and the band scramble around this monster, hanging on for dear life. Everything is thrown into it; horns vie for attention against chanting as all the while the suffocating groove rolls on, relentless in its insistency. The riff of "America" appears from nowhere, loud and proud in the midst of the chaos of the song, its guitar stanza standing alone above the din before that too disappears into the mass of the groove. The song seems never ending, but as it does come to a finish it leaves you wishing for more. The final crowd chanting of "it ain't over" is part groove and part wishful thinking.

If this bootleg consisted of nothing more than this final "Days Of Wild," it would still make it on any essential list; yes - it is that good. However, at two and a half-hours and with most of *The Rainbow Children* album and a run through the back catalogue, the show is much more than this final song. This bootleg is a recording of one of the best shows of the *One Night Alone* tour and, no matter how people may feel about the album, that tour was brilliant as Prince recaptured some of his magic. As such, this bootleg is essential and worth the effort to track it down.

SET LIST

1. The Rainbow Children
2. Pop Life
3. Xenophobia
4. Money Don't Matter 2Night
5. The Work, Part 1
6. Purple Rain
7. 1+1+1 Is 3
8. Strollin'
9. Gotta Broken Heart Again
10. Strange Relationship
11. When You Were Mine
12. Sign O' The Times
13. Take Me With U
14. Raspberry Beret
15. The Everlasting Now
16. Delirious

17. Adore
18. I Wanna Be Your Lover
19. Do Me, Baby
20. Condition Of The Heart
21. Diamonds And Pearls
22. The Beautiful Ones
23. Nothing Compares 2 U
24. The Ladder
25. Starfish And Coffee
26. Sometimes It Snows In April
27. Days Of Wild

RELEASES

- Antwerp 2002 - *4DaFunk*
- Lost And Found - *Eye Records*
- One Nite Alone Antwerp - *Fan Release*
- One Nite Alone… In Antwerp - *Enigma*

26TH OCTOBER 2002
VEGA, COPENHAGEN

The year 2002 saw some fantastic aftershows and some equally fantastic bootlegs. Of the circulating shows, this has to be one of the best of not only this tour, but of Prince's career. The *One Night Alone* tour sees Prince taking on a new lease of life as he regains his feet after drifting in the late '90s. The main shows are long and relaxed yet focused, while the aftershows see Prince playing in an even more laid-back manner. The bootleg from 26th October 2002, is an excellent (I can't stress the word *excellent* enough) soundboard recording of a show that is simply incredible. It is even more so when considering it was a recorded a week after the Antwerp concert and days before the infamously long Bataclan performance. The first part of the gig is guitar-heavy rock before Prince moves through funky jams, ballads, and ends with a knock-out version of "Dolphin." Top-notch in every aspect. The show is heavily bootlegged, and being a soundboard, it sounds fantastic on all releases. However, one of the best in circulation is the Ladybird release, which is a matrix of the soundboard recording and an audience recording. The audience is an integral part of the show, and this release captures the mood of the show with an even balance; as such it is a cut above the rest.

The recording starts with the end of the DJ's set. It is a nice touch and sets the scene for what will follow. Even in this early part of the show, the recording is pristine. The mood is set as the DJ spins "Gett Off," "Poom Poom," and then some hip hop before a flurry of guitar work has Prince warming up his fingers. He plays fast and furious from the start, and after a minute of fret work the band begins with "Who Knows." It is a showcase for Prince to dazzle with his guitar skills, and he delivers with a fast and furious statement of intent. It is a hot beginning, but the show has plenty more to come.

Keeping with the guitar-based songs, "Bambi" follows. Prince is out front with the guitar, but the band is really pushing it along -

especially the drums and bass. There is a sense of excitement in the air as Prince calls, "turn me up Scotty - want to feel it in the whole house" which is the cue for more guitar heroics. The guitar comes in waves, before pulling back to give Prince space to sing, "All your lovers look just like you." It is a thrilling ride and a genuine rock 'n' roll moment that provides excitement and danger in a four-minute package.

The song segues into the main riff of Led Zeppelin's "Whole Lotta Love," and again there is the sense of the live show on the recording, as the riff blasts out and in the left speaker someone clearly loses themselves in the moment with a wild yell of "Whhhooooaaaa." The guitar is deep and throaty, offsetting Prince singing in his usual falsetto. There is a rush as Prince pulls out not one but two spectacular, psychedelic guitar solos. Just as things look like they couldn't get any better, Prince ends the song with a "turn it up!" and yet another killer guitar solo.

> **THERE IS A RUSH AS PRINCE PULLS OUT NOT ONE BUT TWO SPECTACULAR, PSYCHEDELIC GUITAR SOLOS**

The pace is brought down considerably as Prince plays the opening refrains of "The Question of U." The keys enter, and the mood and tempo of the evening is changed. As he sings "what is the answer to the question of you?" the quality is apparent. His voice is crystal clear, perhaps the one instrument people forget that he most proficient with. Of course, there is an inevitable guitar break after a sublime piano solo, but again Prince springs a surprise by moving onto "The One." As one of the most underrated songs in his catalogue, it gets a deserving moment in the recording with the heartfelt lyrics prominent. However, this is a band full of talented players and none more so than Eric Leeds who brings a delicate saxophone solo to the table.

"On the one" Prince stops the band in an instant. "Didn't they tell you no cameras?" he asks the audience. A drama unfolds as Prince chastens the crowd for taking photos. With "I got a nice warm hotel bed waiting for me," he then instructs the crowd that next time someone takes a picture, the person next to them should grab him or her and twist his or her neck. After saying one more time "No pictures, please," the band resume. This incident demonstrates Prince's respect for the music and the performance. He wants the audience to be in the moment themselves without modern distractions - the music is key.

Upon resumption, the band play across genres - Candy Dulfer with a saxophone solo and Prince singing some lines of Alicia Keyes's "Fallin" before the horns and keyboards drift into "Take 5." Then, just as it looks like it couldn't get any better, the song ends with a drum solo. It is an amazing sequence of music, the ten minutes featuring a taste of everything.

With the bass rising to prominence, the recording becomes funk fueled as the band tackles "Brick House." Prince is singing, but it is the bass and horns that are the heroes. As Prince name checks Eric for a solo, things stay in this vein as the band plays "Skin Tight." This version is too short, it is heavy with funk, and highlighted by Prince's singing which carries an innate rhythmic sound, especially as he sings the lines "she's a bad, bad lady, in skin-tight britches." There come several teases, first the bass plays the distinctive introduction of "777-9311," before the band quickly moves to "Hair" - notable for a fine trombone solo. Candy too gets another chance to play before the song ends with a distorted Prince guitar shriek drowning out all else. Again it is another spectacular ten-minute sequence that leaves you shaking your head at the virtuosity of this band.

With some record scratching and sampling, the band enters for another groove. Prince sings "one more jam, one more jam for Prince and the band" as the crowd immediately takes up the cause and keeps the chant going. The lightheartedness and sheer joy of the show can be heard in Prince's next comment as he says, "Ain't you gotta go somewhere tomorrow? Ya'll as crazy as me!" This is where the matrix recording of the show pays dividends - as the audience continues the chant, there is the feeling that they don't need any encouragement from Prince to be part of the show.

Finally, Prince plays the main riff of "Peach" and serves up a version that is not so saturated in guitar. The verses have plenty of horns, keyboard, and sampling, and the guitar only really dominates at the end of each chorus when Prince lurches into a solo. The crowd is still very much part of the show and the recording as Prince leads them into "Copenhagen, we be shaking." The band picks up the mantra as the funk continues before a "from NPG we love you all, good night" from Prince brings the song to its climax.

The best is yet to come. At this point the crowd claps and chants "Copenhagen, we be shaking" for two minutes without pause. It is impressive and adds to the feeling of this recording. The band obliges with an encore as the drums take up a new beat supported by a sampler and scratching. This is one of the funniest moments of the bootleg, although cringeworthy, as Prince sings a version of "Prince And The Band" that is disjointed and ends in a mess. It is hard to pinpoint who is in the wrong, but the song seems to be at the wrong speed, and it is obviously distracting to Prince who is thrown off his flow, fluffing his lyrics several times in the process. For all that though, it doesn't detract from the recording, and it is refreshing to see that even Prince can have his problems onstage - he too is sometimes at the mercy of temperamental technology.

"All The Critics Love You In Denmark" follows. From the title alone, it is an obvious crowd-pleaser. With a long groove, it has plenty of time for the horns to marinate. It continues with an insistent beat and as always it hits the right note with the audience.

"Dolphin" ends the show with a slow introduction featuring gentle guitar from Prince. The song is kept in this low-key style, slower and minimal throughout. In a bootleg full of outstanding moments, this one tops them all. It gains more power in a slow and soulful delivery as it moves in its own gentle grace. One can feel Prince's emotion as he sings; he is investing plenty of himself in the lyrics, giving them a soulful connection. There is only one word for a performance like this - beautiful. It is beautifully sung and beautifully played as highlighted by Prince's guitar solo that closes the song. It is restrained and right on the money, serving as the perfect way to end the show.

> **ONE CAN FEEL PRINCE'S EMOTION AS HE SINGS; HE IS INVESTING PLENTY OF HIMSELF IN THE LYRICS, GIVING THEM A SOULFUL CONNECTION**

This has to be one of the best bootlegs of the second half of Prince's career. Not only does it sound great, but the show itself is wonderfully intimate and highlights the bond between Prince and the audience. It is rare to have a match between the quality of the show and the quality of the recording, and this is the real strength of the bootleg. An unforgettable show, a beautiful recording - bootlegs don't come much better than this.

26TH OCTOBER 2002 - VEGA, COPENHAGEN

SET LIST

1. Guitar Intro - Who Knows? - Voodoo Chile (Slight Return)
2. Bambi
3. Whole Lotta Love
4. The Question Of U
5. The One
6. Fallin'
7. Take 5
8. Brick House
9. Skin Tight
10. 777-9311
11. Hair
12. Peach
13. Copenhagen Jam
14. Prince And The Band
15. All The Critics Love U In Denmark
16. Dolphin

RELEASES

- Copenhagen We Be Shakin' (Clean Version) - *Fan Release*
- Funkin' Copenhagen - *Sabotage*
- My Band's Tight - *Ladybird*
- One Nite Alone In Copenhagen - *Sabotage*
- One Nite Alone... Vega Aftershow - *Pure Funk*
- Prince & The Band III - *Eagle*
- The Copa Vega - *NPR Records*
- Vega Lyrae - *Ride Recordz*

29TH OCTOBER 2002
LE BATACLAN, PARIS

This bootleg is recorded just three days after the Copenhagen concert and is in many ways similar. The set list draws from the same material, and Prince is playing with the same band. The difference is that it runs for two and a half hours, a whole hour longer than the Copenhagen bootleg. The additional songs bring a lot to the party, with "Something In The Water (Does Not Compute)" and the "Santana Medley" essential in their sincerity. The Copenhagen show is one of the best bootlegs in circulation, and although this one doesn't quite reach those heights, it is still an essential part of the *One Night Alone* tour and the aftershow experience.

The show opens with an instrumental that has plenty of the wow factor. With only a drum behind him, Renato Neto adds a mature jazz performance that is warm and inviting. The song has a series of movements as it rises and falls, heats and cools, each movement drawing the listener further into its web. Things get serious as Prince adds his powerful guitar tone, and at this stage the warm-up is all but over, the band cohesive and ready to go. With the funk of the horns making an appearance, the stage is set for one of the great aftershows. The following guitar jam takes things in a different direction from this jazz/funk as Prince riffs and sings to the crowd "good morning to you." It couldn't be more fitting, and afterward there is some suitably heavy guitar as the horns join in. With the crowd picking up the chant of "good morning to you," it is simple yet just as enjoyable as the complexity of the opening jam.

The show changes again with the appearance of "Bambi." It may not be the heaviest version in circulation, but Prince generates an impressive amount of noise from the guitar. His soloing in the latter part of the song swirls around, and this would be the early peak of the recording if not for an even better solo that closes the song. Although an audience recording, the bootleg does justice to all these moments.

29TH OCTOBER 2002 - LE BATACLAN, PARIS

It is well and truly a rock show as the set list continues with Prince's take on "Whole Lotta Love." Prince nails the main riff, but Renato Neto tops this with a fantastically futuristic solo that opens the door for Prince to respond in kind on his guitar. This is a show where the quality of the musicians makes it possible for anything to happen at any given moment, and a close listen reveals plenty of these moments to be treasured.

This is brought into focus with the following "Family Name"; the band can turn their hand to any style and make it their own. It may start with Prince and his guitar, but with the arrival of the horns, it moves quickly along with the band offering their input. The music is first and foremost, and Prince lets his guitar sing out with an emotive solo that finishes with a quip, "Ain't too loud, am I?"

The band stays the center of attention for a different take on "Something In The Water (Does Not Compute)." It is almost mellow sounding; the cold feel of the drum machine is missing and replaced with an organ. The band puts their own spin on the song with a Candy Dulfer saxophone solo followed by rolling tom toms providing warmth. With Prince playing shards of guitar, it is unique, and there is a sense of camaraderie in the way the band play as a whole entity.

> **WITH PRINCE PLAYING SHARDS OF GUITAR, IT IS UNIQUE, AND THERE IS A SENSE OF CAMARADERIE IN THE WAY THE BAND PLAY AS A WHOLE ENTITY**

The opening riff of "The Question Of U" is more conventional with Prince's stark guitar motif matched by Renato Neto and his piano solo. It is all in keeping with the mood set by the previous song, and things stay on a low ebb as the next few songs come bundled together.

An easy transition into "The One" is predictable, the following "Fallin" less so. It is all kept brief as Prince is eager to play guitar, and in the following minutes his sound is superb. With Prince keeping it short, every note is in place and carries equal importance. "Take 5" sees the band demonstrating their chops, and Renato in particular excels as they play. With Maceo adding his signature saxophone, the audience can be heard yelling their approval, although they don't detract from the recording. The music becomes darker and quieter as Prince sings "Ain't No Sunshine," before an ending that sees the men and women in the crowd trading lines.

Surprisingly good is apt for the next song, for it is both surprising and outstandingly good. "She's Always In My Hair" features some of the best guitar work of the show. It is heavy when it needs to be, but also light when Prince demands it. His latter solo in particular is a showstopper and is a spectacular way to end the song.

This is the guitar section of the performance, as Prince solos for a minute before the band picks up the groove that will become "Peach." The music takes some time before it ignites into "Peach," although there are plenty of horns before it reaches that point. The guitar doesn't re-enter the fray until late in the piece, when it appears from nowhere as it kicks off with a suddenness.

"Shake" is the surprise package of the bootleg, with Prince leading the crowd in the singing of "shake!" while he provides the lines in between. It is refreshing to hear it in this set list and Candy gives it a new angle with her energetic solo. It sees the return of the "it ain't over" chant, and this carries across to the funk of the following song.

An unsurprising cover of James Browns "I Don't Want Nobody To Give Me Nothing (Open Up The Door, I'll Get It Myself)" is next on the agenda, and Prince does well to weld it to his own "The Work, Pt 1." There is a natural fit and Maceo is right in his element, charismatically playing the saxophone. This is the moment where all the horns get a chance to blow, and Candy on the saxophone gives a worthy performance.

"777-9311" is short but one of the funkiest parts of the show. It showcases Prince jamming on the bass, and he is sounding fierce as he slaps and pops. These few minutes alone are worth the price of admission as Prince demonstrates his mastery over the bass. As he thumbs it easily into "Hair," things become considerably more laid-back than the previous half hour - the songs continue with this flow, Prince playing bass through "Brick House" and "Skin Tight."

"Cool" makes it into the show, and it is a pleasure to have it on the bootleg. It is not overworked and the mood stays chilled. A trombone solo from Greg Boyer sets the standard early, and midsong it is the bass work of Prince and Rhonda that catches fire. There are some great moments, and as the crowd cheers Prince encourages them to "touch the bass," but it is the bass that touches the crowd.

Some spirited clapping and chanting brings the music back with "All The Critics Love U In Paris." A pounding beat and some great electronic noises get things moving, complete with futuristic keyboard solo that gets pulses racing. With a rhythm track running through the heart of things, the band jams over the top. It seems simple, and with both keyboards sounding excellent, the song is nothing short of fantastic.

"Alphabet St." comes and goes quickly before a slow groove sees the crowd picking up the chant "NPG in the motherfuckin house." The recording captures a funny moment as Prince stops the music to admonish the crowd, "We aren't going to do nothing to nobody's mamma up here tonight." The music resumes with the crowd chanting "NPG in this funky house," suitably chastised and playing the game. The jam continues to flow as Candy provides the main interest with her playing - she is at her finest throughout this tour.

"All The Critics Love U In Paris" is next and this time it is in a different form to earlier in the show. As a longer, danceable number, it works well; the band has found an extra gear, and there is a renewed vigor throughout the song. With Maceo doing his best to blow the roof off and Renato keeping the up-tempo groove, there is a sense of urgency in the music that provides the emphasis and drive.

The opening guitar riff of "Dolphin" is soaked in emotion, and it is a credit to Prince and this band that they can still play something so heartfelt after such an extraordinary show. Prince's vocals are as clean and beautiful as his guitar playing, and during the chorus he switches from singing to playing his guitar instead; just the sort of thing that makes this bootleg so good. Individually all the parts are great; together they become mind-blowingly so. This song is what makes this bootleg so highly regarded, a fantastic moment forever captured on tape.

> **"PRINCE'S VOCALS ARE AS CLEAN AND BEAUTIFUL AS HIS GUITAR PLAYING, AND DURING THE CHORUS HE SWITCHES FROM SINGING TO PLAYING HIS GUITAR INSTEAD; JUST THE SORT OF THING THAT MAKES THIS BOOTLEG SO GOOD"**

The "Santana Medley" that follows seals the deal. There is plenty of Prince on the guitar as well as some frenetic keyboard from Renato. Prince excels in these medleys, and he mimics the sound of Santana well. Renato Neto on the keyboards can match him for style and pace, and the two of them trade solos on their respective instruments. In a show that has already delivered so many highlights, this is another one.

Even after two and bit hours, the crowd still chant for more, and they are rewarded with an instrumental "Come On." The bass is fat and full, a sound offset by the keys and some scratching. Prince starts a chant and very aptly it is "party till the sun come up."

"Housequake" comes on slow and relaxed, a twist on the album version. A rhythm guitar, bass, and drum are the main building blocks as Prince sings his lines slowly before building the crowd to a chant of "time to get funky." The horns swell through the song and there are a couple of solos, all of them on point. It looks as if it might slide by in this manner until the end, but there are more fireworks from Prince and his guitar as the song gains in intensity. Summing up the performance, he finishes with his solo as the crowd continues the chant for another minute.

Third in a series of fine bootlegs covered from the *One Night Alone* tour, this matches the others in performance, quality, and length. The *One Night Alone* tour is well documented, and there are some worthy bootlegs in circulation from most concerts, yet the three that make essential listening contain that little bit more. Although the band isn't held in the same high regard as some other configurations, they still provide a foil to Prince and have the ability to stretch both themselves and him throughout the performance. This bootleg contains some inspiring music, along with wonderful memories of a period when Prince found direction for the next part of his career. He is playing with a love of the music that carries through the bootleg and makes it an essential part of the listening experience.

SET LIST

1. Instrumental Jam
2. Guitar Jam
3. Bambi
4. Whole Lotta Love
5. Family Name
6. Something In The Water (Does Not Compute)
7. The Question Of U - The One
8. She's Always In My Hair

9. Peach - Shake
10. The Work Pt.1
11. 777-9311
12. Hair
13. Brick House
14. Skin Tight
15. Cool
16. All The Critics Love U In New York
17. Alphabet St.
18. Johnny
19. All The Critics Love U In Paris
20. Dolphin
21. Santana Medley
22. Come On
23. Jam

RELEASES

- Body Don't Wanna Quit - *Premium*
- One Nite Alone… In Paris - *Premium*
- Sound & Vision Volume 6 - *Sabotage*
- Whole Lotta Love 4 Paris - *Sabotage*

29TH MARCH 2004
STAPLES CENTER, LOS ANGELES

The *Musicology* tour is when Prince took on the role of a senior statesman in the music world. No longer pushing his current music, he is more than happy to play the part of an icon, giving the audience the hits in a concert tour that showcases not just his back catalogue, but also his musicianship. Commencing a week after his induction into the Rock & Roll Hall of Fame, this is Prince accepting that he is a living legend with a catalogue of music to back him up and a show that gives credence to his induction. He had always embodied the full gamut of performance stardom, but here he makes a point to highlight it, and the concerts are a celebration of his career to date. With a name like Musicology, Prince was schooling the audience on what he considered to be real music, much as you'd expect from his mantra of "real music by real musicians." The concert draws heavily on this, and Prince alludes to it several times before later in the show demonstrating it with his acoustic guitar set, a set that not only spotlights his well-known ability but the songs themselves.

The opening show of the tour at the Staples Center in Los Angeles is widely bootlegged. It was professionally filmed and shown in theaters, making it an easy target for bootleggers. It also gives us one of the best-filmed shows of Prince's career. It may lack the punch and artistry of his earlier tours, but the bootleg is great watch as Prince gives a smooth, professional show that is highly enjoyable. As such, it ranks as one of the best concert bootlegs in circulation and is a fine addition in any collection.

Alicia Keys opens the shows with her subsequently well-known hall of fame induction speech in which she reviews Prince's achievements, the amazing standards he has set and lived up to, and lays down a challenge for him to continue to impress. With a now fully educated audience, the pressure is on for Prince to deliver an incredible performance, but he seems unconcerned.

Musically the performance opens with a rousing rendition of "Musicology" that makes the album cut sound tepid. The performance, stage, and theater of the show are designed with television in mind, which is why this makes such an excellent bootleg. This opening number sets the theme of the evening and a high standard for the rest of the bootleg.

The show is Vegas-like as Prince runs smoothly through a string of hits that would please most crowds. The songs may not have the force or youthful newness that they once had, but Prince knows what the audience wants to hear, and he is more than happy to give it to them. "Let's Go Crazy" doesn't have an inner fire, but it does have Prince showboating on guitar. "I Would Die 4 U" is equally nostalgic and provides Prince the opportunity to preen and play with the audience. "When Doves Cry" is the pick of the opening songs, the earworm of a hook ringing out several times in the arena with an elastic bass giving it an extra layer of funk. Prince may not give a complete lyrical performance, but he doesn't have to as the band and the music are central. This string of *Purple Rain* era songs is rounded out with Prince and the band ripping through "Baby I'm A Star." With plenty of input from the horns and a crisp, clean sound, it does come close to a Vegas revue, especially as Prince leads the band through several turnarounds. Again, he is demonstrating the showmanship side of his personality as well as playing bandleader.

> **THE SONGS MAY NOT HAVE THE FORCE OR YOUTHFUL NEWNESS THAT THEY ONCE HAD, BUT PRINCE KNOWS WHAT THE AUDIENCE WANTS TO HEAR, AND HE IS MORE THAN HAPPY TO GIVE IT TO THEM**

The bootleg takes on a different mood as the rendition of "Shhh" that follows adds a serious tone to the recording, and for the first time Prince can be heard engaging with the music rather than the audience or the band. This is a glorious sum of its parts as Prince's vocal performance is amply matched by his guitar playing and the quality of the recording itself. There is a restrained emotion present through the song; Prince's forceful playing transports the audience away from the glitz and glamour that came earlier.

The next portion of the concert sees Prince shifting gears, and the performance moves from the gravity of "Shhh" to a more lighthearted selection. The show is designed to engage the audience, and what follows is a selection of songs to get them up and dancing. "A Love Bizarre" and "The Glamorous Life" come bundled together, serving as little more than an introduction for the two songs that will keep the audience on their feet - "I Feel For You" and "Controversy." "I Feel For You" plays on nostalgia value, while "Controversy" brings some funk into the picture, the horns announcing it as a different arrangement from the early '80s. It still has the desired effect, it both sounds and looks like a party starter. It also sees Prince returning to his "real music by real musicians" manifesto, something he highlights as Candy Dulfer plays later in the song.

The following piano interlude by Renato Neto is a pleasant surprise, an interesting diversion made even more so by the appearance of the "she's crying, it is backwards" dialog. This leads naturally enough into "God," with Mike Phillips adding his saxophone to the mix. It has a tender sound, although without the emotional heart of the original.

Prince breaks the concert into blocks of music, each one focused on one style. The dance section of the performance ends, a Renato Neto and Mike Phillips interlude follows, and then the show enters into what one could call slow jams. It is one of his most famous slow jams that he begins with "The Beautiful Ones." He gives the expected performance and then follows with an equally lush "Nothing Compares 2 U" and "Insatiable." These songs are not just about the music; Prince knows how to give a performance that matches the songs contents, and he has the crowd in the palm of his hand the entire time.

"Sign O' The Times" introduces the most interesting part of the show. Prince stalks the stage, giving a strangely laid-back version that has a swing rather than a snarl. The intensity arrives late with the appearance of his guitar. This opens the door to "The Question Of U" and the medley often heard during the One Night Alone tour. Initially it is Prince and his guitar that holds the spotlight, but this medley has always been about the band, and after some soulful moments, they step forward and wrap the song in their own music and style. "The One" is the bridge between the two styles, Prince leading "A Question Of U" into a more soulful place with the lyrics of "The One" before his final guitar break puts an exclamation point on it.

"Let's Work" reignites the audience while "U Got The Look" sees the stage filled with dancers from the audience. It is not the best part of the bootleg by any stretch, although it was undoubtedly fun for those who were there. Prince then adds "Life O' The Party" and "Soul Man" to the set list, both keeping the atmosphere at the concert up without adding anything extra to the recording. "Kiss" and "Take Me With U" are in a similar vein, part of the greater medley as the audience continues to dance onstage.

There is a long break next, and for simulcast in theaters this is an opportunity for the video to show some Prince facts, reminding the audience again just what a megastar he is. It is a good promotion for his arena tour, and tour dates are listed before the music resumes with Prince appearing with just his acoustic guitar.

With the house lights up, Prince plays an intimate solo set, letting the songs and music speak for themselves without distraction. "Forever In My Life" glows in this setting, Prince's vocals are warm and inviting while the guitar keeps the song quickly moving along. It segues into "Real Players" and, although different in character, it is a perfectly natural fit. So too is "12:01." In the stillness of the arena, every word carries importance, and the clever lyrical content is brought to the fore. "On The Couch" is the last of these songs to be played with a wink, and there are some sweet couplets to smile at before the acoustic guitar set moves onto surer ground.

> **WITH THE HOUSE LIGHTS UP, PRINCE PLAYS AN INTIMATE SOLO SET, LETTING THE SONGS AND MUSIC SPEAK FOR THEMSELVES WITHOUT DISTRACTION**

"Little Red Corvette" is heartwarming and Prince's performance brings a freshness to the song. It is the high-point of the miniset and the audience has a chance to sing softly along before ending it with applause and cheering. With an emotional charge in the air, "Sometimes It Snows In April" out-does "Little Red Corvette." Prince's vocals soar above the guitar, and even with whistles and shouts from the audience, it has an innate sadness and solemnness that can't be shaken. The final dedication to David Coleman adds some poignancy to an already touching performance.

"7" uplifts the spirits, and Prince brings the audience back up with a rousing rendition. It is not a long song, but it does bring the band back to the stage and sets things up for the final act.

That final act is, of course, "Purple Rain," and it does its usual job of closing the show with an epic performance. Prince tells the crowd that he loves playing this song and from their reaction they love hearing it. It begins without fuss, Renato Neto playing a quick piano line before the audience immediately warm to singing. The song ebbs and flows until Prince unveils the guitar break that will carry it to the end of the show. After a two-hour show, he wraps it up with one last feeling of togetherness and positivity.

Musicology and its subsequent tour ushered in a new era for Prince. The previous One Night Alone tour saw him regain his confidence and muse, but it was also the last time that he properly toured new material. The *Musicology* tour did feature songs from *Musicology*, but it was primarily about the hits and his status as a star. A heavily promoted album, this bootleg is a happy spin off as Prince used the cinema simulcast to promote the tour. The show may not offer anything that hadn't been heard before, although the acoustic guitar set was a worthy addition, but one can't quibble about the quality of the concert or the bootleg. For a run through of the hits and an overview of what Prince does best, this would be a key starting point for any fan new to the world of Prince and Prince bootlegs.

SET LIST

1. Rock & Roll Hall Of Fame Induction
2. Musicology
3. Let's Go Crazy
4. Baby I'm A Star
5. Shhh
6. D.M.S.R.
7. A Love Bizarre
8. The Glamorous Life
9. I Feel For You
10. Controversy
11. God
12. The Beautiful Ones
13. Nothing Compares 2 U

29TH MARCH 2004 - STAPLES CENTER, LOS ANGELES

14. Insatiable
15. Sign O' The Times
16. The Question Of U
17. The One
18. Fallin'
19. Let's Work
20. U Got The Look
21. Life 'O' The Party
22. Soul Man
23. Kiss
24. Take Me With U
25. Forever In My Life
26. Real Playas
27. 12:01
28. On The Couch
29. Little Red Corvette
30. Sometimes It Snows In April
31. 7
32. Purple Rain

RELEASES

- Los Angeles Big Screen - *Sabotage*
- Kick Out The Tour - *Xpert*
- Musicology Los Angeles - *Fan Release*
- Musicology: School's In LA - *RWS Productions*
- Live From Los Angeles - *Fan Release*
- Los Angeles Big Screen - *Sabotage*
- Opening Night - *Phoenix*

1st AUGUST 2007
THE O2, LONDON

Prince took on the mantle of a legacy act and icon in 2004. With his induction into the Rock and Roll Hall of Fame and the following Musicology tour, he was again in the public spotlight and received all the praise he deserved. This momentum carried him for the next few years, and his renaissance continued with *3121* and then the Super Bowl half time show of 2007. Prince continued riding the crest of this wave, taking residence in London for his twenty-one-night stand at the O2 Arena. Heralded by the media and public alike, these shows captured the public's imagination with sell-outs night after night. All twenty-one nights are bootlegged in various forms, as too are all the aftershows he played. Prince offered up a variety of set lists and experiences, a different set list every night with several guest appearances across the run of performances. The first concert of the *21 Nights in London* residency is the most important; the success of the following shows was based on the word of mouth and reviews of this performance. Suffice to say, Prince delivered a knock-out, and the event is well covered on serval different bootlegs.

The opening pre-recorded UK Music Hall Of Fame introduction cements Prince's status as an icon and is a necessary part of the show. Not only does it build anticipation for what will follow, but it also reminds the younger generation just how influential and talented Prince was. With previous band members and musicians speaking about his abilities, the scene is set for what will follow. Unexpected on a bootleg, but it does add to the concert experience when listening to it.

There has been a variety of crowd-pleasing favorites to open shows over the years, but "Purple Rain" is a rare choice. Unusual but perfectly understandable, Prince is signaling his arrival in London with his signature song and dousing the arena in purple from the beginning. He makes the song a statement of intent, playing the full version complete with an elongated guitar solo that glows and growls in equal measure as the crowd sing their "owww, owww, owww." It feels like a concert closer as the audience sings, but there is plenty more yet to come from this bootleg.

The recording then takes off with the next song, an up-tempo "Girls And Boys." After the slow start of "Purple Rain" it gets things moving, especially the horns headed by Maceo Parker and their sharp intensity. The set list is uneven though and the following "Satisfied" sees things slow down after this stomp. "Satisfied" comes off as a smoky seduction piece and makes for a strange bedfellow coming after "Girls And Boys."

Things get back on track with the following two songs - a horn-infused "Cream" and a guitar-lite version of "U Got The Look." Both are an early peep into Prince's back catalogue and, as hits in their own rights, the audience can be heard responding to them on the recording. They are almost throwaway in their delivery, and "U Got The Look" especially suffers from Prince's watered-down guitar sound.

"Shhh" sees the return of the emotive, passion fueled guitar driven song that Prince specializes in. His voice sounds fine for the verses, but the guitar speaks volumes in comparison as he unleashes a torrent of guitar work later in the song. It may suffer from being an audience recording, but the song and the performance are both compelling. The final half minute features some furious guitar work that can be compared favorably to his best.

Being both nostalgic in sound and lyrical content, "Musicology" works well in this context, presenting Prince as the consummate band leader. He lets each member of the band have their moment, the song serving as an introduction to each individual. Although it is long on the recording, the audience seems to like it and Prince gets a positive response throughout. It is tailor-made for this sort of show, and the sound of the party starting begins right here.

> **HE LETS EACH MEMBER OF THE BAND HAVE THEIR MOMENT, THE SONG SERVING AS AN INTRODUCTION TO EACH INDIVIDUAL**

The next portion of the concert is where Prince introduces himself and his music in the manner we expect. The bootleg drags for the first couple of minutes as Prince talks about his stage, his band, and the excitement of playing in London. It is a necessary part of the show before "I Feel For You" and "Controversy" sees him again dipping into his back catalogue to bring a buzz to the arena. "I Feel For You" has an inner energy with Shelby J. giving it a push, while "Controversy" is balanced with Maceo bringing extra vitality. With the other horns also joining the fray, it has a brassy sound that lifts the audience.

The momentum of the performance and recording is lost as the concert takes a downswing when Prince leaves the stage, leaving Renato Neto and Mike Phillips playing an instrumental "What A Wonderful World." While I have been effusive in praising the horns thus far in the show, this is a bridge too far and interest levels drop considerably at this point.

"Somewhere Here On Earth" is not the song to get the crowd back on their feet, and despite an excellent vocal performance, it barely raises above what has come previously. There is no denying that it is a good performance, the only fault being that it is dangerously close to the middle of the road.

Despite its questionable lyrics, "Lolita" has an infectious, up-beat pop sound that injects some much-needed life back into the recording. It is undone by poor sound at times, but the O2 does have a dubious record with sound quality, and we can therefore blame the venue. Overall the bootleg doesn't suffer too much, apart from when some of the lyrics can't be understood, although that may be no bad thing in this case. Prince trots out his familiar (some would say quaint) "I got more hits than Madonna got kids," which may raise a smile for some people - although he doesn't play these hits he is alluding to, instead playing a reprise of the "Lolita" chorus.

The show, the recording, and the bootleg all regain momentum in the next fifteen minutes as Prince plays a consistent run of well-known and well-loved hits. "Black Sweat" may not be technically as much of a hit as the other songs in its company, but it does bring a heavy dose of funk into the equation. "Kiss" ups the ante, and the crowd is all in as Prince gives them a

> **THE STANDOUT MOMENT THOUGH DOESN'T COME FROM THE SINGING; RATHER IT IS THE BRIEF GUITAR BREAK THAT BRINGS A CHEER FROM THE CROWD**

chance to sing. The standout moment though doesn't come from the singing; rather it is the brief guitar break that brings a cheer from the crowd. Likewise, the lyric change of "Watch Desperate Housewives" is another crowd-pleasing moment that, although corny, works. "If I Was Your Girlfriend" surprisingly maintains this upbeat mood, and the deep organ groove underpins the party feel of this performance. A rousing cheer greets Prince as he asks the audience if they are having a good time, suggesting that the show is now running in top gear.

Things take a slow, smooth turn with the appearance of "Pink Cashmere." It is velvety smooth to listen to and is certainly what some might call baby-making music. This is highlighted by Prince, who replies to Mike Phillips's bright saxophone solo with "Careful, Mike, you might get someone pregnant." It is a throwaway comment that accents his easy humor, demonstrating that the stage is his natural environment and a place he can be his true self.

The performance of "7" and "Come Together" sees the energy levels dipping again. "7" is played straight; the bootleg however contains a loud handclap from an audience member that mars the recording and makes the next few minutes an unenjoyable experience. The band moves deftly into "Come Together," a song Prince has dabbled with many times over the years, and this performance is an obvious nod to the UK audience. The insistent hand clap is still on the recording as Shelby J. comes to the fore for the first half of the song. As good as she is, the performance sounds forced, and it makes for a clunky few minutes. The second portion of the song picks up immensely with Prince playing his best guitar break of the show, coming as redemption for the previous few minutes and nearly, but not quite, saving the song.

The show takes another upswing with the double hit of "Take Me With U" and "Guitar." Both songs are upbeat and the bold keyboard of "Take Me With U" lifts the song above the murky noise of "Come Together." The sound isn't perfect - there is some echo present - but it is better than the annoying hand clap of the last couple of songs. Likewise, "Guitar" isn't great, but it is an improvement and the second guitar break in particular is crisp and clear. Prince gives it a full airing, and it is no surprise at all as the final minutes are dedicated entirely to his guitar playing histrionics, something he throws himself deep into judging by the crowd reaction and incendiary guitar heard on the recording.

Things cool with "Planet Earth," a beautiful song that is emotionally cold in this performance. The recording sounds good, yet the song fails to connect throughout, the substance of the band stealing some of the emotional weight that Prince imparts in his lyrics.

The encores don't offer much more at the outset. Shelby J. leads the band through a robust rendition of "Crazy," a song that is redundant in this context and fails to add anything of interest to the show. The following "Nothing Compares 2 U" has Prince back to form, a fantastic performance that has him wringing something extra from the song. He may only sing the first verse, but it is all he needs before he lets Mike Phillips have his moment with a saxophone break. His vocals after the saxophone break see him singing passionately, the saxophone unlocking something deeper inside of him.

The final song of the encore is a crowd-teasing "Let's Go Crazy." Prince doesn't show much respect for the original, the bootleg revealing that it is now little more than the spoken introduction; followed by more guitar heroics and audience chanting. Predictably enough it ends with guitar howl and Prince intoning, "Thank you, and good night"

The second encore has Prince alone playing a stripped back version of "Little Red Corvette." Much like the *Musicology* tour, it is just Prince and his guitar (in this case the Horner), and the audience for accompaniment. In a mark of just how well written the song is, it more than stands up in this arrangement. The lyrics and basic melody are all that are needed, and it gains something more in the simplicity of it.

"Raspberry Beret" is played in similar fashion, Prince and his guitar leading the crowd through a simple rendition. The recording captures the intimacy of the moment as Prince and the audience sound more like friends singing along at a house party rather than a 17,000-seat arena.

Keeping in character, it is "Sometimes It Snows In April" that follows. Another intimate moment caught on tape, this time Prince shows off his guitar playing and vocal skills as he weaves in and out of the song. He isn't totally unaccompanied; Renato Neto is lending some soft keyboard to the moment, yet it has the feel of a solo performance. It is fresh sounding and still has legs, providing yet another highlight to finish this miniset.

The soft intimacy is washed away as the rush to the finish line comes with the following songs. "Get On The Boat" is brassy and brash, the calls of "oh funky London" signaling Prince's intent for the next few minutes. It has a jump to it with the horns onboard, but it is cut down in its prime as "A Love Bizarre" begins. With the girls' vocals behind Prince, it has a nostalgic feel that harks back to the Sheila E. days. The horns again shine out, only let down by the dreary "oh funky London" chants that lead into "Sexy Dancer." The lyrics to "Sexy Dancer" are dispensed with, replaced with Shelby J. singing "Le Freak," which will become a regular arrangement over the next few years. There is not a lot of Prince, however it is enjoyable and enthusiastic with Shelby and the saxophone leading the way. Prince can be heard in the mix late, but it signals the end of the show as he leads the crowd through the "oh funky London" chant one last time.

Superficially this bootleg doesn't look like much. It is a greatest hits show (for the last time, if you believed the publicity) and is squarely pitched at the general public. With the following twenty nights on the line, this opening show sets the standard and ignited the summer for Prince in London. The hits are there, played well and sounding fresh, and this is what the show is about. *21 Nights in London* is still talked about it the Prince community as one of his great achievements and as such this bootleg is an essential document of the moment. *21 nights in London* starts right here.

SET LIST

1. UK Music Hall Of Fame Video Intro
2. Purple Rain
3. Girls And Boys
4. Satisfied
5. Cream
6. U Got The Look
7. Shhh
8. Musicology
9. I Feel For You
10. Controversy
11. What A Wonderful World [Instrumental]
12. Somewhere Here On Earth
13. Lolita
14. Black Sweat

15. Kiss
16. If I Was Your Girlfriend
17. Pink Cashmere
18. 7
19. Come Together
20. Take Me With U
21. Guitar
22. Planet Earth
23. Crazy
24. Nothing Compares 2 U
25. Let's Go Crazy
26. Little Red Corvette
27. Raspberry Beret
28. Sometimes It Snows In April
29. Get On The Boat
30. A Love Bizarre
31. Sexy Dancer

RELEASES

- Down By The River Thames - *Eye Records*
- For Your Memories Volume 1 - *O2verload*
- London 1st August 2007 - *Freddy G*

29TH AUGUST 2007
INDIGO O2, LONDON

Prince flirted with playing in a trio several times over the years, especially after the positive fan response that the Undertaker project, with Michael B. and Sonny T., received in the mid-'90s. With Michael B. and Sonny T. the title power trio could certainly be applied, and although the trio of Josh and Cora and Prince doesn't exude quite the same power, the title can safely be bestowed upon them for this performance. This bootleg takes in an aftershow during Prince's run of twenty-one nights in London in 2007, and it gained a lot of attention from fans at the time; many fans had wanted to see a show like this for a number of years. It was highly regarded when the recording was first released, and it is still a great bootleg today. The concept of Prince in a trio is a mouth-watering prospect, and the bootleg is a fine record of a hot and heavy London night.

The audience recording eases into the show gently with some crowd noise before the trio of Prince, Josh, and Cora are unveiled with a slow groove. The bootleg sound is excellent, clearly capturing Prince's raw, organic guitar from the beginning. The volume is low as the laid-back groove moves into "Thank You For Talkin To Me Africa." The beauty of the show at this point comes from the strength of the three instruments; with only three players, the music isn't at all crowded and Prince's guitar playing is clear. After some early strumming, he proceeds to give a couple of ice-cold lead breaks, each getting a hearty cheer from the crowd. As an instrumental it does its job as an introduction for the show and the band.

"Anotherloverholenyohead" works well in this context, rocking out well as the crowd is obviously swept up by the song and offer plenty of singing themselves. It takes on an extra element of fierceness in this context with Prince's vocals and guitar taking a star turn in the stripped-back setting. However, it is not well served by the recording, and it doesn't have the jump and pop one would expect from this arrangement. However, despite missing some crispness, it does rock, and the segue into "Rock Lobster" keeps this aspect to the fore. It gives Prince an opportunity to up the intensity with his guitar playing, and his break comes in a flurry of notes and screams from the fret board. The closing drumming from Cora grounds the song, the return to earth noticeable after the fury unleashed by Prince.

"Calhoun Square" is firmly rooted in the Michael B./Sonny T. era, yet that doesn't matter at all to Josh and Cora as they make it their own for the next few minutes. Initially the music sits in the background as Prince opens the singing, but soon enough his sound is turned up and primed for another round of guitar work. It is an enjoyable performance, the crowd appreciatively chanting and cheering throughout. The final minutes are focused on Prince's guitar as he plays as fast and furious as he ever has, displaying the same raw power in middle age as he had in his early twenties.

The trio is a perfect match for "Chaos And Disorder," they seemingly become tighter and faster as they go. The drums lack the pounding weight of a Michael B., and that lack of punch is the only point that lets the song down. Everything else is powerful and strong. Cora is playing well, and as a trio they have plenty of enthusiasm, although it is still Prince's guitar that holds it all together.

The lack of power in the drums is again noticeable for "I Like It There." As compensation, there is plenty of noise on the cymbals, and Prince sings passionately to fill out the sound that is missing. Although the trio isn't a power trio in the powerful sense, they are still muscular and moving singularly to create a full sound together.

> **ALTHOUGH THE TRIO ISN'T A POWER TRIO IN THE POWERFUL SENSE, THEY ARE STILL MUSCULAR AND MOVING SINGULARLY TO CREATE A FULL SOUND TOGETHER**

The best minutes of the song are the final few as Prince lets the guitar do all the work and that is where the real joy of the bootleg lies - moments like this as Prince throws it all to the wind.

The bootleg slows as a long introduction appears; with plenty of grooves and some lead guitar before Prince begins to sing. "All Shook Up" has been played plenty of times over the years by Prince, but none quite like this rendition. The trio makes it work for them with a choppy guitar underlying it before the chorus opens out with some lead guitar similar to the songs heard previously on the recording. It is far removed from the original and in addition is band centered rather than focused on Prince. Prince is not to be forgotten however, claiming the spotlight for a laser-sharp solo to finish with.

"Empty Room" is phenomenal and easily the highlight of the show. Some might say Prince's vocals are recorded as well anything else on the bootleg, but the guitar is the thing and is other-worldly in its tone and voicing. With passion and panache, the guitar silences the audience; they are quite literally awestruck as he delivers a powerhouse performance. Prince plays with a tone previously unheard from his guitar. After this glorious guitar extravaganza, the song unexpectedly ends with a whimper.

> **WITH PASSION AND PANACHE, THE GUITAR SILENCES THE AUDIENCE; THEY ARE QUITE LITERALLY AWESTRUCK AS HE DELIVERS A POWERHOUSE PERFORMANCE**

"Spirituality" will always be "Sexuality," no matter how Prince dresses it up. If "Empty Room" was the highlight, then "Spirituality" would be a close second. While the drums aren't as strong, the guitar drives it and serves as the backbone. Prince plays an assortment of fills that compensate for the lack of keyboards, his guitar a jagged, raw edge that makes it a gritty must-listen. The lyric change may not be to everyone tastes, but the rest of the song commands attention and is an arresting moment.

The following "Johnny B. Goode" is predictable. and although the guitar is present and the mood is high, the rest of the song is a disappointment and the one flat spot of the show. There isn't a lot to it, barely a couple of verses with some frantic guitar work by Prince tacked on. By most standards it's not bad; the key element that is lacking is the soul that Prince usually injects into his shows and performances.

A surprising addition to the set list is "Elephant & Flowers," and it immediately scores for novelty value. It is less flowery than the album version, played in this case with a straightforward delivery. Obviously, it is another opportunity for Prince to display his prowess on the guitar, something he does with great aplomb as he again reaches into his bag of tricks during a remarkable few minutes. This time he injects considerably more spirit into it, something well captured on the bootleg - the power and passion is there for all to hear. There is some mind melting guitar work that bends space and time; the next few minutes feel like barely a minute passed as he distorts the space-time continuum.

Another outstanding performance comes hard on the heels of "Elephants & Flowers" in the form of "When Will We B Paid." Opening with a couple of minutes of gentle lead guitar, the hurricane of the previous song is soon forgotten as Prince shows a completely different aspect of his playing. With a few beautiful runs, he demonstrates a considerable amount of soul and this mood persists. It is timeless, and with the recording capturing the vocals cleanly, the lyrics and message are laid bare. In keeping with this gentle tone, the guitar laps at the song, only rising late as it picks up considerably in the final moments. It is the whine of the guitar that carries to the next song before breaking into a heavy riff. Shelby emerges though the noise to sing "Baby Love," something she was born to do. With her full voice over Prince's guitar riff the song gains a push that drives it home. On the downside there is Shelby's "put your hands up, put your hands up," chant, but to be fair this is only brief. The juicy guitar comes forward as Shelby steps back, and it is this that carries the song before Shelby returns to machine gun the final chorus.

"Alphabet St." gets a verse before a fast guitar solo kicks it into high gear. The lightness returns for another verse before the guitar hammers home another attack. The song is structured this way throughout, light verses followed by the sledge hammer of a guitar flurry. The singing is secondary; it is the killer guitar licks that make this moment unforgettable.

There is no better way to finish the show than the song "Guitar," which is entirely fitting considering the last hour. The song epitomizes the preceding performance with light, almost throwaway verses followed by explosions of guitar frenzy. The drums lack presence and defer to the guitar from beginning to end. It is not a bad thing as Prince is in fine form and delivers fireworks every time his hands flash across the strings. The recording is flooded with guitar as Prince begins to shred; for many this is the highlight and what they want to see and hear. With Prince playing at a frenetic pace, the song speeds by and the ending comes much too soon.

After the crowd-pleasing greatest hits shows of the *Musicology* tour and twenty-one nights in London, this stripped-back appearance is what many fans craved to see. Prince delivered on every front; in the smaller setting his musicianship is emphazised and the flash and brilliance of the main shows replaced with something heavier and organic. There is some power missing in the performance, be it the band or the recording I can't tell. What I do know is that this is must have bootleg, a recording that shows off the other side of Prince away from the bombastic main shows. He shines just as brightly with three people onstage as he does with twelve, and this show is all about his musicianship and guitar playing, something all fans can appreciate.

SET LIST

1. Thank You For Talkin' To Me Africa [Instrumental]
2. Anotherloverholenyohead - Rock Lobster
3. Calhoun Square
4. Chaos And Disorder
5. I Like It There
6. All Shook Up
7. Empty Room
8. Spirituality
9. Johnny B. Goode
10. Elephant & Flowers
11. When Will We B Paid?
12. Baby Love
13. Alphabet St.
14. Guitar

RELEASES

- For Your Memories - 21 Nights In London Vol. 12 - *O2verload*
- Prince, Josh & Cora @ Club 3121 - *Fan Release*
- Greenwich Mean Time - *Eye Records*
- The Indigo Chronicles Chapter 3 - *Sabotage*

22ND SEPTEMBER 2007
INDIGO 02, LONDON

Over the course of his career Prince played with a great many different guest musicians, and listening to bootlegs over the years with these appearances we come across all sorts of names and faces. Some guests are legendary and icons in their own rights, while others are lesser names who nevertheless bring something new to the table. Amy Winehouse may have had a short life, but she is most certainly a legend. One of the most unique and talented voices to emerge in the 2000s, her loss was felt keenly among music fans across the world. She may have been a firm fixture in the tabloids, but this didn't represent who she was or what she stood for on the music scene. Like Prince, she was purely about the music and the performance, these two key elements central to her character. She was unforgettable in both aspects, and we are all the poorer for her passing. The show from 22nd September 2007, with Prince is another highlight in her career, and of all the guest appearances over the years, this one carries the most weight, especially as late in the show Prince asks the crowd to take care of Amy. Sadly, nothing could prevent what happened four years later, and we are still feeling that loss today.

It is not all about Amy Winehouse, however, and the first minutes feature a delicate instrumental that serves as a sound check. With the piano and keyboard leading the way, the band feels their way into the show, easing into the music while doing a live sound check. This is confirmed later as the bootleg clearly captures the Prince testing the microphones.

Some soft guitar leads ever so gently into "Love Is A Losing Game." The guitar and piano interplay is spellbinding and lays out what will follow. Amy's vocals have a tenderness to them yet sound luxurious as she begins to sing, and she deserves every bit of applause she gets from the appreciative crowd. With an angelic voice, she is further uplifted by Prince's lead guitar that complements the performance by providing a bed of chords for her to sing across. Prince normally commands attention onstage, but in this case it is impossible to get past Amy's unique and wonderfully expressive voice. As the song finishes, Prince captures the moment perfectly with his comment "I got tears."

The guitar is heavy and raw as "7" begins and sweeps away the last few minutes. After letting the crowd sing early on, Prince picks up the baton to sing the rest of the song himself. Although he is in fine voice, nothing can match the previous song. The show threatens to be overwhelmed by Amy's earlier performance, and even though she has left the stage, Prince is heard playing strongly in an effort to restore some balance to the show.

That raw sound persists into a pumped up "Come Together." "Come Together" is a repeated favorite of the *21 Nights in London* residency, and after hearing all of them I can safely say this is the best. With fiery guitar coming from Prince, the song goes through the stratosphere; the solo he plays is head spinning and leaves one gasping for air in its wake. The song is turned into a Prince extravaganza as it is stretched out for ten minutes while the instruments battle it out for control, a battle that is never decisive.

> **WITH FIERY GUITAR COMING FROM PRINCE, THE SONG GOES THROUGH THE STRATOSPHERE; THE SOLO HE PLAYS IS HEAD SPINNING AND LEAVES ONE GASPING FOR AIR IN ITS WAKE**

Things stay with rocky cover versions as Prince follows up with his much-loved cover of "Honky Tonk Woman." In a full-blooded rendition, Prince and the band fill the smaller venue with a glorious noise that translates well to the bootleg recording. With Shelby taking on vocal duties, the song gains from her boundless energy and takes on a new lease on life. In an unexpected highlight, Morris Hayes plays a spirited piano solo that entirely befits the song and performance, blindsiding the band and anyone listening to the recording.

The band doesn't deviate from this path, and with the rock platform firmly in place they quickly move on to "Rock Steady." With an ominous tone, it is driven by the bass line lifted from "A Whole Lotta Love," and this tramples over the song when it begins. The singing bumps up hard against the bass line, and it sits with unease against its power. Asides from the singing, the band is in hot form, the keyboard swells, guitar chimes, and horns giving the performance plenty of life.

It is a treat to hear Beverly Knight performing vocal duties, but the assessment by the end is that the horns stole the moment from her with their outstanding contribution.

Prince riffs the opening chords of "A Whole Lotta Love," and an excitement immediately fills the air and the bootleg. This initial rush gives way to an instrumental version of the beloved classic. Without lyrics, the song features plenty of Prince howling on guitar, and it doesn't get much better than the face-melting solo he plays to end the song.

The guitar is king as "Shhh" begins with a heavy start and more pyrotechnics from Prince. The music envelops the recording as things pull back and allow Prince to step into the space to sing. Prince is everything to everyone in this performance, going from quiet to loud, smooth to rough, all the while with a passion and emotional pull that is undeniable. As good as the vocals are, the main attraction is his guitar playing, which is monumental in the song and indeed the whole show.

The guitar and rock are finally put to one side as the strong groove of "All The Critics Love U In London" brings the show to its next phase. The keyboards, horns, and guitar play in step and lock in for a long, danceable groove that serves as an introduction. At seventeen minutes long, it is easily the longest song of the performance but never once loses its way, maintaining a high energy level from start to finish. The horns are particularly alluring and add much with their dominant sound that carries through this section of the recording. Despite all the highs and lows around it, this song is the central hub of the bootleg, and the performance pivots around this moment.

There is more funk on the menu as the pounding bass drum carries over into "Sexy Dancer - Le Freak." Prince slips into the background, allowing Shelby to come to the fore to sing these party songs. It is something she takes to with great relish, and as to be expected she extolls the audience to get up and party during the course of the song. There is a lot of satisfaction to be taken from the trombone solo that appears, and it is this solo that carries the music through to the next track, "Chelsea Rodgers."

> **" AT SEVENTEEN MINUTES LONG, IT IS EASILY THE LONGEST SONG OF THE PERFORMANCE BUT NEVER ONCE LOSES ITS WAY, MAINTAINING A HIGH ENERGY LEVEL FROM START TO FINISH "**

"Chelsea Rodgers" is an easy listen with the bass providing a buoyant pop sound. Shelby J. is still in control of the microphone, and it is similar to the previous song with the trombone providing a fatness. Prince is briefly heard later, singing along with Shelby, but his vocal contribution is weak and negligible.

There is an alluring horn introduction to "Misty Blue" that invites further listening. Shelby has settled down by this point of the show and she sounds all the better for being laid-back and singing rather than hyping the crowd. Her version is a corker, but no matter how good, she isn't Prince, the man himself, the entertainer people have paid good money to see. With this in mind, the listener can't help looking forward to Prince's next appearance rather than enjoying Shelby's.

Mothers Finest don't get nearly as much credit as they deserve, so it is pleasing to hear Prince play plenty of their songs over the years. In this case he plays "Baby Love." Although not a patch on the original, Shelby nevertheless is wild on vocals while the band rocks on behind her. On paper it looks like it should be a knock out, which makes it hard to understand why it doesn't quite come across as good on the recording. It does lift the levels after the previous songs, helped largely by the Prince guitar solo that contains just the right amount of malice and venom.

The next part of the show takes time to warm to as there comes a series of excerpts while the band circles around the next song. "Love Changes" is briefly heard, as is "Kiss," before the band turns their attention to "Alphabet St." With Maceo joining the fray, his trademark horn is distinct, the song gains extra shine and a wow factor. This adds considerably to the level of funk in the song, and for a while Maceo takes possession, despite Prince's best efforts to reclaim it with his guitar groove. The bootleg almost loses its way at this point, but there is just enough structure that it doesn't collapse in on itself.

"Love Rollercoaster" is less impressive, although mercifully kept short. The segue into "Play That Funky Music" doesn't improve things, although with very little singing it quickly becomes an exercise in Prince's guitar playing. He plays some lead guitar without getting overly heavy and manages to play some fast and sharp runs.

Prince next takes his time to address the audience, asking them to take care of Amy Winehouse. There is some sadness to this comment, especially in retrospect, and it is telling that Prince felt the need to speak out in her defense. Although he didn't mention her problems, it was all over the news at the time, and there is no doubt he was alluding to the claims and her stints in rehab.

The proceeding "Anotherloverholenyohead" hits like a hammer, and any thoughts of Amy Winehouse are swept away as Prince demolishes the song in a rock-heavy rendition. The singing and band are faultless, yet it is the guitar that draws all the headlines as Prince again canes it for all he's worth. It is close to the version played at the Super Bowl press conference, and it ups it in the hard rock sound. The "Rock Lobster" coda is unsurprising yet perfectly in tune with the performance.

This is a rock-based show, so the following "Villanova Junction" is again unsurprising. Prince does slow it down with Morris Hayes simmering underneath. It is a smoking rendition, highlighting Prince and his guitar once again. Although it does draw to a close after a few minutes, it makes its mark on the evening.

Guitar strapped on, Prince next steams into "Peach." Although offering nothing new, it is infused with an infectious energy that draws shouts of delight from the crowd.

"Stratus" is normally played earlier in shows, so it is surprising to see it late on the set list. After so much guitar and rock, it is refreshing to hear Renato playing. He captures the mood of the piece perfectly and adds to a complete performance from the band. The second half of the song is complete contrast as Prince lets his guitar do all the talking. While he has the same spirit as Renato, he additionally injects a lot of fire and ferocity into his playing, something Renato does not. The two different styles complement each other well, and it demonstrates the strength of this band, the contrast creating a good tension.

> **AFTER SO MUCH GUITAR AND ROCK, IT IS REFRESHING TO HEAR RENATO PLAYING**

The steady beat of "The Question Of U" begins with a somber guitar opening before it gives way to a soulful saxophone solo from Mike Phillips. Things go further down this path as Prince quietens the crowd, having them snap their fingers, while an emotion rush comes to fill the gaps. "The One" has a grandeur to it, the music sweeping before it as Prince unleashes some screams that convey the emotional intensity of the song. Anything following this is a letdown and although Renato and Maceo play some fine music, the best moments had already passed.

Things are shaping up to become funky again with a quick bass line signaling the beginning of "What Have You Done For Me Lately." With a lively groove, it becomes a medley beginning with "Partyman" and ending with "It's Alright." "Partyman" has no shape to it; it spirals around the horns playing the main riff without ever settling into anything more. Maceo is the highlight with his exciting and energetic playing, and this vibe is sustained through "It's Alright." Undoubtedly a fun medley, it all seems light after the heavy emotional songs from earlier in the set, and it is a deflating end to a great bootleg.

This recording has a mixture of genres and styles, some work better than others, and it is fascinating to hear them playing next to one another. The songs that are strong on guitar or pack an emotional punch overwhelm some of the lighter moments, yet all of them belong together. Prince is renowned for throwing everything into the pot when it comes to his shows, and this performance is typical of the type of aftershow we have come to expect over the years. What lifts it above other recordings is not just the appearance of Amy Winehouse, but the emotion that is infused through the entire concert. This concert is one where the feel of the songs is just as important as the sound of them, and in that respect this is one of the best. There is no better way to remember Amy Winehouse and Prince than this recording where they lay it all on the line.

SET LIST

1. Love Is A Losing Game
2. 7
3. Come Together
4. Honky Tonk Women
5. Rock Steady
6. Whole Lotta Love
7. Shhh
8. All The Critics Love U In London
9. Sexy Dancer/Le Freak
10. Chelsea Rodgers

11. Misty Blue
12. Baby Love
13. Alphabet St.
14. Get On The Boat
15. Love Rollercoaster
16. Play That Funky Music
17. Anotherloverholenyohead - Rock Lobster
18. Villanova Junction
19. Peach
20. Stratus
21. The Question Of U/The One
22. What Have You Done For Me Lately
23. Partyman

RELEASES

- 21 - *Eye Records*
- 3121 London Week #7 - *Eye Records*
- Encore - The Final Aftershow - *Purple House*
- For Your Memories Volume 21 - *Overload Records*
- The Indigo Chronicles Chapter 6 - *Sabotage*
- The Final Aftershow - *Freddy G*

28TH MARCH 2009
THE CONGA ROOM, LOS ANGELES

The show of 28th March 2009, is one of the three shows played that night in promotion of the *Lotusflow3r* release. All three shows are recorded and bootlegged, but this show is by far and away the most interesting as it sees the long awaited, much anticipated reunion of the New Power Trio that gave us the unreleased *The Undertaker* album (later released as a home video). With Sonny T. and Michael B. backing Prince, the show is a hard-hitting affair that appeals to those who like to see Prince in full-on rock mode. *The Undertaker* album of the mid-'90s is much loved by the fan community, and the prospect of the trio playing together again was something fans were clamoring for. There is an equally intoxicating set list, including the first-ever live performance of "I'm Yours." After waiting only thirty years, it finally gets a worthy performance and an audience hungry to hear it. A sensational show by any standard, the bootleg is a great document of an amazing night.

The recording opens with an intimate few minutes while Prince sets up the sound and speaks to the awaiting audience. It is a peep behind the scenes and adds a human element to the show that will follow. Prince is gently playful as he asks who is smoking the funny cigarettes and asks for a fan, presumably to blow the smoke away. He is light hearted as he politely asks them not to smoke, and although he's firm you can hear the smile on his face. The tone is set, and he continues in this vein as he talks about Sonny T. when he was a teenager. Most fans could listen to this type of stage patter for hours, but the music that follows will banish this early chat from memory; what comes next is extraordinary. As "I'm Yours" begins, the lightness of the chat is washed away as the band plays a storming version of this early song, making its live debut after thirty years. They deliver a powerful performance, especially Prince's vocals, which are strong and loud. The crunching guitar and drums hit all the sweet spots, and

Prince's soaring guitar solo sets hearts aflutter as the band shows their rock credentials. They are going to rock and rock hard.

"Colonized Mind" is a song of the period, and it slots easily into the set. It is much stronger than on album, something that can be said about a great many of Prince's songs, and it is the vocals that gain an extra charge in the live show. With a passionate delivery and a guitar snaking in and out, Prince turns it into a storm of emotion and passion. He plays furiously as the band creates a whirlpool of sound around him, impressive considering there are only three of them onstage.

It goes without saying that this band owns "Chaos And Disorder." They tear into it with great gusto, and even while the music is energetic, Prince still manages a relaxed delivery. It all comes too easy, and the band demonstrates what years of playing together can achieve - an effortless cohesiveness that is a power itself. The fierce guitar break tugs at the leash, but Prince keeps it reined in for another day.

Prince takes "With A Little Help From My Friends," shakes it up, and makes it his own. Pitching it halfway between the push Joe Cocker gives it and the lightness of Ringo Starr, he gives it the vocal performance it deserves and literally makes it sing. It is the guitar that gives the performance a lift, and coupled with Prince's vocals, makes the song distinctly his interpretation. This is the surprise package of the bootleg, an unexpected cover version that Prince brings his own touch to.

There is a pleasant break in the action as Prince takes time to tell a story about Michael B. With some audience chat, it gets better as someone calls out for "I Like It There." Prince asks him, "What you wanna hear?" as he calls out again. Prince obliges and as he begins to play, the audience member can be heard in a moment of unbridled enthusiasm, shouting, "Thank you, Prince, oh yeeeaaaah, oh my God!" The rest of the song sees the obligatory rock, as well as some singing from the crowd. The guitar work from Prince becomes unhinged, and as his solos branch further out, there is a genuine excitement on the recording.

> **THE GUITAR WORK FROM PRINCE BECOMES UNHINGED, AND AS HIS SOLOS BRANCH FURTHER OUT, THERE IS A GENUINE EXCITEMENT ON THE RECORDING**

The band follows this with a rendition of "All Shook Up," which is played with a heavy crunch. Prince calls that it is time for audience

28th MARCH 2009 - THE CONGA ROOM, LOS ANGELES

participation, which is normally a sign that it is not going to be a great listen on a bootleg. On the plus side, even as the crowd begins clapping, there are some raw guitar riffs that demand attention. "All Shook Up" isn't the first song you would choose to see on a bootleg, but in this case the version played is perfectly serviceable and worth a listen.

This is a great set list exemplified by the appearance of "Empty Room." It starts appropriately slow and emotional, and when Michael B. and Sonny T. join the fray, it kicks up a notch - several notches, in fact. The recording isn't perfect by any means, and the limitations are obvious. However, the brilliance of the song shines through, and the band provides another quality performance. Prince pairs impassioned vocals with an equally emotive guitar, a killer combination in any circumstance. The soul and passion is there in his playing for all to hear, and it only adds to the luster of this show.

"Peach" is obligatory for a concert like this. It is only a few minutes, but the band manage to cram a lot in as Prince tears through his vocals and then proceeds to tear it up on the guitar. It is not spectacular, but it is definitely rock 'n' roll, and these few minutes are among the rockiest of the show.

People assume that Prince is a good match for Jimmy Hendrix songs, but this does not stand up under closer scrutiny. He has covered a number of Hendrix songs over the years, and although there are some good ones, mostly they underdeliver and fail to live up to expectations. "Spanish Castle Magic" is good in its own way, but Hendrix is uniquely Hendrix and Prince doesn't surpass anything that he has done before. The band is ripping it up on the recording, with Michael B. and Prince making a glorious noise together in their own style; it is good but not better than the original.

"When You Were Mine" has a fantastic raw sound, and Prince has the crowd eating out of the palm of his hand with an easy singalong. Prince sings enthusiastically through the vocals before the inevitable guitar break comes with the crowd chanting "hey." It has that basic rock template, pure and innocent, even if the lyrics aren't so. It is a great throw back to a simpler time, and it works well for this show.

With guitar featuring prominently at this performance, there is no surprise at all as the band next break into "Guitar." The lyrics are empty, and Prince plays a strong guitar break in compensation. It has a moment but pales in comparison to other numbers at this concert.

The last song of the show sees Morris Hayes and Frederic Yonnet join the band for a boisterous rendition of "Dreamer." Frederic is very prominent with his harmonica, quiet but distinctive in the tumult of the other instruments. It adds plenty of color to the performance, and he plays a break that cements his moment in the song. The concert ends in style as Prince takes to riffing his guitar against the harmonica before soloing with freedom to a note-perfect finale

This bootleg is a must have, there is no doubt about it. It is not on the genius level of some other recordings, nor is it as historically momentous, but it is a great band of musicians doing what they do best. Prince often gets credit for his funk and for his guitar abilities but rarely for delivering a straight-up rock performance like this. With a decent audience recording to back it up, the show deserves to be heard by a wider public, and for anyone who enjoyed the original New Power Trio it is an unforgettable show.

SET LIST

1. I'm Yours
2. Colonized Mind
3. Chaos And Disorder
4. With A Little Help From My Friends
5. I Like It There
6. All Shook Up
7. Empty Room
8. Peach
9. Spanish Castle Magic
10. When You Were Mine
11. Guitar
12. Dreamer

RELEASES

- C3L.A.BRAtION - *Eye Records*
- LA3: The Conga Room - *Akashic Records*

18th July 2009
MONTREUX JAZZ FESTIVAL, MONTREUX

Prince first played Montreux in 2007, and while that is a good bootleg, the bootlegs from the 2009 shows are much better. Rather than just an audience recording of the audio, we have a full blown pro-shot show - and what a show it is! With a stripped back band, Prince gives a performance that is light and airy, never getting bogged down as it floats with a tenderness from the first moment until the last. The camera crews at Montreux know how to film a show, and we are rewarded with a bootleg that more than matches the quality of the performance. Prince is spotlighted throughout, with only John Blackwell, Renato Neto, and Rhonda Smith onstage with him. There is plenty of room for him to shine without ever having to try too hard to perform. It is one of the most mature performances of his career as he plays a variety of songs that showcase his voice, perhaps more than any other show in circulation. There are no stomping anthems, no dance numbers, and although he does give plenty of time to the guitar, there are very few moments where it feels like a rock concert.

Prince played two shows on the 18th of July, and both have been bootlegged in the same quality with a pro-shot DVD circulating. There is very little difference between the shows (only a couple of songs and the running order). I've elected to select and cover the earlier show due to their similarity.

From the darkness and ominous tones of Renato's keyboard emerges the caressing opening of "When I lay My Hands On U." The first minute may be gentle, but in the next few minutes Prince brings an intensity with his guitar playing and singing, an intensity that will not be matched anywhere else on the bootleg. With powerful chords and howls at the chorus, the song takes on a murderous tone that Prince emphasizes with his later solo. With a name check to Santana and a solo to match, Prince is bordering on something that my inner punk would dismiss as guitar wank.

The show will later ease into smooth jazz and sultry ballads, but for now Prince is still sticking to his guitar songs. The debut appearance of the "slow down" "Little Red Corvette" makes this bootleg essential. The song is slowed as Prince makes the guitar his second voice, adding anguish and hurt to a pop song, forming a lament that cries out as the guitar voices its haunting refrain. The breakdown pushes this further, with Prince wallowing in this guitar tone before the crowd picks up the "slow down" chant that sees the song though to the finish.

The recording is perfectly represented with "Somewhere Here On Earth." The band plays in a smooth style, only coming to the fore for their respective solos as Prince's vocal performance and Renato Neto's keyboard dominate for the next few songs while the concert becomes a light jazz showcase. "When The Lights Go Down" is in a similar vein, only tempered by some guitar playing by Prince that gives it a point of difference. There is an extra energy to the "When The Lights Go Down" performance; an energy that the crowd picks up on and responds to. The natural segue into "Strollin" highlights this as Prince turns it into a call and response moment, ending on a feeling of intimacy and togetherness.

One of Prince's most underrated songs, "I Love U But I Don't Trust U Anymore" comes next and as the hall quiets it has the feel of a showstopper. In the quiet setting with Prince's vocals isolated, every lyric, every word and nuance becomes important and is colored with emotion. It is a scintillating performance as the audience hangs off every word, and Prince ends with some vocal acrobatics that swing up and down.

> **IN THE QUIET SETTING WITH PRINCE'S VOCALS ISOLATED, EVERY LYRIC, EVERY WORD AND NUANCE BECOMES IMPORTANT AND IS COLORED WITH EMOTION**

"She Spoke 2 Me" picks up the jazz vibe, especially as Renato takes up a long solo. Prince's contribution is some jazz-on-a-summer's-day vocals and a guitar solo adds intensity before it gives way to a drum solo from John Blackwell. It is an interesting diversion, but the real fireworks are still to come.

"Love Like Jazz" and "All This Love" pick up all these strands and bring them together in a ten-minute highlights package that is the essence of the show. The vocal work of Prince and the keyboards of

Renato make the first impression, but John Blackwell and Rhonda Smith are equally involved, Rhonda's solo comes as a surprise package and encourages the crowd to further ecstasy. It is perfectly placed, and paced, at this point of the concert, adding some impetus just when it needed it. As the music plays, there is an element of funk underpinning it all and adding a fluid energy to the song.

The first encore opens with the exceptional "Empty Room," a song with a sense of drama from the opening moments. It is a drama that is pushed through the stratosphere with an emotive guitar break that takes the lyrical narrative and turns it into a firestorm of guitar; Prince twisting and torturing the notes as they spew forth. The song burns with such intensity that the following "Elixir" is barely a footnote; it comes and goes while one is still digesting "Empty Room" that came before.

"In A Large Room With No Light" had already debuted in March 2009, but that in no way detracts from the shock and awe of its appearance at this show. It comes as a gift to those that have followed Prince his whole career and dug deep into his unreleased catalogue; the song finally gaining a wider audience after twenty-three years locked in the vault. It slots easily into the set list, its jazz flavors further emphasized by the playing of Renato who draws the jazz further from it. Prince makes the exercise all the more interesting with some quiet beatboxing and guitar in the final minute, which adds a touch of weirdness and unworldliness to the song and makes its appearance all the more special and unusual.

The encore begins with a warm and alluring "Insatiable," the warmest and most inviting song in the show. Prince draws in the room with his vocals blanketing the listener in a soft velvet. With Morris Haynes joining the band, it transitions into a lush "Scandalous," the band playing with a luxurious ease. Prince matches with them with a vocal delivery that carries a chocolate and champagne sound, gradually upping the performance as he goes.

Staying with the seduction ballads, "The Beautiful Ones" gets an airing. It may not be as intense as expected, but it does make an impact. Without it ever becoming a barn burner, Prince does his best to insert raw emotion in the song, something that he only succeeds with in the final moments.

The last song of the show is "Nothing Compares 2 U," Prince singing it alone but ably supported by the keyboard work of Morris

Hayes and Renato Neto. It is a beautiful song, but feels like bit of a letdown after some of the earlier antics. After a fantastic hour and a half of music, the show drifts to an unsatisfying conclusion.

Don't be misled by the final ten minutes. This bootleg is worthy of a place in the fifty essential Prince bootlegs. With a curious set list, the likes of which is not found anywhere else in Prince's bootleg catalogue, and a quality performance by a quality band, this is a show that lives up to expectations. The Montreux DVDs are widely circulating and held in high esteem. As far as a pro-shot show (and a one-off special), they don't come any better than this. Essential for the inclusion of "Empty Room" and "In A Large Room With No Light," this should take pride of place in any collection.

SET LIST

1. When Lay My Hands On U
2. Little Red Corvette
3. Somewhere Here On Earth
4. When The Lights Go Down
5. Willing And Able
6. I Love U, But I Don't Trust U Anymore
7. She Spoke 2 Me
8. Love Like Jazz
9. All This Love
10. Empty Room
11. Elixer
12. In A Large Room With No Light
13. Insatiable
14. Scandalous
15. The Beautiful Ones
16. Nothing Compares 2 U

RELEASES

- From Dusk Till Dawn - *Eye Records*
- Montreux 2009 First Show - *Fan Release*
- Montreux Enhanced - *DaBang*
- Montreux Jazz Festival - *4DaFunk*
- Montreux Jazz Festival - *Sabotage*
- Montreux Like Jazz - *Irukandji Music Ltd*
- Montreux Jazz Festival 2009 - 2 Shows 1 Nite - *Purple Gold Archives*
- Montreux Jazz Festival - *Irukandji*

7TH NOVEMBER 2010
VIAGE, BRUSSELS

The shows of 2010 were a standard run through of his hits and saw Prince playing it safe with his set lists and performances. However, he did play some of the longest shows of his career (both in the main shows and the aftershows), and this makes several of the bootlegs more interesting than perhaps they would otherwise be. The main concerts don't offer too many exciting moments; it is the aftershows that stand out and offer something special for the careful listener. The Viage performance from November runs for almost three and a half hours and offers a touch of everything that Prince and this band could do. It is a classic aftershow performance, and at more than three hours offers a rewarding listen for anyone who has the time.

Prince and the band know they are in for a long show, and the show begins with a string of instrumentals. Prince isn't present for "Joy In Repetition," and it is Renato Neto who makes the first impression on the bootleg with his smooth keyboard guiding the first song. It is pleasant enough, but without lyrics it lacks the emotional depth of the original. However, it is an interesting opening and offers the suggestion that this show will contain few surprises.

Even with Prince onstage, the music continues in this instrumental form, each song showing a different side to the band or highlighting a different instrument. "Stratus" has Prince playing over an ominous roll, his guitar solo a black hole that has galaxies appearing and disappearing as he plays. "Sometimes It Snows In April" showcases another type of his guitar playing, a soft introduction demonstrating a light touch that is later eclipsed as the rest of the band join in. The guitar is back as it plays a stellar version of the main melody, both enticing and entrancing, the twenty-year-old song resurrected as Prince breathes new life into it.

"Delirious" becomes a different beast altogether in its instrumental form, and it needs a whole thirteen minutes to contain its uniqueness and wiriness. The synth lines may be familiar, but Prince's guitar leads it into places previously unknown. And it is not just his guitar that challenges preconceptions; the keyboard too wanders into the darkness, encouraged by Prince and his "take your time, brother." By the time the song comes to an end, the former incarnation of "Delirious" is all but forgotten, buried under bleeding guitar and keyboard that comes not just from the head but the heart.

There are nods to the even more distant past with both "Soft And Wet" and "I Wanna To Be Your Lover" making cameo appearances. With synth squiggles and driving bass that reinforce the funk credentials of the band, it continues on without ever becoming too taxing or demanding.

The guitar bubbles up as Prince teases with "Why You Wanna Treat Me So Bad?" before Shelby brings some dancers to the stage for the next part of the show. As "Sexy Dancer" begins, the lead guitar signals that things are going to stay on this instrumental route; the only vocals to be heard are Shelby's as she encourages the crowd. Things do open up later with Shelby singing "Give It To Me Baby," her voice carrying soul and more than a touch of funk. The bootleg nicely captures the band as they are heating up, and the intensity noticeably increases at this stage.

The instrumentals return as "Party Up" plays, although the audience does provide some lusty singing of the lyrics. The audience is still onstage, and will be for some time - some of them can be heard providing overzealous vocal work on the mic. The song sees some crisp funk guitar from Prince, which brings things into focus after the wayward moments with the audience.

> **THE SONG SEES SOME CRISP FUNK GUITAR FROM PRINCE, WHICH BRINGS THINGS INTO FOCUS AFTER THE WAYWARD MOMENTS WITH THE AUDIENCE**

With the bass grooving on "Uptown," Prince takes to the microphone for the first time in the show. Still accompanied by the crowd, there is no need for him to sing all his lines and he doesn't, leaving several opportunities for the crowd to have their fifteen seconds of fame. With the guitar sitting low in the mix, it is the vocals that command attention, and Prince is finally upfront and ready for his moment.

With the audience still onstage, the show is one big party. Prince obliges with a selection of party songs, the audience singing and dancing beside him every step of the way. While "Raspberry Beret" is predictable enough, "Cream" is far more rewarding. Prince sings, the crowd sings, the girls sing, everyone is happy. It organic and fun, with Prince's guitar break stamping his authority on the song.

"Cool" works for the audience, and it works for the bootleg. It is good and is cool before a fiery "U Got The Look" follows it. Prince may not have his guitar for "U Got The Look," but the song has all the attitude one would expect, and with Prince and the audience singing, the normal guitar set associated with the song becomes secondary.

The dance party ends on a high with a stomping "Controversy." The band tears into it with a loud in-your-face rendition that punches above its weight. Prince squeals, sings, and encourages the crowd, even getting them to chant "oh Belgium" before asking them to get their cell phones out. He doesn't revert to his "clap your hands, stomp your feet"

> **AS THE CROWD CHANTS, PRINCE DOES PLENTY OF TALK HIMSELF, AND IT IS ALL JOLLY GOOD FUN THAT COMES TO A HEAD WITH SOME BRIEF LEAD GUITAR BY PRINCE THAT HARKS BACK TO HIS '80S SOUND**

until well into the song, giving the song time to ferment before the climax comes. As the crowd chants, Prince does plenty of talk himself, and it is all jolly good fun that comes to a head with some brief lead guitar by Prince that harks back to his '80s sound.

It is Liv who takes the show in a new direction, providing a different twist on "Free." With a soft piano, Shelby lends her weight at the chorus, the two of them with a pure sound that is nostalgic and beautiful. It sparkles in its simplicity and brings the show back down to earth. The segue to "Pearls B4 The Swine" has them continuing to cast their spell together, although Prince is notably lacking in both songs.

"Love Thy Will Be Done" is full, and with the beat overtaken by other instruments it moves away from the basic template of the original. It's crowded in its sound and looks better on paper than it is in real life.

Next Prince and his guitar return to front and center. As he plays the opening of "Always In My Hair," the recording is reenergized and has a spark to it that will carry the rest of the song. The larger band brings a more keyboard influenced version, and it is the band that dictates the following direction of the concert.

The band switches gear with "Dreamer," although the guitar remains the main focus. It is a step up from "Always In My Hair," with an increase in energy and liveliness. The vocals are secondary, and even when Prince does sing, the music remains the center of attention. Prince has the band on a tight leash, and they are pinpoint accurate as he works them "right back where we were." It is all very professional and sharp, but lacks joy and a lighter touch.

The joy returns though, with the upbeat synth playing "I Feel For You." With Shelby, Liv, and Elisa taking on the vocal duties, the lightness returns, and even with Prince not contributing much vocally, it is still a gem.

The energy levels of the recording go up further as the next few songs are aimed squarely at the dance floor. Shelby leads the band through a storming version of "Chelsea Rodgers" before "Disco Heat" keeps things moving in the same direction. While Shelby is outstanding on "Chelsea Rodgers," "Disco Heat" is a bridge too far and interest begins to wane. Like all Prince shows, things move along quickly, and "Baby I'm A Star" appears with an enthusiastic shout and the band fires through the song, Prince ending it all with a loud "Vegas" over the crescendo of the band.

"The Love We Make" is a nice comedown after all the previous noise. Prince and the piano are heard above a low-key melancholy drum-beat, yet an uplifting chorus brings balance. The guitar tone offers hope, and despite the early downbeat feeling, it finishes up on a higher plain. One of the outstanding songs of the show, this is a slow-burning number that sees Prince coaxing a spiritual sound from his guitar.

> **PRINCE AND THE PIANO ARE HEARD ABOVE A LOW-KEY MELANCHOLY DRUM-BEAT, YET AN UPLIFTING CHORUS BRINGS BALANCE**

The show veers off again with another party piece coming with "Get On The Boat" and "Which Way Is Up." The first minutes has the crowd singing "America" while the band plays smoothly behind, worth hearing in itself. The song builds, released at the five-minute mark by Prince and his call "one, two!" as the jagged riff cuts deep. The groove features solos by all and it is Cassandra who plays the transition to

"Which Way Is Up," bringing Shelby again to the microphone. With the funk right out front, Shelby is at her very best during the next few minutes, the song and the room shaking in all directions.

"Mountains" is thin and a lost opportunity as Prince elects to play an abridged version. It is missing the x-factor, and it fails to impress on a bootleg already full of great moments. It is shallow, and there's no disappointment as "Shake Your Body Down To The Ground" is sung over the last minute of the song.

With a pounding beat, the band breezes easily into "Everyday People." The show begins to accelerate to an end, "Everyday People" becoming "I Want To Take You Higher." With Prince trading lines with Shelby, the song is quickly driven along, the crowd becoming more vocal as the tempo increases. With some stormy guitar by Prince, the song comes to a halt, leaving the audience orphaned and singing alone.

> **WITH SOME STORMY GUITAR BY PRINCE, THE SONG COMES TO A HALT, LEAVING THE AUDIENCE ORPHANED AND SINGING ALONE**

This doesn't last long on the recording as the funky bass of "All The Critics Love U In Belgium" soon begins. Prince sings just as he has always done, this time with "in Brussels" at the end of the appropriate lines (as usual personalizing it for his location). With twists and turns, the song is kept interesting, and the snaky synth solo sees the song go to another level before Prince's bass solo has the crowd singing his bass parts back at him; yet another highlight on the recording. As Prince resumes with "body don't want to quit; gotta get another hit" he is just as fresh as he was three hours earlier. A couple of turn arounds from Prince followed by a call of "end" finishes the show, and as he says, "We the best," one is inclined to believe him.

This show is a real gem. If it was a scratchy recording from the '80s, it would have a mystique to it and people would hold it in higher regard. As it is, it is a clean recording from recent times, and that seems to count against it. Don't be mistaken - this show is one of the best, not only because of the length of it, but because the band performance is outstanding. They put their mark on the concert with the instrumentals that begin the show before following Prince wherever he wants them to go. This bootleg may not be spoken in the same breath as some of the greats, but it deserves its place and demands more attention than it gets.

7TH NOVEMBER 2010 - VIAGE, BRUSSELS

SET LIST

1. Joy In Repetition [Instrumental]
2. Stratus
3. Sometimes It Snows In April [Instrumental]
4. Delirious [Instrumental]
5. Soft And Wet
6. I Wanna Be Your Lover [Instrumental]
7. Why You Wanna Treat Me So Bad? [Instrumental]
8. Sexy Dancer [Instrumental]
9. Give It To Me Baby
10. Sexy Dancer [Instrumental]/Le Freak
11. Partyup [Instrumental]
12. Uptown
13. Raspberry Beret
14. Cream
15. Cool
16. Let's Work
17. U Got The Look
18. Controversy
19. Free
20. Pearls B4 The Swine
21. Love… Thy Will Be Done
22. She's Always In My Hair
23. Dreamer
24. I Feel For You
25. Chelsea Rodgers
26. Dance (Disco Heat)
27. Baby I'm A Star

28. The Love We Make
29. Get On The Boat
30. (Theme Song From) Which Way Is Up?
31. Mountains
32. Shake Your Body (Down To The Ground)
33. Everyday People
34. I Want To Take You Higher
35. All The Critics Love U In Belgium

RELEASES

- The 20ten Tour Recordings Volume 8 - *Sabotage*
- Viage - *Eye Records*
- Viage 2 - *FBG*

15TH JULY 2013
MONTREUX JAZZ FESTIVAL, MONTREUX

Prince played at the Montreux Jazz Festival in 2007, 2009, and 2013, each time delivering a completely different type of show that touched on all the musical genres he had dipped his toe into over the years. The 2013 Montreux shows bring all these strands together at once as over three nights he played two sets of funk and jazz, while the third night (which this bootleg was sourced from) was heavy on rock before eventually giving way to a funkfest of a finale. The show was eagerly anticipated due to the expectation of the first appearance of 3rdeyegirl in Europe, something that many fans were clamoring to see, especially in light of the reviews from across the Atlantic. The bootleg does the evening justice, professionally filmed with every shot framed to show Prince and the band in the best possible light while they roll out their form of rock 'n' roll to an appreciative audience.

"Let's Go Crazy" is largely forgettable and doesn't give a true representation of what will follow. It is labored and heavy and the following "Endorphinmachine" and "Screwdriver" are light years away from it considering the key ingredients that make a great rock show - spontaneity, energy, and passion. "Endorphinmachine" has all three in spades - from the opening riff and Prince's howl at moon, the song accelerates into a brighter future. The dreariness of the previous song, and indeed life, all but forgotten as Prince and the band tear it up. Prince clearly enjoys the guitar solos; he plays with his expression as much as his hands and this carries through to the music he is creating. They may not have the seriousness of earlier years, but they are sweet ear candy that almost makes one wish to be driving on the open road with a full tank of gas while listening to them. "Screwdriver" also comes at breakneck speed, all light and blistering sound as the band gives the performance of their lives.

Prince rewinds the clock as the opening riff of "She's Always In My Hair" floors all those in the arena. This is the one Prince song that

3rdeyegirl took and made their own; the band steps into the heart of the song and plays as if they wrote it. This is their centerpiece and where they are best as a cohesive unit. Prince leads the way, but Donna matches him early on in guitar heroics before he reclaims his rock-god crown as the music increases in intensity again. The breakdown sees Prince initially play a guitar solo that burns down the house before forgoing the guitar. The music quietens as the crowd, the band, Prince, and the music become one - living and breathing the same emotion, the same magic. Prince sings, the crowd sings, Ida plays bass - it all seems so simple, but this is more than the sum of the parts; this is live music at its best, a moment that can't be captured in a bottle or easily explained away. Even on the bootleg, it is apparent that this is what concerts are all about, the heart and soul of the music.

At first appearance, "The Love We Make" wouldn't seem to be a good match for this band. A long-lost gem from the Emancipation album, it is a surprisingly good fit for the band with Donna playing an instinctive and nuanced solo that captures the spirit of the song. With Prince on the keyboard, the band has a more balanced look and sound, but soon enough he is back on guitar for "I Could Never Take The Place Of Your Man." Playing guitar with a mournful howl, he adds some sense of despair to a previously bright pop song. Slow and intense, the song burns with an inner angst that is released in the guitar break that straddles remorse and anger, the guitar howl picking up where the lyrics leave off.

> **SLOW AND INTENSE, THE SONG BURNS WITH AN INNER ANGST THAT IS RELEASED IN THE GUITAR BREAK THAT STRADDLES REMORSE AND ANGER, THE GUITAR HOWL PICKING UP WHERE THE LYRICS LEAVE OFF**

The mood of the bootleg lifts with the trio of songs that come next. A sudden burst of light comes into the building as "Guitar" rings out. Light and fast, it is played with a smile as Prince and the band know the game they are playing. It is both joyous and energetic, as is "Plectrumelectrum" and "Fixurlifeup" that follow. "Plectrumelectrum" is the heaviest of the trio, but it keeps things moving along before "Fixurlifeup" brings a bounce to the recording and to the crowd.

"Bambi" was bound to get an airing with this band, and the show resumes to a more predictable sound as Prince and the girls do their work on it. Crisp and clean, it serves as a final workout for the guitars before the concert turns the corner.

The bootleg becomes more interesting as "Sometimes It Snows In April" ushers in the next stage of the performance. Prince returns to the keyboards, and rather than taking away from the rock aspect, it actually highlights how good Donna is. She steps up with a delicate solo for "Sometimes It Snows In April," while the following "The Max" sees her playing equally well.

> **PRINCE RETURNS TO THE KEYBOARDS AND RATHER THAN TAKING AWAY FROM THE ROCK ASPECT, IT ACTUALLY HIGHLIGHTS HOW GOOD DONNA IS**

She comes into sharp focus with a style that mimics Prince's before finally making the song her own style.

Rounding out the first part of the show is a fresh and energetic "Cause And Effect" that has Prince and the band rocking hard again after the diversion. Prince takes his time with a finely pitched solo that has a lightness to it not heard elsewhere in the evening. The song may not be classic Prince, but it does suit the band and keeps in the tone of the concert.

The music resumes with Prince dialing the clock back to the early '80s for "When We Are Dancing Close And Slow," a song that has lost none of its power over the years - in fact, it is even better in this modern context with the lyrics touching on clever and sweet rather than gauche and dirty. With a guitar solo that would melt the hardest of hearts, Prince weaves a tapestry of music and words that blankets the recording in a warm nostalgia that is sincere and has a solid emotional core.

The next few minutes of the bootleg fail to live up to this moment as Prince follows it with "Play That Funky Music (White Boy)" and "Dreamer." Of the two "Play That Funky Music" is the weaker; it fails to reach the funk levels of Prince's own repertoire, and he would be better served playing one of his own funk songs. "Dreamer" comes from a different place, and even as Prince and the band do their best to enliven it, it still feels laborious and overworked. Overstaying its welcome by several minutes, its redeeming feature is the guitar storm that Prince rains down on the audience.

The third and final part of the recording sees Prince bring the NPG horn section to the stage as he takes his place at the keyboard. There is plenty that could be read into "Breakdown" retrospectively, Prince openly reflecting back on his life, and it is another highlight as it hits all the emotional hotspots. After a light and ethereal introduction, Prince sings in a world-weary voice that captures the spirit of Jay Gatsby, the lyrics hinting at past regrets and memories. Prince connects with the song, and the recording connects with the listener; as he sings, each lyric comes from something he knows as real. There is the final release as Prince howls into the microphone, but even after the music has finished, the feeling and emotion hangs in the air until the next song picks up.

Still at the keyboard, Prince begins the sampler set with a strung out "When Doves Cry." Prince knows how to change the mood into one of a party, turning the lights off and calling people to the stage to dance. With the lights off and Prince lost in the crowd onstage, it does become a house party, Prince providing the tunes to keep the crowd moving. The groove of "When Doves Cry" is interrupted by a sample of "Nasty Girl." Prince is perfectly content at this point - the crowd responds well to the party he is playing out onstage as he brings "Sign O' The Times" out. It is obvious that musically things are cooking, the crowd chanting along as "Sign O' The Times" becomes less of a social commentary and more of a groove to dance to. With the horns adding light to the groove it becomes far more nuanced and colorful, with things are just about to get even better.

The show cleverly balances the sampler, the live band, and the horn section. "Hot Thing" may start with the sampler, but soon enough the horn section is making itself heard as all the while Hannah keeps the beat. As "A Love Bizarre" explodes out of the blocks, the show is intimate and big at the same time, a fat and full sound while the performance is one of togetherness and inclusivity. Prince himself stands alone at the eye of the storm, neatly cocooned behind the keyboard and horn section as the audience dances around him. He is a man in his element, hunched over the sampler, hat pulled low, in his natural environment. If the crowd and band were to suddenly disappear, one feels he would still be the same, lost in his music as he plays for himself as much as anyone else.

But Prince is not an island as the next song clearly demonstrates. He may be at the center of it, but he still knows how to bring others into the fold and get the best from them. "Love" starts with his sampler and heavy groove, but soon enough it is the horn stabs that draw the ear and the eye. The show is about to ignite, and Prince throws a match on the gasoline as he unleashes Larry Graham with some of the heaviest and funkiest bass playing heard in the last few years. The stage is ablaze now in heavy bass, electronic squeals, dancers, and horns, all of it demanding attention, all of it eye-catching, and all of it funky. Prince brings things to fever pitch as he swings his microphone around to catch a saxophone solo that does the impossible and elevates things to an all-time high as the song enters the final couple of minutes.

"Housequake" is the final performance of the show, and again it sees the band playing in with the sampler. It is a fine mix of styles and made all the more interesting by a sharp solo provided by Donna. She bends the music to her will, temporarily making "Housequake" a different song altogether before it snaps back to its usual shape. Ida too has a chance to stand out and briefly proves that she can match it with anyone as her bass pops and snaps in the spotlight. In a show that has been about the band and the music rather than Prince himself; this is completely in character, and the concert is finishing in the same manner as it started.

> **IDA TOO HAS A CHANCE TO STAND OUT AND BRIEFLY PROVES THAT SHE CAN MATCH IT WITH ANYONE AS HER BASS POPS AND SNAPS IN THE SPOTLIGHT**

Prince played three nights at Montreux in 2013, and on first listen this would appear to be the weakest of those shows. Subsequent listens and viewings reveal this to be a show of much more color and depth than first appearance. It is a band performance, and even as Prince plays his guitar solos out front early on, the band is still the central element, and Prince does his best to draw attention to every player onstage. The show features something for everyone, from its opening blitzkrieg of guitar histrionics through to the sensitive ballads before the final party and the unstoppable horn section. There are weaker songs in the performance, no doubt, but there is much more to this show. The final twenty minutes are as good as anything else in his bootleg catalogue. Essential viewing for anyone who wants to see how Prince works to embed himself in the band and reinvents the set list for these tailored performances.

SET LIST

1. Let's Go Crazy
2. Endorphinmachine
3. Screwdriver
4. She's Always In My Hair
5. The Love We Make
6. I Could Never Take The Place Of Your Man
7. Guitar
8. Plectrum Electrum
9. Fixurlifeup
10. Bambi
11. Sometimes It Snows In April
12. The Max
13. Cause And Effect
14. When We're Dancing Close And Slow
15. Play That Funky Music
16. Dreamer
17. The Breakdown
18. When Doves Cry
19. Nasty Girl
20. Alphabet St.
21. Sign O' The Times
22. Hot Thing
23. A Love Bizarre
24. Love
25. Raise Up
26. Housequake

15TH JULY 2013 - MONTREUX JAZZ FESTIVAL, MONTREUX

RELEASES

- 3 Nites, 3 Shows - *Eye Records*
- 47th Montreux Jazz Festival - Show 3 - *Fan Release*
- Days of Montreux - 3 Nights - 3 Shows - *Irukandji Music*
- Montreux Jazz Festival 2013 From The Soundboard Vol. 3 - *FBG*
- Montreux Jazz Festival Volume 3 - *Silverline*
- Montreux Musicology - *Original Master Series*
- Montreux, Night 3 - *Confusion Records*
- 3 Nights, 3 Shows - *Eye Records*

9TH APRIL 2015
FOX THEATER, DETROIT

The 3rdeyegirl band prompted Prince's return to a simpler, smaller scale stage show and performance. However, the concept of a small band wasn't quite enough to fill out a whole set list and most of the concerts through 2013 featured an extended sampler set. With that in mind, members from NPG began appearing alongside 3rdeyegirl, augmenting the newer core band with keyboards, backing singers, and a horn section. The shows of 2015 are well represented, with several of them circulating in soundboard quality. With lively performances and a different twist on many of the more familiar songs, all of them are interesting enough in their own way. I've selected this one as the most essential, being longer and featuring the best of both worlds. There is plenty of rock guitar on the recording, and this is tempered by a sampler set that covers all the jewels of his career and more. At over two hours, it is a lengthy listen with something for everyone thrown into the mix. It demonstrates every facet of Prince's talent, be it guitar playing, keyboards, vocals, stagecraft, and of course at the heart of it all, his songs.

It isn't surprising to hear "Let's Go Crazy" as the first song; it was the opening number for almost all the 3rdeyegirl shows. What is surprising is how heavy and downright interesting it is. 3rdeyegirl play a heavier incarnation of the song, and although it bashes and crashes, it never gets bogged down in its own weight. The guitar solos have classic rock written all over them, propelling and driving the song forward

Prince shows his songwriting skills next as the show moves into the pop realm with "Take Me With U" and "Raspberry Beret." Forever paired by Prince, they retain the guitar influence while bringing the keyboards and the wider band into the frame. Prince has his feet planted in both the rock and pop worlds, but here he leans firmly toward the pop world in several minutes that get the crowd going.

Prince colors his palette further as the normal guitar-driven "U Got The Look" sees him calling for horns. He then plays his sweeping guitar break that unfurls with the horns into "Musicology," itself another showcase for the many talents of the band. It may not be the first song one thinks of when considering 3rdeyegirl, but with the horn section playing strongly, it is just as good as any other rendition heard during the *Musicology* years.

The first sampler set opens with the timeless "When Doves Cry," before a funk-laden "Sign O' The Times" and "Hot Thing." "When Doves Cry" sets the bar high, three minutes of Prince's catchiest hook over a foundation of pure bass heaven. "Sign O' The Times" is its equal as the bass lays a foundation for Prince to deliver his vocals with both a seriousness and funk-fueled delivery. "Hot Thing" rounds out the funk trilogy with the horns bringing a classic sound to the otherwise futuristic rendition.

Prince may not sing the following "Nasty Girl," but it is as nasty as ever with the sampler playing a minute of it before "Housequake" brings more of Prince's unique style to the show. The opening few rock songs of 3rdeyegirl are well and truly forgotten as Prince showers the concert in this funk that is based solidly on the horns and rhythm section. Despite its familiarity, Prince reinvents the track by keeping it unusual. Uniquely, Ida and Donna both show a different side of their playing as they take a solo.

The show continues to roll backward, first with a short yet perfectly pitched pop song in the form of "I Would Die 4 U," before the trio of Liv, Saeeda, and Ashley take on the vocals for "Cool/Don't Stop 'Till You Get Enough." As Prince steps forward for his vocals on "Cool," he is indeed the personification of cool; the lyrics flow out of him, describing a life that only he could live, or even sing about, without sounding boastful.

The natural pairing of "Thank You (Falettinme Be Mice Elf Agin)" and "Play That Funky Music" sees the band further mine this vein of funk. They make a good fist of it, before Prince laces it with a poisonous guitar break that brings an intoxicating sense of urgency and energy. The funk levels are further raised with the appearance of his own "Controversy." Rather than being a nostalgic trip, it is unhinged and deranged with the horns giving it a wild, untamed sound that spreads in all directions. The inner energy is unleashed, and the song becomes a celebration of horns as it slips and slides toward its climax.

The *1999* album comes into the spotlight with a trio of songs from the era making up the next section of the show. It isn't as straight forward as it sounds - while "1999" is as expected, the following "How Come U Don't Call Me Anymore" is a much-loved B-side and "Little Red Corvette" gets a different arrangement that is far removed from the *1999* album. More adult and mature, it is dangerously pedestrian until Prince gives it an emotional heart at the breakdown and an emotive sing along. The song dissolves away under the spell that is cast as the crowd sings back and forth.

> **MORE ADULT AND MATURE, IT IS DANGEROUSLY PEDESTRIAN UNTIL PRINCE GIVES IT AN EMOTIONAL HEART AT THE BREAKDOWN AND AN EMOTIVE SING ALONG**

The opening keyboards of "Nothing Compares 2 U" generate a Beatlesesque vibe that could have been plucked straight from "Strawberry Fields." Normally Prince would bask in the spotlight, but on this occasion it is Cassandra O'Neal and her exquisite keyboard solo that sparkles like sunlight on the ocean.

While the arrangement of "Kiss" is also perverted from the original, it can't beat the previous few songs for pure soulfulness and suffers in comparison. Nevertheless, it is a great performance and only suffers due to its position in the set list rather than the song itself.

The difference between "Clouds" and the previous tracks is so stark the listener could be forgiven for mistaking it for a different show entirely. It has a contemporary feel and signals a change in direction from the previous rock 'n' roll segment.

Liz, Saeeda, and Ashley come into their own as the following medley of "Yes We Can Can," "Thankful N' Thoughtful," "You're The One," and "Green Garden" spotlights their considerable talents. The final "Green Garden" stands head and shoulders above all else as Judith Hill brings the house down with a vocal performance that has a deep-bellied fire to it. Prince is equally able to channel that fire with the guitar break he bestows on the song, giving it an exclamation point to end with.

The concert again becomes a 3rdeyegirl show with appearance of "She's Always In My Hair." It has always been a stirring rock song, and in the hands of 3rdeyegirl even more so, as the bass of Ida and the natural rock chops of Donna cut through and add an extra layer of depth. Prince stakes ownership with his guitar break before the twinkling breakdown gives him a chance to coax further tears and a hint of sadness from his instrument.

"Purple Rain" may be the most overplayed song in the Prince canon, yet he still manages to find a way to add depth to it night after night. The version on this bootleg sees him open with some lead guitar that has the listener transported away before the song settles into its familiar arrangement. Its final minutes sees Prince encouraging the crowd to do better before it all comes to a head in a wonderful combination of guitar and crowd singing.

A flurry of horns opens the first encore, as an upbeat "Act Of God" that swings and funks easily through "What Have You Done For Me Lately," "Northside," "Theme From Which Way Is Up," "Partyman," and "Dancing Machine." It is a classic Prince medley, with the band running seamlessly through the songs while the backing singers and horns lead the way. It is a great showcase for the band, but it never reaches the heights it threatens and overall ends up being less than expected. A joyful romp toward the finish line, it holds its place without adding too much to the show.

> **IT IS A CLASSIC PRINCE MEDLEY, WITH THE BAND RUNNING SEAMLESSLY THROUGH THE SONGS WHILE THE BACKING SINGERS AND HORNS LEAD THE WAY**

After the sensory overload of the full band rushing through the medley, the show slows as Prince takes the keyboard for a brief yet much loved tease of "Diamonds And Pearls" and "The Beautiful Ones." Each gets a few lines and a flourish on the keyboards and while the crowd cheers for more, there is enough there to be enjoyed. Of the two, "The Beautiful Ones" is the biggest tease, with just a couple of drawn-out lines that have the crowd howling.

A second sampler set sees plenty more teases as the concert draws to an obvious close. "Darling Nikki" has the audience on a string, before a brief "If I Was Your Girlfriend" gives way to the opening verse of "Forever In My Life." It has the feel of the small venue as Prince's vocals have a reverb on them that adds to the live feel. The following "Alphabet St." is even shorter before he switches to a snatch of "The Most Beautiful Girl In The World." "A Love Bizarre" signals that perhaps Prince will give a complete performance, but that too quickly morphs into "The X's Face" and "U Know," both so short that there is barely enough time to register them before Prince moves to the next song. The sampler set is rounded out by "Pop Life" (better served by a one minute rendition) and "777-9311." With its popping bass, it is the best and longest part of the sampler set. Featuring Prince on the bass it has a slimy pop that is a throwback to his early days, and it saves the sampler set from being little more than a quick shuffle through the iPod.

"The Love We Make" was resurrected for *Live Out Loud* tour and the following *Hit N Run* tour. With this band configuration, it gains a brighter and stronger backbone, much more organic and natural as it rises from the silence. Prince's lyrics are pitched firmly at the heart, but it is the band that brings it to life and makes it resonate in the way it does. The show ends on this spiritual high as Prince sings of love for one another.

> **PRINCE'S LYRICS ARE PITCHED FIRMLY AT THE HEART, BUT IT IS THE BAND THAT BRINGS IT TO LIFE AND MAKES IT RESONATE IN THE WAY IT DOES**

The 3rdeyegirl concerts never delivered fully on what they promised; a sharp rock show with Prince featuring heavily on guitar never materialized. The reality was a compromise with Prince leaning on the sampler set and a horn section to pull a well-rounded set from his back catalogue. In many ways it is all the more rewarding for this: the shows are three dimensional and have something for everyone in the audience to grab onto. This Detroit concert is the perfect example and with every listen something more can be heard. There may be rockier 3rdeyegirl bootlegs in circulation, especially from 2013, but this one is essential for the balance that Prince has brought to his performance by 2015.

SET LIST

1. Intro
2. Let's Go Crazy
3. Take Me With U
4. Raspberry Beret
5. U Got the Look

6. Musicology
7. When Doves Cry
8. Sign O' The Times
9. Hot Thing
10. Nasty Girl
11. Housequake
12. I Would Die 4 U
13. Cool - Don't Stop 'Til You Get Enough
14. Thank You (Falettinme Be Mice Elf Agin)
15. Play That Funky Music
16. Controversy
17. 1999
18. How Come U Don't Call Me Anymore?
19. Little Red Corvette
20. Nothing Compares 2 U
21. Kiss
22. Clouds
23. Yes We Can Can - Thankful N' Thoughtful - You're The One - Green Garden
24. She's Always in My Hair
25. Purple Rain
26. Act of God
27. What Have You Done for Me Lately - Northside - Theme Song From Which Way Is Up - Partyman - Dancing Machine
28. Diamonds And Pearls
29. The Beautiful Ones
30. Darling Nikki
31. If I Was Your Girlfriend
32. Forever In My Life

33. Alphabet St.
34. The Most Beautiful Girl In The World
35. A Love Bizarre
36. The X's Face
37. U Know
38. Pop Life
39. 777-9311
40. The Love We Make

RELEASES

- Fox Theater Detroit From The Soundboard - *FBG*
- The Symbol And The Girl - *Grexit Records*
- The X's Face - *Irukandi Music*

21st JANUARY 2016
PAISLEY PARK, CHANHASSEN

The final of our fifty essential bootlegs is also the most personal of Prince's performances and therefore the most essential of them all. Prince never finished his biography, nor was he one for interviews; everything he needed to say he said through his music. Nowhere more so than this one-off gala where for the first time he offers an intimate glimpse into his world with a performance littered with personal memories, titbits, and history. Prince revealed himself in a way few artists ever have - not with a performance punctuated by good natured antidotes, but rather a performance where every song, every sentence, every note contained a part of his story, a part of his life, a part of his very soul. With no distraction of a band or a stage show, it is Prince at his most vulnerable, just him and his beloved piano playing his story with his songs. Like remembering a fast-receding dream when you first awake, Prince's reminiscences are intangible, just beyond consciousness, yet fully realized if you listen close enough and know what you are looking for.

The show itself neatly bookends Prince's career and completes the circle. Beginning with teaching himself piano, through his early days in the intense cauldron of a small band playing small venues, on to his glory days and the ever-expanding NPG lineup, his career ascended. Then returning to his roots with 3rdeyegirl and smaller venues before he is finally back where he started, alone at the piano with only his songs for company. It is a soulful and spiritual performance that sees Prince pull back the curtain to reveal himself at his very core to be a spiritual man who is never happier than when he is alone playing his beloved music. The fame, fortune, and fandom mean nothing; his beliefs and his music are everything, and this show is the epitome of this.

From the first moments there is the sense that this is something special. Prince shows have traditionally had their share of the unexpected and weird, but nothing like the distorted reverberation that begins this one. With a vocal effect that sounds as if it is coming from another world, Prince sings lines that cryptically hint at what will follow. Things come into focus a little more as the room quietens to a hush while Prince whispers his first memories, not just telling the moment but living it with the words he speaks. In the reverberation and echo of his voice, the thoughts and memories of the piano bleed into one another, becoming one, just as the memory exists in his head. As he swings into the "Batman Theme," one of the myths of his biography is confirmed; it has always been said this was the first song he taught himself, and here it becomes much more than a run-through of a familiar favorite. He pours the spirit of his father into the keys, taking the swing of the "Batman Theme" and giving it a light jazz touch as he pulls it apart in an intimate and crowd-pleasing moment.

Intimacy is the key to the show, and even as he sings other people's songs, he infuses them with heart and soulfulness. It hardly matters that they aren't his words; the feeling is of utmost importance. The words cease to mean anything at all as he caresses the melody and brings it into his world. "I Second That Emotion" and "Who's Loving You" come from a much earlier time, but they root Prince and his music and give perspective and a sense of history to the show. As he holds the notes, quivers and inflects, the walls and venue disappear from view leaving just Prince and his voice.

> **"INTIMACY IS THE KEY TO THE SHOW, AND EVEN AS HE SINGS OTHER PEOPLE'S SONGS, HE INFUSES THEM WITH HEART AND SOULFULNESS"**

The show steps out of the shadows and into the light as Prince finally plays a full song (and one of his own) with "Baby." It is all part of the story that is unfolding onstage, the spoken line of "I need to write some songs" placing it at the beginning of his musical chronology. With vulnerable and youthful lyrics, the song comes from the teenage Prince, still onstage living on in the heart of the man who is playing. The tenderness of the performance and the song itself is apparent, the bootleg capturing the magical moment unfolding as Prince pulls a performance out of himself that delves deep back into his past.

It becomes a fully formed Prince concert as "I Wanna Be Your Lover" and "Dirty Mind" both get a celebratory performance. The inner energy of the songs and the audience are drawn out into the light as

Prince plays as if the song has just come to him, new and exciting, eager to share this new music. Both fit to the story he is telling, "Dirty Mind" prefaced with a brief comment that he was trying to discover who he was. The two songs spiral upward, pulling the sound, Prince and the audience with them as they go, ending on a higher plain as Prince pulls the next surprise from his bag of tricks.

"Do Me, Baby" may well have been written with such a setting in mind. The main component of the song, Prince's voice, is compelling with only the piano for accompaniment. He gives the sort of performance that hasn't been heard for years - half lust, half love - and the song twists both emotions up tightly, making it a ball of pure feeling that is impossible to pull apart or properly define.

The *1999* album gets two entries into the set list with "Something In The Water (Does Not Compute)" and "Free" making the cut. "Something In The Water (Does Not Compute)" experienced a renaissance later in Prince's career, appearing regularly in the 3rdeyegirl set lists. Although this rendition doesn't come across as powerful as some of those performances, it still has a beating heart at the center of it. The anger of those shows is here replaced with a mournful tone that is further emphasized by the piano flourishes. "Free" is lighter, but there is a serious note tagged to the start of it as Prince comments that he has the best fans. It is almost offhand, yet it is entirely sincere, and the words and thoughts seep through the rest of the song, giving it new depth.

The most moving part of the show, and the bootleg, comes in the next few minutes as Prince plays an unforgettable version of Joni Mitchell's "A Case Of U." It was a highlight of the Dance Benefit show way back in 1983, and here thirty-three years later it is again an emotional charged moment. This version trumps that earlier performance as Prince produces a dazzling rendition that is in a realm of its own. This isn't a pop or rock show; this is something new as Prince doesn't so much play the music as he feels it. He adds pauses to the music, bringing the shadow of funk to the table as it segues into "(Sometimes I Feel Like) A Motherless Child," a song that is innately soulful and here even more so.

> **THIS ISN'T A POP OR ROCK SHOW; THIS IS SOMETHING NEW AS PRINCE DOESN'T SO MUCH PLAY THE MUSIC AS HE FEELS IT**

Prince attempts to undermine the emotion of "The Beautiful Ones" with his throwaway comment at the start of the song that musicians write songs to cop girls. That may be true, but the next few minutes sees him give a heartfelt performance of one of his most enduring and universally appreciated love songs. The emotion isn't overwrought though, as he plays he tempers the music with a smooth delivery that sees him forgo the shrieks and screams at the end for a more measured and mature performance.

The spell is broken as Prince plays "U're Gonna C Me." The dense emotion of the first part of the show lifts as he plays, leaving a clean and simple sound. Prince gives it a full performance before starting a tease with the first minute of "How Come U Don't Me Call Me Anymore." The audience and listener don't miss much.

On the other hand, "Condition Of The Heart" demands to be played, and Prince obliges with a special performance that focuses on not only his vocal ability but also his finesse on the keyboard. With his voice dipping in and out, sometimes impassioned, other times quietening to a whisper, he brings a new dimension to the show. This is further demonstrated as his hands run up and down the piano, matching his vocals for range and delicacy. The moment ends in the best way possible with a note-perfect performance of the heavenly "Venus De Milo."

Prince returns to a conventional form of storytelling as he begins "Raspberry Beret" by acknowledging Wendy and Lisa and providing a quick anecdote about the latter. "Raspberry Beret" is another repeat favorite, but here it becomes a must-listen as Prince does his best to imitate the feel and vibe of Lisa's jazz playing in the opening minutes. The story he tells is good, but the music is key and the notes he plays in her style more telling than any words. It is a thoughtful and intimate piece; he speaks in the language he knows best, music. The music hints at past memories, part mournful, part celebratory, but all of it coming from the heart.

> **THE MUSIC HINTS AT PAST MEMORIES, PART MOURNFUL, PART CELEBRATORY, BUT ALL OF IT COMING FROM THE HEART**

Rhythm comes to the fore with a rendition of "Paisley Park" that swings on the rhythm of Prince's playing. Like a drunken uncle at a house party, Prince plays heavy on the keys, the melody secondary to the swing and feel of the song. The lyrics and melody hardly matter as Prince comes to the center of all great music; the feel and motion of the song as it moves back and forth at his will.

"Sometimes It Snows In April" doesn't carry the emotional weight often associated with it, surrounded as it is by other stripped back and emotive songs. "I Love U, But I Don't Trust U Anymore" stands up better, the lyrics given space to float out into the audience, settling like snow with their melancholy story. It is an airy and space-filled performance; everything is laid bare, and even though Prince doesn't pour over the lyrics, there is enough in the music to make this another heartbreaking performance.

Things become upbeat and rhythmic again with "The Ballad Of Dorothy Parker" and a well-considered cover of Ray Charles's "Unchain My Heart." "The Ballad Of Dorothy Parker" isn't as muted and down beat as one might expect, and the rhythm in Prince's hands becomes apparent later in the song as he swings the last minute before the segue into "Unchain My Heart." It is only a couple of minutes, but again it points to Prince's history and some musical roots that aren't always easily seen at first glance at his catalogue. These roots seem obvious in this context, especially when one looks to the earlier "Paisley Park", again Prince is telling his story in his way - with music.

Two songs from the *HITnRUN Phase Two* album follow; an album that seems to be a disconnected collection of songs, yet here they find a home where they naturally fit. "Baltimore" gets a warm response, Prince's lyrics gaining more in the piano and microphone environment, each word sounding sweeter yet carrying more meaning and weight. "Rocknroll Loveaffair" is lighter in its lyrical content, yet it too shines on the bootleg as it is appreciated fully. It hasn't had the life squeezed out of it by a full band performance and overproduction and it is all the better for it. The two songs are a natural fit and sit easily alongside the other songs in the evenings set list.

In a show that already pulls at every emotion, there is more to come with the final two songs going further than any of the songs preceding them. First, there is the briefest of entrees in the entirely predictable "Starfish And Coffee," before the first heavy blow comes in the form of "The Breakdown." The lyrics may or may not be autobiographical, but they speak of looking back and remorse, made all the more poignant by the piano that plays underneath, only rising up for the chorus. As Prince sings "give me back the time, you can keep the memories," it is hard not to believe that he is feeling every word. In an evening that has looked back over his life, he is still reaching deeper inside of himself to draw on the well of emotion that exists.

After so much emotion, the show ends on a spiritual note with "Anna Stesia." The opening chords giving way to an uplifting performance of Prince's most spiritual song. Prince holds back nothing in a bold and powerful performance that adds a solid core to all that has come before. The song returns to his lifelong theme that God is love, and as he whispers it the audience picks up the chant, thus ending the show with the essence of Prince. He is passing on a message in the music for the audience to carry onward, and that message is God is love.

SET LIST

1. Intro
2. Batman Theme [Improvisation]
3. I Second That Emotion
4. Who's Loving You
5. Baby
6. I Wanna Be Your Lover
7. Dirty Mind
8. Do Me, Baby
9. Something In The Water (Does Not Compute)
10. Free
11. A Case Of You
12. (Sometimes I Feel Like A) Motherless Child
13. The Beautiful Ones
14. U're Gonna C Me
15. How Come U Don't Call Me Anymore [Instrumental]
16. Condition Of The Heart
17. An Honest Man [Instrumental]
18. Venus De Milo

19. Raspberry Beret
20. Paisley Park
21. Sometimes It Snows In April
22. The Ballad Of Dorothy Parker
23. Eye Love U, But Eye Don't Trust U Anymore
24. The Ballad Of Dorothy Parker - Four
25. Unchain My Heart
26. Baltimore
27. Rocknroll Loveaffair
28. Starfish And Coffee
29. The Breakdown
30. Anna Stesia

RELEASES

- Paisley Park, Piano & A Microphone Gala Event - *Fan Release*
- Piano & A Microphone Volume 1 - *Silverline*
- Revelation - *Sabotage*

PRINCE

7th June 1958 - 21st April 2016

Thanks for the music and the inspiration.